PRAISE FOR DONNA GRANT'S
BEST-SELLING ROMANCE NOVELS

"Grant's ability to quickly convey complicated
backstory makes this jam-packed love story accessible
even to new or periodic readers."
–Publishers' Weekly

"Donna Grant has given the paranormal genre
a burst of fresh air…"
–San Francisco Book Review

"The premise is dramatic and heartbreaking;
the characters are colorful and engaging;
the romance is spirited and seductive."
–The Reading Cafe

"The central romance, fueled by a hostage drama, plays
out in glorious detail against a backdrop of multiple ongoing
issues in the "Dark Kings" books. This seemingly penultimate
installment creates a nice segue to a climactic end."
–Library Journal

"…intense romance amid the growing war between
the Dragons and the Dark Fae is scorching hot."
–Booklist

THE SHIELDS SERIES
A Dark Guardian ~ A Kind of Magic
A Dark Seduction ~ A Forbidden Temptation
A Warrior's Heart
Mystic Trinity (a series connecting novel)

DRUIDS GLEN SERIES
Highland Mist ~ Highland Nights ~ Highland Dawn
Highland Fires ~ Highland Magic
Mystic Trinity (a series connecting novel)

SISTERS OF MAGIC TRILOGY
Shadow Magic ~ Echoes of Magic ~ Dangerous Magic
Books 1-3: Sisters of Magic Box Set

THE ROYAL CHRONICLES NOVELLA SERIES
Prince of Desire ~ Prince of Seduction
Prince of Love ~ Prince of Passion
Books 1-4: The Royal Chronicles Box Set
Mystic Trinity (a series connecting novel)

DARK BEGINNINGS: A FIRST IN SERIES BOXSET
Chiasson Series, Book 1: Wild Fever
LaRue Series, Book 1: Moon Kissed
The Royal Chronicles Series, Book 1: Prince of Desire

Shecrish
Human Land
Dragon Land
Zora
Orgate
Stonemore
Iron Hall
Cairnkeep
Belanore
Flamefall
Rannora
N
S
E
W

This is a work of fiction. All of the characters, organizations, and events portrayed in this novel are either products of the author's imagination or are used fictitiously.

THE BASTARD KING
© 2024 by DL Grant, LLC
Cover Design © 2024 by Hang Le
ISBN 13: 978-1-958353-40-0
Available in ebook, print, and audio.
All rights reserved.

Peek at THE UNCROWNED KING
© 2024 by DL Grant, LLC
Cover Design © 2024 by Hang Le

All rights reserved, including the right to reproduce or transmit this book, or a portion thereof, in any form or by any means, electronic or mechanical, without permission in writing from the author. This book may not be resold or uploaded for distribution to others. Thank you for respecting the hard work of this author.

www.DonnaGrant.com
www.MotherofDragonsBooks.com

THE BASTARD KING

THE BASTARD DUOLOGY

NEW YORK TIMES & USA TODAY BESTSELLING AUTHOR

DONNA GRANT

CHAPTER 1

Northern Territory

Crisp, cool autumn air brushed against Kora's cheeks like a soft caress as she walked among the trees, admiring the orange, yellow, and red of the season. It was her favorite time of year. The crunch of the leaves on the ground, the nip in the late-morning air. For a brief second, she could get lost in the moment and forget the past.

As well as her uncertain future.

Her good mood quickly evaporated. It always did when she thought about what was to come. Why she returned to a land she had hoped to never see again. She had run from the past and the promises she'd made for too long. Fear forced her into hiding. She roamed the realm in a futile search for more of her kind. She had been so sure there were others out there hiding as she had been. It had kept her going after her family was stolen from her. But she had been wrong. No longer could she deny that she was the last.

And with that realization came a cold, hard truth.

Everything rested on her shoulders—and hers alone. There was no one else to step up and make the hard choices. No one else would—or *could*—wipe out the evil spreading across the land. It was why Kora had returned to the Tunris Mountains.

Walking through the forests brought back all the painful memories. She had neglected her duties and forgotten who she really was. It had taken her years to get where she was now, but she intended to do what her family had attempted before.

A nagging worry kept popping up, though. The one that asked what made her think she would be successful when her family hadn't been. Her response was always the same: There is no one else.

She might die in her attempt, but that was better than knowing she was the last. It didn't matter how far they had traveled in the universe. They were always found. Villages obliterated. People exterminated.

Somehow, she was the lone one standing.

Denial had given her nothing but tears and panic. She had never stood out among her people. She had always been perfectly adequate. But it would take much more than that to survive.

Her steps halted when she found herself near a shallow stream. The shore had rocks scattered along the edges. She looked across the water to the slope of the mountain rising to the sky, and her heart clutched. She took a step back in shock. She hadn't meant to come here. Unable to stop herself, she searched the mountainside until she found the entrance to a tiny cave, barely big enough for a child.

"Run!"

She jerked at her uncle's voice ringing in her head as the memory swelled and yanked her back in time.

"KORA!"

Her brother, Kayden, screamed her name. Kora heard the whoosh of wings, a heartbeat before the roar that deafened her. She hastily scanned the forest for her brother and found him near her uncle and cousin as the three stood ready to battle the dragon diving for them.

Kayden turned and looked at her, his dark eyes meeting hers. He gave her a nod, urging her to run and hide. She wanted to stand with them. They were all that remained of her family. How could she leave them?

"Go," her brother mouthed.

Then he turned and faced their greatest enemy. Kora spun and raced through the trees as fast as her shaking legs would carry her. She plunged into the water, tripping over larger rocks as the roars grew ever closer. She didn't notice the frigid temperature of the river as she crossed to the other side and stepped into the snow. Her heart slammed against her ribs, and her stomach churned with dread, but she didn't stop. They had located the cave months ago, just in case.

But just in case *had become a certainty.*

Kora heard her brother shout and chanced a look back. The dragon hovered above the trio, the trees bending and swaying each time it beat its navy wings. She scrambled up the rocky slope as screams rent the air. Her hands clawed at the hard, frozen ground, fisting snow and anything else she could grab to pull herself up. Each time she wanted to look back, she forced her eyes to stay where they were. The shouts and roars told her all she needed to know.

She slipped on a rock and lost her hold, only to slide down. There was a loud crack, and trees began slamming into the mountain a heartbeat later. One landed above her and started rolling toward her. Kora quickly scrambled to the side before climbing the slope once more. The muscles in her legs ached, and she had a stitch in her side, but she didn't stop.

Then, finally, she reached the narrow cave entrance. It wasn't big enough for her. She had told Kayden that when they found it, but he'd insisted. She twisted herself at odd angles to get inside and pressed against the stone wall with her hands over her ears. Unfortunately, nothing could drown out the screams of the dying.

The same sounds she had heard when her parents and their village were attacked.

The same wails she would one day release when they came for her.

Kora wrenched herself from the memory. She sucked in a mouthful of air as her eyes snapped open, and the memory faded. But the sounds reverberated in her head. She slowly turned to look where Kayden, her cousin, Zak, and her uncle, Rylan, had faced the dragon, giving her a chance to get away. They had sacrificed themselves for her. It was a difficult weight to carry. One she did bitterly.

She shouldn't have run. She should've stood with them. If anyone got away, it should have been one of them. They were fighters. They knew what to do. Instead, she had been left on her own to figure it all out. And she had done a terrible job.

The scent of evil suddenly assaulted her. Kora winced, repulsed. Since returning, she had been dodging Stonemore's soldiers. They were everywhere. They made so much noise it was easy to dodge them, but not everyone was so successful. She had witnessed clashes between the soldiers and others they came across. They enjoyed the fear in their foes' eyes. They took delight in harming the innocent. It was why the stench of evil followed them like a thick fog.

Kora turned to leave when she heard a child's scream. She shouldn't get involved. It wasn't her business. She had another task, one that was more important. Yet she lifted her head and listened. The shout came again. She turned to the river and crossed it.

Kora moved near the mountain, keeping as close to the trees as possible. It didn't take her long to come upon the soldiers surrounding a young boy. They were tormenting the boy. Their laughter infuriated her.

Maybe it was returning to a place of such painful memories. Maybe it was because she had finally accepted what she was meant to do. Maybe it was because she was tired of turning away and hiding.

Whatever the reason, Kora walked to the group. They were so intent on their young victim that no one took notice of her. Her anger grew with every step. The soldiers were like the dragon, and the boy her family. It was time to stop running.

It was time to take a stand.

Kora shoved aside the soldiers and walked into the middle of their circle. The group quieted instantly. They'd discarded their helms, but there was no mistaking the breastplate mimicking dragon scales. They were from Stonemore.

She glared at each of them as she turned in a slow circle, halting before the woman who had a hold of the boy. "Release him."

Surprise flickered in the soldier's eyes, but her grip held.

Kora raised a brow. "It takes eleven soldiers to detain a lad? How about you face someone your own size?"

The tall female shoved the boy away. "Are you offering?"

"I am." Kora nudged the boy. "Once he is safely away."

The boy attempted to leave but couldn't find an opening. Kora glared at a pair of soldiers. They stepped aside. She walked the boy to the opening and watched him hurry away. He looked back once. She nodded, much as her brother had done with her, and the lad started running. The hole closed once more, locking her within the circle.

"I've seen some stupid things in my time," the female said.

The others smiled and nodded excitedly, their eyes brightening at the thought of a fight. If only Kora could show them who she really was. But now wasn't the time to reveal that truth. She would take this beating if it meant the lad was safe.

"What the fuck is this?" a male voice boomed around them.

The group lowered their gazes to the ground and bowed their heads. Kora turned at a sound behind her and watched a man stride through the circle to stop before her. She stared at the square areas of his eyes before glancing at the wing-like ornaments attached to the forehead area of the helm.

Large hands reached up and yanked it off before he tucked it against his side. A blue gaze was leveled on her before it slid to the others. His eyes narrowed as he looked at each of the soldiers. Kora took the time to admire his broad shoulders and handsome face. His blond hair was firmly tied in a queue at his neck. Nothing about this man was out of place.

His attention stopped on the female Kora had spoken to. "One day. You had the chance to prove yourself when I left you in charge, Liisa. Not only are you off course, but you've disgraced yourself and this regiment. We do not detain children. The fact that you did says a lot about your character."

When others chuckled, the commander's gaze snapped to

them. "Don't think I didn't see what each of you did. It took an outsider to break it up," he stated, pointing a finger at Kora.

The soldiers were silent, defeated. Though Kora noted that Liisa's gaze was locked on her, the look in her eyes promising retribution.

"Get in line!" the commander barked.

The soldiers instantly moved, and Kora turned to walk away.

"Wait," he called.

Kora studied him before glancing at the soldiers.

"It took guts doing what you did," he said. "Not many would have dared."

"It was something you should have done."

"I was on my way."

"Not fast enough," she countered.

A muscle moved in his jaw. "It isn't safe to travel alone."

"Because of you and your regiment?"

His gaze briefly lowered to the ground. "We're here to protect."

"I witnessed that protection. I think I'm safer on my own."

"Let me repay your kindness to the lad and escort you to your destination."

Kora could just imagine having them bring her to Stonemore's gates. That wouldn't go over well. "There's no need."

"I'm Makhi."

She studied him, noting his interest. He was a fine-looking man, even if she questioned his choice of loyalties. If she were someone else or had another life, then she might consider giving him her name. But she wasn't someone else and she didn't have another life. She had this one, as fucked up as it was.

"Good luck." Kora turned and walked away.

She never gave her name away. It was better to stay anonymous. And Makhi was a Stonemore soldier. She would likely face him in battle soon. Kora ducked behind a tree and watched Makhi march the squad away. The sight of their retreating backs didn't give her any relief. They would return. Especially Liisa. Kora leaned against the tree and considered her next move.

There was no going back for her. She was there to face her past, regardless of the outcome. If her community and family couldn't win, she didn't stand much of a chance either. But she was done running and hiding. She would eventually be found anyway. At least this way, it was on her terms.

Her gaze lifted to the skies. She hadn't seen any dragons. That didn't mean they weren't out there. They were there. They were *always* there.

She got comfortable and tracked the sun across the sky. Her stomach rumbled with hunger. She should be hunting. It was what she had set out to do that morning before the past overwhelmed her, and she decided to interfere with the soldiers. She drank the last of her water in an effort to curb her hunger.

It was midafternoon when she heard the clanking of armor. Kora sighed as she got to her feet. The soldiers were nothing if not predictable. If they wanted a hunt, she would give them one. And she would take them far from their comrades and show them who they were dealing with.

Kora peeked out from behind the tree and spotted Liisa. She had four others with her. Three males and another woman. Given how they kept looking over their shoulders, they must be concerned about the rest of the unit coming for them.

If Kayden were there, her brother would say she was being reckless. She was, but something about seeing a child abused for the fun of it rankled. She couldn't let it go. Just as Liisa couldn't let go of the slight Kora had delivered. Those soldiers loved the pain and power that came with their position, and Liisa intended to put Kora in her place.

She removed her coat and dropped it. There had been too much fury in Liisa's eyes when she departed. She intended to hurt someone. It was why Kora remained. She'd caused the ire, and she would be the one Liisa took her anger out on. Kora briefly closed her eyes before stepping from behind the tree. "Looking for me?"

Five heads whipped in her direction. Liisa pulled her lips back in a snarl and unsheathed her sword. Kora grinned. So damn predictable. She spun and started running, taking them away from the roads and up the mountain before going back down. Arrows whizzed by as she ran across the stream and into the forest.

She scanned ahead, noting fallen trees, rocks, and gullies. Animals darted away at their loud approach. They were deep in the woods, far from others, so it came as a shock when Kora saw someone. She lengthened her strides to put some distance between her and her pursuers and maneuvered into sections to obscure her as she headed toward the person.

The moment his light olive gaze met hers, she stumbled. Winded, she came to a stop beside him. Glancing behind her, she made sure the soldiers were still heading where she wanted them.

"Stay down so they don't see you. I'll lead them away," she told him.

CHAPTER 2

The berries in his hand were forgotten as Derek watched the hunched woman run away. She jumped onto a boulder and straightened as if to declare her presence. The jangle of armor announced the soldiers before he saw them racing after her.

He couldn't remember the last time a human had been friendly. Men avoided him. Women only wanted to get into his bed. But not a single one had ever put themselves into harm's way for him.

Until her.

Derek rose to his feet. He looked from the soldiers to the woman. The path she took only led to one place. And he knew what the soldiers were about. None of this involved him. He had no reason to meddle. But she intrigued him. He couldn't remember the last time he had been fascinated by anyone. Especially a human.

He started running, slowly at first but then he increased his speed. Derek kept her in his sights, and as expected, she ran toward the blocked valley near the wetland. Was she leading them there on purpose? She was fast. Not as fast as him, but faster than the soldiers. She could have outdistanced them quickly, but she hadn't. Instead, she slowed so they could keep up. How...odd.

She wanted them in that part of the valley for a purpose. Five against one wasn't good odds. Maybe others were waiting to help her. His curiosity was piqued. Nothing would stop him from seeing the outcome.

Derek diverted and took another route that cut through the marshland. His feet slapped the water, spraying it as he ran. He arrived, waiting within the thick mist, when the woman rushed into the valley. She slid to a halt and spun to face her pursuers. Long, dark hair had come loose from its bindings and hung to her waist. She stood with her feet apart, her hands at her sides. Her chest heaved from the exertion while her gaze was locked on the approaching soldiers.

"Seems you have nowhere to go," a female soldier stated.

The woman smiled softly. "I'm the one who stopped."

"Because no one goes in there." The soldier jerked her chin toward the swamp.

Derek was well hidden, but everyone knew the swamp was a dangerous place.

Because of *him*.

A crossbow being fired broke the silence. The woman leaned to the side just before the bolt struck her. Derek marveled at her ability to dodge it. In seconds, the soldiers surrounded her. He took a step forward, only to stop. He was curious about the human, but it didn't go further than that.

She ducked and dodged, spun and sidestepped. She even

managed to block a few blows, but she was up against weapons with only her wits. A part of him wanted to help. As he considered it, she suddenly jerked when a quarrel impacted her chest. There was a slight tightening of her face before she ducked a sword aimed at her head. Another blade cut her thigh when she lunged. One of the soldiers stabbed her in the back.

It was a bloodbath. And he had seen enough. Derek shifted into his true form. He stalked forward, knocking over trees as he did. The mist swirled around him as if trying to keep him hidden. It parted when he pushed onward, revealing his face first.

Four of the soldiers caught sight of him and froze. The female leader was too intent on the woman to notice. She swung her sword down and around, embedding it deeply in the woman's side. Derek growled. She lifted her eyes to meet his. Her face drained of color as she tugged her blade free.

The woman dropped to her knees before listing to the side and rolling onto her back. The scent of blood filled the air. Derek stood over her. He didn't know why. There was no saving the human. Not that he would if he could. He looked down. Her eyes were open, but she didn't show any surprise or fear at seeing him. She must already be dead.

And that infuriated him.

"We're leaving," the female soldier announced. "We're sorry to intrude on your territory. We had to take care of business."

Derek looked at her and let smoke roll from his nostrils. His fury grew: with the woman for not getting away when she had the chance, with the soldiers for ganging up on her and killing her, and at himself for not intervening before it was too late. He drew in a deep breath, feeling the fire within his chest flare and expand.

They tried to run, but it was pointless. One breath of fire took them instantly.

He could have made them suffer. Maybe he should have. Derek looked down at the female again. Her eyes were closed now. Her injuries were fatal. He hadn't even gotten a chance to thank her. It wasn't something he did. There had been no need for her to warn him, but she hadn't known that. She deserved better than this.

Derek returned to human form and squatted naked beside her. Why had she brought the soldiers here? There hadn't been anyone to help her. She should've escaped when she had the chance. Why hadn't she?

Her blood spilled into the packed earth as mist curled out of the swamp to lick at her boots. Derek tugged at a lock of hair that had fallen across her face. He dropped to one knee on the ground. Her hair was like aged mahogany, rich and deep. The strands were cool against his fingers.

Her oval face was beguiling. Her full lips could have lured him into temptation with the barest of smiles. Dark brows arched pleasingly over large eyes. He had only briefly looked into those clear brown eyes, but he could describe every detail. They had been bright like a sunrise. Swirling in the dark rays were bronze and amber, all trapped by a thick ring of black.

He skimmed the backs of his knuckles along her cheekbone. Who was she? He would never know. And that was a pity.

She was attractive, but more than that, she had been brave and kind—not something he said about anyone, much less humans.

Derek straightened but didn't walk away. He stared at her for a long moment before he bent and gathered her into his arms. He walked past what was left of the soldiers to the path the animals used to ascend the mountain. She deserved a warrior's death, and while he couldn't give her that, he could give her the next best thing. Derek carried her to the top and gently laid her on the slab of rock.

He stared at her face to commit it to memory, then looked down at her body. She was dressed in all black. Her shirt was threadbare at the wrists and had stitched holes. Her pants weren't in any better condition. It seemed she'd spent most of her coin on her boots. They showed solid craftsmanship that would've lasted her years.

The wind picked up the ends of her hair and danced it around. Derek took a step back. He let his gaze take in the view. He stood on the northernmost point of the Tunris range. Rolling valleys of grass that went on for miles stretched before him. Beyond that was a lake and land as wild as his heart.

He would give her the burial she deserved so her ashes could be scattered into the beauty of the realm. Perhaps that would allow her to return one day as fierce as she had been today.

Derek's eyes lowered to her face again. He couldn't fathom why she hadn't let her speed take her far from the area. She shouldn't have stayed. He had decimated humans time and again, and he would continue to do so in order to free the dragons. Yet he was greatly saddened to see this one dead.

"Dederick."

He fisted his hands at the command that filled his mind. He didn't dare ignore it. His life was pledged to Stonemore, and if Villette summoned him, then he must go to her. Derek debated whether to incinerate the human now or wait. He had seen other mortals gather around their dead. She deserved at least that. If he didn't have time to watch her body burn, then he would do it when he returned.

Derek held out his hand and created an area around the slab with magic so no one could get near her. He looked at the silver cuff on his wrist. No matter how often he traveled using Villette's magic, it still felt wrong.

He caught sight of his nudity and reluctantly used his magic to clothe himself. He spent most of his time doing what he wanted, but there were other times, like now, when he bent to another's rules. His gaze lingered on the dead human a moment more.

Derek touched the cuff. One moment, he was outside. The next, he stood in the center of a chamber deep within a mountain. Flames danced in the enormous hearth, the red-orange glow reaching out to him along the floor with flickering fingers.

He knew this chamber well since it was where he met Villette. There were no windows. A single door marred the simple walls. Despite its size, the room only had one chair. There was no need to use his enhanced abilities. He turned his head to the left and found his mistress sprawled on a chair covered in fur pelts.

"Took you too long."

Derek frowned at the pain in her voice. He caught a glimpse of the new burns that covered her face, arms, and torso. "What happened?"

"Nothing for you to worry about."

He drew in a breath and smelled the familiar scent of dragon fire. "You fought dragons?"

"I told you not to worry about it."

He curled his hands into fists when she didn't elaborate. Villette wasn't just his leader. She had saved him. He owed her his allegiance *and* his life. He gave both freely.

She sighed loudly. "I've already given you my word that you will be by my side when we free your kin."

"There you are. I wondered when you would return."

Derek jerked at the female voice in his head. He inwardly shook himself. "Tell me who did this to you. I will hunt them down."

"I want that pleasure," Villette stated icily. She cut her eyes to him. "Has anything out of the ordinary happened?"

Derek observed her for a silent moment. He could tell her about the female, but then he would have to explain why he cared. Villette would become worried, and there was no need for that. "Nay."

"You need to be extra vigilant. Don't stray far from the marsh."

"You expect someone to come?"

"I'm being cautious. It's how we've gotten this far."

Someone had spooked her, and she wasn't giving him any information. Villette was one of the most powerful beings alive. She was a Star Person, moving among realms by mere thought alone. She ruled Stonemore as the Divine. Few knew her as anything but the Divine's right hand, however. It was a deception she enjoyed. Villette had gained influence and dominion by weaving a complex web of deceit and trickery to gain the upper hand in the battle for Zora.

And she was winning.

There had been setbacks before, but they were getting closer to freeing the dragons. He could feel it.

"Find me while she's still weak."

"I'll see it done," Derek declared, ignoring the other voice.

She swallowed, a grimace of pain creasing her face. "Dederick," she called.

He hated that name, but he bit back his response. "Aye?"

"The next time I call, come immediately." She slowly sat up, but it cost her, and she began shaking. "I may need you soon. Don't let me down."

"I would never," he vowed.

"Check the swamp. I want you to be sure no one has found it."

He took a step to her. "No one has."

"Check the entire area. Go. Now," she bit out.

Derek bowed his head and touched the cuff. Seeing Villette injured worried him. Something had spooked her, and he wished she would tell him who or what it was. In the meantime, he would do as she asked.

He reappeared atop the mountain, only to stare in disbelief at the empty stone slab.

CHAPTER 3

Kora's eyes flew open as she sucked much-needed air into her starved lungs, and her heart began to beat once more. She hated this part. She was disoriented and sore. She sat up, anxiously looking around in the fading light to make sure she was alone.

She was always grateful when no one else was around. She swallowed and grimaced at her ruined clothes. The blood on the tunic had dried, and the material now stuck to her skin. She needed her other set of clothes and a bath. Kora looked up and stilled at the view before her. How had she gotten to the top of the mountain?

There would be time to answer that later. Right now, she had to leave. She swung her legs over the side of the long, flat stone and jumped to the ground. Her legs were wobbly, but she quickly got them under her and found a game trail heading down. The path was narrow and dangerous. She slipped twice but managed to catch herself.

The moment she came off the slope, she started to run to where she had left her coat. The sight of the blackened skeletal remains brought her up short. Her stomach tightened with alarm as she slowly looked to the right, where mist shrouded a band of trees lurking in the growing shadows. The expanse behind the tree line looked even more foreboding and unsettling.

She told her feet to move. She even took a step forward. Until she looked down and saw the pool of blood near the trees. That was where she had stood when she fought the soldiers. Her gaze slid to the burned bodies again. The air whooshed from her lungs. She hadn't dreamed the dragon as she lay dying. It had stood over her, looking down at her with fiery red eyes. There was a dragon.

Kora started running and didn't look back. She cut back to where she had left her coat and bent to swipe it up without breaking her stride. She thought she heard the beat of wings at least a dozen times, but there was nothing when she looked behind or above her. Still, she didn't stop until she reached the ruins of the home she had taken up residence in.

She burst into the cottage and slammed the door so hard that it fell off its last hinge. She propped it against the wall and stumbled backward, her heart in her throat. She had unknowingly walked into a dragon's den. She knew better than to blindly enter an area. Yet that's exactly what she had done to get back at the soldiers.

Her knees buckled. She dropped to the rickety floor and covered her face with her hands. Images of the dragon filled her mind—pictures she had believed were conjured from her subconscious because she feared them so. It had emerged from the fog and stood over her. She had felt the heat of its breath, saw the smoke curling from its nostrils. The huge teeth.

She didn't know how or why it hadn't burned her with the

soldiers, but she had been given a second chance. One she wasn't about to blithely disregard. She had to pull herself together. She needed to think, plan.

"Stop being reckless, Kora."

She squeezed her eyes closed at Kayden's voice in her head. Her brother was right. She had nearly died before going after Villette. She couldn't let the soldiers irritate her again. She had to think several moves ahead. They were predictable. And today, she had fallen into the same trap.

"Not again," she vowed aloud.

First, she needed to clean up. The sooner she got out of the ruined clothes, the better. Kora sat on her haunches and looked at the blanket she had spread on the floor next to the bag with her meager belongings. She rose and grabbed her only other set of clothes before walking from the house to the lake. She stripped and set her ruined clothing in the shallows to soak before wading in. The water was frigid, but she didn't have the luxury of a tub to heat water.

She was shivering by the time she emerged after washing her body and hair. Before dressing, she knelt at the shore and scrubbed her clothes until she had gotten all the blood she could from them. Only then did she dress in her spare attire and make her way back to the hut. She built a fire inside and set out her clothes to dry while combing through her tangled hair. When she couldn't bear her growling stomach another moment, she ate the last half of an oatcake and went to bed.

But there was no sleep to be found. Whenever she closed her eyes, she pictured the dragon's head materializing from the swamp and the soldiers' bodies. Maybe the dragon hadn't burned her because she was already dying. Why bother if she didn't pose a threat? Then again, humans didn't generally pose a threat to dragons.

She might be able to explain why she hadn't felt the heat of dragon fire, but she couldn't explain how she'd gotten to the top of the mountain. It hadn't been one of the soldiers. She had counted five bodies. Perhaps a nearby villager had taken pity on her. As soon as that thought came, she wrinkled her nose. No one would be stupid enough to go near a place where a dragon was. Which meant she still had no idea who took her.

Kora tossed and turned throughout the night and finally gave up near dawn. She put on her boots and walked outside. Some berries helped take the edge off her hunger, but she would need something more substantial. She looked northwest, toward a settlement she knew was there. She had a few coins left. That might get her enough food for the day, but she would have to earn more soon. She couldn't make her way into Stonemore empty-handed.

She could hunt—and would have to eventually—but she wanted to know more about the area. A lot had changed in the time she had been gone. How much of the land had the dragons taken? She would keep clear of the beast at all costs.

When she was dying, she had seen its red eyes, not its scales. So, she didn't know if it was the dragon that had killed the last of her family. Not that it mattered. All dragons were her enemies.

The sky was turning a soft gray as dawn approached. Kora returned to the cottage and put out the fire, then inspected her clothes. Black hid the bloodstains she couldn't get out, but there were a significant number of cuts this time. The tunic couldn't be salvaged. Thankfully, the pants only needed minor stitching. She jingled the pouch that held her money. Food was more important than a new shirt right now.

Kora left the hut and headed in a northerly direction. The sky was clear except for a few puffs of lazily drifting clouds. The wind kept moving her hair into her face and irritating her, so she pulled the top portion back and fastened it with a strip of leather. Despite her distance from the marshland, she continued looking for the dragon. It was there. Somewhere. Waiting to strike.

Almost two hours later, she reached the small village. Unlike other nearby settlements, Stonemore hadn't attacked this one. Those who didn't die in the battles were brought to the city. It was only a matter of time before Stonemore made it to this village. Unless someone stopped Villette.

The street was busy with horse-pulled carts and residents moving about. Kora followed the sounds to the market. It buzzed with people and voices. Children wove among the adults, playing and laughing. Hawkers shouted about their wares. Kora milled through the crowd, taking her time to look at everything. A tunic caught her attention.

She paused beside it and fingered the material. It was nice—nicer than anything she had purchased in a long time. The smell of freshly baked rosemary bread reached her then, and she forgot all about the shirt. Her mouth watered as she followed the scent to a stand on the corner. She haggled her price and got a loaf before going to another stall and buying some dried meat and fruit. She was fingering her last coin when she saw him.

He walked through the crowd, commanding and imposing. The sea of people parted for him. Rich, deep brunette hair fell to the middle of his back. He wore brown trousers and a tan tunic stretched across broad shoulders. His clothes were simple but clean. She moved to see his face, but he turned away at that moment. Something about him was familiar. Kora kept out of sight and followed him. When he glanced over his shoulder, and she spotted the light olive gaze, she immediately knew who he was.

His face was branded on her brain in that second. Strong jaw. Thick, slashing eyebrows. Intense eyes. Wide lips. He was dark and seductive. A man used to getting what he wanted, whenever he wanted it.

"Don't be shy, honey."

Kora startled at the woman's voice beside her. She jerked her head to the side, but the woman only had eyes for the man.

"He welcomes anyone." The woman looked at Kora and smiled. "I spent a single night with him and couldn't walk the next day. But, oh, what a night," she murmured breathlessly.

Kora looked back at him. "Who is he?"

"Derek is his name. He comes around every few months. Chooses a woman or two for a night. Then he's gone."

The man in question paused and bent to pick something up. He squatted and handed a ball to a young lad, who quickly ran off. Kora caught the breadth and width of Derek's shoulders as he stood. His sleeves were rolled up to his elbows, showing the thick sinew of his forearms. She saw the cuff of braided silver at his wrist.

"You best make yourself noticeable," the woman urged before walking away. "Others are already after him."

Eight of them, by Kora's count. The women went up to Derek, rubbing their bodies against him. Kora kept close to the stalls, continuing to watch him. All kinds of women came to him. Tall and short, thin and curvy. Young and old. He looked at each of them. She couldn't tell if he spoke, but he wasn't rude. That surprised her somehow.

Kora pulled her gaze from him and looked about the town. Women all over were ogling him, their hunger obvious. Some smiled dreamily as if remembering something special. Perhaps their night with him? The men looked on with a mixture of envy, hatred, and yearning of their own.

When she looked back at Derek, she saw that he had extracted himself from the women and continued on. Kora found herself following him. She kept her distance, but if he thought he was being trailed, he never let on. He didn't look behind him once.

He stood a head taller than the tallest male in the village. His very presence sent an air of excitement through everyone. From the youngest to the oldest, all were aware of his presence. Most gave him a wide berth. He didn't smile that she could see, nor did he speak. And yet, he held everyone in thrall.

She recalled his shocked expression when she'd spoken to him the day before. Looking at him now, he could probably have taken the soldiers on himself. But she hadn't known that when she glimpsed him. She only knew how bloodthirsty the Stonemore soldiers were and hadn't wanted him involved. Maybe she shouldn't have worried, but that wasn't who she was.

He walked out of the village. Kora could've stopped following him. She probably should have. Instead, she kept shadowing him. To be fair, she wasn't the only one. Women trailed after him, their hopeful expressions almost painful to look at. One by one, they turned back when he continued without choosing them. Until she was all that remained.

Kora paused and glanced back at the village. She should turn around and go back to the cottage, have a nice meal, and mend her pants. Plan what she needed to do next. She had promised herself she wouldn't be reckless again.

She looked for Derek. He was nowhere in sight. She leaned from side to side, trying to see beyond the bend in the road. She considered turning around for a moment, but that didn't last long. She continued in the direction he had gone, reminding herself not to be rash. She came to the curve and slowed, once again leaning to the side to peer around it. There was still no sign of him.

Kora sighed. Perhaps it was an indication that she should leave well enough alone. She didn't know what she would say to him anyway. That's when the hairs on the back of her neck prickled. She slowly turned and found Derek on the road behind her.

CHAPTER 4

She was alive.

When Derek had caught a glimpse of her in the village, he couldn't believe his eyes. He wondered how he could get near her to talk when she followed him. It was easy enough to lead her out of the village and get her alone.

But now that he had her, now that she was close enough to confirm she was the same woman he had carried to the top of the mountain, he only had one question: What was she?

Magic was seen as something evil and malevolent by the majority of Zora. Anyone who possessed any kind of unnatural abilities was an outcast. Some were even killed. Whatever she was, she would likely keep it to herself. He hadn't been there to see her get up and walk away. There was no reason for her to willingly tell him anything. So, he didn't ask.

He stared at her. She held his gaze, unflinching. Who was this woman who'd warned him about the soldiers and then stood against five alone, only to die, come back, then follow him without hesitation?

Only someone who didn't fear anything did that. If she couldn't die, then she had nothing to be afraid of. He should know.

"All right," he said.

One delicate brow arched. "What?"

"You can share my bed."

She slowly ran her gaze down his body. He grew instantly, painfully hard. But he was always hard. No matter how many women he took to his bed, no one filled the empty hole inside him. He got a moment's pleasure before needing more. Always more.

Hunger lit her eyes. The pulse at the base of her neck beat erratically. She swallowed, her tongue peeking out to lick her dusky lips. She hadn't followed him to be bedded, but she wasn't turning away from the offer either. He wanted her in his bed.

And he would have her there.

"Tempting," she said, her voice husky with desire.

It was his turn to quirk a brow. "Is that no' why you trailed me?"

"Nay."

"Then why?"

Her gaze briefly lowered to his chest. "I...I'm not sure."

He took a step toward her, and she retreated. Derek inwardly smiled. She might not fear him, but she sensed there was more to him—something leashed. Something primal. And she was right to back away.

Women begged for his touch, but if they knew him—the *real* him—they would run in terror. They would try to hunt him if they knew what he had done and would do again. It would end in their deaths as it always did, but humans never learned.

This woman had tried to help him. She hadn't known he didn't need it. He had wanted to return the kindness but had only watched her die. She was everything he wasn't. Everything he couldn't be. His future had been mapped long ago. There was no changing it.

And he wouldn't want to even if he could.

"Leave," he said and turned to walk away.

She made to follow him. "Wait."

Even though he knew better, Derek paused and swung his head to the side. He said nothing, just waited.

"It was me yesterday in the forest."

He faced her then. "I know."

"Did any other soldiers come?"

"A small contingent. I gathered they were searching for those chasing you."

She nodded absently. "I see."

"What did you do to incur their wrath?" He shouldn't ask, but the words were already out.

"They were tormenting a boy. I took offense."

"Against Stonemore soldiers?" he asked in shock.

She shrugged, the corners of her lips lifting slightly. "Someone has to stand up to them."

"And that someone is you?"

"No one else was."

When he stepped toward her this time, she held her ground. He closed the distance between them until only a foot separated them. He wanted to rip away her tunic and see if there were scars from her injuries or if she healed as he did —completely.

Instead, he stared into her eyes, noting the amber and gold

mixed with the deep brown. His hand rose as if to run his fingers along her cheek again. He lowered his arm to his side.

"You presume a lot," he said.

She looked up at him, her eyes searching, prodding. He wondered what she saw. Did she see the emptiness, the vacuum that was his soul? Did she glimpse the beast? Could she sense the death that trailed in his wake?

"I do," she admitted with a shrug. "It's a flaw."

He found himself reaching for her again. Derek fisted his hand. "Get far away. Never return."

"I can't. Who are you?"

"Didn't the village tell you?"

She adjusted the bag that held her food. "They said you're called Derek."

"What else did they tell you?"

"That everyone wants in your bed."

He let his eyes rake her body, from her full breasts and small waist he hadn't noticed yesterday to the flare of her hips and long legs. His gaze slowly traveled back up her body. "Not everyone."

"I'm not someone you want to know."

On the contrary, she was exactly who he wanted to know. He would brand himself on her body and touch every inch of her inside and out so he would always be there. No one would ever touch her as he had. No one would ever fulfill her as he did.

"Who are you?" he threw the question back at her.

"No one," she said softly. "Take your own advice and leave. This isn't a good place."

"Tell me your name."

She smiled, but it held sadness this time. "You'll forget me soon enough."

Derek heard the women coming toward him too late. He glanced beyond the female to see them coming. She took off running into the forest. He followed. He didn't catch her, even though he could have. She looked over her shoulder. When she saw him, she stopped and faced him. He didn't slow until he caught up with her.

"What are you doing?" she demanded. "There are plenty of women who want you."

She did, too, but he didn't point that out. "You know my name. It's only fair I know yours."

"Why?"

"Why not?"

"Why are you answering a question with a question?"

"Why are you?"

Her lips compressed. "Names don't matter."

"They hold meaning."

"Kora. My name is Kora." She looked up through the trees, seemingly lost in thought.

Derek watched her. He had spent thousands of years observing those on Zora. He thought he knew all there was to know about humans and other magical creatures. But he didn't know what Kora was. She kept a shield around her, preventing others from getting close. She had something to hide, but he would uncover whatever it was.

If the village got wind that she had an ability, they would hunt her. If they learned she couldn't be killed, they would likely entomb her so she couldn't get out. Living and dying every day for eternity.

Humans took life easily and carelessly. They were heathens, monsters more depraved than any other created. They saw something and took it, uncaring of the consequences. Look what they had done to the dragons.

He wouldn't allow them to do it to Kora. Derek might be friendly with the village, but he would lay waste to it in a heartbeat if it meant freeing his kin—and protecting Kora.

She looked at the ground before her gaze swung to him. "Be careful."

"You're leaving?" It shocked him that she would walk away. Again.

She flashed him a quick grin. "Your ego will be soothed by any number of women back there."

"You shouldn't walk alone."

"I'm always alone."

She whispered it as she turned her head, probably believing it wouldn't reach his ears. He had seen loneliness in humans before, but something about Kora's was different. Mixed with the stark barrenness was shame. Or was it guilt?

Louder, she said, "I assure you I'll be fine. I got away from the soldiers, didn't I?"

Derek almost pointed out that she hadn't but held his tongue. Who was he to call out her secrets when he had so many of his own? "Seems so."

"Goodbye, then."

"Goodbye."

She lingered, and just when he thought she might remain, she turned on her heel and walked away. He watched her for a moment before retracing his steps. He opened his hearing, listening for her movements. He heard the crunch of leaves beneath her foot when she looked over her shoulder to see if he followed. He heard the soft sigh before she continued.

Derek waited half an hour before following her. Her trail was easy to track. When he found the tiny, barely standing cottage, he told himself he had gone too far. He needed to return to the swamp and keep watch. Kora didn't want or need him.

He stayed until nightfall. Then he touched the cuff and returned to the marshlands. He waded through the shallow water. The animals that called it home fell into two categories: the ones who knew he was no threat, and the ammit that swam away using their long, thick tails whenever he was near.

The mist swirled around the knobby trees and hovered over the water. Moss hung from the limbs above him. Humans who came close said the silence unnerved them the most. But the swamp was far from silent. It rang with sound. Silence didn't scare humans. It was the darkness, the ever-present danger just beneath the surface of the water, that did. The same threat that was in their daily lives that they were too blind to see.

Derek walked to the island in the middle of the marsh and stepped onto dry land. He passed through the invisible barrier that had been reinforced numerous times, to the mound of boulders he had created to mimic a cave. The opening was large enough for him to pass through in dragon form. He walked to the two eggs sitting in the middle and put his hands on them. One was a bright magenta. The other a deep forest green.

He had been guarding them for years. Nothing they had tried worked to hatch them. But he wouldn't give up. They would hatch. Just as his kin imprisoned on dragon land would be freed.

CHAPTER 5

Two days had passed since Kora spoke to Derek. Two days of incessant thoughts about him. Two days of dissecting their conversation. Of picturing his face. Of wondering what might have happened had she accepted his offer. Of imagining what it would feel like to be held by him.

Kora sat outside the cottage beneath the cloud-laden sky, twirling a long strand of grass. She had been hiding for so long, she could no longer recall what it was like to be carefree, to give in to simple longings. Because the moment she let her guard down, it could mean trouble. After all, the last time she had ignored the warnings, it had gotten her brother, uncle, and cousin killed.

The remorse and disgrace of that still threatened to choke her. She blinked away the burn of tears and rose to her feet, dropping the grass. It might have taken her this long to return to finish what her family had started, but at least she was here. Though she had no idea what to do next.

She knew little about Stonemore other than it was built into the side of the mountain with massive gates. Uncle Rylan had said there was a back entrance, but he had never divulged where it might be. The information had died with him. She needed to get the lay of the city—and the exits—before entering it.

Even being this close made her uneasy. Villette had hunted her people ruthlessly, relentlessly. She would send every dragon she commanded after Kora the moment she learned of her existence. How could Kora get through the gates and remain undetected? Stonemore was heavily guarded. Just getting inside would be a problem. Then, there was the issue of getting to Villette.

Whether Kora wanted to admit it or not, she needed help. But therein lay another problem. There were those willing to share information about the city, but it came at a cost, and her coin purse was all but empty. She couldn't pay for another meal, much less someone to give her the information she desperately needed.

She walked to the bush and plucked more of the bright red berries before popping them into her mouth. It wasn't just the issue of money. She also had to trust the person. They could give her bad information or lie. She had no connections to the area. With no one to trust, she would have to follow her gut. And that wasn't always reliable.

Kora dusted off her hands when she finished her snack. She needed to hunt. She scanned the trees and began walking. Every moment she spent searching for food took away from the time she required to get to Stonemore. She tried to imagine what Kayden or Rylan would've done. Even Zak. They thought to protect her, and they had. It had also given her a false sense of safety. If she had known their kind had dwindled to just the four of them, she never would've wandered off that day.

But she had.

The drop on her cheek jerked her out of her musings. Kora sighed when she saw the dark cloud overhead. She had been so lost in thought that she hadn't paid attention to the weather or where she was going. She turned and jogged back to the structure.

Her gaze settled on a figure leaning against the outside of the hut. Her steps slowed to a walk, and her heart beat faster when she recognized Derek. He had one foot propped on the house, his arms crossed over his chest, with his face turned toward her. Even from the distance, she could feel the intensity of his gaze.

He watched her like he was a predator and she the prey. When he moved, it was done deliberately, purposefully. He had an animalistic quality, one that screamed, *"Danger!"* And promised untold desires.

She should turn the other way and run. Put distance between them. Instead, she kept walking toward him like a string connected them, slowly pulling her closer.

When she neared, he dropped his foot to the ground and straightened. His pale olive gaze refused to let her look away. Fat drops of rain began pelting them. She stopped before him, close enough to set her hand on his chest. Kora found herself leaning toward him and stopped. It would be so easy to give in to what her body needed. To what she longed for.

She wasn't made to be on her own. She was meant for a community. A family unit. Kora might snatch a night here and there with a willing partner, but it was never anything more. She couldn't allow that. Not until she succeeded in killing Villette.

Her attraction to Derek wasn't the problem. It was the way he consumed her thoughts. She had kept herself free of entanglements. Derek was anything but simple. He would demand she give him everything, and if she did, she would open herself to things she didn't dare face until the past was put to rest.

The rain fell faster. Neither moved. They were locked in a silent debate, neither willing to surrender. Kora shivered as a drop of rain fell on her neck and slipped down her back. If she didn't make the first move, they might be standing out there for hours, and she had hunting to do. Though letting him inside could be a deadly mistake.

She watched the water caress the firm planes of his face from his brow to his cheekbone and down the hollow of his cheek to his jaw. The drop sat there a moment before dripping onto his chest. Even just this close, she could feel his warmth. She fought against the need to move closer.

Kora suppressed another shiver. No matter how she studied her instincts for an answer on what to do, they gave her nothing. She finally gave in and walked to the door. There, she paused and cut her eyes to him. Derek's gaze remained on her. She lifted the door and set it aside before walking in. He followed soon after.

She added wood to the fire as he placed the door back over the opening. The cottage was so small that every movement was loud. She remained facing the flames because she didn't trust herself to face him again. If he had filled her thoughts the past few days, she would never get him out of her head now that his scent was here.

The silence became unbearable. She reluctantly straightened and turned. Derek hadn't moved from the door. His presence filled the entire cottage. She tried to swallow and wet her dry mouth. Droplets of water fell from the ends of his hair to land on the wooden floor. He moved toward her. Instinctively, she stepped back.

His eyes narrowed briefly, but he kept coming. In two steps, she was against the wall with nowhere else to go. He halted in front of her and flattened his hands on either side of her head. Then he leaned in close. His warmth enveloped her. She inhaled, the scent of water, pine, and smoke filling her senses.

She wanted to lay her hands on him, rip away his tunic, and bare his chest to her eyes, hands, and mouth. Desire throbbed between her legs. Her nipples hardened as her lips parted of their own accord.

He brushed his cheek against hers, rolling her head to the side. Then he put his face against her neck and breathed deeply. When he lifted his head, his eyes smoldered with a hunger that matched hers.

"Why are you here?" she asked.

His gaze dropped to her mouth. She bit back a moan, even as she arched her back, pushing her chest toward him. "You know why."

Kora shook her head. "Find another."

"I want you. And you want me."

She couldn't deny it, even if she wished she could. And that terrified her. Just as her reaction to him did. He hadn't even touched her yet. A moan passed her lips when she imagined what it would be like when he did.

She turned her head away. "I can't."

"Do you belong to another?"

"Nay."

He shifted closer, his body stopping just short of touching hers. "What's stopping you?"

"People close to me get hurt."

"Not me."

"Everyone."

He placed a finger gently against her chin and turned her head to him. His eyes blazed with a fierceness that surprised her. "Not. Me."

"Who are you?" she whispered.

"The one who is going to make you scream with pleasure."

She couldn't have told him to go if she wanted. "One night only."

A slow, sexy grin was his only reply.

Kora waited for him to kiss her, but she soon realized she had to make the first move. She peeled her hands from the wall and placed them on his waist. Slowly, she smoothed her hands up his stomach to his chest and then over his thick shoulders before her fingers tangled in his long hair.

A muscle ticked in his jaw, his body stiff as he waited to see what she would do. She cupped the back of his head and pulled it down as she raised her face to his. His lips were soft, pliant beneath hers. She kissed him again and again, allowing her mouth to linger against his longer each time. Then she slid her tongue along the seam of his lips.

A ragged moan rumbled in his chest as he pinned her between his hard body and the wall. He seized her mouth, deepening the kiss. He ravaged her until she was breathless and shivering for more.

She yanked his tunic from his pants and slipped her hand under the hem. The instant her palms met flesh, there was no turning back. He broke the kiss to yank the shirt over his head and toss it away.

Kora lightly ran her fingers over the masterpiece of his torso.

Strong shoulders and a wide chest tapered to a trim waist. His stomach rippled with defined muscles. Thick sinew corded his arms. She couldn't stop touching him. And she wanted to see the rest of his body.

It was all Derek could do to keep his hands off Kora. He had imagined fucking her in every way possible. It had driven him to her every day. He had stayed hidden, hoping for a glimpse of her, but it hadn't been enough. He had to have her to ease the ache she had created.

He watched her face as she caressed him. She left a trail of fire everywhere she touched. He burned. The hunger, the need blazed brighter than ever. And it was soon to rage out of control.

His eyes fastened on her tempting lips. Her mouth parted, breath rushing past. Her fingers skimmed the flesh that met the fabric of his pants. She bit her bottom lip, her chest rising and falling rapidly. His control snapped.

Derek bent and captured her lips, sliding his body up hers. She groaned and wound her arms around his neck. There was a fire in her, begging to be released. She tried to temper it, but he would settle for nothing less than everything from those who shared his bed.

He kissed her deeply, thoroughly. He was momentarily shaken when she kissed him back with as much fervor. Derek fisted a hand in the long, cool strands of her hair and tugged her head back. Her lips were swollen from his kisses as she stared at him, her chest heaving. By the stars, she was a sight. And he had yet to fill her.

He put his nose to her neck once more and inhaled. Something about her earthy scent stirred something within him—a familiarity he couldn't place. But it didn't matter. There was nowhere she could go now that he couldn't follow. He lifted his head and caught her gaze. Lust burned in her eyes.

He put a hand between them and tugged on her belt. Derek added magic, and it fell away in his hands. For a heartbeat, he almost gave in to the desire to discard her clothes with a thought. He usually enjoyed the slow removal of clothing, but not this time. Not with Kora. The urgency, the *need* to fuse their bodies had consumed him since he'd first spoken to her.

He felt the loss of her hands when she grabbed her tunic and removed it. Derek had to force his fingers to loosen on her hair. Then she stood in the bindings around her breasts, looking at him with excitement and anticipation. He grabbed her hands when she reached to unhook the binding.

Derek lifted her arms above her head and held her wrists in one hand. His gaze lowered to the swell of her breasts before he pressed his lips to each one. He unwound the bindings until they, too, fell to the floor.

Her hips rocked against him seductively as she moaned. He captured her mouth in a kiss. She raised a leg, hooking it around his waist. He ground against her, as needy as she. Kora was tipping him into a place he had never been before, somewhere he hadn't thought existed. Nothing mattered but her and the pleasure that awaited them.

Impatience rode him. He glided his free hand down to her boot and tugged. It thudded to the floor. Her kisses were intoxicating, and he couldn't get enough. Each taste was enthralling, calling him back for more. His cock throbbed as it became impossibly hard. He released her wrists and moaned when she spread her palms over his shoulders.

Their bodies rocked against each other until they were mindless with need. Derek lifted her, using magic to remove her remaining boot as well as his. Then he turned and laid her on the blanket.

CHAPTER 6

She was on fire. Every part of her burned for him. He was the breath that filled her lungs, the blood that pumped through her heart. The heat and yearning that swelled within her.

The desire that blazed in his eyes took her breath away. She tried to pull him down on top of her, but he resisted, reaching for the fastening of her pants instead. He removed them and her underwear with the same speed as he had her other garments. Her skin flushed with need as his gaze ran over her from her breasts to her waist to her hips to her sex and then down her legs before slowly moving back up her body with the same hunger.

His hand flattened on her stomach, his thumb sliding along her side. He wore a curious expression she couldn't read. Just as she was about to ask him what was wrong, he stood and removed the last of his clothes.

All thought left her mind when she saw the size of his arousal jutting outward. Kora rose onto her elbows, eager to take him in hand. He kneeled between her legs and settled over her like a prowling animal. She lowered onto her back and watched him as he moved over her. His thick arousal lay between them. Then, he was kissing her again. A slow, deep, seductive, soul-stealing kiss.

It was amazing. It was glorious.

But she needed more. She needed him *inside* her.

She tore her mouth from his. "Please."

"What do you want?" he asked in a voice roughened by need.

Kora stared into his beautiful eyes. "You."

Her words sent a rush of thundering need through him. Derek touched her face and stroked down her neck to the outside of her breast. He cupped the globe, letting it fill his hand before bending and wrapping his lips around her pert nipple.

He felt the tremor that went through her. She moaned, her nails digging into his back as she rocked against him. He suckled the turgid peak until she was moaning incoherently. Then he moved to her other breast. The moment he cupped her sex, she came apart in his hands.

Derek watched the pleasure that washed over her face and through her body. He slid a finger into her wet heat and circled her clit with his thumb. She sucked in a breath, her eyes flying open to lock with his. Her mouth was open in a silent scream as her eyes rolled back in her head, and another orgasm ripped through her.

Warmth spread through her, sending her floating on a wave of ecstasy the likes of which she had never felt before. And she never wanted to come down.

Derek's delicious weight was atop her. She whimpered when he removed his hand from her. A moment later, he rubbed the length of his cock along the swollen folds of her sex. She opened her eyes to see him looking down at their bodies. The elation she saw on his face sent a thrill curling through her. Then he maneuvered the head of his arousal to her entrance.

His gaze lifted to meet hers as he slowly pushed inside her. Kora gasped at his size. He planted his hands on either side of her, holding his body up. He pulled out of her and gradually filled her again, going a little deeper. She looked between their bodies, watching the way he moved in and out of her.

She spread her legs wider as her body began to adjust to him. Their gazes met, held. He moved with measured movements until he was seated within her. He kept up the slow, deep thrusts. She thrilled at the movement of the muscles in his back and shoulders. Their bodies grew damp as they slid against each other.

He gradually increased his tempo until he was driving into her, hard and fast. Desire twisted low in her belly, building toward another climax. She reached for it, eager for more. He didn't disappoint either. She wanted. He gave. It wasn't long before she cried out from the intense orgasm that ripped through her. She clung to Derek, her body shuddering.

He held her tightly, never letting go, not even when he buried himself deep and his seed filled her.

Kora woke to the feel of fingers inside her. She moaned as Derek nestled his chest to her back, her top leg thrown over his.

"I'm no' done with you yet," he murmured huskily, rocking his hard cock against her bottom.

She sucked in a breath when he circled her swollen clit with his finger. Then it was back inside her, pumping. A second joined the first. Everywhere he touched, pleasure followed. She could just lay back and experience it all. But that wasn't the kind of lover she was.

Kora flipped and rolled him onto his back before straddling him. He shot her a smile as she brought his rod to her entrance and lowered herself. He reached for her breasts and teased her nipples, sending pleasure straight to her sex. The feel of him moving inside her was bliss. Her body was an instrument, and he played it to perfection.

She dropped her head back as she rode him. His long fingers gripped her hips, holding her as he urged her faster. She came apart when his thumb found her clit.

And when he held her after she collapsed atop his chest once they'd orgasmed together, she told herself it meant nothing. She needed a release, and he supplied that.

The next time she woke, he put her on her hands and knees and filled her from behind. He held her firmly as he thrust hard and fast, their bodies slapping together. She didn't think she had any more to give, but she came alive in his hands. A moan fell from her lips when he reached around and stroked her clit.

Their harsh breaths filled the room. She wanted to touch him, but each time she tried to move, his fingers dug into her hips more.

"Next time, you get to choose," he ground out.

Kora smiled, pleased to know he wanted more. Thoughts soon halted as desire swelled. She pushed back against him, meeting Derek each time he drove into her. He hit just the right spots, sending her spiraling to climax.

"Now," Derek growled as he reached down again and found her clit.

Her body reacted on command, shuddering around his cock as he gave a final thrust.

Rain beat a steady drum atop the roof of the hut. Water dripped inside from holes in the ceiling. Kora opened her eyes to find herself on her side, facing the hearth, where a fire burned. She slowly looked behind her, but Derek wasn't there.

She didn't know whether to be glad about that or not. After all, she had said only one night. She blew out a breath and rolled onto her back, wincing at the delicious soreness of her body. She had needed a night where nothing had mattered but pleasure, and Derek had delivered, just as she had known he would.

Kora sat up and looked around for her clothes. She rose and quickly dressed before glancing outside. The dark skies made it difficult to determine if it was day or night. She was chilled and didn't relish going outside in the rain, but she was hungry. There were still some berries on the bush. They would have to last her until the rain let up.

She went to the hearth to warm her hands and spotted a sack

hanging on a peg. Kora frowned. It wasn't hers. She looked around the small hut again, then removed the bag from the hook. She peered inside to find dried meat and bread. She wasn't too proud to accept food. She had gone hungry enough to know only fools turned away such things.

It rankled that Derek wanted to pay for their time together. Still, she pulled out a slice of meat and bit into it. It wasn't until she had eaten half that she realized he might have accidentally left it. She hastily returned the bag to the peg but finished the slice she had already taken. He hadn't had a sack when she saw him yesterday. Though he could have put it inside before she arrived. She hadn't noticed anything other than him after returning.

Kora walked around some leaks in the ceiling. She went to the door and moved it to look outside. There was no sign of Derek. His clothes were gone. The likely reason was that he had left. She wasn't a deep sleeper. She should've heard him moving about.

She leaned against the doorway, watching the rain as she combed through her hair with her fingers. Her thoughts drifted to the hours spent in Derek's arms. He was a skilled, demanding lover. And nearly as insatiable as she was. A smile pulled at her lips. She didn't regret a single moment. While she hadn't planned such a meeting, it seemed fitting as a last hurrah before the end. Because whatever happened to her, it would be an end. Either her life or Villette's.

Movement caught her eye across the grass near the trees. A murky figure took shape, striding toward her. She recognized Derek's tan shirt that was now plastered to his hard body—a body she knew intimately. It wasn't until he was nearly upon her that she noticed he carried something. She looked down at the skinned ritbit to his face and moved aside for him to enter.

Water dripped from his long, black hair onto the floor. He set the small animal over the fire to cook and then faced her.

"I was hungry," he stated.

She glanced at the bag she'd found earlier.

"Everything all right?"

Kora hesitated. Was everything all right? She had convinced herself that Derek had left. It had been convenient so she didn't have to get through an awkward farewell. She had been happy about that. Sort of. The night had been incredible. In fact, it had been the best night of her life. But now he stood before her again. He didn't just know where she slept. He had returned. She didn't know how she felt about that. He had stripped her of more than her clothing during the night. He had somehow divested her of the walls she'd put around herself. She was exposed, bare in a way she had never been before.

And she wasn't sure how to reverse it.

Or even if she could.

Or wanted to.

She realized he was waiting for a reply. "I don't know."

"You'll feel better when your belly is full," he said matter-of-factly.

Kora stood mutely as he stirred the fire before lowering himself to the floor and leaning back against the wall. She should tell him to leave or leave herself. Yet she needed someone who knew the area. Derek just might be that someone. If she could trust him.

The danger she sensed in him hadn't vanished after sharing his bed. Derek wasn't a man to be messed with. All someone had to do was look at him to know that. Even if she hadn't seen the villagers treat him with respect, awe, and trepidation, she would've known to be cautious around him.

It was that same danger that drew her.

He didn't carry weapons that she could see, but she recognized a fighter when she saw one. It was in how he viewed others, in the way he carried himself. And in the manner he spoke. He could rule the village if he wanted, but he didn't. Maybe he led another group. She looked at his large hands and long fingers. Those hands had held weapons before. She was sure of it. Her gaze returned to his to find him studying her as intently as she was him.

If she was to triumph over her enemy, she needed to plan, and the only way to come up with a solid scheme was with information. That meant trusting others. She just hoped she was making the right decision.

"Have you lived in the area long?" she asked.

"A very long time."

"Then you know about the dragon that's near."

CHAPTER 7

So, she had seen him in his true form. Derek propped his feet on the floor and rested his arms on his knees. Just what did this female want with him? Did she know he was the dragon who'd stood over her? Her gaze was calculating, her body tense. The answer was important to her. Well, he wanted answers, too. And he always got what he wanted.

"I do," Derek answered.

Kora lowered to the floor, propping her back against the opposite wall as if she tried to get as far from him as she could. It was laughable. All he had to do was stretch out his legs and touch her foot. But he gave her the space she seemed to need. It hadn't been that way a few hours earlier.

"Tell me about the dragon," she urged.

Derek let the statement hang between them for a long moment. "You don't intend to do something foolish, do you?"

"I want to know if it leaves the swamp."

All the fucking time. What would she do if she knew he was the very thing she asked about? "Dragons are part of our world."

"Unfortunately."

Her words struck a nerve. It wasn't the first time he had heard such talk. Normally, it didn't bother him. But it cut painfully this time. "They do what they do. Like all animals."

"Are you not afraid?"

"Are you afraid of the beasts in the forest?"

She tucked her hair behind her ear. "I can defend myself against them."

"Even a brineling?" The huge, smelly animals had a single-minded focus when they set their sights on someone. They never quit until they killed what they were after. Their hide was too thick for any human weapons, making them extremely dangerous predators.

"I avoid them. Just as I avoid the dragons. Can you tell me if the dragon leaves?"

"It does."

"Do you know where it goes?"

It was obvious she was after something in particular. "I do not."

"Have you heard of Stonemore?"

"Everyone has."

"Have you been to the city?"

Things were getting more interesting by the moment. He had walked the city once before Villette thought it better if others didn't see him. "I have."

"What can you tell me about it?"

"It's overcrowded and loud."

"Is it easy to get past the guards at the gate?"

He tilted his head, regarding her as he picked through her wording. "You're looking for someone."

"I am."

"And you think they're in the city?"

"I know they are," she replied.

Derek scratched his chin. Stonemore was Villette's domain. He didn't want Kora anywhere near the city, but he could see by the stubborn lift of her chin that nothing would dissuade her. "The guards determine who gets in."

She nodded absently, her gaze briefly dropping to the floor. "Is there any other way to get into the city?"

There were several ways, but he wouldn't share them with anyone. Not even Kora. "There are soldiers everywhere in the city. There's no getting around them."

"How hard is it to get in?"

The more questions she asked, the more worried he became. He recalled touching her side where he had seen the sword embedded. There wasn't any sign there had been an injury. She didn't just come back to life. All her wounds had vanished as if they never were. Kora was just the type to draw Villette's attention. He had seen it before, and it rarely turned out well for the individual.

He thought about how Kora had told him to hide from the soldiers. He hadn't saved her from death, but he could keep her away from Villette.

"Getting through the gate is just the first obstacle. Each level is controlled by soldiers, and they can close it off at any time. If the one you're looking for is on the lower levels, you should be all right."

Kora pressed her lips together. "How do I get to the upper levels?"

"Only the wealthy are given access."

She leaned her head against the wall and looked at the ceiling, seemingly lost in thought.

Derek turned the ritbit over on the spit. The growling of Kora's stomach had sent him out into the night to hunt. He had used his magic to create the bag of food but then decided to get fresh meat. She had survived on berries and small animals in the days he had observed her.

He hadn't meant to stay. He'd intended to drop off the meat and leave, but something about seeing Kora standing in the doorway and how she looked at him... He craved her taste even now.

She had been a wild and sensual lover, giving as good as she got. Demanding as much as he. The fact that he had been content to hold her as she slept had surprised him.

But not nearly as much as the satisfaction that filled him after their first encounter. She had touched him in ways he hadn't believed possible. He had come harder than ever.

And was startled to find that he had been satisfied. Truly and utterly satiated. It hadn't been emptiness that had him reaching for her again but hunger to see if he could replicate the feeling.

And he had.

"Maybe this person doesn't want to be found," he said into the silence.

"I have to do this."

"That's why you've come to the mountains?"

She raised her head to look at him. "Aye."

"This isn't a good place." He should know. He was responsible for causing the stark terror among the humans.

"Why do you remain?"

"Because I must."

She flashed him a quick grin that held no mirth. "I, too, must be here."

They fell into silence then. Neither moved until the meat had cooked. Derek took the ritbit off the spit and pulled off a large piece before handing it to Kora.

He couldn't stop thinking about her scent. It was familiar, but he couldn't place it no matter how he searched his mind. He would, though. He wanted to know what she was. He didn't know about any humans who could come back from death.

Derek hadn't cared about any species—magical or not—other than his. His entire purpose was to free the dragons from their captors once and for all. If that meant wiping out every human, then he would do it. Villette had a plan, and he was following it. Though it was taking longer than he liked.

There had been setbacks, which only incensed him more. He had been patient, but every day his kin were trapped was another day of torment. Villette promised her plan was nearly ready, but that was before she got injured. She was a Star Person. Part of a group of beings more powerful and formidable than any other in the universe.

He had seen her heal serious wounds, but she never spoke of the burns on her neck and face. Now, she had more. Despite her potent magic, Star People could be killed. If she died, then everything he had fought for all these centuries would be for nothing. He couldn't lose her. Villette was the only Star Person willing to free the dragons.

Derek slid his gaze to Kora. Who was within Stonemore's gates that drew her to the city? He didn't know why anyone went. It was loud and smelly. Even in the bowels of the mountain, he was overcome by the taint of the place. The starving and needy, the religious fanatics who believed everyone should worship their gods, the swindlers and charlatans, and the soldiers taking power however they could.

Villette welcomed them all. He didn't understand why she encouraged humans to visit the city. He had asked once, but she hadn't answered.

"There's a back entrance," Kora said. "I know there is."

Derek quirked a brow. "How do you know that?"

"Someone told me."

"Did they tell you where it is?"

She sighed. "Nay."

"Stonemore's army is huge. Like I said, there are soldiers everywhere—as you've seen."

"Destroying villages. I know. They'll come for yours soon."

He shrugged. "It isn't mine."

"You wouldn't protect the people within? They're innocent."

"No one is innocent."

She stretched her legs out and crossed them at the ankles. "That's a bold statement."

"It's the truth."

"Maybe," she conceded. "I think most people are doing the best they can. The Divine attacking villages is solely about power. The soldiers kill and maim, and the survivors are told to go to the city."

Derek didn't reply. There was nothing to say. Everything she said was the truth. There were parts she didn't know, but he doubted learning them would cause her to feel differently about Stonemore or Villette.

Or him.

"How much power does one ruler need?"

He ran a hand down his face. "Are you sure the one you're searching for is in the city?"

"Positive."

"Can you get a message to them and lure them out?"

Kora shook her head.

"I take it they don't know you're coming?"

"They do not."

Derek understood then. He should have pieced it together sooner. "You're attempting to locate an enemy."

"Does that bother you?"

"It does not. My warning still stands. Don't go."

"I didn't come all this way for nothing."

He slowly released a breath. "What do you plan to do with this nemesis?"

"I'm going to exact my revenge."

"You're going to kill them."

She nodded once.

Derek could give her a speech about how retaliation was never the answer, but he thought that was bollocks anyway. His entire life had been about exacting payback on those holding the dragons prisoner. He was many things, but he wasn't a hypocrite.

"You're going to stand out," he told her. "Not just the way you dress, but your manner."

"Then give me all the information I need. I'll change my clothes. I'll do whatever it takes."

And there it was. She had given him the means to ensure she

was caught the moment she entered the gates, thereby preventing her from seeking whoever she was after. If he did that, it would alert Villette.

He wouldn't have hesitated to notify Villette of her presence before. But Kora had shown him kindness and lost her life in the process. It wasn't just that he needed to discover what she was. For the first time, he couldn't shake the feeling that he owed her. At the very least, he should return the favor.

Maybe Kora was someone dangerous. She might even be a species that endangered the freedom of his kin, but he would uncover that for himself. He didn't know why it was so important, but it was. It became clear from the instant of their first kiss. Villette need never know about any of it.

"You'd be a fool to take anyone's word," Derek told her.

Her lips curved into a half-smile. "I asked for information. I never said I'd believe you."

"With that attitude, you just might survive the city."

"Stonemore has taken in people from many villages. They'll dress and act differently. I'll blend fine."

He grinned and bowed his head to her. "Right you are."

"Does that mean you'll tell me about the city?"

Derek only knew what he heard from others. It had been ages since he had actually walked Stonemore's streets. Villette had made it clear she didn't want anyone to see them together and word to get back to those holding the dragons. But that didn't mean he couldn't go to the city.

"Derek?"

He was supposed to guard the eggs, but he had watched over them for several hundred years now. No one had come to steal them, and they hadn't hatched. His magic protected them. No one would get near them. The cuff allowed him to check on them whenever he wanted.

A small frown wrinkled Kora's brow as she watched him. She was capable, and whatever magic she had gave her an advantage. How long would that last when she was killed inside Stonemore's gates and came back to life?

"I'll do better than tell you. I'll take you."

CHAPTER 8

"You what?" Surely, Kora hadn't heard him right.

"I'll take you."

She couldn't decide if she was thrilled about having a companion to help her navigate the complexities of the city or worried Derek would get in the way. "Why?"

"Why not?"

They were back to that again, then. She rolled her eyes and blew out a breath. "I think I have the right to an answer. And if you tell me it's because you don't believe I can take care of myself, then you won't be going."

"You couldn't stop me."

"Try me." It galled her when he grinned.

Derek shrugged. "I have business there."

"What business?"

"Who are you trying to find?"

Kora balled her hands into fists. The man had a special way of irritating her. She dropped her gaze to his mouth, remembering how his tongue had wrung screams from her while licking her. How could he vex her yet also make her crave him?

If he came with her, she would have use of his body again. The moment that thought came, she knew it was wrong.

"Traveling together will benefit both of us," he told her. "I know the city and can get you inside. I have business to see to anyway. You can't argue with that."

She couldn't, damn him.

"There's also the added benefit of us continuing to share a bed."

Did he read minds now? Kora couldn't make such an important decision because her body hungered for more of his. Yet he made valid points. She needed to get inside the city, and he promised to get her there. That in and of itself was worth it. Once inside, they could go their separate ways.

"Are we in agreement?" he asked expectantly.

Kora waited several long moments just to annoy him before saying, "Aye."

"Good. Get some sleep. We leave at dawn."

She wasn't tired, but talking to him was exhausting. Kora gladly crawled to her blanket and put her back to him. She sat stiffly for a long time, waiting to hear if he intended to join her. She couldn't decide if she wanted him to or not.

That was a lie. She wanted him. Desperately.

She closed her eyes and tried to forget him. But there was no forgetting or ignoring a man like Derek.

Kora woke against a hard body. Once more, she'd slept through Derek moving about. This time, lying next to her. His chest made a comfortable pillow, though. His heartbeat was strong and steady, his chest rising and falling regularly.

She carefully lifted the arm draped across his flat stomach and her leg thrown over his. Then she took the arm that held her and slowly removed it. She sat up and moved away. Only then did she release her breath.

Her head swiveled to look over her shoulder. Derek lay on his back, one hand under his head, and the other lying open as if waiting for her to return. Sometimes, the act of sleeping with someone was more intimate than a sexual act. A person let their guard down when they slept. They were vulnerable, defenseless.

She moved silently to the window and cracked it open. The storm had passed, leaving the world covered in droplets of water in the softness of the dawn. The sky was streaked: pale blue, yellow, and pink. Birds sang loudly as they fluttered from tree to tree, greeting the new day. She had returned to the place of her nightmares to fulfill her family's obligation. It started now.

A flutter of worry filled her stomach. Everything hinged on her as the last. It was immense pressure, and she hadn't been able to handle it before. But no matter how far or fast she fled, there was no outrunning the past. It was always there, waiting to remind her of what she had done.

What she *still* needed to do.

The ghosts of her ancestors watched her, waiting expectantly. Their silent accusations had stung worse than any injury. They couldn't rest until she had completed their mission and put the universe back into balance.

She didn't want the responsibility. While she had battled her inner demons that told her she wasn't strong enough to take down Villette, others had died. While she huddled in fear and let her anxiety dictate her life, evil had spread like a disease. If she didn't cut out the infection now, then it would blanket the entire realm.

Did she have what it took to win? The only way she would know that would be to face Villette. There was no one to back her up. No one to help her plan. No one to keep her in check so she didn't do anything rash and foolish.

And no one to get her out of trouble.

Kora glanced at the blanket, only to find it empty. She spun to look behind her. Derek squatted before the hearth, banking the coals. "How do you move so quietly?"

He didn't look her way as he said, "I move normally. You were lost in thought."

She tried to run her fingers through her hair again but gave up after a moment and dug the comb from her bag. Her hand grazed the money bag and the single coin within. She couldn't go to the city empty-handed. With the overcrowding, she didn't imagine there would be many opportunities to find employment.

Kora sat and combed her hair. The repetitive motions helped to soothe the riot of emotions swirling within her. She glanced over to find Derek watching her with a curious expression. He looked away when he noticed her eyes on him. Then he stood and dug in the sack of food. He handed her some dried meat and bread.

"Aren't you going to eat?" she asked when he didn't take anything.

"I'll eat when I'm hungry."

She watched him walk out of the cottage. Kora braided her hair and then ate. It felt good to have her belly full of food. Afterward, she gathered her things and put them in her bag, setting it by the door. She peered outside as she shrugged on her coat. Derek stood to the side of the hut, looking back toward the village.

Kora walked to him. "You don't have to come with me."

His head swung to her. "Me standing here makes you think I don't want to accompany you?"

"It makes me wonder if you have reservations or perhaps that you've changed your mind."

"I'm looking at the birds," he said, returning his gaze to the sky.

She saw them then. The two birds gliding through the sky. "What kind are they?"

"Lonin. The largest birds on the realm. You can spot them by their white feathers. They mate for life."

Kora watched the duo circle elegantly among the clouds, moving farther away and taking their haunting calls. She had seen a lonin up close once. It had been terrifyingly huge, its wingspan twice the length of a person. Its beak had been frightening but it was nothing compared to the talons.

She tore her gaze from the birds to Derek. He seemed in awe of the lonin. Almost as if he were imagining himself flying with them. She looked at the birds again and wondered what it would be like to soar among the clouds. She would be able to go anywhere. Get lost in the puffs of white. Maybe even above them. Possibly high enough to touch the stars.

"I wonder if the air smells different up there," she said.

"It does."

Kora looked at him. Before she could ask how he knew, he turned and walked to the cottage. She followed to see him grab the sack of food. She slipped the strap of her bag over her head and through one arm to settle across her body.

"Ready?" he asked.

No one would know if she didn't go to Stonemore. No one would know if she never confronted Villette.

No one but her.

She lifted her chin. "Aye."

Derek set a grueling pace. He didn't take the easy paths either. Kora kept up, but barely. She quickly abandoned her coat, stuffing it into her bag in an effort to remain cool. The route through the trees had been the easy part. After they refilled their waterskins, he led them straight to the mountain. The incline was steep and grueling. The only respite she got was when she reached each of the three ridges that flattened out enough to give her legs a break.

While she was winded and sweaty, Derek looked as if he were taking a leisurely stroll. She managed to keep up, but he occasionally looked back at her and called for them to rest. She wished she could've told him to keep going, but she wasn't stupid. Each opportunity to rest was one she relished.

Kora drained her waterskin while Derek had barely touched his. He eventually handed his over, and she gratefully took it. She didn't know if he took them to a water source because she was in such need or if it had been part of their journey, but she nearly cried when she heard it. She plunged her hands into the cool water appreciatively and splashed it onto her face before cupping her hands and bringing them to her lips.

While she contemplated stripping off her clothes to plunge

into the fast-moving stream, Derek filled both their waterskins. Then she was on her feet again to keep trudging up the mountain. Her stomach growled with hunger, but she wasn't about to ask to stop for food. Though she glared at Derek's back, wondering how he could look so composed during such a climb. Granted, he was in excellent shape, but she had thought she was in pretty good form herself. He proved her wrong.

Her thigh muscle gave out when she tried to step. She windmilled her arms to try to stay balanced. Suddenly, Derek was there, his hand on her arm, steadying her. He pulled her up, and she realized they had reached the top of the mountain. Tears of exhaustion threatened. She had never been so tired in all her life.

"Sit," he commanded. "We're stopping for the noon meal."

Kora didn't point out that it was past noon. She was just happy to hear that she could sit. When she tried to lower herself onto a rock, her fatigued muscles couldn't hold her. She ended up falling unceremoniously, hurting her arse in the process.

Derek tossed her the sack of food. She grabbed the first thing she touched. As she chewed the dried meat, she peered down the mountain they had just climbed. It looked a lot taller from where she was than when she had seen it from the bottom. There was no way she would've made the climb as quickly if she were by herself. Nor would she have known where to go. It had all been Derek.

The sun beat down on them relentlessly. She longed for an autumn breeze to cool her heated skin, but the chilly temperatures seemed to abandon them, even at the top. Kora fanned herself as she looked at Derek's profile. He stood at the edge, looking down the other side where they would descend. Dark stubble shadowed his jaw. Even among the rocks and trees, he appeared larger than life. Nothing seemed to faze him. She wondered what it would be like to face the world in such a manner.

His pale olive eyes met hers. Who was this man who had sought her out, pleasured her mercilessly during the night, and held her as she slept? She wasn't sure she would ever be able to peel back all the layers to find out. Or if she even wanted to. Sometimes, it was best to let the secrets be. Then again, he might surprise her and answer if she dared to ask, but would it be the truth?

If she were someone different, she might try to find out what his secrets were.

If he were someone different, he might want to share them.

But they were who they were.

Kora finished eating and put away her waterskin. It took her two tries to get to her feet. She walked to Derek, noting he hadn't sat during their meal. He still watched her. He kept his emotions behind a thick wall, not allowing her to see his thoughts or feelings. She understood since she hid things herself. It was easier that way. Just as it was easier to pretend that everything would work out in her favor when things pointed in another direction.

"Ready?" she asked.

"The descent is tricky."

"I'll be careful."

He looked as if he were about to say something, then nodded and started down. Kora realized they were on a game trail. She used the trees for balance as she passed them. The decline was so sharp that she had to walk sideways so she didn't go sliding down. It put a lot of strain on her already overworked leg muscles.

The descent was done at a much slower speed than their trek up. Her thigh muscles began to cramp. She rotated her ankle in an effort to work out the kinks in her calves, but that stopped working after a while. She couldn't hold back her sigh of thanks when they reached a ridge.

Kora was so happy to be off the incline that she didn't pay attention to where she placed her foot and slipped on a cone. Her body lurched, and she reached out for something to grab. She tried to steady herself with her legs, but the muscles wouldn't respond. Her mouth opened on a silent yell as she started falling to the side. Suddenly, Derek was there again. His hand wrapped around her arm and yanked her roughly against him.

Instinct had her clutching him. When she realized what she was doing, she forced her fingers to loosen and released him. "Thank you."

He grunted and walked away.

Kora glanced over the side to the rocks below to see where she would have fallen had he not caught her. Again. She had taken such a plunge once. It had been excruciating, and she had no interest in repeating it. Besides, she didn't want to have to explain broken bones that healed in hours to Derek.

They continued their journey. It took the rest of the afternoon to get down the mountain, especially because Kora was careful how and where she placed her feet. When he brought them to a section of boulders and dropped the sack, she was too tired to question him. She found smaller rocks to make a ring for a fire. Derek returned with wood, and she stacked it before she lit it. Fatigue weighed on her as she scooted back to rest against one of the immense boulders.

The sky was beginning to darken, the first blink of stars appearing. She took a closer look at their location and was impressed at the seclusion it offered. The mountain rose behind them with deadly sharp rocks. They would be able to spot anyone coming down the slope. The boulders shielded them from view on the other three sides, with only narrow entry and exit points.

Derek returned shortly with another ritbit. She was a decent hunter, but he seemed to excel. As he did with just about everything she had seen so far. Her stomach rumbled with hunger at the smell of the cooking meat.

She had questions, but she was too tired to carry on a conversation. It seemed Derek was, as well, because he didn't talk either. She ate with her eyes closed, and once she was finished, Kora curled up on her side and promptly fell asleep.

CHAPTER 9

Wind shuffled through the weeds to join the creatures of the marsh for a cacophony of sound. The wetland came alive at night with insects and animals. Water splashed softly, followed by the flicker of a snake's tongue. Derek walked the perimeter of the swamp, looking for signs of another.

Folklore about the swamp—and him—had been handed down through generations of humans. Stories he, himself, had begun. But it kept the mortals away. Their fear was vital in order to protect not just the area but also the eggs. He headed toward the nest once he was assured that no one had entered his domain. The magical fires burned continually, adding smoke to the wetlands while thickening the fog and giving yet another element to the legends.

Derek flattened his palm against the barrier he had erected around the stone structure. Animals entered as usual, but nothing human or magical could get in. He sent magic out through his hand, boosting the shield. It was enough to keep mortals out, but nothing could keep a Star Person away.

He walked through the imperceptible barrier and inspected the eggs. Another day without any signs of hatching. Maybe they never would. He turned and walked away. Each day the dragons didn't emerge from the eggs reminded him of his failure to free his kin. He was tired of waiting and doing nothing. Villette had nearly been ready to put her plan into action. Now, she was injured. That would set things back. He couldn't stand alone against other Star People. She was the lynchpin to everything. So, he had no choice but to wait.

At the edge of the island, he heard an ammit hiss a warning. Derek swung his gaze to the large reptile with its long, armored body, floating on the water's surface. He growled a warning that had the ammit quickly swimming away.

Derek watched the animal retreat before stepping back into the water and heading to where he had seen Kora die. When he got there, Derek squatted next to the area still darkened by her blood. He glanced at his hands, remembering how they, along with parts of his body, had been stained with it after carrying her. There was something at the edge of his mind, a memory he couldn't quite pull into focus. It was the same with her scent. He knew it but couldn't place it. Yet. There were too many years of memories to search through, but he would find what niggled him.

He straightened and touched the cuff to return to Kora. He made sure to arrive outside the boulders. A quick look around confirmed that no one had ventured close. Derek entered through the narrow opening and came to a halt at the sight of Kora.

The firelight danced over her like mystical beings trying to entice her. The red-orange glow brought out the auburn highlights in her hair, like he had glimpsed in the sunlight. Her face was slack in sleep, her breathing even and deep as she lay on her side with one hand beneath her cheek. Just looking at her took his breath away.

The more time he spent with her, the more she intrigued him. He wanted to know everything there was to learn about her. The obsession alarmed him. No one in all his very long years had stirred such...fervor in him.

He ached to claim her again. To bury himself in her wet heat and feel her walls tightening around him as she came in his arms. The need was so profound that he was already reaching to unbuckle his trousers. Derek stopped himself and carefully leashed his desires. He had kept Kora up for most of the previous night. Not to mention how hard he had pushed her today. No human could have covered the distance they had in such a short time. But he knew she wasn't human.

While he wouldn't give in to his desires, he couldn't deprive himself of the feel of her body. He silently walked to Kora and lay beside her, molding his front to her back. He draped his arm over her waist. She shifted against him, pressing herself closer. Even in sleep, she reacted to him.

The attraction between them was powerful. The way they came together, the pleasure each gave to the other. He, better than most, knew they'd experienced something different. Something he wasn't done enjoying.

Derek closed his eyes and settled comfortably. He liked Kora's warmth against him. He didn't need sleep. There were times he rested and shut his eyes as he had the night before, simply because he wished to. He still wasn't sure why he had pretended to sleep when she woke. Everything about her drew him. It would end once he discovered her secret. Just as the persistent hunger to fill her would diminish. He would tire of her eventually. It was just the way it was for him. She had already lasted longer than most.

"You've returned."

He clenched his teeth at the woman's voice in his head and disregarded it. So much for enjoying the evening.

"There's no ignoring me. I've waited too long."

Derek imagined a door in his head and then slammed it, hoping it would shut her out.

"Nice try."

"What do you want?" he demanded.

"Freedom."

"Who are you?"

She laughed softly. *"You know."*

"I don't."

"She's weakened. Find me. Free me."

Derek frowned. *"Who is weakened? Are you a dragon?"*

"I can't hold this connection much longer."

"Are you a dragon?"

"How many times has she wiped your memories?"

The question rang through him like a bell. *"Who?"*

But there was no reply. The voice was gone, her question bouncing around in his head, growing louder each time. Had someone meddled with his memories? Nay. That was impossible. Whoever was getting into his head was doing it to make him doubt. And it was working.

It was all he could think about as the hours slowly slipped by and night gave way to morning. He didn't pretend sleep this time when Kora woke. She stiffened when she felt him behind her. It rankled, adding to his sour mood.

Derek rose without a word and sat on the opposite side of the fire. He took food from the sack and tossed it to Kora. She caught it effortlessly. He watched her withdraw some bread.

"How close are we to Stonemore?" she finally asked.

"Half a day's walk."

She nervously glanced around. "I've never been on this side of the mountains." Her gaze landed on him. "Too close to dragon land."

"They won't hurt you."

"I've heard talk that dragons have been seen around the city recently."

Derek paused in chewing. For a second, he thought she'd meant that dragons had crossed the border. But Villette would have told him if that had happened because that would mean they had escaped captivity. Nay. Kora likely referred to him. Derek gave in to the need to be in his true form sometimes and took to the skies. It wasn't often, and he was quiet. But he could sometimes hear his kin's roars when he was high enough.

"None will harm you," he told her. He was the only dragon around, and he had no intention of hurting her.

They were soon packed up and headed toward Stonemore. Derek skirted the mountains on his right and walked along the border of the forest to his left. The temperature had dipped during the night. Kora shrugged into her coat to ward off the chill. He saw the way she furtively glanced into the trees, as if she thought dragons might burst from them at any time.

"Ferdon Woods," he explained. "It covers a large portion of land from the northern tip of the Tunris Mountains, then runs past the southernmost hills, nearly to the coast. It is filled with brineling and wildcats, along with a host of other animals—some dangerous, others not so much."

"Hmm. Sounds like a cheery place."

"It's beautiful, actually."

She glanced at him. "I suppose danger doesn't bother you."

"There are different kinds. That is a natural habitat for the animals. If you enter their home, you need to be prepared for the consequences."

"And Stonemore?"

He turned his head to look into her eyes. "The same applies. You're walking into a human habitat. And they can be infinitely more lethal than any animal."

"A person can be reasoned with."

Derek laughed and shook his head as he looked forward. "Some, maybe. There are always those who believe their way is right and nothing will alter their thinking. They'll kill and destroy anything in order to get what they need."

"Are you speaking from experience?"

He cut his eyes to her. "I make no apologies for who I am."

"And who is that, exactly?"

"The one leading you to Stonemore. The same one who made you scream in pleasure. You didn't seem to have a problem with me then."

Kora blew out a breath, her lips twisting. "I didn't say I had a problem with you."

"I beg to differ."

"I don't know you."

"And I don't know you."

She grunted. "That's not entirely true. You know more about me than I do you."

"You shared that you were looking for someone."

"An enemy," she added.

"That isn't telling me anything personal about yourself." Even as he said the words, Derek realized he might have to tell her something about himself.

Kora adjusted the strap across her body. "Do you know anyone in the city?"

He let her change the subject. "To help you search?"

"I'm just trying to get a sense of what will happen once we're inside."

That was the question, wasn't it? Derek didn't intend to let Kora out of his sight, but he expected her to have a different opinion on that. No need to tell her his plans now. She would only balk. Until he knew what she was, he was sticking to her.

And if she could help save the dragons, then he would do whatever he had to do.

"Let's get inside first," he answered.

Whether his words satisfied her or not, Kora didn't ask any more questions. But without her conversation, his troubled thoughts returned. Specifically, the one about his memories. He didn't doubt that it was possible for a powerful being to mess with someone's mind. But why his? There were all kinds of magic and many different species who could wield it. He had witnessed some incredible displays over his vast years. It wasn't *if* someone could take his memories, but *why*?

The voice in his head kept saying *her*. Was she alluding to Villette? The woman had never mentioned a name. She could, in fact, mean anyone. Derek contemplated asking Villette, but he wanted to know more before he did that. If anyone had the kind of power to delve into someone's mind and remove memories, it was a Star Person. There was no reason for Villette to mess with his head, though. He had sworn his allegiance to her.

The humans holding the dragons was another matter entirely. They would have to know who he was in order to delve into his memories. That meant they needed to track him, and Derek was nothing if not wary. He noticed everyone. And looked at all suspiciously. He would've known if someone were after him and ended their lives immediately.

If it wasn't Villette or the humans, then who?

Kora's hand tugged his arm to get him to stop. He swung his head to her. Before he could ask, he heard the noise of the city. They were getting close.

"You've been frowning for the past hour," she said.

He ignored her statement. "We've made good time."

"It's no wonder with your quick pace." She held up her hands when he shot her a look. "I'm not complaining. Just stating a fact."

Derek looked in the direction they were walking. He could just make out the top of the vaulted, red-sandstone arches and columns of Stonemore. "Stay close."

She kept next to him as they set off again. The nearer they came to the city, the louder the din became. He spotted the buildings long before they stopped before the tall, stone gates. Derek noted the soldiers standing along the battlements, looking down at them. A group stood outside, talking to one of the guards.

"They're not going to let us in," Kora whispered.

Derek wrapped his fingers around her wrist and tugged her closer. "Let me do the talking."

"Fine by me."

They came to a stop behind the group. Derek tuned out the

exchange between them and the guard and opened his hearing to listen to the other soldiers.

"We should hang a sign out that says 'go away.'"

"I should hear this week if I'm getting transferred to an outside unit. I can't wait to get away from the stench here."

"The wealthy need to stop giving invitations. Don't they realize we don't have any more room? Lady Maiju and her stupid parties."

Derek heard someone shout at him. He lifted his gaze to the soldier. "I have an invitation from Lady Maiju."

"You do?" Kora whispered.

Derek put his hand in his pocket and formed a small scroll with his magic. He held it out to show the guards.

"You two, come through," the soldier snapped from above. "Only them!" he added when others tried to follow.

The heavy gates groaned as they slowly parted. A dozen soldiers spilled out, swords drawn to keep others out while he and Kora slipped inside. She jumped at the boom of the gates closing behind them. Derek looked over to find her eyes wide as she took in their surroundings.

The gate area was packed with bodies. Soldiers milled about, vying for space, along with hundreds of the unhomed. The smell of unwashed bodies and waste was overpowering, especially to his heightened senses. Kora coughed and covered her mouth and nose with her hand.

He guided her away from the gates along the road. It had once been wide enough for two carts to pass but was now filled with people and barely wide enough for anyone to walk side by side. Hungry children wailed, and animals whimpered in starvation. Over it all, Derek heard the sound of fists meeting flesh as someone fought. He heard a woman yell and the slap that quickly followed.

His gaze moved around quickly, sickened by everything he saw. It didn't make sense for Villette to keep this many people in the city. Derek did a double take when he saw children being rounded up by priests in red robes. At first, he thought it might be to help them, but then he saw how the children flinched whenever a priest was near. Just what the hell was going on?

Kora was glued to his side, her gaze sweeping from side to side like his. He knew the moment she saw the baby lying listlessly in its mother's arms as she cried silently. Derek hurried Kora away from them, up the street's incline, and around the corner to the next level, which wasn't any better. He didn't slow until they reached the third section.

"How many levels are there?" Kora asked.

Derek took in those around him, particularly the red-robed priests. There were many more of them here. He didn't remember such priests from before. "Eight. The wealthy keep to the top four. Every section has a squad of soldiers who can close off a level with gates."

"I still think that's wrong."

"The gate to get to level five is always closed. The wealthy never wish to mingle with those below them."

She eyed him. "Will your invitation get us to five?"

"I can get us in anywhere."

Kora's lips curved into a smile. "I'm beginning to think you might."

CHAPTER 10

Stonemore was everything Kora had thought it would be. And so much more she hadn't. The noise was so loud she could barely stand it. The press of people made her want to scream. And the smell was intolerable. She didn't understand why anyone would remain. At least people had a chance to find food out in the forest. Here, they were waiting for handouts that would never come. She thought of the dead infant she had seen and had to shove it from her mind.

She looked upward to the top of the mountain and the palace. That's where Villette would be. The ruler upon her throne.

"Come," Derek murmured, tugging on her arm as they moved to the fourth level.

Kora tried to move behind him, but he kept her beside him. He put himself on the outside so others ran into him instead of her. Derek's protective nature was surprising. It was a side she hadn't expected to see. She didn't know why he had offered to take her to Stonemore, nor did she entirely trust him.

But she couldn't deny that it was nice not being alone. She never would've gotten through the gates without him. Though she had to wonder if entering the city had been the right thing. Soldiers really were everywhere. Then there were the red-robed priests. She didn't like the look of them. Nor the ones who wore armor beneath their robes. What were priests doing wearing armor, anyway?

Too many eyes watched her.

Too many ready and willing to stop her.

Derek slowed as he looked at a building. It appeared to be some kind of living quarters and based on the number of red-robed individuals around it, it was theirs. He then walked to a large semicircular overlook with a stunning view of the city below and the forest beyond. She saw the tops of the trees extending far into the horizon. Kora placed her hands on the stone and peered down. Seeing so many out in the elements without food and very little water sickened her. She wanted to scream at them all to get out. But they wouldn't listen to her. Fear kept them rooted. And she knew all about how such trepidation could take hold of someone.

Kora glanced at Derek to see what he thought, but he stood with his back to the wall and his gaze beyond. She turned and followed his line of sight to the tall building near the barracks. "What is that?"

"My guess is a temple."

"For?"

"They call themselves the Priests of Innus."

She scanned the area to find a sea of red around them. "I've never heard of them. Or priests who wear armor."

"I have heard some rumors."

The way he bit out the words had her swinging her gaze to him. Derek clenched his fists, fury rolling off him. "What do they do?"

"Not here."

She was prepared when he took her hand and led her to the gates. Every street was angled, winding up or down the mountain depending on which way you were headed.

The soldiers straightened as they approached the gate. Derek said nothing, simply handed over the invitation. The guard read it and gave it back before nodding to another to allow them entry. Kora released the breath she had been holding as they made their way up the fifth level.

The difference from the lower four levels was markedly noticeable. The streets were absent of the unhomed and trash. Everything was clean and orderly. Those walking were dressed to show the wealth of their station. Even the businesses were beautiful. And it was evident that she and Derek stuck out against such grandeur.

If Derek saw the stares, they didn't seem to bother him. She, however, felt every gaze. Would they try to throw them out? She wasn't entirely sure she and Derek were supposed to be here at all. When he started to enter an inn, she didn't follow. He paused and turned, lifting a brow in question.

"I can't stay here," she whispered.

He walked to her. "Why not?"

In their haste to get to Stonemore, she hadn't thought about the very thing she would need above all else: coin. Kora glanced around and moved closer before lowering her voice to say, "I can't pay."

"Good thing I can."

"I can't ask that of you."

"You aren't."

She searched his eyes. "In exchange for?"

"I didn't ask for anything."

"But you want something."

He moved closer until their bodies touched. "So do you."

Waking up with his body molded to hers had been incredible. Until she remembered where she was headed and why. She'd thought they would go their separate ways once they were in the city. Having Derek around only put him in danger. She also couldn't let him get in her way. Nothing would stop her now.

"I ask nothing of you. I demand no repayment. Come in or don't," Derek said before entering the building.

Kora watched his retreating back and went through her options. It didn't take long because she only had two. Then she followed him inside. By the time she reached Derek, he had already handed over payment and was being led up the stairs. He didn't look behind him once. He walked into a room and left the door open, assuming she would follow. Which she did.

Derek made his way to the window and opened the shutters. "What are you afraid of?"

So very much. "Nothing."

"Then close the door."

Kora did as he instructed and got her first look at the room. It was three times the size of her hut. There was even a square tub in the far corner. The bed was a grand affair adorned in cream and red. There was a table, chairs, and a plush settee upholstered in deep crimson.

Her gaze slid back to Derek. Just when she thought she had him figured out, he surprised her. He didn't dress as if he had wealth, nor had he acted like it. He didn't walk around with a weapon either, yet everyone gave him a wide berth. Sensing how dangerous he was, just as she had. Even the soldiers in Stonemore had acted nervous around him. He was an enigma she would likely never sort out.

But, oh, how she wished to.

He turned to face her. "Food will be brought up soon." Then he walked past her to the door.

"Where are you going?" she asked, rotating with him.

He paused with his hand on the door and looked back at her. "I have an errand. I thought you might like some privacy. Don't leave."

She met his gaze and realized he waited for an answer. She nodded. With that, he was gone. Kora turned back to the room, her gaze landing on the tub. She imagined sitting in the hot water. It had been a very long time since anyone had told her what to do. But he was right. She did want some privacy. And a long soak.

Kora walked to the tub and ran her fingers along the edge. It was stone carved right out of the mountain. She noticed handles at one end and was reaching for one when a knock sounded, startling her. She yanked her hand back and whirled in the direction of the sound.

"Get it together," she chided before going to open the door.

A young girl greeted her with a smile while holding a tray laden with food. "Hello, miss. Shall I put this on the table?"

"Oh, yes." Kora opened the door wider.

The servant placed the tray on the table and then faced her. "Is there anything else?"

"I would like to bathe."

"You can find the drying cloths on the shelf. There is a basket filled with different-scented soaps just here. However, if there is another scent you would prefer, I'll try to find it."

Kora hadn't even seen the shelves. It was difficult to see much when Derek was around. He filled spaces to capacity. Not just spaces, though. He filled her senses and her mind, too. Utterly. Completely. "Do I need to bring up water?"

"Not at all," the girl replied with a smile and walked to the tub. She pointed to the far handle. "This one is for hot water." She pointed to the one near her. "This one for cold. Press the plug at the bottom to hold the water in and pull it out to release it."

Incredible. Maybe she was beginning to understand why so many flocked to the city. "Thank you."

The door closed softly behind the girl. Kora immediately turned the handles, and water flowed freely. One hot, one cold. She adjusted until she got the temperature the way she wanted it and pushed the plug closed. Then she yanked off her boots and clothing in record time. She took down the basket of soaps to smell each one. She chose the one with bits of rose petals.

The smell of the food pulled her to the table as the tub filled. She nibbled on different dishes, trying each of them, her gaze going often to the depth of the water. When it was high enough, she stepped into the tub and lowered herself until she rested against the gently sloped back. Nothing had ever felt so decadent.

Steam curled from the surface and wafted around her, making her hair stick to the sides of her face. Her eyes closed as the water lapped at her skin. Her tense muscles began to ease. The aches in her body softened. She might never leave. How many cold baths had she taken? How many quick scrubs in rivers and lakes? This was how one was meant to bathe.

She didn't know how long she lay in the water before she realized she wasn't alone. Her eyes snapped open to find Derek standing beside her, his eyes locked on her body. His hair was still damp from his bath, and he wore new clothes. His hands fisted, then flexed at his side. She spotted the bulge in his pants that made her squeeze her legs together as desire pulsed greedily.

"Woman." His voice was rough, the word a warning and an endearment.

Kora lowered into the water until only her face was visible, then sat up and smoothed her wet hair back with her hands, wondering—hoping—he would join her. She glanced at him when she reached for the soap and lathered her hands. She scrubbed her arms first and then her breasts. He groaned—or was it a growl?—before stalking to the table, his back to her.

She grinned and finished washing her body and then her hair before rinsing. Reluctantly, she lifted the plug and rose to reach for the drying cloth. Derek was there in a heartbeat, holding her flush against his body. He looked deep into her eyes before claiming her mouth for a deep, all-consuming kiss.

She was breathless when he lifted his head. She tried to pull him down for more, but he leaned back.

"I want you in my bed. Not as payment but because you want to be there," he said.

Her lips throbbed from his kiss, and blood whooshed in her ears. What was it about Derek that made her throw caution to the wind? What did he have that made her forget all reason just to be with him? To have him inside her, touching her. Kissing her.

"Will you?"

She swallowed and nodded.

"Say it," he insisted.

"Aye. I want to be in your bed."

He lifted her from the tub and dropped her onto the mattress. Kora bounced once before he covered her body. She wondered how he had removed his tunic so quickly, but she quickly forgot when he kissed her again. Then he was inside her, thrusting in and out in time with his tongue in her mouth.

They came together frantically, as if each would die without the other, as if they hadn't been together in eons. She locked her legs around him. He angled her hips and drove deeper. Harder. Faster.

He brought her hands over her head and threaded his fingers with hers. She felt the potency of his body, the vitality that rippled through his muscles before sliding inside her. He ended the kiss and looked at her. She was trapped in his eyes, lost in the desire that curled around them, through them. In them.

It was charged, carnal.

Utterly primal.

He gazed at her, and she yearned. He touched her, and she was lost. There was power there, a kind she didn't understand or care about. Not when he made her feel so good.

And she knew in that instant she was lost to him, to the power he had over her body. One she gave willingly, readily.

Eagerly.

CHAPTER 11

Derek reclined naked against the headboard with the pillows at his back and watched Kora, one foot propped on the bed with his knee bent. The woman captivated him in everything she did. Watching her bathe had been a lesson in torment. Even now, she held his gaze as she plucked food from one of the many platters and brought it to her mouth—a mouth that had recently been wrapped around his cock. Her long, bare legs were stretched out to rest on the chair beside her.

"Purple," she stated.

He shot her a flat look. He never carried on conversations with his bed partners. Whenever they got chatty, he silenced them with his tongue. It worked every time. And while he wanted Kora again, he also found himself eager for her conversation. That was the only reason he went along with her curiosity in discovering his favorite color. It was a safe topic since neither wanted to give up anything personal.

She shifted, causing her breasts to sway. Her nipple hardened beneath his gaze. He swallowed as his cock stiffened. His craving continued to intensify. It boggled his mind, but he was enjoying himself too much to look deep into what it could mean.

Kora tilted her head to the side, and the dark curtain of her hair tumbled past her shoulder. "Blue," she said around a mouthful of food.

"I told you that you wouldn't be able to guess it."

Her throat moved as she swallowed. Then her eyes dropped to his cuff before meeting his gaze. "Silver."

He shook his head.

Kora threw a piece of bread at him, which he snatched out of the air. "All right. I give up. What is it?"

"The orange at sunset."

Her face softened as she smiled. "Nice choice. I never would've guessed that."

"I know," he replied with a grin.

She shot him a look, her brows raised. "Your turn."

He did not play these sorts of games. Derek didn't care enough about anyone to want to know such trivial things. It gave the impression that he might stick around. He thought about Kora's blood on his hands that day. A memory of the feeling of her lifeless body in his arms as he carried her to the top of the mountain rose.

Then he did something he had never done. He tried to guess her favorite color. "Black."

Her laugh bounced off the walls. "Questioning my choice of clothing?"

"I wouldn't dream of it."

"It's a practical color, but not my favorite."

As soon as she said the words, he realized she chose black because it hid bloodstains. It also explained the mending he had seen. Then another thought made him frown. Just how often was she injured? And even more importantly, how often did she die? He would find out. If it was the last thing he did, he would discover everything there was to know.

Derek studied her. What was a color someone like her might like? "Pink."

"Not even close," she teased.

He rested his arm atop his knee and let his wrist dangle. What would she do if he told her he knew she had come back from the dead? But he knew the answer. She'd likely clam up and leave the first chance she got. It's what he would do. "Green."

Her mouth slackened in surprise. "How did you figure that out?"

"Lucky, I guess. Why green?"

"It signifies life." She wrapped her arms around her middle and shrugged. "Even rebirth if you think about spring and how everything blooms to life after vanishing during the winter."

Or someone returned from the dead. Derek observed the subtle play of emotions that moved over her face when she looked away. He wondered what she was thinking. It wasn't something he asked anyone because it invited them to ask him the same questions. Yet he was about to break another of his rules.

Thankfully, Kora spoke before he could. "I didn't get a chance to comment on your new attire earlier. They're nice."

Derek glanced at the new clothes piled on the floor after he'd used magic to remove them. He jerked his chin to the settee. "You have some, as well."

She held his gaze for a long moment before turning her head to look at the small sofa. "I can't accept that."

"You can."

"I can't." She cut her eyes to him, her chin lifting defiantly.

He quirked a brow at her. He had expected this, and he had come prepared. "Earlier, I said I wanted nothing in return, but that wasn't entirely truthful."

"It never is."

"Yet you came along."

"What do you want?" she demanded instead.

He glanced toward the shuttered window. "Nothing more than for you to remain with me while we're in the city. A couple walking through the streets can go unnoticed."

"Whereas a man on his own can't? I'm not buying it."

"I need to visit some places. You need to search. I need someone to accompany me, and you need access to areas you otherwise wouldn't be able to enter. As I said when I first offered to accompany you, it will benefit us both."

Silence stretched as she studied him. From the moment they'd entered Stonemore, Derek knew she was taking it all in so she could sneak away. He didn't want to spend his time searching for her when he could be helping her. The only problem was that she didn't trust him. He hadn't ever wanted someone's trust before.

And he wasn't quite sure why it was suddenly so important that he had hers.

"Why didn't you say that from the beginning?" she asked.

"I'm telling you now."

"That isn't what I asked."

He released a long breath and went with the truth. "I'm used to working alone."

In answer, she dropped her feet to the floor and rose to walk to the settee. She fingered the dark blue material. "Nearly everyone I saw once we reached the fifth level was in this color. Why?"

"Only the wealthy are allowed that color. The lower classes wear green, brown, red, and orange."

"The blue also stands out."

"Aye."

Her head swiveled to him. "This will make me look the part."

"Clothes are only a portion of it. You have to believe you belong. When you believe, so will everyone else."

"Do you come to Stonemore often?"

"Rarely, in fact."

"You're here," the voice cooed in his head.

It came from nowhere and made him close his eyes and turn his head away.

"Derek? Are you okay?" Kora asked.

The sound of his name on her lips pulled him into the present. He looked over to find her brow wrinkled in concern. For him? He wanted to pull her into his arms as he sank into her body once more.

"It's been a long time since you've walked the city streets. There is much you don't know."

"Derek?"

"Aye," he said and rose from the bed. He stalked to the window and threw it open again to stare out at the stone wall covered in flowering vines that led to level six. In his head, he asked, *"What don't I know?"*

"Free me while she's still weak, and I'll tell you everything."

"Tell me now," he demanded.

"I don't have long."

"Then you'd better talk fast."

An aggrieved sigh filled his mind. *"Those with magic are killed. Don't let anyone know who you are. And stay away from the priests."*

"They can't hurt me."

"Not you, but others."

That made no sense. Why wouldn't those with power use magic to protect themselves?

"The priests target those who don't know how to protect themselves," the voice answered.

Shock ran through Derek. *"You can't mean...?"*

"I do. Free me. We will end the priests once and for all."

"I don't need you for that."

"But you do need me to fill in the past."

Derek clenched his teeth and curled his fingers around the bottom of the windowpane.

"Time is running out," she said. *"I need you, and whether you want to believe it or not, you need me to fight her."*

"Derek?"

He jerked at Kora's touch. When he looked over his shoulder at her, her frown had deepened. "I'm all right."

"You don't look it."

He was done talking—to Kora and the disembodied voice in his head. He turned and wrapped his arms around Kora. Then his lips found hers.

A mist hung around the city when morning dawned. Kora made use of the tub again. Derek had wanted to join her, but if he did, they wouldn't leave the room for hours, and there were things he needed to see to.

He managed to wait until she finished her bath before using the tub himself. Derek stepped out to dry off when he caught sight of Kora. The dark blue breeches skimmed her legs like a second skin and were tucked into her boots. But it was the long-sleeved top with its plunging neckline that fell nearly to her belly button and showed her incredible cleavage that caught his eye.

"Everything fits perfectly," she said as she ran her hand over the soft material on her arm.

He followed her movements as she skimmed her stomach under her breasts, moving downward to her hips.

"How do I look?" she asked.

His eyes jerked to her face. He said the first thing that came to mind. "Stunning."

"What should I do with my hair? Leave it down, or put it up?"

"Down." He cleared his throat when he heard the hoarseness in his voice. "Down."

She ran her hands through the thick strands. It parted naturally to the side and framed her face. Kora walked to the table as she eyed his body. "You wear clothes well, but I like you just like this."

"Is that your way of saying you want to stay inside?" he teased.

"That's a rather tempting offer."

He dropped the drying cloth and closed the distance between them. "Just tempting?"

"More than you know," she whispered huskily.

Derek gazed into her brown eyes flecked with amber. He knew exactly what she meant. He had remained with her all night instead of checking on the eggs. "Good," he told her and gave her a quick kiss.

He turned to dress and felt her eyes on him. His pants were thicker but just as supple as hers. His shirt had the same plunging neckline that stopped at his stomach. Kora had no embellishments on her garments. She didn't need them. He, however, had a mixture of different-colored blues embroidered along his neck and wrists.

"I like the color on you," Kora said.

He brushed his hair and readied to pull it into a queue when she made a sound. Derek raised a brow at her.

"Leave it free."

"All of it?" he asked.

She considered for a second and then nodded.

Derek dropped his arms. Once outside their room, anything could happen. He almost tossed her onto the bed to stay inside for another day, but he knew they had to get out eventually. "Guard your words and expressions once we're out of this chamber."

"Are you expecting trouble?"

"I always expect trouble."

They left the room and walked downstairs before leaving the inn.

"Any destination in particular?" she asked.

The streets weren't nearly as full as the lower levels, but Derek still kept her beside him. "Just having a look around."

Many met his gaze and quickly looked away. Kora smiled and nodded to those they passed. Some were openly friendly, while others were more reserved. They walked the length of level five before the switchback took them to six. There were more homes there but enough businesses to draw people.

When Derek saw a crowd, he turned them toward it. Kora tensed slightly as they entered a jewelry store. Everyone wanted to see some necklace he couldn't care less about. He had other reasons for being there.

He watched as others gravitated to Kora. She was approachable with a pleasant smile, and the owners were quick to talk to her. Derek introduced himself but didn't say much more. Once the couple learned that he and Kora were new to Stonemore, they readily shared some of the city's ins and outs.

"You must attend any event given by Lord Martti. His cook is amazing, and his parties are talked about by all," the wife said.

The husband nodded. "Anyone from level five and up is invited, so you don't need an invitation. As a matter of fact, there's a gathering tomorrow evening."

"We'll be there," Derek said. "We would love to get to know others."

Kora glanced at him and nodded. "It sounds like fun."

"Anything else we should be aware of?" Derek asked.

The couple exchanged a look before the man leaned forward. "Stonemore is safe from any of the outcasts."

"Outcasts?" Kora asked.

The woman nodded and whispered, "Those with...*magic*."

She said the word as if she might go up in flames at any second. Kora stiffened beside him. "How can you be sure no one has magic?"

"The Priests of Innus protect us," the husband stated. "They find anyone with abilities."

The woman shuddered. "It starts with the children. There were regular sacrifices until recently, when some of the kids escaped. The priests won't be stopped, though."

"Then we chose the right location to live," Derek said, forcing a smile.

The man nodded. "I wouldn't live anywhere else."

CHAPTER 12

The rush of blood in her ears drowned out the rest of the conversation. Kora didn't remember leaving the store. Suddenly, she was on the street, Derek's hand gently but forcibly guiding her.

"Don't say anything," he whispered. "Not now."

The faces and places she passed were a blur. She somehow put one foot in front of the other and stayed upright, even as a scream of denial rang through her mind. She kept thinking about all the children she had seen after entering Stonemore. How many had been killed because she was too afraid to finish what her family had begun? How many more were being rounded up to die even now?

She stumbled. Derek steadied her. His hold was firm and strong. Without him, she would be a puddle on the ground. He kept her from causing a scene. But more than that, he kept the soldiers' attention away from her. How much longer did she have before her magic was discovered? How many hours did she have to get to Villette with a vague, impractical scheme that was sure to end in her death?

"Kora."

What was she doing? She had returned to face her destiny, but she hadn't planned, she hadn't learned about her enemy. She was as reckless and rash as always, running headlong toward something without so much as an idea of what to do. Villette needed to be brought to justice for more than her family. It was for every innocent life that had been violently taken on Villette's orders.

"Kora."

Derek's voice was low and hard, breaking through her thoughts. She blinked and found his face inches from hers, his eyes searching hers. She swallowed an inner scream of denial. "They're killing children."

His lips flattened as he drew in a deep breath. "It appears so."

"Did you know?"

He gave her a hard look.

That was a *nay*, then. She dashed away a tear that had escaped and looked to the side. They were in a corner alcove at the end of the street, hidden from view. She wanted to curl up and cry, but there was no time for that. Someone had to take a stand for the children, and it looked like that someone was her.

"You can't stand against the priests," Derek stated.

She looked at him. "Someone needs to."

"They'll surround you and kill you along with the kids."

"Maybe." What would the priests do when she came back to life? It was something she didn't want to think about. The thought of them killing her over and over made her sick to her stomach.

"You came to find someone. Focus on that."

Kora stepped back to separate herself from him. "And forget about the children? They're innocent."

"The practice has been going on for some time. One person will not stop it."

"It only takes one to bring about change."

His entire demeanor altered. He stiffened, and his face shuttered as he reinforced the walls around his emotions. "If you have a death wish, there are other ways to achieve that."

"Would you not give up your life for another?"

"Nay."

She was shocked by his reply. "How...sad."

"You think that's sad?" he asked with a sneer.

"There has to be someone or something you share a bond with. Something you believe in strongly enough that you would die to protect it. Someone you love."

He looked away. "You have no bond with anyone here."

"These are children we're talking about. They're meant to be loved, cherished, and protected. None of us chooses to be born as we are. Not our hair or eye color, not the tint of our skin. The only thing we *can* choose is who we love and how we live. No one gets to choose whether they have magic. Why should anyone be punished for it? Especially children."

"People will always kill what they fear."

She swallowed and leaned back against the wall. "Are you one of those?"

He slowly turned his head to her. "I fear nothing."

"Must be nice."

"What are you afraid of?"

Everything. "Failing."

"Maybe you put too much pressure on yourself."

Perhaps she had trusted the wrong person. Kora scrutinized Derek. She knew next to nothing about him but hadn't exactly opened up to him either. They had been warily circling each other since they met, waiting for the other to give in before they did. The only time the walls came down was when they were in each other's arms.

It wasn't as if she would bare her thoughts, fears, and dreams to him now. They stood in the middle of a city that had outlawed magic. For all she knew, he could turn her over. She had encountered few who *didn't* fear those with abilities.

"We can't stand here all day. Are you coming?" he asked sharply.

She needed to learn the layout of the city to form the beginnings of her plan. So, while she wanted to slink away and rail privately at what was happening, she had to put it aside and focus. Kora nodded, and they walked out onto the street together. He didn't place his hand on her lower back this time. She liked the feel of him touching her, but it was better this way. She couldn't allow herself to believe he cared. Derek's only concern was for himself. So, she kept some distance between them—physically and figuratively.

They leisurely strolled along the sixth level, stopping at different shops and pretending all was right with the world. She took notice of where the soldiers were stationed. They were more at ease on the upper levels without the crush of bodies and crime that happened below.

In the seventh section, she noted soldiers standing at certain gates that led to homes. Those inside must be important to have their own contingent of guards. Kora made a mental note of each location in order to steer clear of them.

To her surprise, she and Derek were allowed to enter the top level, where the palace was located. Kora stood at the base of the steps leading up to the fortress gates and observed others milling about, awe on their faces as they stared at the impressive building. She noted the open-air corridors and hundreds of arched windows. Flowers and plants of every size and color enhanced the outside of the palace, in pots or hanging from archways. Guards stood sentry everywhere her eyes touched, most notably at the gate, which was presently closed.

The palace was a stunning display of architectural style, with attention to every detail on a grand scale she had never seen before. It announced the wealth of the city and the power of the one who ruled it.

But she knew the foul entity who called it home.

Kora wouldn't be able to enter through the front gate, but she had never expected to be able to. There were other entrances. The servants and soldiers would enter by another access point. Villette wouldn't allow them to come through the front. Kora need only wait and follow one to find her way inside. That was her way in. The soldiers. No one stopped them. No one looked too closely at them. It was perfect. She didn't know why she hadn't thought of it before.

Stealing a uniform and getting into the palace would be easy compared to the difficult task of locating Villette.

"You can't be serious."

She glanced at Derek to find him staring at her with a deep frown. "What?"

"You're looking for someone in the palace," he stated in a hushed voice as he faced her.

Kora flashed him the flat look he often gave her. "I've never seen anything of this grandeur up close. I'm merely taking it all in."

He snorted and put his back to the palace. "Of course, you are."

"Believe what you will."

"We should leave before someone notices your intense perusal."

"I'm not the only one ogling," she said defensively.

Derek said nothing as he walked away. She gave the palace one last look and then followed. Kora held her arms against her when a cold wind blew around them. Only the very old and very young wore cloaks against the chill. She couldn't imagine how dreadful the winters were so far up the mountain, but she wouldn't be here long enough to find out. The quicker she put her plan into action, the better for everyone.

To Kora's surprise, Derek stopped at a café for lunch. They sat outside with the mountains as their view. Sometimes, the buzz from the first four levels would reach them, but it was rare. Being so far above the others, it was easy to forget what was happening below. But she had seen their deplorable living conditions up close. Animals didn't even live in such squalor. It was just one more reason to go after Villette immediately. She wanted to sink into her thoughts and begin planning, but the way Derek watched her made it impossible.

"Say whatever it is you want to say," she told him when she couldn't take his silent stares any longer.

"I'm not sure you would listen."

Her smile was tight as she lifted her glass in a mock salute. "You know me so well."

"I know your heart bleeds for everyone. Maybe you should focus on yourself instead."

"Like you?"

He shrugged one shoulder. "Is that so bad?"

"You have nothing you live for."

"What do you live for?"

She looked out to the mountains. "For entirely too long, I lived for myself. Now..." She paused and sighed. "Now, I live to make up for my mistakes."

"Everyone makes mistakes. What makes yours so different?"

"It cost my family their lives." She met his gaze, her smile sad. "Didn't expect that, did you?"

He refilled her glass with wine. "I doubt the blame lay squarely on you."

"It does. I denied it for many years, but I've finally accepted the truth."

"Is that why you're here? To make up for your family's death by finding someone?"

She shrugged and took a bite of the delicious food. She could really get used to having food around anytime she wanted. "It's part of it."

"And you intended to do it alone?"

"I'm good at improvising."

Derek nodded slowly. "I bet you are."

The intensity of his gaze made her uncomfortable. She ate three more bites before she looked up. He still watched her. "What? Do I have something on my face?"

"Did you lose your entire family?"

She leaned back in the chair and scratched her temple. "Aye."

To her surprise, he didn't ask any more questions. As if he didn't want to know how they died or what she had done to cause it. Which was good because she didn't want to talk about it. She expected they would return to the inn after the meal, but Derek surprised her a second time when he took them to a clothing shop. She balked at the idea until he stopped her in front of a cloak. The blue color was so deep it was nearly black. She fell in love with it immediately.

He didn't stop there, though. A woman came out bearing an armful of gowns.

"I don't need anything else," Kora quickly told the owner.

Derek leaned close and said, "We have the gathering to attend. We need to look the part. We have a deal, remember?"

Kora wanted to refuse, but he was right. They had made a deal, and they were attending the party. Still, she was uncomfortable accepting his coin again. Yet she couldn't remember the last time she had been surrounded by such beautiful things. And she certainly had never worn anything so nice before. Her heart yearned to be carefree, just once.

She nodded in acceptance and was swiftly ushered into a dressing area. Women came out of nowhere to help her disrobe. She was given the softest underthings. They felt like a whisper of a cloud against her skin. If she left with only that, she would be dancing on air. But the owner of the shop and her helpers brought in the dresses.

Kora tried on gown after gown, each one more decadent and beautiful than the last. There was a mirror in the dressing room that she twirled in front of as everything else fell away. She was just a woman putting on pretty frocks in front of a mirror.

That continued for what felt like hours before she finally found a dress. The dark blue was accented with midnight thread and had small, silver beads sewn into tiny clusters that looked like stars around her wrists, along the hem, and following the V in front and back. Then came another flood of women pinning and tucking to ensure the perfect fit.

They brought in jewels and glittering hair combs, and even gleaming sandals, but she waved them all away. Derek was spending too much already.

By the time she came out, the sun was sinking behind the mountains. Derek rose from his seat, seemingly unperturbed by the time it had taken. The shop owner confirmed where they were staying and promised to deliver the gown the following day. Kora put on her cloak and walked out with Derek.

She shot him a glance. He threw around money as if it meant little. If she hadn't seen him pay for things herself, she never would've thought he had that kind of wealth. Why keep that to himself? Most people liked others knowing they had money. And if he kept being wealthy a secret, what other things did he hide? She wouldn't go looking to find out because he might attempt to poke around in her secrets. That didn't mean she wasn't curious, though.

The man was gorgeous, with a body she couldn't get enough of. She looked around at the other women and saw them staring. She wasn't the only one who noticed his good looks. There was no blending in for Derek. He was a man remarked on by all.

Their bodies brushed. Instantly, her breasts grew full. The fabric grazed her nipples, hardening them as her sex throbbed. Thankfully, the cloak hid all of it. The need, the *hunger* for Derek was overwhelming. He had that kind of hold over her body.

It was irritating.

It was also heady.

By the time they returned to the inn, the dining area was crowded and loud. She wanted to go up to the room, but he put a hand on her lower back. She shivered, wanting his touch yet hating it and the power he had over her at the same time.

"The fire should warm you," he said, his breath brushing her ear.

He was warming her just fine. He could do it even better in bed with their clothes off. His hand was firm as he steered her to an empty table near the hearth.

CHAPTER 13

Derek pretended to sleep as Kora slipped from the bed and dressed. She hadn't been interested in the gossip around them at dinner. After she'd finished her meal, she excused herself and came up to their room. By the time he joined her, she feigned sleep. And he let her. Because he knew what she was about.

He waited until the door closed behind her before he rose and called his clothes to him with magic. There was no need to chase after her. He had her scent. He could find her anywhere. Derek went to the window and opened it. He peered outside to make sure no one was near, and then he jumped. He landed softly with bent knees before walking to the edge of the building.

A couple was kissing passionately in the alley. He looked around them and spotted Kora walking toward the gates. And just as he expected, she was headed down. She had been smart enough to wear the new clothes, which would allow her reentry into the upper levels.

He walked down the alley past the couple, who paid him no heed. When he came to the street, he paused and leaned out, checking to see who was about. Then he crossed the street and ducked into another alley a few buildings down. This one was so narrow he had to turn himself sideways and shuffle his feet until he reached the back. A tall wall separated each level, so no one dared to try to get from one to the other any way but through the gates. But he wasn't just anyone.

It might be the wee hours of the early morning with darkness hanging over the city like a blanket, but like most cities, this one didn't sleep. He easily scaled the back of the building to reach the roof. Then he jumped over the back alleyway to land on the wall before dropping to the ground on level five. He repeated the process, following Kora to four.

Derek found her in the shadows, glaring at the temple. There was no way she was getting inside. Her anguish at learning the children's fates had sat uneasily in his chest ever since. She had asked if he would give his life for anything. He hadn't been able to tell her there was only one thing he cared about: freeing the dragons.

Everything he did, every action he took, was to that end.

Or it had been.

Now, he snuck away to check on the eggs while she tried on gowns and pretended sleep when he should have stopped her before she left. She had turned his world upside down. It would be better for him to walk away. He had even attempted it, but the question of what she was kept him from leaving.

But it was more than that. To his shock, he worried about her. Not just her wanting to save everyone but also the way she stared at the palace with open hostility.

Her admission about her family stunned him. He was eager to know more, but he hadn't asked. How could he when she had sat still as stone, her eyes bright with unshed tears just from mentioning them? He had felt the walls coming down around her for protection. She was strong and determined, but she also carried deep emotional scars.

Still, she had allowed a few things to slip—whether on purpose or not. The one she searched for was to make up for a mistake. And they were in the palace. What she would do when she found them was still in question. Her face had given nothing away, but the way her fingers curled on the table had told him plenty.

Shouts from the next level down yanked him from his musings. A child's terrified scream split the night, followed closely by a woman's wail. Kora rushed to the gate, but the guards held her up. Meanwhile, he got over the wall without anyone the wiser.

The sight of the armored priests surrounding a woman with a girl only a few years of age drew him up short. A crowd was rapidly forming, their macabre need to watch the potentially gruesome proceedings overwhelming their better judgment. They knew what was happening. Sadly, so did he. And he wanted it finished before Kora reached them.

Luck wasn't on his side tonight. Kora pushed her way through the crowd until she reached the priests. Then, somehow, she got through them until she stood in the circle with the woman who clung to the child by one arm as a priest yanked angrily on the other.

"Stop!" Kora bellowed to the priest.

The shouts in the street silenced, more in surprise than anything. Derek looked around at the faces, eyes bright with excitement at the prospect of something happening. The residents' lives were abysmal. They looked for anything to take their minds off how bad things were, and right now, a child being taken from its mother was just what they wanted. Add Kora to the mix, and everyone knew there was about to be bloodshed.

Derek could get to Kora in time. But she wouldn't leave without the woman and child. Did he dare interfere and alert Villette that he was in the city? Or did he let things play out and get Kora away before she could be hurt? It was an easy decision.

He shifted to the left to better see her. Everyone now looked at her: the priests, the woman and child, and each spectator. No one noticed him, which was exactly what he wanted. Derek noted the faces of each of the priests. It was easy to pick out which of them would go for Kora first.

"Who are you?" one of the priests demanded of her.

Kora lifted her chin, her brown eyes blazing with fury. "A citizen. What right do you have to take this woman's child?"

"The right of our gods."

Was it his imagination, or was smoke coming from her? Derek fisted his hands when Kora wrapped her arms around the child and held her tightly. If he took her now, she would yank the child, the mother, and the priest with them. Fuck.

"That's not good enough," Kora said.

Murmurs of disbelief and shock rippled dangerously through the crowd. Derek moved closer, his gaze shifting between Kora and the priests. Things were about to get ugly.

"We do not abide the evil that is magic," a priest declared, his voice ringing with authority. "We will wash the wickedness from the realm, one devil at a time!"

"You mean with the blood of an innocent child?" Kora argued.

The priest pulled back his lips in a sneer. "There is nothing innocent about this fiend."

"You act as if the child chose to have magic."

"No one questions us. Grab her!"

Shouts of fear rang out while others cheered at the spectacle. The priests had drawn their weapons and began to close in on Kora, the woman, and the child. Derek touched the cuff and appeared in the circle behind Kora. He grabbed the priest nearest him and shoved him to the ground so hard his head hit the stone. Derek lunged for Kora, his fingers reaching for her wrist as the priest holding the child's arm swung his blade down and severed the limb. The girl's shriek of pain was only drowned out by the mother's screams.

Pandemonium erupted. The scent of blood filled the air, and like crazed animals, the priests had their single-minded focus on Kora and the woman. Derek grabbed a discarded sword and started swinging. The crowd pushed inward, some trying to get away, others attempting to join the fight. But it separated him and Kora.

Derek fought his way through again and was nearly upon her. He reached for her once more, but she was yanked away. A bellow of fury erupted from him when he watched multiple blades viciously pierce and slice her upper body. He felt himself shifting. And for just a second, welcomed it. Then he remembered where he was and managed to get himself under control.

He then hacked his way through the crowd until he reached Kora. She lay unmoving on the ground, piled on top of other bodies. Blood gushed from her to mingle with others' that pooled on the stones. The priests had turned their bloodlust on the crowd and were slashing their way through whoever remained. Derek ignored the cries for help and gathered Kora in his arms. Just before he touched his cuff, he saw both the mother and the girl lying dead among the others.

Derek lay Kora gently on the bed. Her heart had stopped beating. She was dead, but she had been dead before. He stripped her of the ruined clothes and threw them in the hearth to burn. Then he began cleaning the blood from her. He counted eight different wounds on her upper body, some so deep they pierced through to her back.

His ire festered. Each time he remembered seeing a blade puncture Kora, his rage burned brighter. He should've stopped her. He should've intervened. Instead, he had stood there and watched, protecting himself.

After her body was clean, he used magic to replace the ruined sheets. Then, he waited for Kora to come back from the dead. Every second was an eternity. He checked her breathing and listened for the beat of her heart. He studied her wounds, trying to determine if they were healing. But everything looked the same.

The hours stretched as dawn arrived. He didn't leave her side as the noon hour came and went. He rubbed his forehead. Why hadn't he asked her questions about what she was? Would she always come back? Was there something special he needed to do? Maybe he should return to the top of the mountain and put her where he had before.

What if the priests were responsible for her not being able to regenerate?

Derek was debating taking Kora from the city when a gasp sounded from her lips. He was on his feet in an instant, standing beside the bed. Her mouth was open, her back arched as she sucked in a huge breath. Then she collapsed and dragged in another large inhale. Her eyes slowly blinked open to look at the ceiling. She scanned the room, stopping when her gaze landed on him. Fear flashed in her eyes, and it tore him in two.

"I followed you," he told her.

She held the covers against her nakedness as she sat up. "How long was I out?"

"Ten hours."

She tried to swallow. He brought her water and watched as she gulped it down. He refilled it, and she drank that one slower.

"How much did you see?" she asked hesitantly.

He studied her wary expression. He could lie, but he didn't want to do that. "Everything."

"The child? Did she get free?"

He glanced at the floor before shaking his head. "Both she and the woman were killed."

Kora squeezed her eyes closed for a heartbeat, her pain obvious. "I suppose this is where you tell me I was foolish to intervene."

"You did what you thought you had to do."

She turned her head away. "It was reckless. One more mistake. Two more lost lives I'll carry."

"Those aren't on you. That's on the priests. They were going to kill the child regardless of what you said or did."

"That doesn't make it easier to bear."

He blew out a breath. He wouldn't tell her about the other lives that had been taken. She would try to claim those, too. How many others did she carry that weren't hers? He was afraid of what the answer might be. "Nay, I don't suppose it does."

"I know you want to ask, so ask."

Derek hated that she wouldn't look at him. She had held

nothing back as his lover. The desires of the flesh exposed people in ways they never understood. But few cocooned themselves like Kora. Or him. He wanted to know what she was. It was the very reason he was in Stonemore. He could find out right then and end his curiosity.

But should he? What would it cost her to share that? He was afraid it might be more than she was willing to give.

Her head swung to him. "Do you fear me now?"

"Nay."

"Then ask."

It was on the tip of his tongue, but the words never passed his lips. "I'm going to get us some food and make sure no one saw either of us."

He was at the door when she called his name. He looked over his shoulder at her. Twice now, he had carried her bloody, lifeless body. And twice, it had hit him like a gut punch.

This last time, though, he had experienced emotions he couldn't name. Feelings he didn't want to feel. They were dangerous. Just as she was.

"I'll understand if you don't come back," she said.

Is that the kind of person she thought he was? It bothered him more than it should, especially because he *would* leave if she were anyone else. Actually, he never would've gone this far to begin with. "I'll be back."

"You shouldn't say that until you know."

He held her gaze, waiting.

"I'm...I'm a hellhound."

All the air left him. The scent he had recognized but couldn't place suddenly made sense. He could do nothing but stare at her while trying to reconcile her words.

"I'll understand if you leave. Or if you tell someone."

He somehow managed to say, "I'll be back."

In the hallway, he leaned against the door and closed his eyes. No wonder he hadn't placed the scent. It had been ages since the last hellhound was seen. Villette had them exterminated, relentlessly hunted until they were no more.

Yet one lived.

And he had brought her to Stonemore.

Derek's duty demanded that he slay Kora and bring her body to Villette. But he couldn't. He *wouldn't*. Every instinct he had urged him to take Kora and get away from the city before it was too late.

The sound of water reached him through the door. Derek straightened and made his way downstairs. Everything felt just out of focus as if the world was distorted and he needed to catch up. There was no way Kora could learn that he was a dragon. Her fear of dragons made sense now. Of course, she would be terrified of them. They were the only ones who could kill a hellhound.

He was her enemy.

Derek stumbled and grabbed the wall to steady himself. He suddenly knew exactly why Kora was in Stonemore. If dragons were the only ones that could kill hellhounds, her kind were the only ones who could slay a Star Person. It's why Villette had sent Derek and Bryok to hunt them.

The room began to spin. Kora was there to kill Villette. He couldn't allow that to happen. Villette was the only one who could free the dragons. He needed her. But he wouldn't report Kora to Villette either. Villette had stopped looking for hellhounds because she believed they were gone. She had no need to search for more. That kept Kora safe.

Derek looked up the stairs to the door. For now.

CHAPTER 14

Kora stared at the closed door long after Derek left. The way he had gone utterly still after she told him she was a hellhound, as if every muscle in his body clenched, kept flashing in her mind. He hadn't outright rejected her, but it felt the same.

She threw off the covers and stood. After one last look at the door, she walked to the tub and turned on the faucets. Kora stared at the flow of water as it filled the container, but she couldn't stop thinking about Derek or his reaction.

It wasn't until she was about to step into the water that she looked at her body. There wasn't a trace of blood anywhere. Her head swung to the bed. There was none on the sheets either. The clothes she had worn were gone, but her boots sat by the settee. Clean. The only explanation was that Derek had wiped the blood away and gotten rid of her clothes in case someone came looking.

Kora wasn't sure what to make of that. She sank into the water and drew her knees up to her chest, wrapping her arms around her legs and resting her cheek on her knees. She had been sure he was asleep when she left the night before. There was no way she had woken him. He must have only pretended to sleep.

She ran through the events of the previous night from the time she left their room. All she had wanted was a closer look at the temple without others watching her. She had been right in thinking that most residents had taken to their beds. While she studied the building, she'd heard a child cry out in pain. That, with the clink of armor, had pushed all reason aside. She took off toward the sound without even wondering what might be going on —or if she should get involved. Then she saw the soldier priests and the one who had the girl by the arm.

Fury had swept through her. She felt the heat of flames licking her skin but somehow kept them from erupting. No one commented on the smoke around her. After ignoring her responsibilities for so long, she needed to do *something*. Unfortunately, she had once more been reckless about it instead of coming up with a plan.

She should have hidden and watched where the priests took the girl and *then* gone in to save her—and potentially others. Instead, she had gotten the mother and child killed, along with herself. Her blunder had also shown Derek she had magic. Something she had never intended to reveal.

"What am I doing?" she whispered.

Everything she touched fell apart. Her good intentions got others hurt and outed her. How soon before Villette knew a hellhound was in Stonemore?

Her gaze slid to the door again. Derek had said he would return, but she wasn't so sure. Her admission had shocked him. There was no doubt about that. He had cleaned her wounds and seen her come back from the dead. That hadn't bothered him. He could've left well before she woke. He could have even turned her in. Yet, he hadn't.

So, why the reaction to the confession?

She frowned as she thought over his words. He'd said he followed her. That meant he saw everything. How had he gotten to her without sustaining any injuries? The soldiers wouldn't have left her body in the streets. They would've likely taken the dead. Which begged the question: How had Derek gotten her body?

Moreover, how had he carried her back to the inn and past numerous soldiers without being stopped?

She'd had to talk her way past guards just to get to the lower levels. She couldn't imagine them freely opening the gates for Derek while he carried her bloody body. None of it made any sense.

A knock yanked her from her musings. She lifted her head. Derek wouldn't knock. He hadn't before, and he wouldn't now. "Enter," she called.

The door swung open to reveal the young servant from the previous day. She carried another tray of food inside.

"Your gentleman said you weren't feeling well," she said.

Your gentleman. There was nothing about Derek that was hers. Nothing about him belonged to anyone but him.

Kora wanted to ask where Derek was but was proud of herself for not giving in. The servant wouldn't know anything anyway. "Thank you."

"Let me know if you need anything else," the girl said and left.

A great sadness filled Kora. She had never told anyone she was a hellhound. She wasn't sure why she had with Derek. She could have told him anything but the truth. But she hadn't. She'd said the words that would condemn her. He wasn't coming back. She should dress and leave the city immediately while she still had a chance. Hide out until she knew for sure she wasn't being hunted. But that meant more innocents dying. All because she was scared.

She was tired of being afraid. Tired of running. Tired of all of it.

Yet she didn't move. She remained until the water turned chilly. Kora let it drain and refilled the tub. Heated water was a luxury she rarely got, and she planned to take full advantage of it while she could. She stretched out and let the heat ease her muscles. Her body had healed on the outside, but it took the muscles and tissue longer to stop hurting.

Kora washed thoroughly, even though there was no blood on her. She had felt it gush from her with every stab and slice. The screams of the child and her mother had penetrated her cloud of pain. She had tried to reach them to help, but the only way she could have saved them was by letting loose the hound within her. She hadn't.

To save herself.

She stood and let the water sluice down her body. Kora stepped out of the tub and dried off before putting her black garments on. Then she stirred the embers in the hearth to life before sitting before the flames and combing her wet hair. It was always tangled and took forever to dry.

When that chore was done, she attempted to eat. She was normally famished after coming back from the dead, but the thought of food turned her stomach. Her thoughts shifted to Derek again and how he had gotten them to the inn, but no matter how she looked at it, she realized he must have had help.

Was he part of the soldiers? Did he know someone? Was that

how he had gotten them into the city and up to the sixth level? When he offered to accompany her, he never said anything about an invitation. Had that even been real? Had *anything* been true?

But there was a more alarming question. Did he work with Villette?

She had known Derek was dangerous and idiotically found that appealing. Her attraction obscured any misgivings. After being alone for so long, it had felt good to have someone share her bed. She had known not to let it go further. She should've walked away and forgotten him. Shouldn't have agreed to travel with him to Stonemore.

Rash and reckless. No matter how many times she messed up, no matter how many people died, she hadn't learned anything.

Kora stood and walked to the window. She felt the coolness of the day even through the closed blinds. She raised them and peered outside to see the overcast skies and plants swaying in the breeze. She snapped the shutters closed and stood in front of the fire to warm herself. Did she dare stay and see what happened? Or did she stuff the food into her bag and run?

She was the closest to Villette she had ever been. She might not get another chance. Nay. There would be no more running. But if she was to get inside the palace, she had to do it the right way. That meant she needed a plan.

Kora considered the plan she had begun the day before. She needed a backup, however. There had to be more than one way to move between levels. There must be secret passages that weren't guarded like the gates. They would be tucked away somewhere. It would take time to find them, but she could do it. The wee hours of the morning provided the best cover with the least number of eyes.

Once she got to the palace, she needed a way in. Soldier or servant. She still leaned toward soldier. Everyone was used to seeing them, and they likely moved about in places servants couldn't go—they were usually restricted to certain areas.

Each level had a station of guards. There had to be someone near her size. Finding them would take more time, but that was the easy part. Then again, if she got the armor first, no one would stop her from moving between levels, and she wouldn't have to worry about finding any secret passages.

"Looks like my first order of business is staking out the soldiers," she said aloud.

Since she knew nothing about the palace, it was impossible for her to plan anything for when she was inside. She needed to get in, and she would. After that, it was a matter of learning the layout and determining where Villette was before she was discovered. There were likely a dozen other things she was forgetting to consider or factor in, but she had the start of a really good plan. It would work.

It had to.

For the second time that day, a knock startled her. Her heart sank deeper because she knew it wasn't Derek. She told herself she'd stayed to plan, but she had remained in hopes he would return. Even when she knew he wouldn't.

Kora walked to the door and opened it. Standing there was one of the girls from the clothing shop. She carried a large box wrapped in a pale blue bow.

"Sorry this is late. The extra order took more time than we thought," she explained.

Kora stared at the package, remembering the gown she had chosen for the party. "I won't need that now."

"It's already paid for," the young girl said with a shrug. "It's yours."

Kora hesitantly accepted the box and closed the door. New clothes, a soft bed, ample food, and as much hot water as she wanted. She had been indulged beyond her wildest fantasies. It had been great, but it was over now.

She placed the package on the bed, intending to leave it. But the more she stared at it and recalled how she'd felt in the dress, the more she wanted to peek. Kora untied the bow. Then she lifted the lid and looked inside. She smoothed her hands over the gown's supple fabric. She lifted it from the box and held it up to her. She had been excited to dress in such finery and stand beside Derek.

The realization that she wouldn't get that opportunity was like a kick to the stomach. She sighed and began folding the gown when she glanced inside the box and stilled at the sight within. Kora set the gown aside and pulled out two tunics and two pairs of pants. Beneath them were sandals meant for the gown. There was also a small box nestled to the side, wrapped in another blue bow.

Her hands shook as she opened it to find a decorative hair comb with vibrant blue and white stones. She ran her fingers lovingly over the gems. The only time she had come close to anything so fine was when she'd held her mother's alabaster hair comb.

By the stars, she missed her family. Sometimes, the ache was so deep and all-consuming that she thought it might swallow her whole.

And other times, she wished it had.

She didn't want to be the last. The weight of that responsibility was too much. She had stumbled repeatedly over the years. She couldn't fail. But she feared that was exactly what she would do.

Warmth suddenly spread through her. Her stomach fluttered because she knew that feeling.

And she knew the cause.

Kora turned and found Derek standing in the open door, watching her.

CHAPTER 15

"You came back."

The surprise in Kora's voice contradicted her carefully controlled expression. Derek softly closed the door, unable to tear his gaze from her. He had spent the past few hours arguing with himself about what to do. He knew what Villette expected of him, and he comprehended the vow he had given her. But another truth struck him. He wasn't giving up Kora. He intended to keep her by his side. As for the rest? Well, he'd figure it out as he went.

"I said I would," he replied.

Kora glanced at the comb in her hand before gently setting it in its box. "I know, but...we're both aware of what others think of people like me."

"And you believed I would use that information against you?"

"I wouldn't have blamed you if you did."

Was that really how she saw him? Nay. This wasn't about him. This was about others and how magical beings were banished or killed. That, combined with her family being slain, would cause anyone to expect the worst.

Kora pressed her lips together. "I shouldn't have told you."

"But you did. Why?"

"I wish I knew. I've never told anyone."

"No one?"

She met his gaze. "No one. Ever."

Derek walked to stand before her. He had been confused about what to do, but no longer. "No one has ever entrusted me with such valuable information before. Your secret is safe with me." And he meant it.

"It's knowledge some would pay handsomely to obtain."

"Coin means nothing to me."

She walked to the table. Her body was tense, her lips compressed.

He followed her with his eyes. And then it struck him. "You don't believe me." When she didn't reply, he asked, "Which part? About the coin or your secret?"

"I don't know. Both?"

There was a way to prove himself about the coin. All he had to do was show her he had magic. But that would raise questions about what he was, and he would lose her if she knew he was a dragon. He knew that to the very depths of his soul. He didn't consider *why* he couldn't let her go. That was for another day.

"What do you know about...my kind?" she asked.

Derek chose his words carefully. "A few things."

"Like?"

"That you're hard to kill."

She swiveled her head to look at him, the walls around her fortified and solid. "And?"

"You erupt into flames."

"Both are true. Did you also know that we're able to smell evil? That, when we do, we're bound to find and kill it to keep the balance of the universe?"

Derek frowned and shook his head. Villette had conveniently left out that part. She knew everything about her enemies, so she had known and not shared.

"Once, there was a woman who could tell if an infant had magic merely by touching them. She traveled from village to village, giving insight to parents about the babies they had taken in. No one ever knew where she would travel next or how long she would stay. No one even knew her name, but she was known by all. Always traveling alone. Some claimed the magic of others called to her, that she could sense it. I'm not sure what brought her to the village. There are so many things we don't know. Why can't women become pregnant? Is it us? Or does the fault lie with the men? Why do infants just appear in random places? Where do they come from? Who is bringing them? Are they taken from families and given to others on Zora? So many questions. But she had an answer."

"If the babies had magic."

Kora sank into the chair and rested an arm on the table. "I had been found in a field two days prior. The elders of the village gave me to a young couple who'd just married. It is said the woman walked into the village and straight to their door. I was lying in a cradle. When she touched me, I erupted into flames, burning the blanket and cradle. I can't imagine what the couple must have thought. Magic is one thing. Flames are another. The woman told the elders I belonged with my kind, and they gladly handed me over. She brought me to a hidden community where everyone had magic, but most were hellhounds. My brother told me the story often. He was five years old when our parents took me in. He remembered that day vividly." She smiled, but it was fleeting.

"For the first eight years, my life was idyllic. I was showered with love. My parents were wonderful, and I adored my brother. I had friends and extended family. No one sneered because I had magic. No one feared me. I didn't have to hide who or what I was. I had no idea how good things were until it was all taken away."

Derek didn't move or make a sound. He wanted to hear this as badly as he wanted to beg her not to tell him more because he knew the story wouldn't end well.

She swallowed, her gaze going distant. "My father was part of a small group of hellhounds that caught the scent of evil. They followed it, doing what we do. They succeeded in ending the malevolence, but a dragon was nearby and caught their scent. They separated, each going in a different direction, knowing the beast could only follow one. They believed they had fooled it, but in reality, the dragon had tricked them. It followed the scent that led it straight to our town."

Derek fisted his hands, his lungs seizing. He shook his head, refusing to believe what he was hearing. It couldn't be the same village. It just couldn't.

"Mum had Kayden take me to safety with some of the others as she hurried to help Dad and anyone else she could. It was the last time I saw my parents. Kayden tried to leave me, but I wouldn't let go of him. My cousin, Zak, kept us both there. The battle was over quickly. When we emerged, there was nothing left of our community. Nothing but fire and smoke. And piles of ash that had once been people. I knew to be afraid of dragons because they were the enemy, but I learned a valuable lesson that day. I learned to fear and hate."

Bile rose in Derek's throat. Because he had been the one who killed her parents and so many others that day. All in the name of protecting Villette so she could free the dragons. Even if he had known then that hellhounds sought evil to end it, he would have carried out his mission. His kin deserved freedom.

He squeezed his eyes shut. It was bad enough that Kora considered him her enemy. If she learned what he had done... He couldn't even finish the thought.

Derek was startled as he realized how long ago that attack had been. His eyes flew open to look at Kora. If his calculations were right, that meant she was over five hundred years old.

She drew in a deep breath, unaware of his thoughts, and slowly released it. "For days, Kayden, Zak, and I thought we were all that was left. Uncle Rylan eventually found us. There were a few other survivors, and it was decided it would be better if we went our separate ways in case the dragon returned. I swung between bouts of grief, rage, and hate. Every night, I woke screaming from nightmares, reliving the sounds of the dragon."

Derek turned his head away. He could try to tell her his reasonings for what he did, but it wouldn't matter. He had destroyed her life. He had done it many times over, and no one had made him feel regretful. Until now.

"The days were long and taxing," she continued. "We were constantly on the move and kept away from others unless we had no choice. If we needed supplies from a village, Uncle Rylan went. I don't know if it was because I was a girl or because I was so young, but they hid a lot from me. They would wait until they thought I was asleep before they talked. And it was always in whispers. I only heard bits about the plan. I got a name—Villette. And I had a place—Stonemore. Maybe if I had known everything, I would've listened to their warning to stay put."

Derek made his way to the table and took the chair opposite Kora. He had no words, at least not any she would want to hear. So, he sat and continued to listen.

"I was restless," she said as she tucked her dark hair behind her ear. "It's a bad excuse, but it's the truth. I was so tired of moving around and being kept out of things. I wanted to be involved, but they wouldn't let me. The more they tried to shelter me, the angrier I got. I should have paid more attention to where we were. I should have *listened* when they tried to caution me. I had so much rage at what'd happened to my parents that all I wanted to do was hurt someone. I know now that's why they kept me out of it. I needed to get past my grief and learn to control my emotions. They told me that repeatedly. I believed I was ready to join the fight."

Derek flattened his palm on the table instead of reaching across it to cover her hand with his. He wanted to touch her, but he didn't deserve that privilege. Not now. Not ever again.

Her gaze lifted to his. "I was too young to realize that I directed my anger at them because I didn't have anywhere else to aim it. It wasn't as if I could go after the dragon. I went for a walk to clear my head. I never even saw the dragon. But it saw me."

Derek searched his mind to see if he had a memory of this. He hoped it wasn't him. He was already responsible for too much when it came to Kora.

"It rose from sleeping on the top of the mountain. I froze in terror. All the times I imagined fighting against one of the beasts vanished as I turned and ran. Kayden, Rylan, and Zak intercepted it when it came after me. Kayden told me to hide, and that's what I did. I saved myself and watched as the three remaining members of my family were killed instead of standing with them as I had demanded they allow for months." Kora paused and drew in a shaky breath. "Surprisingly, the dragon didn't look for me. I didn't leave that spot for days. I stared at their smoking remains and went through everything I should have done. Then I ran far and fast. I've been running and hiding ever since. Their ghosts follow me, a reminder that there was unfinished business." She shrugged. "I'm the last of our kind. It's time I finish what my family began."

"If you're the last, shouldn't you have a duty to stay alive?"

"I used that excuse for a while. It doesn't hold water anymore. I have to do this."

He wanted to reach out and touch her, but he held back. He might have been the one to attack her village, but he hadn't been the one to kill her brother, cousin, and uncle. That wouldn't mean much to her, though, so he kept it to himself.

"The moment my secret is out, a dragon will come, and it will kill anyone near me," she said.

"You expect to be discovered?"

"I'm trying to warn you."

"Warning heard."

She turned her head and blew out a frustrated breath. "Get away from me. Far away."

He couldn't. He had already tried. Twice. "I'm not going anywhere."

"I can't be responsible for another death."

"Then don't be."

She laughed, the sound hollow as she looked at him.

They held gazes for a long moment before it dawned on him

why she had shared her story. "You think I've already told someone about you."

"You were gone a long time."

"I had things to sort through."

She quirked a brow. "Like?"

"Like ensuring no one suspects you in the incident last night."

"Right. Tell me, how did you get me past the soldiers back here?"

He had hoped she wouldn't think about that. It was a good thing then that he had already come up with a good lie. "I said you were drunk and spilled wine on yourself."

"Quick thinking."

She didn't believe him. He saw it in the set of her jaw and the suspicion in her eyes. He hadn't cared about anything but the dragons his entire life. He had never apologized for the lives he had to take that brought him a step closer to freeing his brethren. He did what was necessary at every turn to further his cause. He took women to his bed to ease his lust, but they were nothing but a means to an end. A few hours of pleasure that never quite satisfied him.

Then, one day, a dark-haired beauty unexpectedly came into his life. He had been sad to see her die, but that was when he'd thought her merely mortal. From the instant he discovered her gone from the slab until now, he hadn't been able to get Kora out of his blood.

It wasn't just about lust, though that had a lot to do with it. She captivated and enthralled him. Her strength riveted him. Her smiles beguiled him. The way their bodies came together was thrilling and extraordinary.

He shouldn't trouble himself about children being sacrificed.

People did horrible things everywhere. But he cared now because he had seen how it affected her. It made him take a closer look at himself.

Perhaps that was why he said words that could come back to haunt him. "I'm not your enemy, Kora. I want to help."

"Why?"

"I don't know."

She smirked. "That might be the truest thing you've said."

Derek understood her hesitation. He leaned forward. "Do I smell evil?"

"I don't know."

He blinked, taken aback. "What?"

"A lot changed for me the day my brother died. I repressed many things in an effort to pretend I wasn't a hellhound."

"Then how do you know you're going after the right person?"

"Because she's the one who sent the dragons after my people. She's the one allowing the children to be sacrificed. And she's the one running this city."

Derek had been afraid that would be her answer. "The Divine rules the city."

"The Divine is nothing more than a woman named Villette. She is much more than she lets on, however. She's powerful. Extremely so. And only a hellhound can kill her."

Every argument he had against Villette vanished. No one in the city knew Villette was the Divine. Everyone believed it was a man. It was a ruse she had begun years earlier to allow her to move about the city freely while still maintaining an iron control.

How could he help Kora when he had given a vow to Villette? If either found out about the other, things could go from bad to worse in a second.

"If Villette is as formidable as you say, should you go after her alone? No one would fault you if you went away and forgot about her."

"No one else can do this. It has to be me. Besides, I would never be able to look at another child without thinking of the ones dying here. She has magic, yet she allows anyone with it to be slaughtered. And she's not just allowing it. She's condoning it. Tell me that isn't evil."

He couldn't.

CHAPTER 16

Kora hadn't felt beautiful very often in her life, but she certainly did in the gown. She stared at herself in the mirror, smoothing her hands down the dark blue pleats. The deep V-neck accentuated her breasts before gathering to emphasize her waist. The pleats continued downward to skim the floor. There were even pleats on the long, full sleeves. But her favorite part was the back. Kora turned to the side and lifted her hair to look over her shoulder and see the V that exposed most of her back.

Before, she had purchased clothes when she needed them. They were for function only. She wouldn't have even glanced at anything like the gown because it wasn't needed. She never would've guessed that she might require something so grand. The material was as soft as a feather against her skin but warm enough that she wouldn't need the cloak.

Her only problem was her hair. She attempted to gather it behind her head to use the comb, but nothing she did held for very long. She certainly didn't want her hair falling at the party. Her usual plait or gathering the strands at her neck wouldn't suffice. She didn't know anything about fancy hairstyles. The fact was, she didn't belong with the wealthy, and she was terrified they would see right through her disguise, no matter how pretty it was.

The only saving grace was that Derek wasn't there to see her many failed attempts. She didn't know where he was. Maybe she should've asked when he had slipped out, but she had exposed too much of herself and felt raw. Being alone had helped to scab over the emotional wounds telling her story had caused.

Kora sighed and gave up as she left her hair down. She gently set the comb on the table and walked to the door to find Derek. When she opened it, the serving girl stood there, her hand raised to knock.

"Pardon me, miss," she said. "I was coming to see if you needed any assistance dressing."

Kora hesitated. It wasn't easy for her to ask for help about anything, especially something she felt so inferior about. She swallowed and blurted out, "Do you know anything about hair?"

Her face lit up. "Aye, I do."

"Would you mind helping me?"

"Of course."

Kora stepped aside to let her in before walking to the table. She held up the comb. "Can you use this?"

"I can. Do you have a style in mind?"

"Do whatever you think would look best."

The girl talked as she worked, her fingers nimble as she combed and sectioned Kora's hair. It took barely a push to get her to open up. Kora learned her name was Ada and that she had been born in Stonemore. Ada's family still resided on the third level, but she had managed to land a job well above it, which was a big deal.

Kora hung on every word. She was getting an uncensored view of the city from someone born to the lower levels who now lived in the upper ones. It seemed life in the lower four was even worse than what Kora had believed. Food was scarce, crime was unchecked, and poverty touched everyone. The wealthy went on blithely living as if nothing was wrong. Ada's lover was a soldier, and he had confided in her that many of them were apprehensive about trying to control the lower four levels that always seemed on the brink of something catastrophic.

"There you go," Ada said with a smile as she stepped back.

Kora stood and walked to the mirror. She blinked, startled at the vision that met her. She didn't know the woman staring back at her. With the dress and her long, dark hair swept over one shoulder with soft tendrils framing her face, she looked elegant and beautiful.

"The comb is holding your hair here," Ada said as she brought Kora's hand up and back to feel where it held the hair.

Kora may not belong with the wealthy, but she looked the part. She turned to Ada. "Thank you. You are very talented."

"It's easy with your hair. And I have a love for it. I was always styling my mum's and sisters'."

"You have a gift."

They shared a smile, and then Ada hurried away to see to her other duties. Kora took another look in the mirror. She wanted to remember every detail about the dress and her hair. Then she faced the room. She was tired of staring at the same four walls. Derek had surprised her by returning, but that didn't mean she didn't still worry. He had left again.

Kora blew out a breath. He knew her secrets now while she knew none of his. There was a shift in the dynamic of whatever they were. Lovers, yes. Friends? That might be stretching things a bit. Yet he had gotten her to the inn and cleaned her. Anyone would say that's what friends did.

For anyone else, it might be, but Kora knew how dangerous it was for her to even breathe. Derek held her life in his hands. And she had given him that power. Even now, looking back, she didn't know why she had told him. Loneliness, maybe? The need to have a connection to someone? To belong? To be seen and...loved?

Being alone sent her thoughts to places she didn't want to go. She had to face the outside world eventually. It might as well be now. She walked from the room, pausing as she closed the door behind her. Then she lifted her chin and made her way to the stairs. It was disconcerting to walk down without being able to see her feet. She clung to the rail with one hand while she gathered her skirts in the other. It was a relief to reach the bottom. Ada shot her a grin as she moved about the dining area.

Kora returned the smile and chose a table against the wall so she could see the door and the stairs. The door opened, and the chill of the evening slid inside and directly to her. She missed the sunny days and warmth of her childhood home. No matter where she went, it was never quite right. The sun might be out, but the weather was too cold. Or the temperatures were fine, but the skies were filled with drab clouds. But she couldn't go home. So, she wandered. Forever searching for a home she would never find.

Ada brought wine. It gave Kora something to do as she waited. She caught people darting looks her way. Her body tensed, wondering if they knew she was responsible for the death of the mother and girl from the previous night. No one shouted, pointed, or called for the priests. Yet.

Finally, she spotted Derek as he strode through the door from the outside. His long hair was pulled into a queue at the base of his neck. She liked how the blue shirt molded to the width of his shoulders and skimmed his trim waist. He could wear anything and make it look good.

But he looked best naked.

He nodded at Ada and headed for the stairs but halted when he reached them. Derek slowly turned his head to her. Their gazes locked. She saw the raw desire reflected there, and her stomach fluttered excitedly in response. He turned and walked to stand beside her.

Derek leaned down and brushed his lips against her cheek. "You take my breath away."

Kora shivered at his words as well as the husky timbre of his voice. Her eyes closed for a heartbeat. Then, he straightened. She looked up at him. "You look amazing yourself."

"Shall we?" he asked, holding out his hand.

She took it and stood while he tossed a coin to Ada. His hand on her back guided her out of the inn and onto the street. Once there, he dropped his arm as they made their way to the gate. The clear, navy sky twinkled with stars and the last light of the setting sun. It would have been an enjoyable walk if it was just them. But they were going to mingle with others. With every step, she began to question their appearance at the party.

"Why are we going again?" she asked in a low voice.

He remained near but didn't touch her. "There was a twofold reason, though we no longer need to search for your individual."

She didn't hear any censure in his voice. And she had listened for it. "And the other?"

"Being in the midst of such a gathering is a good way to learn about the citizens and their opinions because everyone has a view on something."

"Ada, the serving girl, shared that her lover and others in the army are getting anxious about things in the lower levels."

"I heard some rumblings about that today while I was out."

She so badly wanted to ask what he had been doing, but she didn't. "It was soldiers?"

"Residents and shop owners on level five. They're the closest to four. Because of that, they hear and see a lot."

"You don't really think that will be a topic at a party, do you?"

He grunted. "I think anything is fair game for the wealthy."

Their conversation ended when they reached the gate and waited for the soldiers to allow them to pass. Then they were trudging up another incline. She had to hold up her skirts so she didn't trip on them. Derek walked as if he knew where he was going, and it turned out he did.

The house had a large fence and an impressive ornamental gate with guards on either side. The gate was open, and no one stopped them, but it still bothered her that there were soldiers at all. Kora glanced over her shoulder as they walked past the gate and saw four more of them standing inside.

A gently curved path led them to the front door, standing open and adorned on either side with a variety of yellow flowers. There was a large overhang above them to protect them from the elements. On either side of that were woody, twining vines that wound their way up the side, branching off in different directions to shroud the house in fragrant, yellow blossoms.

Derek's hand returned to the small of her back as they stepped through the doorway. Servants moved between guests, carrying trays of drinks and food. Kora accepted a slim glass of a pale yellow drink. Someone really liked yellow.

She sniffed it before taking a sip. It was tangy and slightly sweet, but it packed a punch. Derek had chosen a short, fat glass holding an amber-colored liquid. Together, they moved about the front entry, farther into the house. There were guests in every room they ventured into. The clamor of conversation hurt her ears, and it took her some time before she settled and was able to pick up exchanges around her.

"Come back to this room if we get separated," Derek told her.

Separated? Did he plan to leave her? And why did it matter? She had been on her own for years. What was another night? But she still looked for something to remind her what room she was in. She found it in the huge painting of an elegant woman sprawled on a bed with the sheets discreetly covering her nude body. "All right."

"Let me know whenever you wish to leave."

Kora looked at him and teased, "Is now too soon?"

He grinned, and it transformed his face from gorgeous to breathtaking. His eyes sparkled with humor. His lips parted to speak just as a woman walked up. The light that had been there dimmed, and Kora wanted to shove the lady away and recreate the scene.

Instead, introductions were made. To her surprise, Derek gave their real names, but he was vague about how long they had been in the city. She sat back and listened to it all, watching the way he easily deflected questions and turned the conversation.

It wasn't long before there were others in their small circle. Kora traded names, which she forgot almost as soon as she learned them. It was hard to keep all the faces straight, much less their questions. Some were inane, but most probed deeper. She and Derek were new to the city, and that meant there were secrets to be learned.

She began to tune others out. The room was too warm, the crowd too much. She wondered what would happen if she suddenly welcomed the fire within her. Would those around her run away screaming the moment flames erupted over her body? She was suddenly shoved as people pressed in on her. One moment, Derek was there. The next, she couldn't find him.

Kora frantically looked around for him. She caught sight of the painting and released a sigh. At least she was still in the room, but she was near the back now. Each time someone walked up, they moved in closer, and she instinctively shuffled back to maintain some personal space. Everyone wanted to be in her face, and her desire to have some breathing room had moved her away from Derek.

She searched the room for him again and finally caught a glimpse of his head. Someone asked her a question, the same query she had been asked several times that night. The more alcohol was consumed, the more prying the questions became. She ignored the person. It was either that or leave. She opted to leave. She started to slip away, her eyes locked on Derek, when someone touched her arm.

"Kora, dear. There is someone you *have* to meet."

There were dozens she'd *had* to meet, and not a single one of them had been anyone she thought important. She pulled her gaze from Derek and turned to the woman who had stopped her, only to go rigid at the sight of the red-robed armored priest.

The shiny armor and red robes belonged to a man with a pointed face and narrow-set eyes. The dark gaze observed her keenly. "Kora," he said and bowed. "It's a pleasure."

Kora wanted to run, scream for Derek. Images of the priests surrounding her with their weapons drawn flashed in her head. She had been found out. He was here to arrest her, but she wouldn't go easily.

"She's overwhelmed," the woman said with a laugh.

Kora couldn't remember her name. She was draped in expensive jewels and had some sewn into her lavish gown. Kora looked from her to the priest.

"I am just a man," the priest replied with an easy smile.

Was he kidding? He had to be joking.

The woman squeezed Kora's arm. "You are more than that, and you know it."

Kora found both staring at her expectantly. The priest was smiling and relaxed. Maybe he wasn't here to arrest her. She realized she had been holding her breath and relaxed her body so she could draw in air. When she did, a foul stench slammed into her. Evil.

It was so shocking to have that sense return that Kora gagged and coughed. She forced a tight smile as she stared at the priest. The fire within her demanded release to bring him to justice. And she would. Just as soon as she took care of Villette. "I didn't expect to see one such as you at a party."

"We may be priests, but we still like to have a good time," he said with a grin.

The people around her erupted in laughs. Kora forced the sound past her lips as a tendril of smoke wafted from her fingers. She took a step back and felt a familiar, hard body behind her. Derek rested a hand on her waist, instantly calming her.

CHAPTER 17

Derek felt Kora relax marginally at his touch. He had gotten to her the moment he spotted the priest. And he hadn't come alone. Derek noted six others in their room alone who were with the priest. They were easy to spot among the crowd, eating and drinking but not a part of anything. They spoke to no one. Their gazes scanned faces constantly. But most importantly, their focus was the priest. The more Derek saw of Stonemore and its residents, the more he wanted to leave and never return.

"Ah," the priest said with a smile that didn't reach his eyes. "The other newcomer to our fair city. Derek, is it not?"

"Aye. And you are?"

"Everyone knows Aksel," the woman with him said. "He is a true friend to us and Stonemore."

Aksel gave her an unassuming smile that Derek saw through. He knew men like this. They pretended to be something they weren't, but their true colors were eventually revealed.

"You are too kind, dear Carla," Aksel told her. Then he turned to Derek. "I'm not sure I remember. Where do you hail from?"

"The north," Derek answered.

The priest sipped his drink. "Which city?"

"Nothing as grand as this."

"And what brought you and Kora south?"

Everyone leaned in as if eager to hear. Derek stared into Aksel's dark eyes. The priest was trying to determine if Derek was a threat. He was ready and willing to show Aksel just what a threat he and Kora both were.

"Adventure," Kora answered smoothly. "I wanted to travel and experience more. Derek indulges me that way."

Aksel studied Kora before sliding his gaze to Derek. "It seems you're both fitting in well here."

Carla laughed and changed the subject. Derek didn't take his eyes off the priest. When Aksel motioned for Derek to follow him a few minutes later, he moved to do just that. Kora's hand gripped his.

"I'll be fine," Derek whispered. "I'm curious what he wants."

"He doesn't believe us," she said softly.

He leaned down and brushed his lips over hers. "Others with him aren't wearing red. You'll be able to spot them. I'll be back soon."

Derek left her and followed the priest up the stairs to the second floor, through another crowded room, and out onto a balcony that overlooked the city. Aksel rested his hands on the railing and half-turned when Derek approached.

"A grand view, is it not?" the priest asked.

Derek's enhanced gaze saw past the forest to the land where his kin were being held. He strained, hoping he might spot a dragon, even as he knew he wouldn't. "It is. But you didn't bring me out here to talk about the view."

Aksel chuckled. "I did not. Why Stonemore? What made you come here?"

"As you well know, it's the only place for miles that's still standing. We've been traveling and needed a rest."

"Is that a dig at the strength of our city?"

"Stating a fact."

Aksel grunted. "No matter how many say they wish for peace, there are always others who long for battle. It's inevitable for rivalry to happen, and towns go to war."

"Stonemore goes to war a lot."

"Everyone wants what we have."

Derek swung his gaze to the priest. "And what is that, exactly?"

"You've seen it for yourself. Power. Wealth. Abundance. They all wished to take from us."

"Some of those villages were too small to have dared such."

"And yet, they did."

It was a lie. The priest and others believed it with everything they were, and nothing anyone said would disprove it. Derek knew Villette had been building her army, but he hadn't known how.

"You're back. And close. Are you coming to free me?"

Derek gritted his teeth. Now wasn't the time for a conversation with the faceless voice. "Kora has been asking how she can help the needy we saw when we arrived. Many are starving."

"They are being seen to. There is no reason for someone of her position to get her hands dirty with such things."

Derek had seen all manner of behavior from the humans. Some good, some bad, and some deplorable. What kind of priest considered those less fortunate in such a way? Why bring them to the city at all? Why not just kill them instead of making them suffer? It didn't make sense.

"I can see you don't agree."

Derek faced the priest. There was a lot he wanted to say, but it wouldn't do any good. "I'm learning the system here."

"That's good to hear. It won't bode well for you to go against us."

"Why aren't you answering me? I can feel you near."

Derek looked at the priest. "Is that a threat?"

"It's a warning."

"Time is wasting. She's healing. We must act now."

"Not now," Derek stated firmly. He said aloud to Aksel, "What is it you do, exactly? I've never seen a priest wear armor."

"Stop by the temple, and I'll show you. Only you, though."

Derek quirked a brow. "You have something against women? I thought everyone was allowed in the temple."

"Let's just say I think Kora would have a difficult time understanding our ways."

"And I wouldn't?"

Aksel flashed a smile. "That is yet to be determined. Enjoy the rest of the party."

Derek watched him walk away. The conversation had gone pretty much as suspected. The priest had made his stance known and delivered a thinly veiled threat. Derek didn't need to learn their ideology to be sickened by it. There was little he had seen of what humans called religion where someone hadn't misinterpreted divine messages and twisted them to suit whatever they were after. There was also the curtailing of freedoms, instilling fear, and the impediment to the progress of cultures.

Or the extermination of whatever they feared. Like magic.

He thought about the child the night before and how she had been so casually slaughtered. Kora had called children innocent. She was right. The young were taught to believe in things. Everyone in the city feared magic because that is what Villette wanted. There had to be a reason, though he had yet to figure it out. Villette was magic. He was magic.

The dragons they were trying to free were magic.

He had to take a hard look at himself, though. He was wary of religion, but an argument could be made that he was as culpable as everyone at Stonemore. He didn't follow the priests, though. He followed Villette. And when she demanded that the hellhounds be hunted to extinction, he and Bryok had gone after them.

Could he judge religion so harshly, then? Or was he to be judged with the masses?

"I can answer that."

Of course, she would be listening to his thoughts. How did she even get into his head? The only one capable of that was Villette.

"Finally connecting the dots. Took you long enough."

"The other Star People are long gone from Zora. She remained behind to help the dragons."

The woman laughed softly. *"She is not the only one on this realm."*

"If she captured you, it was for a reason."

"I just heard your thoughts about religion, and you want to believe her? There are two sides to every story. You've only heard one."

"Then tell me yours."

"Find me, and I will. I can't hold this connection for long."

"Where are you?"

"You know."

"Stop saying that."

There wasn't a retort. Derek left the balcony and returned to Kora. Her smile was genuine when she saw him, and it eased some of his tension. He shouldered his way to get to her side. Her gaze searched his, eager to know about the conversation. And he was keen to tell her. Whatever she saw on his face must have satisfied her. They remained until after Aksel and his underlings departed.

Neither said a word until they were far from the house. Then Kora asked, "What did Aksel want?"

"What those like him usually want. To threaten."

"Sounds like a good conversation then," she joked.

He looked at her and found himself grinning. "Hardly."

"I was worried he recognized me."

"I was, too." It was the reason he had gotten to her so quickly. "One of them might, so we need to be careful." He paused, then said, "I was invited to the temple."

Her brows shot up as she glanced at him. "Are you going?"

"He wants to educate me on the religion so I can make sure you fall in line."

"Excuse me?" she asked, her outrage matching his.

Derek grunted. "I told him you wanted to volunteer to help with the unhomed and needy. He informed me that the wealthy didn't get their hands dirty with those people."

"*Those people*?" she repeated in a furious whisper. She halted, her hands clenched at her sides.

He put a hand on her back to get her walking again and looked around to make sure no one had heard them. "I am as offended as you."

"She's part of this. You have to see that."

Derek knew Kora spoke of Villette.

"You don't see it," Kora stated.

"I didn't say that."

"You didn't need to."

He stopped this time, turning her to face him. "I see the issues. I see the trouble brewing."

"But?" she pushed when he didn't say more.

"You said it yourself. She's powerful."

"And I can stop her."

"Alone?"

She lifted her chin defiantly. "I'm all that's left."

And that was his fault. "Kora," he began.

"Forget about that for now. I want to know if you're going to the temple."

There was no way he was forgetting things. It was her way of turning the conversation, and he would allow it. For the time being. "I want to see inside. I also want to know what else he'll say."

"I don't think you should go, but it'll look suspicious if you don't. I need them to think we're believers. It'll buy me more time to plan."

Plan? She had been planning? Of course, she had. She wouldn't wait on him. "Promise you'll tell me when you go after her."

"So you can follow me?"

"So I can help."

She rubbed her hands up and down her arms. "You can't. She'll kill you on sight. I can't have that. I won't let that happen."

Derek watched as she walked away. He caught up with her, and they continued in silence. But he had to question his motives. He had sworn himself to Villette and their cause. If he went back on that, the dragons would be doomed forever. Centuries of his life had been dedicated to getting closer to the only thing he wanted. It should be an easy choice.

It always had been before.

But it wasn't. He had already crossed a line by helping Kora get into the city and keeping her secret. Yet he found himself continuing to aid her. He found ways to help her reach her goals, which would only make it that much harder for him when he had to make a decision.

Because he would. There was no getting around that fact. It would come down to Villette and his kin or Kora.

Were his desires more important than the lives of tens of thousands of dragons? After everything he had sacrificed, after all the deeds he had done, there was only one answer.

They undressed when they returned to the inn. Immediately, they wordlessly reached for each other.

CHAPTER 18

Kora once more woke to find Derek gone. The spot on his side of the bed was cool to the touch, but it only took a thought about the pleasure he had wrung from her the night before to cause her body to flush with heat.

Words weren't needed. They had spoken with touch, soothed with their mouths. He'd stroked and caressed, teased and tormented, and coaxed orgasm after orgasm from her. Even now, the memory of him inside her, thrusting deep and hard, made her clench her legs. There had been little sleep, but neither had cared. She'd needed him. It was as simple as that.

There might not be much trust between them, but the one thing they did have was passion. Undeniable, fiery passion.

And if she wasn't careful, it would bypass all reason.

Kora turned her head to look at his pillow and the indentation where his head had been. She had no idea if he was running an errand, getting breakfast, or going to the temple. It rankled that the priest had intentionally left her out. She'd wanted to see inside, but she would gladly miss it if it meant she didn't have to be around any of the priests.

She rose and took a relaxing bath before dressing. Kora hung the gown in the wardrobe next to her cloak before tucking away the sandals. Her feet had frozen at the party. The cool temperature didn't seem to affect others. Or maybe they just hid it better. Many of the guests had commented on how unseasonably warm this autumn was. And all she could think about was how cold she was.

The patter of rain drew her attention, and she peeked through the shutters to see a swath of gray clouds perched over the city. She frowned at the sky before heading downstairs for the morning meal. Ada greeted her warmly and assured her the rain would stop soon. Kora was surprised to discover that the storm had indeed faded to a drizzle by the time she finished eating. Kora retrieved her cloak and set off while the weather allowed.

Kora headed up, looking for signs of Derek as she walked. He had reservations about her going after Villette on her own. *She* had the same misgivings. She had enough doubt without adding his. Wishing she didn't have to do this alone wouldn't change the situation. She had to deal with things as they were.

She strolled through the streets on her way up to the mountaintop. She needed to see the palace on her own. She had a story ready if anyone stopped her, but no one paid her any mind. From their perspective, she dressed in the blue of Stonemore, so that meant she belonged. If only they knew the truth.

Kora tightened the cloak in an effort to keep the cool, damp air off the bare skin of her chest. Surely, the residents wore different shirts during the winter. Not that it mattered. She wouldn't be there long enough to find out. Either she would triumph over

Villette and beat a hasty retreat, or she would perish. One way or another, the nightmare would finally end.

The trip to the top was uneventful. Most were still inside and hadn't ventured out yet. She knew some could be watching her from the safety of a building, so Kora kept up the pretense even when no one was around.

Her steps slowed when she reached the eighth level and saw the palace. The sandstone appeared a deeper red after the rain. Even more so when set against the gray sky. She counted the steps from the entry gate to the door as well as the number of guards. She noted the carriages and the wealthy occupants who disembarked. She debated whether to engage someone in conversation in the hopes of learning who they were going to see, but she decided not to draw that kind of attention to herself. Her plan of dressing as a soldier was still the most solid.

To that end, she focused on the comings and goings of both soldiers and servants. Kora strolled from one end of the level to the other. Many milled about in the palace gardens as if hoping for a glimpse of the Divine. Kora rolled her eyes and wanted to tell everyone it was Villette. That she had lied and deceived everyone.

"I figured you'd make your way here."

She spun at the sound of Derek's voice. He sat on a bench beside a tall pot filled with tiny purple flowers. She had been so intent on watching the servants and soldiers that she had missed him altogether. "Did you?"

"It's where your target is."

So it was. She glanced at the grand structure, hoping to hide the fact that she was perturbed he had left their bed. She had to remind herself that they weren't a couple. They were two individuals with a mutual attraction, sharing a room. That was all. And yet she found herself asking, "How was the temple?"

"I've not gone yet. I had other things to see to."

"You could have woken me." Gah. Why did she sound so peeved? She was, but he didn't need to know that.

He grinned, his eyes crinkling in the corners as if he could read her mind. "Next time, I will. What are you about today?"

"Planning." It didn't go unnoticed that he hadn't said where he'd gone, and she wouldn't ask—even if she *was* dying to know. Secrets. They would be the death of her. The ones she kept and the ones she wanted to pry from Derek.

"Hm," he said and got to his feet. "I can't blame you for not wanting to divulge anything."

She examined his rugged face but couldn't find any anger in his features or words. It was a surprise. He didn't push for anything, which directly contrasted with what she fought within herself.

A muscle ticked in his jaw, and irritation flashed in his eyes before he turned his attention to the palace.

"Everything all right?" she asked.

His face tightened, but he didn't answer.

Kora found herself moving closer to him while glancing around. Maybe he'd spotted something she hadn't. After all, she hadn't seen him sitting on the bench. She saw three women coming up the street and a couple at the steps of the palace, gazing up at it in wonder. Others were in the garden behind them, and one man in particular stared at Derek for a long moment.

She stepped behind a bush and peered through the foliage at the stranger. The muscular body and handsome face had others staring after him. His attire suggested wealth even beyond what she had seen the night before. His hair was a mix of light brown and dirty blond that brushed his shoulders. His hands clasped behind his back, he looked toward Derek each time he stopped next to a flower.

Kora turned her head to her companion to find his hands fisted, and his body rigid with tension. His gaze was locked on the palace, and he seemed unaware of anyone or anything else. Including the stranger. She put a hand on his upper arm and felt the coiled muscle. "Derek."

His gaze snapped to her. Gradually, he relaxed.

"What just happened?" she asked

He shook his head. "It's nothing."

"It looked like something." She turned to look at the stranger again, but he was gone. "I don't want to alarm you, but there was a man watching you."

Immediately, Derek's eyes scanned the area. "Where?"

"I don't see him anymore."

"Would you know him if you saw him again?"

"Aye."

Derek nodded once. "Describe him."

Kora told him what she had noted. It worried her that the stranger had vanished so quickly. She turned in a circle to look for him and caught a glimpse of his backside as he went around the side of the palace. "There."

Derek didn't go after him. Instead, he watched until the man was out of sight.

"Where does that path lead?" she asked.

"Into the palace."

She shot him a glance. How did he know that?

"I asked," he said as if reading her mind once again.

"Should we follow?"

Derek shook his head. "I doubt it was anything."

"I don't know. The way he stared…it was as if he knew you. There was surprise, too, though."

"He probably mistook me for another. It's been some time since I've been to Stonemore. I don't know anyone here. By the way, we received another invitation for tonight. I was told it would be a small dinner affair."

Kora shivered as a gust of wind blew past her, followed by a smattering of rain. She didn't want to go to another party on the off chance she might have to face another priest. Not to mention the relentless questions from those who acted as if it was their right to know everything about her.

"It's a good way to pick up interesting gossip and learn about scandals. People let their guards down at parties with the alcohol flowing." He turned to face her. "But we can decline."

She smiled tightly, recalling the clothes, food, and lodging he was paying for. "I will accompany you as we agreed."

"I won't hold you to that."

"It's our deal."

He bowed his head. "Shall we walk the garden? You might get better views of the palace."

They turned together and walked side by side. She watched droplets of water form at the edges of petals before dropping to the ground.

"Can you discover if there's another exit to the city?" she asked.

He glanced at her. "I can try. Are you worried about something?"

"Me. And leaving."

"No one will ever know," he replied firmly.

She passed a fragrant, dark purple bloom. "Someone will know. Someone will see." If she succeeded. If she didn't...well, it wouldn't matter.

"If anyone comes for you, fight. If they manage to kill you, I'll get your body."

"That isn't what I'm asking."

"It needs to be said."

She shook her head. "You've been seen with me. Regardless of how things go, they will likely tie you to me. You need to be able to get out."

"They won't hold me."

"You don't know that."

"Rest assured, I know places to hide so I can't be found."

Kora swallowed as they turned down a path, the palace now to her right. "You stand out in a crowd. You'll need to be careful."

"I will."

"Can I ask something of you?"

He nodded. "Of course."

"Don't agree until you hear what I have to say."

"All right."

Kora released a long breath. She'd known the odds before she came to Stonemore, but new terrors had awaited once she was inside the city. "It's a lot to ask."

He stopped and faced her. "Kora. Ask what you will."

She looked into his pale olive eyes. They watched her closely, patiently. "If I am captured and the..." Her words failed her. She swallowed and tried again. "If they take my life over and over again, find a dragon. I would prefer death than enduring such torture."

"That's what you would ask of me?"

"You may not even need to. Villette probably has dragons near. They'll catch my scent as soon as...well, when things happen."

Derek continued along the path in silence. Then he said, "I promise not to let them torture you."

"Thank you."

"Do you have a way inside?"

She knew he was asking about the palace. "I'm working on it."

"Be careful."

"I issue the same request to you."

He raised a brow as he looked at her. "About?"

"The priests."

"They don't scare me."

She was beginning to wonder if anything frightened him. "Maybe they should."

"Because they kill? Plenty of others do that."

"Because they do it with impunity. They believe in a cause. Someone who has absolute faith in something is blind to all else. They refuse to see any other side or even look at the facts for themselves."

A frown crinkled his brow, and he looked deep in thought. "Unconditional."

"Aye. They believe unconditionally."

"They are certain their way is the only way."

Kora grunted. For a moment, she wondered if Derek was talking about someone else. "There is always more than one way. Anyone who claims there is only one is delusional. Or a fraud."

"Based on your theory, there is more than one way to get Villette."

She hesitated. He had been talking about something else. "While that's true, it doesn't change the fact that it has to be me."

A dark brow arched. "Are you sure you have all the facts?"

He was throwing her words back at her. While she enjoyed a good debate, and it had been so very long since she'd had one, now wasn't the time for it. She knew what she had to do, and Derek wasn't going to change her mind. "Take a look around. If I had any doubt, it dissolved the moment we came here, and I saw firsthand what she's done. Think of all those below. Their homes were destroyed, their ways of life stolen. Their families taken. Some probably went to a nearby village, only for it to happen again. Eventually, everyone made their way here. And for what? What did Villette gain? The size of her army swelled. What about all those starving, sitting in the elements, and thinking about the lives they once had that were snatched away for nothing? She doesn't care about them. They are casualties of war. They're all dead—they just don't know it yet. They'll suffer, waiting and begging, before death finally finds them. Then there are the children the priests are killing. In my opinion, that alone is enough to bring Stonemore down. She should've been stopped years ago. I lie awake some nights thinking about all the lives she has taken while I've hidden myself away, turning my back on who I am. On what I'm supposed to do." Kora shook her head. "Well, I'm facing things now. Everything Villette has done has brought her more power. It needs to stop."

"Maybe she's after something big and requires an army."

Kora rolled her eyes. "She is a Star Person. They are the most powerful beings in the universe. She doesn't need anything or anyone. If she wanted Stonemore razed tomorrow, she could make it happen with a snap of her fingers. Don't feel sorry for her. She wants control, and she's gotten it by using deception and manipulation. She isn't hiding her true identity for nothing. She has something big planned, and by the time everyone realizes what it is, it'll be too late."

"And you think taking her out will change all of it? There are other Star People."

"True. But I can kill them. They can also kill each other."

He turned his head to her. "How do you know so much about the Star People?"

"I don't know," she said with a shrug. "Some of it just seems to be in my head, but I learned other things from my family. It isn't as if hellhounds were made to destroy the Star People. Or maybe we were. I don't know. The story I heard was that a chance encounter with one of them resulted in their death. From then on, we were hunted."

CHAPTER 19

"The universe is a big place. There might be more of you out there," Derek said.

She shrugged. "I hope there are, but it isn't as if they can get to me. Or me to them. I've searched everywhere for another on Zora. There isn't anyone but me."

There was a way. He just didn't know what it was. And if he did? Telling Kora would pit him against Villette and destroy any chance of the dragons gaining their freedom. But if he could get Villette to move soon against those holding his kin, he would then be able to stand with Kora. His loyalties wouldn't be divided.

It was a good, solid idea. But it wouldn't work. Nothing he'd said or done had pushed Villette to move forward yet. She always had a reason to postpone the attack, always had a new strategy that would ensure victory. By the time she finished talking, he *wanted* to wait. That lasted for a few weeks, but the more time he thought about the dragons' suffering, the more he wanted to go immediately. He would've done it alone if he'd thought there was a chance of success.

Why hadn't he? Why hadn't he done *something*? Instead of waiting, lingering. Planning.

Derek looked over Kora's head at the palace. Whenever he grew frustrated and antsy—which was often—Villette reminded him that the continued survival of the dragons rested with him and the eggs.

"You don't actually believe that."

Just when he'd thought he had shut the woman up, she returned.

"How many times have you tried to free the dragons?" When he didn't reply, she snorted. *"Exactly"*

"You know nothing," he replied.

"I know far more than you. I could give you all the answers. About the dragons, about Villette, and about those lost memories."

"As if I'd believe you. You'd say anything to get free."

"And you'll blindly follow another just because she says the dragons need saving."

"They do!"

Her laughter filled his head.

Derek saw Kora glance at him, a worried expression clouding her features. He realized he was clenching his jaw and forced his muscles to loosen. "Do you plan to remain here?"

"I'd like to look around more, but I can't get to the areas I need to see."

He could take her. He could bring her anywhere she wanted. Right to Villette, even. All he had to do was say the words. She would even take him up on the offer. It wouldn't be until later that she'd ask *how*. Then, all his secrets would come out. There would be fear in her beautiful brown eyes instead of desire. The thought of that was like a vise around his lungs, squeezing painfully.

Fuck. He was in a right fine mess. All of his making. He hated lying. He'd never needed to before. Oh, he might sidestep the truth or ignore something, but he never outright lied. Yet he had found himself being dishonest with Kora multiple times. The lies sat awkwardly and offensively on his tongue.

He wanted to scoop her into his arms and take her far from Stonemore. Far from Villette and anything else that could hurt her. He could find a place where it was just the two of them. Somewhere they could bask under the sky and give in to their passions whenever they wanted.

Somewhere their pasts didn't matter.

He slid his attention to her. The top of her head came to his shoulder. Dark locks swayed as she walked, her back straight. Regal. He saw men run appreciative gazes over her. Kora was a formidable magical creature. Fierce and strong. Much like the dragons.

Derek hadn't understood what'd drawn him to her, but he suspected it was the fact that she was a hellhound. Maybe the magic in him sensed the magic in her. Though he'd never had such a strong attraction to any other magical being. Perhaps it wasn't because she was a hellhound. Maybe it was something unique and extraordinary that only Kora had. He'd walked away and forgotten others without hesitation. But not her. She had gotten into his blood.

"Shall I walk with you back to the inn?" he asked.

Her brown gaze cut to him. "Where are you going?"

"Aksel awaits me at the temple."

"It's a mistake for you to go," Kora said.

He glanced at the palace once more. "It'll raise suspicions if I don't."

"I'm going to remain here a bit longer." Kora stopped and faced him. "I don't want you to go, but I understand. Please, be careful."

Derek tucked a strand of hair that danced near her eyes behind an ear. He caressed his fingers along her jaw, tilting her face up to his. "I urge the same of you."

"I'm merely observing. You're walking into a viper's nest."

"It won't be the first time."

Her gaze softened as she sidled closer so their bodies brushed. "I'd rather be there to watch your back."

"I don't want you anywhere near them again."

"That's a little difficult as long as I'm in the city."

He looked at her lips. "All the more reason for us to leave."

"It's tempting."

His gaze met hers. Would she leave if he asked her? She had to feel what was between them. The way she touched him, kissed him, told him she did. Derek didn't want to lose whatever this was. But even as he tried to hold on to it, he felt her slipping away.

His head lowered until their lips were mere breaths apart. He imagined what kind of life they could have together and allowed it to fill his mind completely before pressing his lips to hers. She melted against him, and he wound an arm around her waist, holding her tightly as their tongues slid sensuously against each other.

By the time he ended the kiss and lifted his head, reality intruded. Kora wouldn't stop hunting Villette, and he couldn't halt his progression to the goal of freeing the dragons. That left them precisely where they had been when he woke this morning.

Derek reluctantly loosened his hold and stepped away. His

hand lingered on her before falling to his side. "I'll meet you at the inn."

He walked away, leaving her staring after him with lust-darkened eyes. Derek's strides ate up the ground as he made his way out of the garden and back to the road in front of the palace.

"Tread carefully with the priests, Derek."

"They can't harm me."

"Those priests answer to only one. Villette."

The soldiers opened the gate and allowed him to pass through on his way down to the next level. *"You tell me nothing I don't already know."*

"You see much, but not nearly enough. Open your eyes fully."

"If you have something to say, say it," he said with a growl. *"Stop speaking in riddles."*

She sighed. *"Come back to the palace. The farther away you are, the harder it is for me to hold this connection."*

Derek stopped in his tracks but didn't turn around. *"Tell me who you are."*

"Free me, and I will. I'll tell you everything."

"I'm not going anywhere near the palace until you tell me who you are."

"Fine," she bit out. *"My name is Miena."*

He had hoped the name might trigger a memory, but there was nothing.

"I can help you," she said.

"Help me do what? Free the dragons?"

"Find the truth."

He hadn't expected such a reply. It unsettled him. *"Why should I trust you?"*

"I'm not the one who took your memories."

"So you say."

"I'm not the one lying to you either."

Derek snorted. *"All you want is freedom, and you'd say anything to get it."*

"And all you want is the dragons. What have you done to get to them?"

He started walking again. To his relief, Miena's voice didn't return. Yet her words disturbed him. By the time he reached the temple, he was in a foul mood. Mainly because she had created suspicion against the only one who had ever tried to help him.

That wasn't true. The suspicion had begun long before now, but he had shoved it aside. Coming to Stonemore with Kora had forced him to see things he hadn't before. It shone an unflattering light upon Villette and her intentions. Miena just added to everything. It had the same effect, however. His ire was swelling.

And resentment brewed.

Derek soon stood outside the temple, gazing up at the pointed roof that soared high above all others. Villette had never hidden her quest for power. She claimed the dragons would help her achieve domination over the humans who had wrought such destruction upon Zora. That was why she agreed to free them. He hadn't given a second thought to the deaths of the humans. In fact, he had been the cause of many.

But everything was different now. It didn't matter why—Kora, being in Stonemore, or Miena's voice in his head. Maybe it was a combination. He didn't just feel different. Things looked different, sounded different. Smelled different. Like he had been walking around in a fog, and it was clearing.

He was being dramatic. There had never been a fog. He had always seen things just as they were.

Hadn't he?

His suspicion wasn't just on Villette. He was growing suspicious of himself and the implication that his memories had been wiped. What if everything he believed was a lie? What if everything he had done was based on propaganda perpetrated by another?

Derek squeezed his eyes shut and halted those runaway thoughts. He could drive himself insane with such contemplations. He opened his eyes and looked around him. The hatred of all things magical wasn't new. He had heard and witnessed it in other villages. But Stonemore took it to a new level. For one crazy instant, he contemplated shifting right where he was just to see how the priests and residents would react.

How long would it take the soldiers to come pouring out, their swords raised and arrows nocked? How many armored priests would stand before him, demanding he leave? Would Villette venture from the palace to reprimand him? What about the residents? From the wealthy to the poor, how many of them would run in terror simply from his existence?

Derek could wipe the priests and soldiers out in seconds. He could topple the grand temple and erase every instance of the priests. He could rise against Villette and set the city ablaze.

But it wouldn't stop the people's aversion to magic.

It would only generate more fear and animosity.

He couldn't be himself and not start a war. Just as he couldn't tell Kora the truth and not lose her. How had he gotten into such a sticky position? More importantly, how did he get *out* of it?

"There you are."

Derek lowered his gaze to Aksel as the priest made his way through the crowd to him. Derek glanced at those nearby to see people quickly averting their gazes in fear at the sight of the priest while others drank him in.

Aksel turned to stand beside him and gazed up at the temple. "It's a thing of beauty, isn't it?"

"It certainly stands out."

"Everyone needs to be able to see it. It beckons all to the calling." Aksel grinned. "Come. Let me show you inside."

Derek walked with him to the door. Armored priests milled about outside, and all looked at him curiously. Even suspiciously. Derek stared down a few before entering the temple. There was a hush inside that not even the racket of the outside could disturb.

Three giant pointed archways greeted him from the vestibule. They walked beneath the middle one and came to the enormous main room. The ceiling soared thirty feet above them. Various colors splashed the stone floor as light flooded through the pointed, arched stained-glass windows. There were more pointed arches on either side of the nave. Ornamentation graced the columns, the arches, around the windows, and even the floor, but nothing compared to the altar.

"We chose not to have seating," Aksel said as they strolled. "It allows more inside. Though not everyone can fit. Most remain outside. But they come. That's the important part."

"Is it?"

"Of course."

Derek stopped before the altar, which was entirely too garish. "They call you Hebronians, don't they?"

"That's right," Aksel said, seemingly impressed. "We follow Innus, the one god. There are three main gods and many lesser ones, but Innus rules them all. He created this beautiful realm and handpicks who to send to Zora as infants in order to fulfill a destiny that will wipe out magic once and for all."

Derek clasped his hands behind his back lest he throttle Aksel. "If that were so, why does he continue to bring children with magic?"

"He doesn't. The Evil One imbues those individuals with powers in an effort to defeat Innus through us."

It was a good thing Kora wasn't there. Derek imagined she would've launched herself at the priest. And he wouldn't have held her back. In fact, he would have joined her.

"It is a great honor to be a Priest of Innus. Those of us in armor are hand-chosen by the Divine," Aksel stated proudly. "We protect the temple and the priests above all else. Even the Divine."

"Were you soldiers before?"

Aksel nodded. "We give up everything to take this position. All family, coin, and personal items. We are dedicated to Innus."

"Have any changed their mind and wanted out?"

Aksel chuckled. "That isn't a choice. Once chosen, you follow orders. That's what soldiers do."

"What if you get tired of fighting?"

"A priest always fights, whether they wear armor or not. We're fighting against evil. Both physical and metaphysical."

Derek faced him. "You believe all magic is evil?"

"Of course. If we were meant to have it, everyone would. We don't have wings because we aren't meant to fly."

"People don't have gills, but they swim."

Aksel laughed and shifted his feet, a hard glint in his beady eyes. "Not quite the same."

"So, you will remain as you are until death?"

"A few who wear the armor will eventually become priests. All of us aspire to that status, but there are only so many positions. Soon, however, groups of us will venture far from this glorious city to spread the important word about Innus and the fight against magic. The wars have put people in dire straits, and it's a good time for them to turn to the only thing that can help."

"Your religion."

Aksel's smile was still in place, but it tightened. "Ours is the truth."

"All the priests stay in the temple?" Derek asked to change the subject.

"Most of us. A few are housed at the palace near the Divine."

Derek looked at the ceiling. "I'd love to see what's on the higher floors. Maybe take in the view."

"Only those in the order get that privilege."

Derek lowered his gaze to the priest. "I heard talk today of a slaughter on one of the lower levels the priests were involved in."

"Ah, that. A child with magic was found and was being taken, as is our right. Someone attempted to interfere. We had to set an example."

Derek recalled how the priests had attacked anyone near them. They hadn't cared if they had magic. They had only wanted to kill. "I'm curious how you know who has magic and who doesn't."

"That is also only for those in the order."

Of course, they wouldn't want the truth getting out. The priests wanted everyone to come to them. It was all a ploy.

"Anything else you want to know?" Aksel asked.

Derek tried to smile. He wasn't sure he was successful. "I like to gather details when I'm learning something new. I had never heard of the Priests of Innus until I entered Stonemore."

"Soon, everyone will know of us. We will be the dominant religion, snuffing out all other impostors. Stonemore will be the capital of the realm, as well as the home base of our faith. Village by village, city by city, we will take control and send the abominations running until we corner them and end them and their evil once and for all."

"What if one of yours has magic?"

"That is simply impossible."

"How do you know I don't have magic?"

He lifted his chin, his smile gone. "We have our ways."

Once more, Derek had the urge to shift, just to prove Aksel wrong and see his expression.

"Have I answered all your questions?" Aksel asked.

"For the time being."

"Then I will see you at service the day after tomorrow."

Derek looked at the altar.

"Attending service is required of all those within our walls."

Derek slid his gaze to the priest, anger churning at being forced to participate in a religion he didn't believe in. "Perhaps the guards should make that known before anyone enters the gates."

"Consider yourself lucky you're inside. Others are being turned away," Aksel replied.

All traces of humor were gone. Apparently, Derek hadn't done a good enough job of hiding his disdain. Not that he cared. He wanted information, and he had gotten more than enough.

"Thank you for your time." Derek turned on his heel.

He got a few steps away when Aksel called his name. Derek paused and tensed. Depending on what the priest tried, he might be shifting in the temple, after all. Slowly, Derek looked over his shoulder.

"Be sure to get here early," Aksel advised. "You'll want to be inside for the best experience. I'll look for you."

Derek didn't bother answering. Thankfully, he wasn't stopped again. He couldn't get out of the temple fast enough. The longer he was inside, the more he felt a crushing weight pressing down on him. He felt the priests' eyes on him long after he walked out of the temple. He caught two following him. It wasn't in his nature to allow such a thing, but he had no choice this time. If he caused a scene, they would take a closer look at him and Kora. That could lead to her being connected to the incident the night before, as well as outing her as a hellhound. He simply couldn't allow the things he was keeping carefully hidden to be exposed.

He returned to the inn. The moment the main door closed behind him, he paused to scan the dining room for Kora. The tightness in his chest loosened at the sight of her. She sat near the hearth, her gaze on the flames dancing within. He couldn't cross the distance fast enough as he drank in her beauty. The moment he reached her, he pulled out a chair and sank into it.

Her head swiveled to him, and she looked him over carefully. "Well?"

Derek swallowed and motioned for Ada to bring ale. He needed to wash away the vileness of the temple. "You don't want to know."

"I don't, but I need to."

After Ada set the tankard down, Derek looked around the room. It was early yet, and many tables were empty. He leaned forward and waited for Kora to do the same. Then, he conveyed his conversation with Aksel.

Horror shuttered her face. "That's…"

"I know," he muttered before downing half the ale.

She slowly sat back in her chair. "They have to be stopped."

"I don't think taking on two opponents at once is the answer."

Kora shook her head sadly. "Those with—" she began but suddenly stopped and furtively glanced around. She cleared her throat. "Those like me need to band together and rise up before it's too late."

"I'm not sure anyone will do that."

"It's either that or die."

CHAPTER 20

Derek tossed back the rest of his ale and motioned for another. Kora's gaze didn't move from him. Everywhere he turned, someone was watching, waiting to see what he would do. Or say. He thought of Miena and what she wanted. Then there was Villette. Aksel. Even Kora.

He tossed Ada a coin when she brought another ale. His gaze collided with Kora's over the stein's rim. "What?" he asked when he lowered the mug.

"I know trust is an issue between us, but would you classify us as friendly?"

Derek leaned back in his chair, wondering where this was headed. "I would."

"I'm not trying to pry, but something is bothering you. I just," —she paused and shrugged—"I just want you to know I'm around if you wish to talk about it."

There were many things he'd like to be doing to Kora at that moment, and none of them was talking. "I'll keep that in mind."

"Is that all that happened at the temple?" she asked in a low voice.

Derek nodded. "Every word."

"Will we be at the service?"

"I don't think we have a choice."

She shot him a dry look. "There is always a choice."

"They'll be looking for us. Or he will be, at least. Unless you intend to carry out your plan between now and then."

"I don't think I can."

He had worried about that. "You need help planning?"

"I'm talking about the service. I won't go. I don't believe in whatever it is they're promoting, and I refuse to have it shoved down my throat."

Derek had to give her credit. If they made a stand, they would be targeted by every priest and soldier. The priests didn't have a way to pinpoint magic, or they would've come after both him and Kora. They were guessing. They might have gotten a few right, but now they were just randomly choosing. Somehow, that made it worse.

"What about tonight?" Kora asked.

Her question pulled him out of his thoughts. The priests worried her. Aksel might be at the party, or another like him. If they were, they would make a point of talking to both him and Kora. How far would she allow herself to be pushed before she broke? How far would he? He had promised to keep her safe, and there was a real possibility he would have to do just that. Unless they didn't go that evening.

"You aren't keen on it, and I've had enough of others for the day," he said.

She gave him a curious look. "Really? You don't need to go?"

"I saw a nice eatery today. We could give it a try for dinner. Or stay in. Your choice."

"Let's try the place you found."

They finished their drinks and rose. Derek turned Kora to the left and headed toward the bistro. She was walking unusually slow, taking time to inspect each building they passed, peering into narrow alleys when she spotted them.

"Looking for something?" he finally asked.

She jerked her head forward. "Just taking it all in."

"You want to know if there is another way to move between levels besides the gates."

"If you must know, aye."

He looked down at the cuff on his wrist. He could make things easy and take her into the palace himself. Handing over the cuff wasn't an option because he needed to be able to check on the eggs.

They reached their destination. The doors and windows of the eatery were open, and many of the tables spilled onto the sidewalk. Music drifted from inside. As the host led them to a table, Derek saw the small stage where some performers sat playing their instruments.

As if they had said all the words they had for the evening, he and Kora sat in silence, watching one set of performers after another move on and off the stage. Their meal came, and they ate while listening to music and singing. A marionette show came on last. Derek watched how Kora's smile spread over her face as she clapped and cheered along with many others. Even Derek had to admit he had a good time.

They left, softly humming one of the tunes as they strolled to the inn. He looked up at the stars and the double moons. It had been a good night. A fun one. He didn't want it to end.

"Is there another way to the levels?"

Derek had wondered if she would ask him. "It seems prudent the city would have such a means."

"Does that mean they do?"

He glanced at her. "Aye."

"Will you show me?"

"Are you asking for my help?" He wanted her to. He wanted it more than he should because the more entangled he became with her, the harder it was for him to see the line he shouldn't cross.

But maybe he already had.

Their hands brushed as they walked. He wanted to reach for her and twine his fingers with hers. It made that line he was so worried about difficult to see. He never used to hesitate. He always knew what to do.

She pressed her lips together. "In this, I am asking for your help. You know why I can't involve you."

If she knew he was a dragon, she'd realize how beneficial he would be. But that came with the flip side of that coin.

"But I also want a good chance at reaching her," Kora said.

Derek gave in to the need and took her hand. He liked how she accepted his hold and even laced her fingers through his. He turned them around to retrace their steps until they came to one of the alleys. He pulled her into it behind him and stopped when he reached a wall of vines.

"Am I to climb over?" she asked.

He grabbed the plants and tugged them to the side so she could see the metal gate.

Her eyes lit up. "This is perfect."

"Not exactly. It's locked."

"I can get through."

He smoothed a lock of her hair that had become tangled in the vines. He had the sudden urge to pull her close and kiss her.

Kora turned her head to him. "Thank you."

The moons lit her eyes as if they shone a spotlight on her. He let the vines fall back into place, and they made their way to the street.

Only once they reached their room did Kora ask, "Would you have shown me if I hadn't asked?"

"Aye." And that was the truth.

"Why are you helping me?" She stared at him, her brow furrowed. "You don't seem the type to go out of your way to help anyone."

He shrugged and sank onto the settee. "I'm still wondering that myself."

"Do you have a way out of the city?"

"Worried about me?" he teased.

She nodded, her expression solemn. "Does that surprise you?"

"A bit. No one worries about me."

"Perhaps that's the problem. Everyone should have someone concerned about them."

"What about you?"

She walked to him and lifted her skirts before straddling his lap. Her hands rested on his chest and slid up his shoulders and around his neck to tangle in his hair. "Do you want to talk or kiss?"

Her mouth was on his in the next heartbeat.

Derek stood next to the bed and looked down at Kora. She slept on her stomach, her wealth of dark hair fanned out around her, one leg outside the covers, and her lips parted. The last thing he wanted to do was leave her, but he had duties.

And he wanted answers.

He held his hand above Kora and waved it over her so she remained asleep until he returned. Then he walked to the door and used magic to ensure no one could enter. He took one last look at her before touching his cuff.

It took no time to check on the eggs and learn they were still undisturbed. Then he returned to Stonemore. Except he went to the palace. It had been so long since he'd stood within its walls that he had almost forgotten what they looked like. Enormous, red-sandstone columns adorned with swirling motifs at the top held up the walls. The edges of the points on the arched windows and entryways were decorated, but none more so than the railings along the stairways, and the balusters. The vaulted ceilings even had decorations as if not wanting to be outdone.

Warm, golden light from sconces cast the sandstone in amber. The large hallways were empty. Derek wasn't sure what he was looking for. He had questions for Villette, but Miena might give him answers. If he dared to give her what she wished. The more he thought about his memories being tampered with, the more troubled he became.

Derek strolled from corridor to corridor past many doors. He had never walked these particular halls, at least that he was aware of. Yet he somehow knew exactly where to go. His feet led him up several floors to a deserted room. He stopped at the doorway and gazed at the wreckage within. It looked as if an explosion had ripped off the balcony and part of the room. There were scorch marks along the stone as well as rubble everywhere. Dark spots of dried blood were still visible. He didn't understand why no one had cleaned up or repaired the space.

Villette had never mentioned anyone attacking her. Though he was beginning to suspect she didn't tell him a lot.

"You came."

Derek's head swung to the right, and a door he hadn't noticed before. He didn't know how, but he knew Miena was behind it.

"Open the door, Derek. Open the door and see me."

He stared hard at the handle but couldn't make himself move toward it.

"I'm not the only one in here. There's another. A human with magic. Listen closely. You'll hear two heartbeats."

Derek opened his hearing and concentrated. He picked up one heartbeat and then another. There were indeed two individuals behind the door. *"Who put you in there?"*

"Villette."

"Why?"

Miena made an indistinct sound. *"I dared to stand against her."*

"Why do I need to be the one to release you?"

"If I had a way to ask the hellhound, I would."

Derek stilled.

"My companion can sense magic. She picked up on your companion. Now, can you please open the door and free me? Or did you come just to prove you could?"

He didn't budge.

"Has my sister rubbed off on you? Have you become like her? Are you here to give us hope, only to dash it away?"

"I want answers."

"Maybe I can give them," said a male.

Derek jerked at the new voice in his head. Movement caught his attention. He turned to find a man leaning against the wall near where the floor crumbled into nothing, his gaze locked on Derek.

"This isna a room anyone ventures to since…" The man waved at the debris.

He had a strange accent Derek couldn't place. "What happened?"

"A battle. Many died." The man's dark blue gaze moved briefly to the door. "You can hear her."

It wasn't a question. There was something about the man. Derek thought he should know him, but he couldn't place why. "How did you know I was up here?"

"I heard you." The man tapped his temple. "You speak verra loudly."

"Who are you?"

"The better question is, who are *you*?"

Derek looked at the door. "Do you know who's behind it?"

"Open it, and we'll both find out."

Derek couldn't. He swung his head back to the man. "Are you a Star Person?"

He laughed. "Hardly."

"Then how can you project your voice into my head?"

"You mean like this?"

"Aye."

The man's eyes narrowed as he looked at him. *"You really doona know?"*

"I wouldn't ask if I did."

"I'm Merrill."

"Derek."

"Well, Derek, what are you going to do? Open the door and get your answers, or walk away?"

Derek studied the newcomer. The way Merrill held himself said he feared nothing. His response to Derek's mention of the Star People said he knew about them. Did that mean he knew Villette? *"You still haven't told me how you can talk to me like this. I thought only the Star People could do that."*

"What Star People do you know?"

"Answer me, and I'll answer you."

Merrill considered him for a long moment. He crossed his arms over his chest. *"It is the way my kind speaks."*

"What is your kind?"

"I answered you. Now, you answer my question. Which Star People do you know?"

"Villette. And recently, Miena." Derek inclined his head toward the door.

Merrill's lips flattened, and his arms dropped to his sides, tension radiating from him. *"How do you know Villette?"*

"Your turn. Who is your kind?"

"Are you blind? Have you not seen them around? Heard them?"

Derek had no idea what he was talking about. He realized then that Miena hadn't said another word since Merrill joined the conversation.

"How do you know Villette?" Merrill demanded.

"I work with her. Have I seen what around? Who *is your kind?"* It was suddenly very important that Derek find out.

Merrill closed the distance between them, stopping only a few feet away. "I doona like games."

"I'm not playing games."

Merrill's head suddenly swung toward the door he had walked through. He held up a finger as he listened. He stood rigid for several long moments before lowering his hand and looking at Derek. "If there is one thing I've learned, it's that nothing is what it seems in this place. You'd do well no' to trust anyone."

"Tell me what you are," Derek demanded.

Merrill simply looked at him with confusion and wariness. "Can you really no' know? It shouldna be possible."

"Just tell me. Please," he added.

Instead of answering, Merrill glared at the door.

Derek moved into his line of sight. "I'm waiting."

"And you'll be waiting longer." Merrill turned to leave.

Derek curled his hands into fists. "You have magic, and you're at the palace. Do the priests know of you?"

Merrill peeled back his lips in a sneer. "Doona ever threaten me. As for those fuckers, they'd do well to stay far from me. They're only alive because the bells have no' tolled, announcing the murder of another child."

"They killed one the other night."

Merrill's eyes burned with hatred. His voice dropped low, danger dripping from every syllable. "Did they, now?"

Then he was gone.

"I'm still here, waiting to give you answers," Miena said. *"Open the door."*

CHAPTER 21

The firm body molded against her back pulled Kora from sleep. She moaned at Derek's arousal pressed into her buttock. He was always hard and hungry for her body. Just as she craved his. It had surprised her at first, but now, she savored it. Relished it, even.

His lips left a trail of heat along her neck to her shoulder. Large hands held her firmly. She felt the need in him. But something else was there, as well.

She turned in his arms to see him but had no chance to ask him what was wrong as he captured her mouth in a kiss that sizzled with yearning and the promise of ecstasy. Her thoughts scattered when he palmed a breast and tweaked her nipple. Desire shot straight to her core as she rocked against him.

No matter how many times they had come together, no matter how many ways, she ached for him. It was a need that swelled and intensified. One that bordered on obsession. She knew it but was powerless to stop it.

Because she found something more than pleasure in Derek's arms. She'd found safety for the first time in a very long time. It would end soon. Perhaps that's why she eagerly and willingly returned to his arms.

She wanted to forget about Villette and the responsibilities she carried. She wanted to forget everything and everyone but Derek and the kernel of bliss she had found in a world of nightmares.

He seemed to want the same as he positioned himself between her legs and thrust into her. Their bodies moved together in a seductive rhythm that soon had her climaxing, with him following closely behind.

They lay locked together until their breathing calmed. She watched as he pulled out of her, but he didn't meet her gaze. He rose and poured water into a goblet before drinking it. He held up the cup to see if she wanted any.

She shook her head and arranged the pillows behind her back to rest against the headboard. "Come back to bed."

He padded over. She took his hand when he went to climb in and drew him to sit between her legs again. Then she pulled him down so he leaned his back against her chest. Kora then wrapped her legs and arms around him.

"What's this for?" he asked.

She rested her cheek against his head. "Sometimes people need to be held."

Derek didn't scoff or move away, and that told her more than any confession would. They sat there for a long while in silence, listening to the fire pop as she ran her fingers through his hair. In the quiet moments when he held her before sleep, or like now as she held him, she allowed herself to wonder what it might be like to have someone to lean on. Someone who would lean on her and also have her back. Someone who accepted her.

Someone who loved her.

It was a precarious diversion because those thoughts spun a future that would never be. It made her long for things beyond her grasp. To hope.

And there was nothing more dangerous than hope.

"Why did you tell me about your family?" Derek asked.

Her hand stilled briefly. "You discovered my secret. It seemed relevant to give a history."

"You would never have shared anything otherwise, would you?"

She couldn't see his face from her position, but something in his voice made her pause. "As I said, it was a secret I never shared. The last thing I wanted was to be hunted."

"But you remember your family."

"Aye. Do you not remember yours?" When he didn't answer, she regretted her question. She had told herself she would never ask about his past or whatever he held secret, though it killed her not to.

Finally, he said, "Nay. Nothing. I tried before and then stopped because it was too painful."

"Something happened to change that."

"Someone recently told me my memories had been wiped."

Shock rolled through her. "Is that even possible?"

"I was hoping you could tell me."

"The only ones I know who can do that are the Star People. There could be others, I suppose, but I've never heard of anyone. I've not exactly moved in circles with others with magic, though. Why would anyone want to do that to you?"

He covered the hand she had resting on his chest with his. "I've been asking myself that same question."

"Have you come up with anything?"

"Maybe," he said after a long pause.

She held him tighter. They could find out. All they had to do was depart Stonemore. Kora desperately wanted to leave, but she had come this far. She couldn't turn back now.

"There is someone who said they can give me answers," Derek told her.

"You don't sound as if you want to take them up on that opportunity."

He grunted. "It's a matter of trust. They demanded something in return."

"Nothing is ever free, and if it is, you should be wary of it. Is what they're asking for more than you want to give?"

"It's not about that. It's about if I *should*."

It would be so much easier to decipher what he was trying to tell her if she knew the details. He kept it from her for a reason, though. Just as she had kept her secret for as long as she had. She respected that, even if it chafed. "Then don't."

"I won't get any answers then."

"How will you know if what they say is the truth?"

He released a long sigh. "That's the problem. I won't."

"What happens if you give the person what they want?"

"There will be repercussions."

That gave her pause. "What kind?"

"I'm not sure."

"To you?"

"And most likely others. There's more."

She waited for him to continue as he let the statement hang between them.

"I heard Villette is weakened now."

Kora swallowed, letting that sink in. "Why didn't you tell me sooner?"

"I should have."

It wasn't an answer, but she suspected it would be the only one she got. "Who told you?"

"That doesn't matter."

"It does. It means you have a connection to the palace. One you didn't mention before."

Derek's shoulders lifted as he inhaled. "Kora," he began.

"Don't," she warned. "Don't you dare try to tell me I shouldn't go after her or that I can't do it. I know she might kill me. It's a chance I'm willing to take."

"And if I'm not willing to lose you?"

He seemed as surprised by his statement as she was. She wished she could see his face, look into his eyes, and attempt to interpret his thoughts.

"You're the last of your kind," he continued. "Don't throw that away."

She closed her eyes. "I'm also the only one who can kill her."

"Other Star People can."

"They haven't exactly done anything about her, have they?"

"And if one in the city were willing?"

Kora dropped her head back against the headboard and tried to stop the room from spinning. "You've known this and haven't told me. Why?" She shook her head and lifted it, her thoughts running haphazardly in her mind. "I know there is little trust between us, but you said we were friendly. And I shared my secret."

"I needed more information before I came to you. I needed to be sure."

She wanted to believe him. She really did. But she didn't. He held too many secrets. They weighed a person down. She should know. She carried enough of her own.

But something kept gnawing at her. Something that kept getting shoved aside with each new revelation. Something she had to know. "How do you know so much about the Star People?"

"I've interacted with them."

"Them? How many?"

"Villette. And the newest, Miena."

She shoved him away and climbed out of bed. She paced the room, alternating between fury and disbelief. "I get it now. You were ready to leave after our night together, but I mentioned Stonemore, and you were all too willing to help me. I was suspicious, and I never should have agreed to..." She threw up her hands. "Whatever this is."

"Kora..."

"Nay," she said, shaking her head. "All this time, I've been telling you about Villette and my past. My *secret*," she hissed angrily. "You knew and said nothing." She halted and glared at him. "Is that where you've been going when you sneak off? Are you warning Villette about me?"

His nostrils flared as he held her gaze. "I've not seen or spoken to her since before we came here."

"Of course, that would be your reply. Why do I even bother asking?" She started pacing again.

"Kora."

"Then you tell me Villette is weakened. You're setting a trap for me. Will there be a dragon there, too? By the stars, how stupid am I?"

"Kora!"

She whirled to find him standing behind her and shouted, "What?"

"I'm not setting a trap. If I was, I would never have told you about Miena."

Her body began to lean toward him, aching for his touch, but she took a step back. She had let her guard down simply because they'd shared their bodies. She had opened herself to him, only to discover his duplicity.

"Let me remind you that you also kept secrets," he said.

"The word there is *kept*. Past tense."

He narrowed his eyes and took a step closer. "Secrets you would still have if I hadn't seen you die and come back to life."

"Speaking of, how did you really get us back here and past the guards that night? Was it your connection to Villette? I'm surprised you didn't take me to her then."

A muscle moved in his jaw. He thrust out his hand to show the cuff. "This is how I got us back."

She eyed the piece of silver he never removed. "That?"

"You want proof? I'll give you proof," he stated as he yanked her to him.

One moment, they were in the room. The next, they were in a forest. The change was so sudden that her knees gave out. She gripped Derek, but his hold was already tight. The next moment, they were on top of the mountain they had traveled. She barely got a chance to look around before they were back in their room. Derek released her, and she stumbled out of his arms, catching herself on the end of the bed.

She looked from the cuff to his face. "You mean you could've gotten us to Stonemore with that instead of walking?"

"Aye."

"You can get me into the palace."

"I can, but you never asked for my help."

Kora looked around for her clothes and hastily dressed. She needed a barrier between them. "And if I ask now?"

"Does that mean you trust me?"

"That isn't what I asked."

A long stretch of silence filled the room. "If you ask. I will."

"That was convincing."

"There are other things I must consider."

"Like?"

A muscle in his jaw tightened. "Miena is being held in the palace. She's able to communicate with me. She says it's because Villette is weakened after a recent altercation with someone."

Kora didn't like the change of subject, but she was more interested in learning how Miena spoke to Derek. "How, exactly, is she talking to you?"

He tapped his head.

"You must be joking," she stated.

Derek shook his head. "The closer I am to the palace, the easier it is for her to reach me."

Then it dawned on her as she recalled the strange way he'd acted the day before. "That's what was wrong when we were in the garden."

"Aye."

"And she's the one who has the answers you seek."

Derek briefly lowered his gaze to the ground. "She is."

CHAPTER 22

Shimmery blue moonbeams spilled through the windows, bathing the palace floors and walls in its mystical light. Merrill had intended to take to the skies that night, unsure if he would remain at Stonemore or venture farther abroad. Meeting Derek had changed everything.

Merrill's boots didn't make a sound as he took the circular staircase down deep into the mountain, where he had followed Villette after she crawled away in agony. She had begged for his help. But he hadn't lifted a finger. She had meddled with his brethren, and she deserved everything she got.

And more.

The few soldiers he passed paid him little heed. They were used to seeing him move about the palace. Once, Villette had restricted him to his chamber. He swore it would be the last time anyone confined him anywhere. He'd thought he was done with humans, as well as whatever vendetta Villette had. Even his own brethren.

His anger had gotten the best of him. There had been no leashing it once it broke free. It still festered inside him, coiled and waiting to strike.

When it did, no one would be safe.

Merrill reached the bottom of the stairs and stalked down the narrow tunnel that snaked deeper into an area restricted to only Villette. He ignored it as he did everything else. Merrill kicked open the door when he reached it, filling the entrance as his gaze landed on the bed. A smile curved his lips at the sight of Villette writhing in anguish.

He felt a particular delight at seeing the burns that covered most of her body. For weeks, he had allowed her to believe that he'd remained in the hated city for her. She had even convinced herself that she held him there. Unfortunately, she had for a short time. But he was nothing if not resourceful.

Anger and resentment had a peculiar way of bypassing emotions that would have otherwise hindered him.

Merrill let her cut off communication with the others because he needed time. To sit with the emotions he had buried for eons. He needed time to think. And consider. He had locked away his indignation and hostility for too long, all because it had been what his brethren needed. And it was easier than dealing with it.

He had been there for his brothers, helping them in their time of need. He had even been as close to happy as he could be. Then again, that was easy to achieve when traumas were buried so deeply that they were ignored and eventually forgotten.

Then they'd come to Zora, and *everything* changed.

Whatever excitement they felt at finally finding the dragons they had sent away from Earth to protect them vanished the instant they crossed through the Fae doorway. Suddenly, the rules the Dragon Kings had lived by for millennia no longer applied. The dragons didn't need or want the Kings.

Then there were the mortals. Somehow, they had found their way to Zora, as well. They were like cockroaches, infiltrating everything.

"Merrill," Villette whispered, holding out a shaking hand. "You've come to help."

Last but not least, there were the Star People. He hadn't thought he could loathe anyone more than he did the humans until he encountered Villette and learned just how wrapped up she was in Zora and Earth.

He leaned a shoulder against the doorway and crossed his arms over his chest. She was weak. He might be able to kill her. At the very least, he could cause her more pain.

His thoughts slid to his encounter with Derek. There was no doubt he was somehow connected to Villette, and Merrill intended to find out how and learn if there were more Dereks out there before he gave in to his need to end her life. "Tell me who burned you?"

"It...doesn't...matter," she said through clenched teeth. "I'm...healing."

Not nearly fast enough. That could benefit him. "It's been over a week."

She winced in pain as she moved, her breaths coming in gasps. "I will...survive." She turned her head to him, her eyes burning with fury. "And I...will...punish you...for this."

"Will you now?" he asked, his brow quirked.

"You answer...to *me*."

Oh, aye. He would enjoy watching the life fade from her eyes. "I answer to me. I'm a Dragon King, lest you forget."

Her blue eyes shot daggers at him. Her lips were pinched, her teeth bright against her burned flesh. "We'll see."

"Tell me about the dragon you have working for you."

A flash of surprise crossed her face. It was so fast Merrill nearly missed it. But he had been watching for it.

"Get...out." She cried out as she moved. Her charred fingers tightened on the mattress. "You...aren't...meant to be...down here."

He shrugged. "And yet, I am."

Her breathing was labored, her body shaking from the pain. It appeared it was taking everything Villette had just to stay conscious while trying to heal. She was weak and vulnerable, and because of it, the shield she used to prevent the other Kings from reaching out to him and he to them had vanished. It was why he had heard Derek.

There was another of them. One he suspected not even Eurwen and Brandr who ruled the dragons on Zora knew about. And if they didn't know, then Con didn't know.

Another dragon who could shift. That made Derek a King. Were there more like him? Merrill had to find out.

"He isn't...your concern," Villette snapped with more vigor than he'd expected.

Rage exploded through Merrill. The inferno it wrought was a storm ready to be unleashed on Villette, the priests, and all of Stonemore. When his ire grew, he didn't become crazed and smash things. He got cold, calm. Calculating.

And even more deadly than usual.

He straightened and dropped his arms to his sides as he went over Villette's words again. Derek didn't know what he was. She had either kept him from the dragons or made him believe there were none. Just what was this bitch up to?

Merrill shouldn't get involved. He had a chance to leave and roam Zora to his content.

But the longer he stared at Villette, the more the flames of fury roared.

"He's a Dragon King," Merrill stated. "Which means he's my concern."

Villette smirked. "You can try...but you'll never...find him."

"We'll see," he said.

As he walked away, he heard her shout of pain. Merrill retraced his steps and left the palace through the front door. He paused atop the stairs and looked at the sky. It beckoned, urging him to shift and spread his wings. To launch into the air and fly among the stars.

He had come to Stonemore with Shaw to find out who was hunting the dragons. It had resulted in a battle that destroyed the room where Merrill had found Derek. Shaw had left with his mate, Nia, and Merrill remained behind. But not before the residents saw Shaw in his true form.

Before that, Stonemore had witnessed Cullen in dragon form as he helped his mate, Tamlyn, stop children from being sacrificed. Then Alasdair entered the mountain through a back entrance, looking for him. The city had seen three Kings in their true forms, yet not one of his brethren had gone after the residents. Still, a fear enveloped the city that was so thick it nearly choked him.

It had been too long since Merrill released his dragon. He fought the urge to do so now, calling to Derek and any others Villette had. Because there were others. He was sure of it. She had a fondness for dragons, but he hadn't figured out why. Yet. He would.

The last time he had walked the streets of Stonemore, he had succumbed to his anger. Which had led him straight to Villette's bed. She had stoked the flames into a roaring blaze that wouldn't go out anytime soon. Milling about the streets of the city could be his tipping point. But he had to locate Derek and figure out what he knew. And what he didn't know. It was best to do that away from Villette and Miena.

"Derek?" he called and waited to see if he would answer.

"Aye."

"I'd like to talk."

"Is that not what we're doing?"

Merrill grinned. Spoken like a true Dragon King. *"I'd like a face-to-face meeting."*

"When?"

"No time like the present."

Derek sighed. *"Where?"*

"Are you in the city?"

"Aye. There's a tavern on the sixth level called The Tiny Root."

"I'll meet you there."

Merrill severed the link and walked down the remainder of the steps. The guards exchanged looks but hurried to open the gate as he approached. He walked away from the palace without a backward glance, still unsure of his plans. A lot would be determined after his conversation with Derek.

His gaze went to the distance, across the forest to the border of the dragons' land, where the rest of his brethren lived. Since Villette's battle, he had heard Constantine calling for him. The

King of Kings was the only one Merrill answered to. It was the first time Merrill had ever ignored him.

Con wasn't the only one trying to reach him. So was his best friend, Varek. If he were going to talk to anyone, it would be Varek, but Merrill wasn't ready to return to the others. He wasn't sure he ever would be. What was the point? He didn't have a clan to rule—none of them did any longer.

When Merrill reached the tavern, he paused. He didn't know what had halted him. Then, just as he was about to walk inside, he caught sight of a woman with long, wavy, inky hair coming toward him. Her steel-gray gaze skimmed over him as if he were inconsequential. He sensed her Druid magic and turned to follow her with his eyes as she walked to the gates. The guards refused to let her pass. She lightly placed her hand on one without saying a word. To Merrill's shock, they let her through.

He took a step to follow but remembered why he was at the pub. There was a Druid in Stonemore. He hoped she had enough sense to keep her magic hidden before the priests got to her. Merrill waited until she was out of sight before entering The Tiny Root. Derek was already seated at a table. Despite the late night—or early morning—hour, the place was packed. Derek's olive-colored eyes scrutinized Merrill as he approached.

He slid onto the bench opposite Derek. "Thank you for meeting me."

"What do you want?"

"The same thing you do. Answers."

Derek rested his arms atop the table. "I doubt we want the same ones."

"Does it matter? We each need something, and I think we can help each other."

"What makes you so sure?"

Merrill bit back a grin. "What makes you so sure we can no'?" When Derek said nothing more, Merrill spoke. "I know you work with Villette. How did that come to pass?"

Derek drew in a breath, then answered. "She found me when I was a youngling. She protected me until I could defend myself."

"You doona sound convinced of that."

Derek's brow furrowed. "Where are you from? I've never heard such an accent."

"I'm from a place called Scotland. It's verra far away. Why are you unsure about your origins?"

He glanced away. "Miena told me Villette wiped my memories."

"Miena is the one in the room?"

"Aye. Have you not spoken with her?"

Merrill shrugged a shoulder indifferently. "She speaks. I ignore her. She wants out and will say anything to achieve that."

"I'm aware. Why haven't you let her out?"

"I tried, but a lass stopped me. Her face and voice told me more than I needed. She was sucked into the room just from the little I had opened the door. It slammed shut behind her. I've stayed away since."

Derek's face smoothed, and his brows lifted. "That's the second heartbeat I heard. Miena said another was with her. You didn't try to get her out?"

"If you had been there that day, you'd understand. Let's get back to the memories. The only reason to mess with another's head is if they become uncontrollable. What do you do for Villette?"

"What are you?" Derek asked instead.

Merrill grinned at a comely serving lass who came to the table. He and Derek ordered ales and waited for her to leave.

"Well?" Derek pressed.

"I'm the same as you."

"I doubt that."

Merrill quirked a brow. "How else can I speak inside your head? As I told you, it's what our kind does."

"That's not possible."

"I assure you, it is."

"And I assure you, it isn't."

It was Merrill's turn to frown as he observed the dragon across the table from him. "You mean you aren't the only one Villette has. So, I take it you can no' communicate telepathically with them? How many others does she have?"

Derek remained silent.

Their drinks arrived, interrupting the conversation. Merrill waited impatiently until they were alone once more, then leaned forward on the table and dropped his voice to a whisper. "You doona have to tell me. I'll figure it out easily enough. I just can no' fathom why you're loyal to her."

"She's going to help free my kin."

Of all the things Merrill had thought Derek might say, that wasn't one of them. He blinked and slowly sat back. Surely, he hadn't heard correctly. "Excuse me?"

"They're being held prisoner."

Merrill flattened his hands on the table and pushed against Derek's mind. *"You're speaking of the dragons."*

Derek's eyes widened slightly. *"You don't seem surprised."*

"What the fuck do you think I am? I told you we were alike."

Derek shook his head. *"That isn't possible. She told me there were only two of us outside the border."*

"She lied. That's what Villette does." Sparks of anger erupted from the inferno within him. Killing her wouldn't be enough. He would make her suffer again and again until she begged for death. Even that wouldn't be enough. Merrill took a drink in an effort to keep his anger in check. Aloud, he said, "Tell me everything."

"Humans are holding them."

"How?"

"She suspects it's with the help of another Star Person."

Merrill tightened his fingers around his tankard. It cracked. He forced his hold to loosen. "Go on."

"She promised to free them but needed to create fear in the mortals first."

"That's what you've been doing?"

"I'm part of it, aye."

Merrill bit back a growl. "And? How is terrorizing the humans helping? They fear anything with magic now."

"Villette said it was paramount to success. That the fear would weaken the humans' hold across the border so we could free the dragons when we attacked."

Merrill scratched his forehead. "What would you say if I told you they've always been free? No one is holding them."

"I would demand to know where they are. This world was meant to be ours."

"Aye, it was. In more ways than you know. Then the humans arrived, and the dragons carved out a place that was all theirs. No human is to cross the border."

Derek flattened both hands on the table and stared down at it. "That's not possible."

"Go and see for yourself. Better yet, call out to them through our mental link. They'll answer. Ask for Con."

"Who is that?"

"He's the one in charge," Merrill answered. He didn't want to reveal everything to Derek at once. He needed to hand over a little at a time to keep drawing him in.

Derek lifted his head and speared Merrill with a look. "This could all be a trick."

"I'm the only one trying to help without asking for anything in return. Villette has her own motivation."

"And you think you know what that is?"

Merrill snorted. "I do. So do you. It's power. Total and absolute control of this realm. Miena wants freedom. You can no' believe her either."

"But I can trust you?"

"You can."

Derek sat back and shook his head.

"Ask around the city. See when they last saw a dragon. They'll tell you it was one with amethyst scales. That was Alasdair. Before that, it was Shaw. He's blue. And before that, Cullen—a garnet dragon. They all flew over Stonemore, causing widespread panic."

"Why haven't you?"

"Shaw and I came together on a mission."

"If he's gone, why are you still here?"

"I had some things to work out." Merrill caught the serving girl's attention and called her over. "Lass, I was just telling my newly arrived friend about the dragons that were seen recently."

Her face drained of color. "It was horrific. Those beasts were right over the city, circling like they were going to eat us." She shuddered and hurried away.

Merrill quirked a brow. "Believe me now?"

CHAPTER 23

The thick, still air of the swamp settled over Derek. He and Kora had been in the middle of a conversation when he left to meet Merrill. She had been furious, and likely still was. Which she had every reason to be. He had been opening up to her only to say he had to meet someone else. Naturally, she wanted details he couldn't give. Because to do so meant revealing that he was a dragon. He wasn't ready to see fear in her eyes when she looked at him. So, he'd told her nothing.

It wasn't a good way to build trust. Quite the opposite, actually.

He would make it up to her. Somehow. The truth she so desperately wanted would solve the dilemma. But he couldn't. Even considering it made his stomach roil.

If he couldn't even think about it, how could he ever tell her? No matter how much he wanted to keep things hidden from her, it would all come out eventually. Whether it was tomorrow or a hundred years from now.

There were no answers for this situation—at least none he wanted to consider at the moment. Derek turned his attention to what he had learned from Merrill. He had divulged, but not nearly enough. Derek had a million more questions.

Merrill was a dragon like him. He could barely wrap his head around that fact. Of course, he was taking it as fact. He hadn't seen Merrill shift. Maybe he couldn't. It might all be some charade—a big joke being played on him. If dragons could speak with their minds, then he and Bryok would be able to do it. Nay, Merrill had to be a Star Person. They were the only ones who could communicate like that.

Then why had Merrill urged him to contact Con? There was also the fact that dragons had been seen around Stonemore— dragons that weren't him or Bryok.

Derek alternated between rage and shock.

And despair.

Someone was lying. Both Miena and Merrill pointed at Villette. He didn't need to ask Villette to know where she would cast the blame. Kora's goal was to end Villette. If given the opportunity to learn all the facts, she would side with Merrill and Miena if only because of Villette.

Derek knew Miena and Kora both wanted Villette dead, but he had yet to determine what Merrill was after. He claimed not to want anything, but as Kora had pointed out, nothing was ever given for free. And Derek had found himself in the middle of all of them somehow.

As for Villette, he had seen firsthand what she condoned—and even encouraged—in the city. He had been party to so much of the same outside Stonemore. If he accepted what the others told him, that meant he was as much of a monster as Villette. If they wanted her dead, then they should be after him and Bryok, as well.

Because he had followed her blindly, accepting everything she told him.

And why wouldn't he? He had thought he and Bryok were the only ones of their kind who were free. The only ones that could liberate the others and protect the eggs. Even Bryok believed as much. Though that didn't make Derek feel less of a fool.

He now had to question everything and everyone to figure out who was lying and who spoke the truth. No longer would he indiscriminately believe anyone. He had no choice but to pick apart every word and action while comparing it to the facts he had and whatever he uncovered. Then hold it all up against whoever he was scrutinizing.

He started with Kora. He had seen her die twice and come back to life. He had seen her wounds heal. He knew about her village since he had been responsible. Derek had also witnessed the soldiers slaughter in the streets. His encounter with Aksel while visiting the temple had laid bare the depravity of the so-called religion.

The only things Kora had asked of him were the way to Stonemore and whether he knew any other routes to the different levels. She hadn't tried to get him to help her kill Villette or even sneak her into the palace. Out of everyone, he believed everything she had told him.

Or maybe he just really wanted to believe.

Merrill was another matter. The citizens believed they saw dragons. Was it real or magic used by a Star Person to conjure the apparitions? That did sound like something Villette would do. Her motivation would be as it always was—terror. She wanted the humans to fear dragons, but it seemed to go beyond that. She wanted them to fear magic. He couldn't figure out how that benefited her or any other magical being. He had to be missing something.

Derek had no discernable reason for why Merrill would lie. Just because he'd mentioned Con and said to reach out mentally meant nothing. For all Derek knew, he could connect with another Star Person. He would have to see the individual for himself before he believed anything. That meant going to the border. Where he believed—or had for so many years—the dragons were being held prisoner. That meant crossing into forbidden territory.

On one hand, Merrill might be speaking the truth. On the other, it might be a trap. Someone could have learned what Villette was planning and sought to take him out of the equation. That seemed more logical than the dragons being free and not coming to find him, Bryok, or the eggs.

Perhaps Villette wasn't the person he believed her to be. But she *had* saved him. She protected and sheltered both him and Bryok. Not to mention the eggs. That had to count for something, didn't it?

Derek put his hand atop an egg. At one time, he had waited anxiously for it to hatch so another of their kind could take to the skies alongside him. Maybe even a mate. Years turned into decades that turned into centuries with no change. He had stopped wishing, stopped expecting, and accepted the reality. It was just him and Bryok.

But that reality had changed.

He dropped his hand as he considered Miena. She had the most reason to lie and twist the truth. She wanted her freedom, and Villette had put her where she was. Derek suspected the reason was exactly what Miena said—she had tried to stop Villette. There had never been any mention of Miena. That was probably because he wasn't meant to be in the palace, so there had been no reason for Villette to tell him about her or spin some story to keep him away.

Derek had few facts about Miena. So few he could count them on one hand. Miena had told him about Villette's weakened state. Whoever Villette had tangled with had left her magic depleted, which had shifted everything, putting him in the position he was currently in.

He needed answers, and Merrill didn't seem keen on handing them over. Derek wasn't eager to test the theory that the dragons weren't prisoners. Kora had shared everything that was relevant. That left Miena.

Going to her was risky. But he had to start somewhere.

His decision made, Derek touched the cuff and appeared outside Miena's door. "I'm here," he said.

"I didn't think you would return," she replied. *"Why aren't you opening the door? Aren't you here to free me?"*

"I'm not sure yet."

"Ah. You and Merrill must have had a nice conversation."

He frowned. *"How do you know that?"*

"The one trapped with me can sense all magic, remember? I know Merrill came into the room earlier. She also told me the two of you met again."

"It's curious that he hasn't freed you. Why is that?"

"Perhaps you should ask him."

"I did."

She paused. *"I see. Yet you're back. Why?"*

Derek looked at the door. *"I'm considering letting you out."*

"But?"

"I need answers first."

"I promised you all when I'm freed."

He shook his head. *"I need some beforehand."*

"You get one."

"Three."

"Two. No more."

Derek narrowed his eyes at the door. *"You want to haggle when your freedom is so close? Maybe I'll walk away, and we can forget all of this."*

She sighed loudly. *"Fine. Three. Do I have your word you'll open the door?"*

"If the answers satisfy me."

"It's an aye or nay response. I'm not going to give you answers only for you to walk away."

"Accept my reply or not. I'm done negotiating."

Her voice was tight, her words hard when she said, *"Then ask. I want out."*

Derek considered all the questions he'd been mulling over. What were the most important? He would have to be specific if he wanted a decent answer.

"Why would Villette wipe my memories?"

"Oh, dear boy. Isn't that obvious? You began asking too many questions. You pushed too hard and demanded too much when things didn't make sense. A lot like you're doing now. She needs you compliant."

He placed his hand on the wall as blood roared in his ears.

"The only difference this time is that she's weak. I don't know what caused it, but if you want out of her hold, then you need to open that door and let me go after her. I can stop all of this."

"Or take her place."

"That is a chance you'll have to take. What's your next question?"

"How many times has she wiped my memories?"

Silence met his words.

"Miena," he growled. *"How many times?"*

"I don't think that's the question you should ask."

Derek dropped his hand and took a step back, the implications clear. Unless... *"You don't know."*

"Not specifically, nay. I know of at least three."

He swallowed and tried to calm his racing heart. Every answer peeled back another layer, and each layer attempted to knock his legs out from under him.

"Next," Miena stated.

Derek focused his mind. *"Are dragons being held captive?"*

"Aye."

So, Merrill had lied. It had been a trick to get him to the border so he could be taken. He had wanted to believe Merrill so badly. The thought of another dragon being near had elated him, but he should've known it couldn't be true.

"Open the door as you promised."

Derek blinked and stared at the door. He walked to it and grabbed the handle.

"We had a deal, Derek. I held up my end. It's time for you to hold up yours."

He tugged at the door. It held for a moment before popping open. Heat blasted him, instantly drenching him in sweat. Near the door to his right was a narrow section of floor untouched by lava that moved sluggishly around the room. Sitting against the wall was a woman. Her damp strawberry-blond hair hung about her. Hazel eyes watched him as she made no move to stand. Then her gaze slid to the side to look deeper into the room.

Derek turned his head to the left and found another woman standing chained in the middle of the lava, her brunette locks hanging past her butt. He knew without asking that it was Miena. Her bright green eyes glowed with anticipation.

"I've waited a long time for one of you to finally open that door," Miena said.

He ignored her and started to walk into the room when the other woman held out a hand before yelling, "Stop!"

Derek stilled. "What is it?"

"If you come in, the door will lock. There's no handle on this side," she explained.

Miena snorted. "It'll be fine once he releases me. I'll get us out."

Derek inspected the inside of the door and confirmed there was no handle. Then he slowly looked at Miena. "You want me locked in with you?"

"I want to be free!" she bellowed.

The sound shook the walls, causing debris to rain down around them. He should've known. "It was all a lie. Just so you could get out. She put you in here for a reason."

"Because I went against her," Miena stated as she yanked on the chains around her wrists. "I dared to stop her."

"Right."

Miena's face contorted with rage. "I've not lied to you."

"You just conveniently left out the fact that I would be locked in with you."

"Not if you release me. Once free of the chains, I can get us out."

He looked dubiously at the lava. "After I go through that."

"If you want to right the wrongs that have been done to you, to the dragons, and even to humans, you'll get me out of these," she said, lifting her hands as far as she could.

Derek turned back to the human. "What's your name?"

"Daelya."

"What about you? Do you want out?"

She bit her lip hesitantly. "I don't know."

He hadn't expected that. "And why not?"

"Villette sent men to kidnap me so I could tell her who has magic."

Miena harrumphed. "Now ask her what Villette does with that information."

Derek glanced at Miena before returning his attention to Daelya. He already had a suspicion, but he wanted it confirmed. "What happens?"

"She gives it to a priest," Daelya answered.

Miena's chains clinked loudly. "It's how the priests know which children to round up and kill. It's also how Villette knew Merrill and his friend entered the city."

"I didn't want to tell her," Daelya added.

Derek nodded. "You didn't have a choice."

"But I do now. If I stay here, she can't get to me. Villette doesn't come here. Ever."

Miena said, "He could get you out of the city."

He shot Miena a look. "If that's what you want, Daelya. I could take you back to your family."

"Villette's men slaughtered them," she answered. "Besides, she would only send more after me."

Derek looked at the lava as it moved closer to Daelya's feet. "I can't leave you here. You'll die."

"The room is filled with magic. It has kept her alive for weeks," Miena stated.

Daelya nodded. "It's true. I've not been hungry or thirsty once."

"What's it going to be, Derek? Are you keeping your word?" Miena demanded.

He gripped the door and considered his options. There were reasons Miena could've lied to him about his memories. She might not have known that Villette had already entered his head, but she added enough that could push someone to her side. Did he dare believe Miena? That was still up in the air. There was a real chance she'd leave him and Daelya locked in the room once she was free.

He believed Daelya. Her distress of leaving the room was too real to be faked. And who would choose to remain in such a horrible place? Only someone who held such fear.

"Don't you dare close that door," Miena threatened.

Derek quirked a brow. "Or you'll do what?"

"You don't want me as your enemy," she warned.

"I'm not making an enemy. I'm getting facts before I decide anything."

"What more do you want?"

He drew in a deep breath. "The truth."

"I have it," Miena proclaimed.

Derek shrugged a shoulder. "Perhaps. But you aren't the only one."

"Fine. Gather your truths, but hurry. Villette is healing. It's slow, but it's happening. Soon, she'll call for you to return. And she'll give you a target."

"And who might that be?"

"The one who injured her. A Druid named Katla."

What exactly was a Druid? Miena hadn't pulled that term out of thin air, though. Derek swung his head to Daelya. "You sensed her?"

"She does more than that," Miena interjected.

Daelya glanced at Miena before she nodded. "My ability also allows me to remotely watch others using magic." She glanced down at her hands in her lap. "I saw the battle between Katla and Villette."

Derek waited, sensing there was more she wasn't saying. "What else?"

"A lot more," Miena said. She yanked at her chains. "You won't get any of it until these are gone. I told you Katla's name. You'll know I'm not lying when Villette sends you after her. Then you'll come to me. If it isn't already too late."

Derek looked at Daelya once more. She shook her head. And with that, he stepped out of the room and let the door close.

CHAPTER 24

Kora was furious with Derek for leaving in the middle of their conversation. He vanished right before her eyes after saying he had to meet someone. She hadn't stormed out of the room to look for him. He wanted his secrets? Well then, fine. He could keep them. She was done with the half-truths and explanations that didn't seem complete. As well as everything else.

The problem was that Kora wanted to storm out. Not to look for him but to leave and do her own thing. She hadn't intended for anyone to help her anyway. Derek's cuff would make things easier, but she wasn't comfortable with it. For many reasons. The least of which being that she didn't trust him. Without coin or a place to go, Kora would only make things more difficult than they already were.

But she couldn't stay either.

She looked down, only then realizing she had put on her black clothes. Then she looked at the door. She had a plan. If Villette was weak, now was the time to put her scheme into action. And if she wasn't? Well, Kora hadn't expected her to be anything but what she was, so it didn't matter.

With her back straight and chin lifted, Kora emptied her pack, slipped it over her head, and walked from the room. She snuck down the stairs as she had done the last time and stole out the door. It was easy to keep to the shadows away from the rare street-lamp. She hastened to the alley Derek had brought her to and found the gate beneath the vines.

It creaked loudly when she opened it, making her wince. She slipped through and closed it behind her. Kora knew she would be traveling fast on her return, so she made sure to turn and look behind her at where she needed to go to get back to her level. Then she headed toward the soldiers' quarters.

None were posted outside, thankfully. It made getting next to the building easy. She kept low, creeping beneath the windows, listening as she passed. Most of those inside were sleeping, and the few who *were* up were drinking and playing a game of dice. They shouted and slammed their tankards on the table. Just the type of noise she needed to drown out any sound she might make.

Kora peered into one of the darkened windows. The shutters were open, and moonlight spilled inside, showing rows of beds. She pushed open the shutters and climbed through the window, landing softly on her feet. Then she began looking for female soldiers.

She stopped at the first she came to and looked at the boots. They were several sizes bigger than hers, which likely meant the uniform wouldn't fit. She checked three more before locating a pair that would fit.

Kora found the other items she needed in the chest at the foot of the soldier's bed. She cringed when the armor clanked as she lifted it. Someone farther down shifted in their bed. Another's snores softened as they turned over, then they grew loud again. She slowly added the items to her bag. She decided to leave the helm since most in the city didn't wear them, but she did grab the boots.

Getting out of the room proved more nerve-wracking than getting in. Every movement she made caused the armor to clink. She finally had to hold the bag out with both hands to stop the noise. That worked until she came to the window. Kora swung the bag outside and slowly lowered it by the strap until it was on the ground. She dropped the boots next to it. Then, she climbed out.

She gathered everything and slunk back around the building, only to come to a halt when the soldiers who had been playing dice walked outside. She flattened herself against the building. The shadows were narrow and thin there, but they concealed her well enough. Unless one of them turned and looked her way.

Kora held her breath, waiting and watching. The minutes lengthened as the group stayed outside, smoking and trading stories of their latest bed partners. Her legs began to cramp from squatting. She debated darting to deeper shadows when one of the soldiers looked in her direction. He must not have seen her as he flicked what remained of whatever he smoked to the ground. The others finished, and, finally, they returned inside to their game.

Relief surged through her. Kora didn't budge until she heard them deep in the game once more. She fought against the need to run. She made herself move deliberately to keep the noise at a minimum and not draw attention to herself. Every few steps, she looked over her shoulder. Then she would look around to see if anyone watched from a window.

The moment she spotted the alley that led to the hidden gate Derek had shown her, some of the tension left her body. Until she tried to push the gate open, and it wouldn't budge. She used both hands and shoved, but it still didn't move. Kora needed the uniform, and this was her only way back to the inn. There had to be a way through.

She looked at her hands. It had been a long time since she'd called on her hellhound magic. Would it even work? Better to find out now. She placed her hand on the pillar where the gate latched and let the flames erupt from her palm. The fire blazed huge, and she hurried to dim the light and concentrate it on the latch.

Smoke wafted from her hand. Then the gate sagged. She jostled it open, tearing a few vines as she did. Once she was through, she shut it behind her and tried to cover the torn vines. She hurried back up to the room, half-expecting to find Derek there. Unfortunately, there was no one to share her victory with. She shut the door behind her.

Kora sighed and dropped the sack. She immediately tried on the uniform. It wasn't a perfect fit, but it did the job. The armor covered the too-long sleeves. She pulled her hair to the back of her head as she had seen the female soldiers do.

Then she stood before the mirror. Not because she cared what she looked like but because she wanted to make sure everything appeared as it should. Her gaze moved to the bed. Unbidden, an image of her holding Derek filled her mind. She squeezed her eyes shut and shook away the image.

"I can do this," she told herself.

She had gotten this far. Albeit with Derek's help. She would do the rest on her own as it was meant to be. Kora looked at the gown hanging in the wardrobe. The woman she had been that night was someone else. The one now was who she was. That other night had served its purpose. Now, she would fulfill her responsibilities.

Derek stood at the edge of the forest, looking to the open expanse that led to the canyon where the border lay. He could be on the other side with just a touch to his cuff. But he didn't move. He wasn't sure what held him back. All he had to do was cross the border and see for himself if the dragons were free or not without anyone knowing. Or trapping him.

A chuffing sound drew his attention. Derek turned his head to find a wildcat sitting a short distance away, watching him with intelligent green eyes. The black spots amid its slightly lighter-black fur were distinctive to the species. The feline was huge and imposing. None had ever gotten this close to him before.

It chuffed again.

The sound was one they made in friendly greeting. Derek looked for a wound, but the beast didn't seem to have any that might make it act strangely. He held out his hand and mimicked the chuffing sound. The feline stood and walked to him, continuing to chuff. To his surprise, the animal rubbed its massive head against his hand.

Derek sank his fingers into the soft, midnight fur. The animal purred loudly before moving to lean its body against his. He had both hands petting the wildcat now, feeling its powerful body. Its paws were larger than his hands, and he had witnessed the speed at which they could run.

"You shouldn't just go up to anyone," he warned in a soft voice.

The cat lifted its head and met his gaze. "Nay, I don't suppose you do that, do you? You're too smart."

The animal leaned its whole head against him when Derek rubbed its ear. He grinned. "You like that, do you, boy?" He took a quick look. "Sorry. Girl."

Derek rubbed the other ear. Before he knew it, he was on the ground with the wildcat lying across one leg as he looked at the border. He stroked the animal from head to tail, repeating the motion over and over again. Her eyes were closed contentedly.

"I've had that feeling recently. With Kora. Shocked me. It also made me do things I never would've done." He sighed. "I don't know which way is up anymore. I don't know what is truth and what is fiction. Will I get what I'm looking for across the border? I might simply be imprisoned like my family."

Family. He winced at the word. Villette told him his family had been captured. She had been trying to rescue them, and his mother sacrificed herself for him.

"Villette isn't who I thought she was. She's kept things from me. But then I've kept a lot from her, too. Does that make me untrustworthy?"

The cat briefly opened its green eyes to look at him.

"Do I discount everything she's done because some people are telling me she's wrong? The rest of the city adores her. Or who they think she is, anyway. I'm not sure many would even care if they discovered she was the Divine." Derek leaned his head back against the tree. "I've trusted her and have believed *in* her for so long that I don't know if it's because I know what she said is true or because it's what I've always done.

"I swore my allegiance to her above all others. I've done all she has asked of me. But it comes back to...why haven't we freed the dragons? I'm beginning to wonder if they are being held captive. By humans no less. Humans with magic along with a Star Person, but nothing we couldn't fight."

Derek thought about the excuses she had given him, as well as the steps to the next plan, only for something to happen and put things off. Then start all over again.

"What if it was all a lie?" he whispered. "What if I've been killing in her name to spread the fear she wants *because* I'm a dragon?" He grunted. "Miena said the dragons are being held. I don't know what to believe."

The wildcat rose and walked out of the trees. It paused and looked back at him as if telling him to follow. Derek got to his feet and watched as the animal continued to the canyon. It looked back at him one more time before jumping over the edge.

Derek started to follow when he realized the sun had come up. "Kora," he whispered and touched his cuff.

CHAPTER 25

The armor was heavy and confining. Kora hated everything about it. But wearing it gave her exactly the kind of anonymity she had hoped for. Citizens nodded wary greetings or ignored her altogether. Despite that, she felt exposed. As if those who looked at her would have her face branded on their memory. Why hadn't she gotten the helm? Sure, it would've been heavy to cart out with the rest of what she stole, but it would have hidden her face. The boots she had believed would be a good fit were actually too small. They scrunched her toes and made walking painful—like everything else about the uniform.

As she neared the gate, Kora's heart hammered wildly against her ribs—part in trepidation but also with a thread of anticipation. Eagerness to fulfill her duty. She forgot about her feet as she approached the gate to the next level. The guards glanced at her uniform and let her through while continuing their conversation as if she wasn't there. Which was fine by her.

Almost exactly the same scenario played out while getting to the top level. The ease of it left Kora edgy. She tensed, waiting to hear the sound of boots running up behind her. But none came. She kept her steps even despite wanting to run. Her plan was working.

Kora gave the palace the side-eye as she walked down the street. She drew in a deep breath and waited for her hellhound senses to kick in. Just like when she faced the soldiers the other night, she caught the scent of evil. It was faint, but there was no mistaking that it came from the palace. The scent would lead her to Villette.

But that was for after she got into the palace.

More people strolled the gardens today. She expected the battle to stay within the palace, but she couldn't guarantee that. Villette would try to get away. And if she ran, Kora would follow. She wouldn't have a lot of time to take down her enemy. A dragon was near. Kora had to be alert for its arrival.

Because while she might have Villette's scent, the dragon could get hers.

An image of Derek flashed in her head. She didn't want to die. She wanted to live. And while she would never say the words aloud, she wanted more time with Derek. To explore if there could be a future.

She slammed the door on those thoughts. It was suicide to dwell on such things when walking into battle. There was only one thing she should focus on: finally ending Villette's reign of terror.

The uniform continued to make Kora unnoticeable to nearly all. She felt eyes on her as she approached the main gate. She nodded to the soldiers standing guard. They responded in kind, saying nothing to stop her. Kora's stomach churned with nerves. It was the reason she had forgone any food. Just in case.

She tried to remember the things her family had taught her about battle. After so many years of not using her abilities and trying to forget she was a hellhound, those recollections weren't easy to bring up. And when she did, they were fuzzy and difficult to piece together. There was no denying that hiding her true nature had damaged her abilities and put her self-trust in serious doubt.

There was no changing any of that now. She would have to trust whatever instincts remained when she stood before Villette.

Kora reached the far end of the palace and followed the curving path around the side. Almost immediately, she encountered a black iron gate. A guard stepped from behind the tall wall of stone shooting out from either side of the gate. He let her inside without a word. Her breathing came fast, and she sought to calm it lest he notice.

She passed him and stayed on the path. It was more crowded than she had considered. Other soldiers and servants walked to-and-fro, going to different buildings. Kora headed toward the palace. No one spoke to her, much less looked her way. Everyone was busy with their duties.

Her steps quickened when she spotted the door that led inside the palace. Within moments, she was standing on the servants' floors. She inhaled and coughed as the stronger smell of evil hit her. She swallowed and hurried out of the way when the door opened behind her. Men and women garbed in simple servants' clothing hurried about the area.

Kora continued to be overlooked except when she got in some-one's way. She hastily walked deeper into the wide hallway and peered through the open doorways to the rooms beyond. There were three different kitchens, a room where silver serving pieces were stored and another where gold serving pieces were. There were at least four different rooms for food storage. She also saw what looked like a dining area where the servants could take their meals.

She continued deeper into the area and spotted servants carrying trays up a flight of stairs. She followed them to the landing, where a section of the wall opened like a door. It was easy to spot once she saw it. And if there was one, there were more. She looked up to see the stairs switch back several floors above her. No one was around, so she slipped out from behind the secret panel.

The instant she stepped out, she found herself within the palace. A tall, wide corridor stretched as far as she could see on either side. The smell of evil slammed into her, so pervasive it made her reach for the wall to hold herself up. She gagged at the stench. Kora stumbled away from the hidden door and tried to right herself.

It took several minutes before she could breathe without retching. A deeper worry slid through her because there were three distinct scents of evil. One far above her, and two deep within the mountain.

The silence of the empty room was deafening. Derek stared at the bed—where he should've been with his arms around Kora.

He should've returned to her sooner. He should have told her what he'd discovered. He should have shared everything. But it was too late for *should haves*. She was gone.

He looked through the open door of the wardrobe to the deep blue gown hanging there. His eyes narrowed when he spotted her blue clothing folded and neatly put away along with her black outfit. She hadn't gone after Villette naked. She'd said she had a plan. He had foolishly believed he had time to earn her trust so she would share it. But trust went two ways, and he had given her very little of his own.

Derek ran a hand down his face, feeling the full weight of his mistakes. He had unsuccessfully attempted to walk two diverging paths. All along, he'd known he would have to choose. He had expected to find some truth before he had to make that decision. He had never waited before. He was decisive. Certain.

Undeniably clear on his decisions.

But that was before Kora got into his blood and wound herself around his psyche. Her single-minded focus should've told him she wouldn't wait. She had given him time. She had been patient. And he had tarried for too long. It didn't help that he had told her Villette was weak. Of course, she'd gone after her target.

He certainly would have.

"Fuck!" he shouted, clenching his hands in frustration.

The decision he had been so hesitant to make was upon him. Did he leave Kora to her fate, whatever that might be? Or did he fight alongside her?

He looked at the bed she had meticulously made, smoothing the covers with nary a wrinkle in sight. The lust that had brought him to her that first time had grown, shifted. He hadn't realized that every time they touched and kissed, each time their bodies joined, a bond had cultivated, strengthening and expanding until it was firmly settled within his heart. Uniting him with her now. And forever.

The realization of the feelings he hadn't acknowledged—or had even been aware of—shook him to his core. Nothing else mattered but Kora. Not his promise to Villette.

Not even the dragons.

Kora couldn't decide which scent to follow. She hadn't thought there would be more than Villette's. She wouldn't get a second chance, so she had to choose wisely.

One up. Two down.

Villette had chosen to build Stonemore along the side of a mountain, with the palace at the peak. She liked to be on top. There could be an argument to head up. And yet, her uncle had been convinced that Villette used the actual mountain to conceal much of her activities. It made sense that someone would dig tunnels for escape. And if they did, then Villette might have a place below to hide.

Two scents below. If Kora followed the stench down, she might indeed face off with Villette. She might also find herself battling two enemies.

"Come on," she whispered to herself. "You can't stand here debating forever."

She looked up and decided to check that first. But her feet wouldn't move. She inhaled deeply and slowly released it. Looked like she was headed down, then.

Kora walked to the left to look for stairs. She went farther into the palace in her search. Over the next thirty minutes, a few soldiers passed her, but she ignored them. Thankfully, they didn't talk to her.

Whenever she saw someone dressed in finery, she hid. The soldiers might ignore her, but that may not happen with others. Kora was trying to be quiet as she walked another long corridor, but the armor clinked incessantly, announcing her to all. Thankfully, the palace was filled with noise that seemed to come from everywhere.

She turned a corner and spotted someone who looked very official, their steps quick and determined. Kora ducked behind one of the enormous columns and flattened herself against it. The armor on her shoulders struck the stone loudly. She held her breath, waiting for the official to call out, but they didn't. Kora slowly and silently moved around the column as the individual passed.

Kora let out a sigh when the woman's footsteps grew distant. She was done searching. If she didn't ask someone, she might be here for days. And every moment wasted looking was one in which she could be discovered.

She stopped the next servant she found. The young boy was tall and reed-thin. His dark hair was cut to his scalp, and his clothes looked as if they were meant for someone years older given how they hung on his body. He carried a tray laden with food.

"Need some help?" she asked with a friendly smile.

Dark eyes ran over her. "You'd drop the tray with all that armor."

She found herself laughing. "Most likely. I'm trying to get below, but I got turned around in all the hallways. Which stairs lead down?"

"Down to the servants' quarters? Or down inside the mountain?"

"The mountain."

He nodded firmly. "Follow me."

She fell into step with him. After a few moments, she said, "You shouldn't be carrying that. Someone older should help."

"I've worked hard to get to this position. It's coveted by everyone. I'm happy to carry food around instead of some of the other jobs I've had."

Kora hadn't considered that. "My apologies. I meant no disrespect."

"None taken." He suddenly halted and jerked his chin to the hallway on the left. "Take that until you find the stairs. They'll lead you down. Hope you know where you're going from there. We aren't allowed below."

"Thank you," she said.

But he was already gone. Kora turned to the left and started walking.

Derek caught Kora's scent the moment he materialized in the palace. He followed it through a maze of passages. It would be easier if he knew where Villette was. Then he could wait there for Kora.

His strides lengthened until he was running. The urgency to reach Kora drummed through him. He had never felt such dread before. Such foreboding. Panic at what might become of Kora drove him harder, faster.

"Wait for me," he pleaded.

But he knew it was too late.

The narrow staircase was tucked into a corner. She had walked the hall the boy told her to take three times before she found it. The steps descended in a spiral that seemed to go on forever. She didn't encounter another soul. Torches hung on the walls, casting meager light upon the stairs. The air became cooler and damper the deeper she went while the scents of evil grew stronger with each step.

Kora's thighs burned by the time she reached the bottom. Just as the stairs had begun, they ended, hidden in an alcove. She had stopped counting them after four hundred. She paused at the landing to get her bearings—and give her legs a much-needed break.

She peeked around the corner and looked down a tunnel. The scents split. One to her left and the other to her right. The one to her left was closer. She decided to check that one first. Her shoulders squared. She was closer than anyone in her family had ever been to getting Villette. Closer than any hellhound had been in centuries. The ghosts of her people stood at her back, watching and waiting.

She couldn't fail them.

If she closed her eyes, she could almost feel her brother to her right and her uncle to her left. How she wished Kayden and Rylan were with her.

Kora stepped out of the alcove and turned left. The evil odor washed over her, making it easy to follow. It took her down a narrow tunnel to a door that stood ajar. Inside, she heard someone moaning in pain. Kora quietly approached and peered through the crack. The room was dark, other than a fire. She saw the edge of a bed and someone's feet as they moved them about.

She nudged the door wider. The rest of the bed came into view as it sat against the far wall. A naked woman with blond hair writhed on the mattress. Burns covered her arms, chest, and face.

The woman stilled as if sensing that she was no longer alone. She turned her head to Kora. Blue eyes locked on her. A moment later, the burns disappeared, but it took the woman considerable effort to hide them. This wasn't just anyone. She suspected it was Villette.

But she had to be sure.

"Get out," the woman ordered.

Kora shook her head.

"No one disobeys me."

Four words, but in them, Kora knew she had found her target. Something in the voice gave it away. The tone and inflection. The anger. Kora removed the vambraces from her arms and let them drop to the floor.

"Who are you?" Villette demanded.

Kora removed the greaves and cuisses from her legs, followed by the breastplate. She welcomed the fire that raged within her as smoke curled around her right before flames erupted over her, burning her clothes away. "The one who is here to end you."

She moved into the room, ready to kill. Three steps in, the floor fell out from beneath Kora.

CHAPTER 26

The shift from the shadowy room to the glare of the sun had Kora off balance. She pitched forward, blinded by the light and reaching for anything to keep herself upright. There was nothing but air as she tripped and fell to her knees. She extinguished the flames and blinked against the harsh light until her eyes adjusted.

Grass cut into her bare flesh, making it itch. A hasty look told her she was alone. But *where* was she? Kora got to her feet and turned in a circle to see nothing but waist-high grass in every direction. No mountains, no tunnel. No Villette.

She could only stare as disbelief rolled through her. She had found her enemy and had been within feet of attack. And now she had to start over.

The difference was that Villette knew a hellhound lived.

Derek sailed down the stairs so fast his feet barely touched stone. He didn't stop when he reached the bottom and continued following Kora's scent. He was rushing down the tunnel when someone yanked him into a room.

He instinctively lashed out with magic. Something connected with his jaw, snapping his head back to smack into the wall. Derek barely noticed the pain as he focused on his attacker. He ducked when he saw a fist coming at him. Then he straightened and threw magic with both hands. The next thing he knew, Merrill had him against the wall, his forearm pressed into Derek's neck.

"We can keep fighting, or I can tell you where the woman is," Merrill stated flatly.

Derek stared into dark blue eyes and released the hold he had on Merrill's shirt. Immediately, Merrill released him.

"Fuck, you're strong," Merrill muttered. He bent over and rested his hands on his knees.

"You spoke of a woman. You saw Kora?"

Merrill straightened and blew out a breath. "I doona know her name. I saw a woman on fire."

"That's Kora. Where is she?"

"Gone."

Derek shook his head, but inside, he roared his denial. "She can't be dead."

"I didna say she was dead. I said she's gone."

That dimmed Derek's panic enough that he could think again. "Gone? Gone where?"

Merrill glanced out the door and lowered his voice. "I saw her head toward the room where I found Villette the other day. I followed out of curiosity. Kora removed the armor she wore and erupted into flames. Then she walked into the room."

"And?" Derek snapped when Merrill didn't immediately continue.

"She fell through the floor."

Just when he thought he had found her. Derek slumped against the wall and tried to drag air into his lungs that now felt as if they were being crushed. "How?" Even as he asked the question, he knew.

"You work with Villette and you ask that?"

He shot Merrill a dark look. "Where would she send Kora?"

"What is it you do for Villette, exactly?"

"If you don't know anything about Kora, then I don't have time to talk."

Merrill stepped in front of him and lifted his arms when Derek went to leave. "If you want to find your woman, then you need to follow her."

It was the only reasonable conclusion. There would be no hiding his choice then. And there would be repercussions.

He didn't care.

Derek strode past Merrill to follow Kora's scent to the door at the end of the hall. He stopped at the doorway, his gaze locked on Villette's body rigid with pain.

Not only didn't Kora know where she was, but she had no clothes or shoes, no coin, and no food. She couldn't remain, though. After turning in another circle, she randomly chose a direction and began walking. The sun beat down relentlessly. She thought about Derek's cuff and how useful something like that would be in her current situation.

Kora had only been walking for about ten minutes when the first roar cut through the air. She immediately dropped, her gaze frantically searching the sky for the dragon. The second roar was louder. And much closer. It shook the very ground beneath her feet. There was no hiding from the dragon. It had her scent.

The need to run thudded through her, but she didn't give in. If she died, then she would do it facing her nemesis. Kora got to her feet and let the flames erupt and cover her once more. The amethyst dragon slammed to the ground in front of her, its wings held wide. It stood on four limbs with long talons.

She tilted her head back to gaze up at the ferocious beast. It towered over her menacingly as its citrine eyes glared down at her. Its skull was narrow with amethyst crystal growths in various places over the scales. A row of horns ran down the sides of its jaw. Its nose was wide with two short, slitted nostrils. Rows of colossal teeth poked out from the sides of its mouth.

The dragon snapped its wings against its body. The edges were tattered and damaged, but it was the armor-like scales that grew on the top of the wing's primary bones that caught her attention. The scales were wide at its back and colored darker on its stomach.

The hate emanating from the fiend was palpable. Fear had controlled her for long enough.

Kora threw her arms out and screamed, "Come and get me then!"

The dragon inhaled. She waited to be doused with dragon fire. Then another earsplitting roar sounded.

Fear and rage mixed within Derek the moment he saw the dragon about to attack Kora, becoming something dark and treacherous. Something unstoppable.

Something inescapable.

He shifted and launched into the air with all the power he could muster. He saw the amethyst take in a breath and roared to announce his presence—and to warn of his intent. The amethyst dragon swung his head around just as Derek wanted, but it didn't come for him. Derek landed behind Kora, his eyes locked on the amethyst before he opened his jaws and roared.

Derek felt Kora's fear. He wanted to look at her, but he didn't dare take his eyes off his opponent. It was a good thing because the amethyst rose on his back legs and spread his wings. Derek saw the fire moving between his foe's scales and quickly shielded Kora with his wing an instant before the flames engulfed her.

The heat of the dragon fire burned his scales, leaving them scorched and stinging. He whipped his barbed tail at his rival. The amethyst bellowed as the barb imbedded in its scales. Derek then launched himself at the dragon, tackling him as they rolled away from Kora, tearing at each other with teeth and claws.

Kora had frozen in place with the arrival of the second dragon when it landed behind her. She had looked between the two as fear turned her blood to ice. The second dragon was larger than the amethyst. It had onyx scales edged with metallic silver, and its red eyes never wavered from the other dragon. Were they enemies? Or were they fighting over who would kill her?

Then the oddest thing happened. The black-and-silver one

shielded her from the other's dragon fire. She was so surprised that she simply stood there in shock while the heat from the amethyst dragon's flames made sweat run down her face.

She snapped out of it when the amethyst bellowed. Before she could react, both dragons were fighting. Kora started running. Her arms pumped, and her feet slammed against the ground as she moved quicker than she had ever done before. She might have said she would stand to face her enemy, but that was before there were two of them.

A large shadow moved over her, and she looked up to find the dragons fighting in the air. Roars reverberated around her. She shifted course and kept running.

Derek yelled as teeth ripped through the scales on his shoulder. Blood gushed down his foreleg, thick and warm. He had a hold of one of the amethyst's wings with a claw as his other hand slashed at anything he could reach. His back talons got in several good strikes, too.

He pulled them higher and higher, keeping the amethyst's attention on him so Kora could get to safety. The dragon was big and old, if the scars on it were any indication. It fought with a ferociousness that stunned Derek. Then again, he had only ever fought against Bryok, and that had never been for life or death.

This was.

The amethyst sank his teeth into Derek's wounded shoulder again, adding a second injury. Derek growled in fury and latched his jaws around his foe's neck, clamping down. The dragon screamed and yanked his head back, trying to get free.

There was something different about the last roar. Kora slid to a stop and looked behind her to see the dragons in a free fall. She couldn't look away as they plummeted to the ground. They were far away, but she still felt the vibration when they crashed.

She waited, hoping both were dead. She spun and started running when she heard the fight continue.

"Why can't they just die?" she murmured.

Derek lay on his back and stared up at the blue sky as his body slowly knitted tendon, muscle, and bone back together. Each breath was agony. No part of him wasn't injured. From tail to head, even his wings. The process was usually quick, but the damage he had sustained in the battle as well as the fall had been substantial. Both of his wings were broken. One had nearly been shorn off.

The battle itself had been long and taxing. A couple of times, Derek had wondered if he would win. He had felt himself close to death several times. Derek turned his head to look at the amethyst who lay unmoving. Even when his opponent had been gravely wounded, he hadn't stopped fighting. There had been no quit in the dragon. But Derek had Kora, and that gave him the strength to keep going.

That ensured he would be victorious.

It had cost him, too. He'd lost sight of Kora. Her scent was still heavy in the air. It would be easy for him or anyone Villette sent after her to follow.

He returned to his mortal form. He needed to get up and go after Kora, but his body wasn't healed enough yet. He waited for as long as he dared before rolling onto his stomach and pushing up onto his hands and knees. Villette wouldn't take his betrayal calmly. It wasn't just Kora's life in danger now—it was his, as well.

Derek climbed to his feet and forced his feet to move. He took one step, then a second. He lifted his foot for another when he saw the amethyst's hand move. Derek didn't hesitate to shift and jump into the air before landing atop his foe. He clamped his teeth around the amethyst's jaw and ripped it out. He wouldn't move again.

This time, when Derek's human body returned, he clothed himself with magic. He looked in the direction Kora had run and fixated on a spot in the distance before he touched the cuff. He repeated that five more times before finally spotting her.

Kora ran until her body gave out. Pulling herself off the ground took energy she didn't have, but she had pushed herself too hard. Fear had a way of doing that. She was covered in sweat, her body trembling with fatigue, and her throat parched as she put one foot in front of the other.

She hadn't heard the dragons in some time. That didn't mean they weren't coming after her, though. She had nowhere to hide or go where they wouldn't find her. She was doomed. She always had been. She just hadn't known it. But even if she was going to die, that didn't mean she had to make it easy for the beasts.

Kora squinted up at the sky, looking for dragons and clouds. She would love some shade. The fact that she was still alive was shocking. She likely wouldn't be if the black-and-silver dragon hadn't protected her. Why? She couldn't wrap her head around it doing such a thing. Kora wished she had gotten a better look at it. She had only caught a glimpse of the gleaming black scales that looked as if silver had been painted along the edges. But she thought it resembled the one who had stood over her when she battled the soldiers.

Which was ridiculous.

Or was it?

Someone had put her dead body on the top of the mountain. Could it have been a dragon?

She snorted a laugh. The heat was getting to her. Dragons didn't care about such things. They certainly wouldn't be concerned about a dead hellhound.

The moment she heard the sound of water, she rushed to it, her exhausted muscles forgotten. Kora splashed into the shallow stream. The liquid cooled her battered feet. She squatted and cupped her hands, filling them with water before bringing them to her mouth. She drank her fill and sat back with a sigh. When she looked up, her gaze snagged on Derek, who stood on the opposite shore.

"How are you here?" she asked, unsure if he was a figment of her imagination.

He walked through the water to her and helped her to her feet. He brushed her hair away from her face with his fingers. "I told you I would find you anywhere."

"There are dragons," she began.

"I saw. The amethyst is dead."

"And the other?"

He shrugged. "Not a threat."

The cold water caused Kora to shiver. She backed out of the stream. The next thing she knew, clothes covered her. She looked down at her black garments then up at Derek.

"I have magic," he said as he moved to stand before her once more. "More than what the cuff does. I should've told you."

Now he wanted to share his secrets. Kora waved his words away. "It doesn't matter. I have bigger problems. I found Villette, but when I tried to attack, I ended up here. Wherever *here* is. She knows what I am. She's the one who sent the dragon. You should get far from me before you're killed."

He put a finger under her chin and gently lifted until she met his gaze. "I'm not going anywhere."

"There's nowhere for me to go. The dragons will find me."

"I know of a place."

Kora was tired and emotionally drained. She needed time to collect her thoughts. Derek offered that. She was tired of being alone, tired of carrying her worry on her own. Now wasn't the time to give in to the yearning to share some of her burdens. That wasn't fair to anyone. This was her mess.

"Trust me," he urged and held out a hand.

CHAPTER 27

"I want to. But I can't."

Derek lowered his hand to his side. He saw the determination in her eyes. She intended to face whatever was to come on her own. Or so she thought. The problem was that he had yet to give Kora a reason to trust him. She wanted to know his secrets, but she would never trust him if he told her everything. He was in a situation he didn't know how to get out of without losing her.

"We're too exposed here. We need to find a place that offers more shelter," he told her.

She raised her brows. "We?"

"I'm not leaving without you."

"Did you hear anything I said?"

"I did."

"Then I'm the last person you should want to be around."

He stared into her deep brown eyes and did the unthinkable.

He bared his heart. "You're the only one I want to be around. Today. Tomorrow. In a million tomorrows."

"Don't. Please, don't say such things. I can't watch anyone else die. It's too painful."

"I'm not going to die."

She scoffed and took a step back. "You can't say things like that."

"I'm here to help you. Let me do that. Please."

Her face crumpled as she glanced away. "I should refuse for your sake."

"You've stood on your own for a long time. You've proven yourself to everyone. Accepting my offer doesn't diminish your strength. We're friends, aren't we?"

"Are we?" she asked softly.

He nodded. "I wouldn't find you if we weren't." Derek held out his hand. "I've protected you before. Let me do it again."

This time, she put her hand in his. "I'm too tired to argue. It isn't as if we have anywhere to go. There's nothing but grass."

Derek pointed in the direction she had been running. "There is a forest that way."

"You know where we are?"

"Nay. I can see the trees."

"You can...?" Her brows drew together. "How?"

He shrugged. "It's just something I can do. It will take hours to walk it. I can get us there faster."

Derek didn't waste any time getting them into the relative safety of the woods. The land was flat, and the vegetation dense, but it was shelter. He let Kora take the lead and followed her as she wove between the trees until she found a place she liked.

The tree had to be the tallest and biggest in the forest. It would take five of Derek standing with his arms out to wrap around the trunk. Kora sank against it and stretched out her legs in exhaustion. He gathered branches and returned to build a fire.

"Let me," Kora said after he'd stacked the wood.

He could have lit it himself, but he sat back as she held out her hand. A flame erupted from her palm and arced across to the sticks. When he arrived, he had gotten a brief glimpse of Kora on fire and feared he was too late, that the dragon had already engulfed her. But they had proven to be *her* flames.

Her gaze lifted to his. Her brown eyes blazed with fire of their own before a red-orange color filled her irises. He stared in wonder as the ends of her glorious hair sparked with embers. Her skin cracked and split into sections as the same red-orange hue could be seen underneath. He had never witnessed anything so beautiful or amazing. Flames shot out of the slits and covered her, disintegrating her clothing but leaving her hair and skin unmarred.

He had seen hellhounds on fire before but never cared about how or why they had such an ability. Or how it was used. He had hunted them so none could harm Villette. Now, he wanted to know everything about Kora to protect *her*.

The flames died, and her skin stitched together as the glow faded. Smoke trailed from her hair before vanishing altogether, and once more, her eyes were the warm brown he knew. She sat naked, watching him.

"That was astonishing," he whispered in awe. "Does it hurt?"

She shook her head. "Not at all. It feels powerful."

"As it should."

"You don't fear me?"

Derek sat across the fire from her. He used his magic to clothe her again before shaking his head. "Do you want me to?"

"Nay," she answered.

This was where Derek should open up and spill his many secrets. He wasn't sure how, though. Where did he start? How did he explain enough but keep what he was from her? He didn't want to lie anymore. He wanted to lay it all out—every offense, every transgression. But he knew what would happen. Her fear of dragons was too visceral. It didn't matter how much time they had spent together. She would believe he had deceived her.

And he had.

That's what gutted him. There was no getting around it. Nor could he keep it from her forever. The truth always came out. It would be better if he told her rather than letting her learn it from someone else. He parted his lips to speak, but the words wouldn't come.

"The fire will attract the dragons," she said.

He tried to smile but didn't succeed. "If any show, I'll get us away."

"With the cuff."

"Aye. Are you hungry?" He snapped his finger, and a ritbit was suddenly roasting over the fire.

Kora nodded to the silver on his wrist. "Are you sure that isn't where you get your magic from? I've never seen anyone do anything like that."

"The cuff was a gift. It's not attached to my magic."

"A gift from Villette?"

He slowly released a breath. The time for lies and half-truths was over. It was time to begin building trust. Somehow. "Aye."

"Why?"

"So I could get to her when she called for me."

Kora snorted. "She's quite full of herself. What exactly are you to her?"

"A means to an end."

"For?" she pushed.

Derek closed his eyes for a heartbeat. This was going to be so much harder than he thought. "She found Bryok and me. We were very young, and she looked out for us. She kept us safe, and when we asked about others like us, she told us the story of how a group of magical humans, along with some Star People, had taken them prisoner. The anger that filled me that day has yet to lessen. It has driven me since."

"I have an inkling of what you felt," Kora said.

"Villette saw that both Bryok and I wanted to do something, and we started to plan. Whenever Bryok or I pushed to free our kin, she would tell us we needed to be stronger. We were too young. So, we grew, and we trained. She told us stories about what those enslaving our kind did to them. It fed our hatred. She pointed us in a direction, saying she had gotten word of a group or person involved in the capture of our kin. We didn't hesitate to retaliate. We went after them. And we destroyed them."

Kora's brow was furrowed. "Did you question them?"

"It's what we should've done. But, nay. We reacted." He leaned back on his hands, the shame of his crimes washing over him. "Until very recently, I never doubted anything Villette said. Or asked of me."

"You never questioned her or others?"

"Who was there to ask? Bryok and I were kept away from everyone. When we were freed, we spent so much time set apart that we preferred it that way."

Kora's eyes widened. "Do you even know if what she said about how she found you or your people is the truth?"

"Nay." He twisted his lips. Looking back on it now, there were plenty of warning signs if he had only looked. "Despite all the training and planning, we never attempted to free my people. She always had a good reasoning—something I couldn't determine might be a lie or not."

"But you stayed loyal."

It wasn't a question. He shrugged a shoulder. "I did. Then I met you."

"So, you knew all along that I was after Villette and wanted to stop me?"

"I had no idea. I felt...compelled to help you. It was such a strong emotion that I was powerless to ignore it. Villette never wanted me in the city. I was warned to stay away. On the occasions she called for me, we met privately within the mountain."

Kora drew her knees to her chest and wrapped her arms around them. "And once you learned I was after Villette?"

"She would expect me to warn her, but I didn't. You opened my eyes to what was happening in the city. What she accepted and intended. It went against what I thought I knew, and I had trouble reconciling that. Doubt set in. The voice in my head gave me another push."

"The voice you said you heard when we were in the gardens?"

"Her name is Miena. She's a Star Person that Villette has imprisoned at the palace. Miena began speaking to me as we neared Stonemore. The closer I am to the palace, the stronger her voice. Villette's weakened, as you saw, which affected her magic somehow."

Kora grinned. "That means other things are weakened. Can you trust Miena?"

"Of course, not. She wants her freedom, and, supposedly, I can give that to her. Though I'm not sure I should. She told me Villette wiped my memories at least three times. I began to doubt if my kin were being held, but she said they were. She also promised to give me answers to all my other questions, but not until I've released her."

"Did you?"

Derek shook his head. "I found her. She's chained in the middle of a room with lava flowing around her. She isn't the only one there, either."

"Villette caught two Star People?"

"Daelya is human, but she can sense magic in others. Villette was using her to find those with it in the city."

Kora's face tightened. "So that information could pass to the priests."

"It seems so. Daelya would rather remain in the room with Miena than be used by Villette again."

"Can't say I blame her."

"Miena said she was chained because she tried to stop Villette. She also claims that once she's released, she'll kill her sister."

"If Miena has answers and can end Villette, then maybe you should grant her freedom."

Derek turned the meat over to cook the other side. "I considered it." If for nothing else than it would keep Kora from confronting Villette. "That seems like the right answer, but something held me back."

"When I was in the palace, I caught three distinct scents of evil. One at the top of the castle and two below. I found Villette below."

"Miena's at the top."

Kora grunted. "I wonder who the third is." She shook her head slightly. "There has to be someone who can give you the truth."

"There is someone who claims to know."

"Who?"

Derek was pleased with how the conversation was going, but their discussion was far from over. They were treading into territory he dreaded, and there was no way he could skirt it. "The man you saw staring at me in the gardens. The same one I went to meet the other night. His name is Merrill."

"How did he contact you? No one came to the room."

He hesitated, debating how to tell her. He finally decided on just saying it. "I heard him in my head."

"He can do that, too?" she asked in surprise.

"The Star People have that ability because they're so powerful. Merrill said it was something our kind can do, too."

Her mouth parted in shock. "You're telling me he's like you?"

Derek watched her carefully. "So he claims."

"You don't believe him."

"Why would I? Bryok and I can't talk mind-to-mind."

Kora wrinkled her nose. "That is a problem. Did you ask him anything?"

"I asked him a lot. He shared that our kind wasn't being held. He urged me to go check for myself."

Kora's throat moved as she swallowed. "Did you? Oh. I see. He could be telling the truth, but it might also be a trap."

"Exactly. I did contemplate it, though. I went and got close, but I didn't go through with it."

"You weren't ready to know the truth. Either way. If they are, indeed, free, it means you would have to face the fact that Villette has lied to you for your entire life. If it is a trap, then you would have to be looking over your shoulder constantly."

Derek shoved his hair out of his face. "As you have."

"You get used to it."

"Nay, you don't."

She smiled sadly. "Nay, you don't."

"Anyway, all that brought me back to Miena, saying my memories had been wiped."

"There's only one reason anyone would mess with someone's mind."

Whenever Derek thought about the people and places that could have been erased, or the person he might have been, he became enraged. "Merrill said the same."

"I can't imagine how I might feel if I thought someone had taken something from me like that."

"If Villette did it, she will pay. Regardless, you won't be fighting her alone. I'll be beside you."

Kora pulled the skewer of meat off the fire to hold between her hands. "Villette has a lot to answer for. If you don't want to see if your kind is being held or not, let me do it. I owe you. Tell me where to go. I won't have much time because of the dragons after me, but you can get us in and out quickly."

"I appreciate it more than you know." Because no one else would have offered. "But I have to see for myself. Merrill said a man named Constantine rules our kind. He urged me to talk to him through my mind."

"But you could be talking to anyone."

"That's why I'd prefer a face-to-face."

"That would be smart. The offer stands if you change your mind." She tore off a piece of meat, popped it into her mouth, and looked at him over the flames. "You never said what your race is."

CHAPTER 28

Kora took another bite. It hadn't escaped her notice that Derek had gone out of his way not to mention what he was. And she knew that, despite her asking, he didn't want to tell her. A flare of irritation rose. They were supposed to be earning trust. It wasn't happening fast, but it wouldn't happen at all if he held on to his secrets.

That made her ask herself why he didn't want to tell her. Was he uncomfortable? Scared? Worried? She had all those and more when she forced the words from her lips. He had given her time. It was only fair that she do the same for him.

Suddenly, his head snapped to the side, and his body went rigid. Kora immediately looked in his direction and listened. She strained to pick up any sounds but couldn't hear or see anything. She was about to ask him what he'd heard when he moved. One moment, he was on the other side of the fire. The next, he was beside her, hauling her to her feet.

He put his mouth by her ear. "Don't move. Don't make a sound. I'll be right back," he whispered.

Derek was gone before he finished speaking the last word. The panic in his words encased her in ice. She flattened herself against the tree's trunk and scanned the forest. There was still enough light from the sinking sun to see. The sounds of the woods continued around her. No predator stalked her. Tension eased out of her muscles, and she couldn't help but wonder if Derek had created an issue to keep from having to answer her.

He reappeared beside her, his hand wrapped around her arm. "We have to go. Now."

"Why?"

"The amethyst is gone."

She frowned at him. "What do you mean, gone? Show me."

"There isn't time," he said between clenched teeth. He moved to touch the cuff when a deep laugh rang out around them.

Kora stiffened at the same time a whiff of evil teased her nose. She couldn't figure out where the laugh had come from. When she turned back to Derek, she saw resignation in his eyes. And something else he quickly hid.

He slipped the cuff from his wrist and discreetly put it on hers. It was so big it nearly fell off. "Return to the city," Derek said in a soft voice. "Go to the room where Miena is and ask Daelya to tell you where to find the Druid, Katla."

"We go together," Kora insisted. She breathed through her mouth as the smell of wickedness grew.

Derek slowly shook his head. "There's no time. I'll keep Bryok occupied. Find Katla. Go after Villette together." He released her and took a step back. "Go," he mouthed.

"When are you going to learn?" asked a deep, gravelly voice that rang through the forest.

Derek turned at the same time a man with straight, flaxen hair that brushed his shoulders stepped from behind a tree. Kora stood frozen, staring at the newcomer's cold, blue eyes. He was dressed in the blue finery of Stonemore with a thick, hammered gold cuff at his wrist. The man was powerfully built and focused solely on Derek. And he reeked of evil.

She started to call to her flames and take out the man when Derek issued a low growl from beside her. She glanced over, and he shook his head at her. Kora frowned, but Derek was no longer looking her way.

"You continue to make the same missteps and mistakes over and over. How many times does Villette need to reset you before she washes her hands completely?" the man said.

Kora's lips parted in astonishment. Had she really heard him admit that Villette had taken Derek's memories? The man's frosty gaze slid to her. A tremor ran through her at his menacing glower. There was no way she was leaving Derek with this man. They would fight him together.

"You want a fight, Bryok? I'm right here," Derek goaded.

Bryok laughed again, the sound as cold as his eyes. "I've come for you both. But you knew that. The little hellhound can run, but I'll find her just as soon as I kill you. There will be nothing left when I'm done."

"Now, Kora!" Derek shouted.

She touched the cuff but didn't return to the city. Instead, she teleported to a limb high in a tree. Because no matter how much Bryok scared her, she would fight alongside Derek.

"A hellhound? Really, Derek. That's a new low, even for you," Bryok said.

Derek and Bryok slowly began circling each other. "You follow blindly without asking questions."

"I never understood what Villette saw in you. She gave us life. But regardless of what we've tried, you always turn on her. Time and again, no matter who you talk to, no matter where you are, you decide she's your enemy. She wanted me to bring you back, but I'm done cleaning up your messes. This ends today."

"You're right," Derek said. "It does. But with your death."

Kora's startled gasp rent the air as Bryok changed into a dragon with navy and gold scales, but it was drowned out by the groan of trees as they split and were thrown out of the way to accommodate his massive size. Bryok lunged at Derek, who transformed into the black-and-silver dragon. Kora's heart dropped to her feet at the sight, fear turning her blood to ice as she grasped what Derek was. She wanted to run, to flee, but she was frozen.

She was so immersed in her fear and the scene that she didn't realize the tree she was on had splintered. It moaned ominously before pitching to the side, sending her flying. She landed on her back; her breath knocked from her. Pain radiated through her. More creaking had her looking up in time to see a tree falling and coming right at her. Kora thought about being outside the forest and touched the cuff.

Breath finally filled her lungs. She rolled over into some tall grass and popped up on her knees to peer above it for another look at Derek and Bryok. Their roars boomed as they clashed with such force the earth shuddered. She spotted the two silver horns atop Derek's head that dripped with Bryok's blood. Derek shoved him.

Bryok slid backward, his long, navy talons scoring the ground.

He roared and sprang forward, his arm reared back as he descended. She watched in horror as four slashes opened on Derek's chest. He bellowed and whipped his tail at Bryok. Then, they were tangled together, rolling out of the forest toward her location. Kora took one more look at Derek and pictured the palace in her mind. Her finger hovered over the cuff as Derek's huge jaw locked onto Bryok's shoulder. She touched the metal.

The dragons' roars turned into the clamor of the city. Kora found herself standing in the corridor outside the stairway down into the mountain. She knew she needed to do something, but her mind got stuck on one simple fact: Derek was a dragon.

A *dragon.*

The sound of voices snapped her out of her musings. She turned to find the stairs that would take her to Daelya. Whether it was luck or some kind of divine intervention, Kora found the staircase almost immediately.

As she ascended, the tap of her boots on the steps made her think of the trees snapping. That brought back images of the dragons fighting. Her steps slowed, and her heart twisted with hurt and anger. Derek was a dragon. One with black-and-silver scales.

Her arm swung down, causing the cuff to bang heavily against her hand. She stretched out her fingers to keep it from falling off. She stopped and looked down at the silver. He had given it to her to escape Bryok. It was Derek who had protected her against the amethyst.

She thought about the dragon that had stood over her. Had that really been Derek? Or was she only imagining it was black scales in the fog?

Kora looked up the stairs and got moving again. She reached

the landing and paused when she heard voices headed toward her. She turned to the next flight and started up them, then kept going until there were no more. When she reached the top, she found herself in a hallway with arched, open-air windows looking out over the city. She glanced left and saw a doorway that led through another passageway. She turned to the right and saw a door down the hall. There wasn't a soul around anywhere, at least that she could see. It was like this section of the palace had been forgotten.

She turned right with the windows on her left and a solid stone wall on her other side. She proceeded cautiously down the corridor. It wasn't long before she noticed small cracks in the floor. The farther she went, the bigger they got. Then she spotted more fissures on the walls.

The closer she got to the door, the more fissures there were. The yawning door stood like a hand beckoning her forward. She stepped over the biggest fractures and slipped through the doorway.

The room was a disaster. The wall facing the city was gone, as was some of the floor. Everything had been blackened by what must have been an explosion. Or a fire. Dragon fire, perhaps? Derek's face came into her mind's eye, but she pushed it away and concentrated on the situation. The floor was littered with debris and dark splotches. Beneath it all, near the outer wall, were cracks big enough to make her wonder if the entire room was about to break apart.

Kora scanned the chamber and found two more doors. One on the opposite side of the room, and another to her right. Did one lead to where Miena and Daelya were being held?

A vision of Derek in dragon form, his mouth open and wings spread wide, flashed in her head. She closed her eyes to dispel the image. Instead, she saw the face of a dragon as she lay dying, red eyes looking down at her. The face became clearer. She saw the black scales tinged with silver.

Did that mean he'd carried her up the mountain? Dragons didn't do that.

Nor did they shift.

She gripped her head as her emotions tangled with facts. Kora wanted to scream. Had it all been a game? Was she nothing more than a pawn?

Had any of it been real?

She drew in a shaky breath and lowered her arms. The heft of the cuff was a constant reminder of Derek. She covered it with her hand and considered flinging it away. Then Derek's words whispered through her mind.

"I'll keep Bryok occupied. Find Katla. Go after Villette together."

Dragons hunted hellhounds. They didn't protect them.

Everything she thought she knew had been jumbled and shaken until she didn't know which way was up any longer. Kora smoothed her fingers over the braided metal at her wrist. The cuff had been Derek's way out. Why had he given it to her?

Why had he done any of the things he had?

Her stomach knotted so painfully she thought she might be sick. Then she remembered what Bryok had said about Derek's memories. She clung to that as if it were a lifeline. Derek's memories had been erased more than once; each attempt meant to turn him into whatever Villette wanted. Most likely, a copy of Bryok.

Anger swelled and returned to where it had always been. Villette. She had to be stopped. All of it needed to end.

Kora stepped over rock and rubble to the door nearest her. Her fingers wrapped around the handle, and she started to open it when it was suddenly yanked out of her hand and slammed shut.

"I wouldna do that, lass."

She turned her head and found herself looking into eyes of the darkest blue. The man had his dirty blond hair pulled away from his face as he watched her. But she recognized him. Derek had called him Merrill. But was he a friend or foe? "This doesn't concern you."

"That silver on your wrist is too big," he stated. "Did you steal it?"

She looked down at the cuff. Pain cut straight through her heart. Derek was a dragon. Derek had protected her.

Kora shook her head. "He put it on my arm and told me to find Daelya."

"Why?"

She lifted her gaze to him. "Why should I tell you anything?"

"Because I can help. If you'll let me." He lowered his arm from the door. "Lass, tell me where Derek is."

"Fighting a dragon." Hearing the words aloud made her wince. "He's one and never told me."

"Aye, he is. So am I."

She tensed, eyeing him suspiciously. She had been surrounded by dragons and never knew it. How many people had she passed, believing them to be human, when they were really dragons? It was too much to take.

Merrill sighed wearily. "If I wanted to harm you, you'd already be dead. Tell me where Derek is."

"I don't know. I'd never been there before."

"Take me to him."

"I'm here to find Katla." Even when she questioned Derek's

motives, she was still following his urging. "She's the one who hurt Villette."

Merrill kept his hand on the door. "And you can do just that. But first, take me to Derek so I can help him."

Kora wanted to believe Merrill was a friend, but she was drowning in doubts and panic. He was offering her support if only she was bold enough to take it. But even Derek hadn't known if he could trust Merrill.

"Shall I shift right here to prove what I am?" Merrill asked heatedly. "We doona have time for that. Take me to him before it's too late."

Kora might very well be bringing death upon herself, but she wanted to help Derek. Even if he was a dragon. She clutched Merrill's hand and tapped the cuff before she changed her mind. In the next heartbeat, roars fell like thunder around her, one on top of the other. She spotted Derek, who fought not just Bryok but also the amethyst dragon. She did a double take at the sight, but there was no denying. The dragon Derek had slain earlier was alive.

Merrill pulled out of her grasp and started running. He got two steps before he jumped into the air and shifted. The shock of seeing him turn into an orange dragon made her stumble back. Merrill flew straight up before tucking his wings against his large body and diving into the melee from the sky, going straight for the amethyst. Being around dragons in a fight was dangerous. Remaining while four were trying to kill each other was a death wish.

Kora sought out Derek. Blood spattered his scales, but she didn't know if it was his or another's. She had shared her bed with a dragon. Had given herself to him more completely than any other. And he hadn't killed her.

She jerked when Bryok threw Derek to the ground. He rose quickly, giving her time to see the wounds covering him. One wing was torn in half. She moved toward him without realizing it. What could she do against dragons? She didn't belong in that fight. Her quarry was elsewhere. Merrill had restored the odds. She had done what she needed.

Kora lingered for a second more and then returned to the room in the palace. She didn't hesitate to throw open the door this time. Heat blasted her, snatching her breath and drenching her in sweat.

"Well, well, well. The hellhound has finally arrived," said a voice from deep within the room. "What took you so long?"

Kora looked inside to find who she assumed was Miena chained and standing in thigh-deep lava, just as Derek had described. Kora scanned the rest of the room and located Daelya near the door. "Derek told me to find Katla. Will you tell me where she is?"

"All Derek had to do was release me, and I'd have taken care of our mutual enemy," Miena said. "Where is he, by the way?"

Kora wiped the sweat from her brow before it dripped into her eyes. "Fighting Bryok."

"Ah. I had hoped he might succeed in learning the truth this time." Miena shrugged, causing the chains to rattle loudly.

"What is the truth?"

"That is something he needs to discover on his own. It's the only way he'll believe it."

Kora now understood why Derek hadn't freed Miena. She turned her attention to Daelya. "Please. Can you help?"

CHAPTER 29

Derek was losing. Badly. He had been holding his own against Bryok, but then the amethyst he'd killed earlier returned. It was all he could do to stay alive and give Kora a chance to kill Villette, but he had few opportunities to make contact. His injuries barely healed before he sustained more. It got to a point where the magic couldn't heal him quickly enough.

He heard Merrill shouting his name in his head right before a deafening roar resounded above him. Derek glanced up to see orange scales diving straight for them. It gave him time to lean away as Merrill slammed into the amethyst dragon, sinking his talons into its scales.

Derek and Bryok were locked in combat. He whipped his tail around and thrust the barbed end in Bryok's back. The shout of pain that echoed around them was music to his ears. Derek yanked his tail out and rushed his foe. He flipped Bryok onto his side. Derek stepped on him with one foot and slashed at his face with his talons. The sound of scales splitting brought a wave of satisfaction, but it didn't last long.

Bryok got to his feet and engulfed Derek in fire. The flames licked hungrily at his injuries. The heat sizzled in his open wounds. His muscles locked in agony. Derek opened his wings and tried to fly, but the one hadn't healed yet, leading to a clumsy attempt that infuriated him. There was no getting away. He had to face the fact that he might not survive this battle.

Derek tried to fight against the pain, but he was too weakened. He wasn't ready to die. Not without seeing Kora one more time. He gathered the last ounce of his strength and slashed at Bryok, shredding and ripping more scales. The assault surprised Bryok enough to cut off the dragon fire. Derek didn't let up on the assault. He forced Bryok to stumble back. But then he made a mistake. He got too close. Bryok's teeth clamped down on his throat. Derek bellowed and tried to break free, but it was too late.

He was dying. There was no denying it. Derek let his thoughts drift to the only person who mattered to him—Kora. He should've told her the truth. Should've explained everything. He'd been a coward. All because he had developed feelings and didn't know what to do with them. He wished he could be there to see her take down Villette. Kora would win. He was sure of it.

Bryok swung his head from side to side, his teeth cutting through scales and into Derek's muscle and tendon down to the bone. Blood poured down his chest. The edges of his vision were beginning to darken. As his life was draining from him, all he could think about was Kora and the mistakes he had made.

Shame had kept him from telling her that he was a dragon. He deserved her loathing. She had every reason to hate him. Everyone did. He had taken innocent lives because someone told him to. He should've asked more questions, looked deeper for facts. He should've seen for himself if the dragons were imprisoned. There was so much regret that it nearly swallowed him whole.

But if he was going to die, then so was Bryok. Villette wouldn't send him after Kora.

Power Derek had never felt before surged through him. He slammed his hand against Bryok's head, raking his claws down the side. One of Derek's talons cut into his eye. Bryok's jaws immediately released him as he threw back his head and roared. Derek saw a thick, green liquid dripping from Bryok's teeth. When he raised a hand, that same liquid oozed down his talons. Derek didn't move back quickly enough as Bryok slashed his chest.

The power Derek had felt swelled and surged like a tidal wave. It flooded every neuron. He opened his mouth, but it wasn't dragon fire that spewed from him. It was ice. It targeted Bryok's head first, coating him in white. Bryok stiffened before shaking the ice away, but Derek layered more until Bryok's entire body was covered.

Derek put his hand to his still-bleeding neck and looked at his handiwork. Blood spurted between his fingers. He wasn't mending, and he didn't know why. Breathing was difficult. The pain was excruciating. He shifted to his human form, hoping that would start the healing process. His legs buckled. He landed hard on his knees and sat back on his haunches to look down at his chest. Four deep slashes ran from his left shoulder to his right hip.

He looked for Merrill and found him putting out the fires that had spread during their battle. The amethyst dragon lay dead once more. How long before he regained life? Would he?

"Would you like the honor?" Merrill asked as he walked up beside Bryok's frozen body.

Derek motioned for him to do it.

Merrill slammed his fist against Bryok. The ice cracked and began to split. Bryok's hand fell off, splintering into tiny pieces when it hit the ground. The gold cuff Villette had given him rolled near Derek. Bryok's jaw was next. The cracks continued over his body as pieces fell off and broke apart. Derek hadn't just frozen him from the outside. He was solid all the way through.

"You should be healing," Merrill stated, worry tinging his words.

Derek felt himself falling to the side. Merrill grabbed him and held him upright.

"Why the fuck are you no' healing?" Merrill demanded.

Derek shook his head and tried to keep his eyes open. He attempted to talk, but his throat was too damaged. He sought Merrill through their mental link. *I think I was poisoned.*

"I know someone who can help."

He put a hand on Merrill's arm and nodded to the cuff. *Put it on. Picture where you want to go. Touch it, and it'll take you there.*

"Great. Now, come on."

Nay. Kora needs you.

"You need me," Merrill argued.

Derek shook his head. *There's no saving me. I can feel the poison in my blood.*

"You're no' going to fucking die. I'm no' going to allow it."

Derek didn't have the energy to argue. He fought to keep his eyes open long enough to watch Merrill slip on the cuff.

Dragon Land

. . .

"Co–!"

At the sound of Merrill's interrupted bellow, Constantine's head jerked up from the table where he had been poring over maps. *"Merrill?"* he called, but there was no reply.

"What is it?" Rhi asked.

He swung his gaze at the sound of the Irish accent to look into the silver eyes of his Fae mate. "It was Merrill."

"Is he returning?"

The hope in her voice cut through Con because it was the same optimism everyone had. He, more than any of them. "He was shouting my name, but it was cut off. Something's wrong."

"We know where we have to go, then," she stated, lifting her chin.

He faced Rhi. Her long, black hair hung loose down her back. She wore her usual all-black attire, from leather pants to a body-hugging shirt that molded to her seductive curves. He cupped her cheek. She closed her eyes and leaned into his palm.

"If we go to Stonemore, it starts the verra war Villette wants," he said. They had fought enough battles. He wanted peace, but too many worked against that.

Rhi's lids opened to look at him. "Then perhaps you and the other Dragon Kings don't go."

"Doona say it," he began and dropped his hand to his side.

"Leave things to me and the other mates."

He shook his head. "I can no'."

"You forget, we have our own Star Person. Lotti has made great strides in learning the extent of her powers."

"But is she ready to face Villette again?"

"We may not have a choice."

Con blew out a breath. Merrill was in trouble. It was time they brought their brother home. "Talk to Lotti. I'll alert the Kings."

"Derek."

The voice came from far away. He thought he recognized it, but the throbbing in his chest consumed him.

"Open your eyes, Derek. Now."

Rage dripped from each word, but something else niggled in the back of Derek's mind. Something that sent a prickle of wariness through him, snatching him from the comforting hands of oblivion. He lifted his lids, shaken to find himself alive. Had Merrill found someone to heal him? Derek moved his arm and quickly clamped his teeth together to hold back a shout of pain. Then a face moved into his line of sight.

He caught his breath, thinking it was Kora. The image cleared, and he found himself looking into the murderous rage flaring in Villette's blue eyes. Any hope of a future or happiness instantly evaporated. Her lips were pinched, her face a mask of cold fury. She turned her back to him.

"You." The one word spoke volumes. "How dare you go against me? You think yourself a King. I'll show you what real power is."

Derek frowned. He didn't know what she was talking about. He had never thought himself a *king*.

"I did warn you."

"Fuck off."

Shock slammed into Derek at the sound of the voice. He turned his head to the side to find Merrill on his knees beside him, straining as if held by invisible bonds. Derek searched for the power he had used against Bryok, but he couldn't find it now. Or any of his magic.

"I sacrificed Bryok for this." Villette laughed then. "Who knew it would be so easy to get the cuff on you? You're mine now, Merrill. You have to obey me."

Derek might not have his power, but he could still move, though it was painful. He reached out to tear the gold from Merrill's wrist, but Villette slapped his hand away.

"As for you," she said, "apparently, wiping your memories isn't enough. You've left me no choice." She glanced at Merrill. "Pick him up. You'll carry him back to the palace."

The knot of anxiety in Kora's stomach continued to expand and tighten. She had used Derek's cuff to return to their room and change into Stonemore clothing to blend in. Now, she walked the streets, searching for Katla. It had taken some doing, but Daelya had eventually given Kora a description of Katla, as well as an approximate location.

Kora looked at every woman with long, black hair. There were quite a few, but nearly all wore Stonemore blue. Maybe Daelya had gotten Katla's location wrong. Miena hadn't been happy that Daelya had given over the details. Daelya could have lied. Or perhaps Katla hadn't reached the sixth level yet.

It was Kora's third pass on the street when she paused. She had assumed Katla would head straight to the palace, but she hadn't. She had taken time to get to know the city. Maybe Katla was doing the same. Kora changed her tactics and started looking inside each business.

Searching for anyone not wearing blue was the easiest way to pick out an outsider. She went up one side of the street and moved to the other. Her anxiety and dread ramped up with each place she came up empty. Kora stepped into a tavern and scanned the space quickly. As she was turning away, she spotted a white top that caused her to do a double take. There, at a table toward the back, sitting with her back to the wall, was a woman with long, black hair.

Anticipation spiked through Kora. She wove around chairs and people to halt beside the table. She waited until the woman lifted her gaze. Kora smiled when she stared into the steely gray eyes Daelya had described.

"May I help you?" she asked in a strange accent.

Kora nodded. "I think you can. I'm Kora. Mind if I sit?"

"I do, actually. State your business."

"We have a common enemy."

"I doubt that," the woman stated and looked away.

Kora stared at her face and said, "Villette."

Katla's gaze slid back to her. "Seems I was mistaken." She motioned to the chair. "Sit, please."

Kora sank onto the chair and looked across the table at her potential ally. "Whatever you did to Villette weakened her. I'm going after her, and I'd like you to join me."

"Why should I trust you? Villette might have sent you."

It was the same thing Kora had said to Merrill a short time ago. "I understand your hesitation. I have a difficult time trusting, too. I'll put it bluntly." She glanced around and lowered her voice as she leaned closer. "I can kill her."

"And I'm to believe that...why? Her kind is particularly hard to destroy."

"Besides another Star Person, hellhounds are the only beings that can kill a Star Person. Villette hunted my people to near extinction. I'm the last of my kind."

Katla idly drummed her fingers on the table. "I've never heard of hellhounds."

"And I've never heard of a Druid. Yet, here we are."

Katla eyed her before bowing her head slightly. "Go on."

"Villette imprisoned her sister, Miena, in the palace. There is also a human in the room with a talent for sensing..." Kora glanced around, realizing where she was. "Us," she finally said. "Daelya told me your name, what you looked like, and where I could find you."

One of Katla's dark brows lifted. "Or it was Villette."

Kora tried not to let her distrust get to her, but time was of the essence. She lowered her voice to just above a whisper. "Villette used Daelya to uncover who was different and send that information to the priests, who used it to find the individuals—mostly children—who are then sacrificed."

Katla's fingers curled into fists, and her eyes blazed with the promise of a reckoning.

"Exactly," Kora said. "She has to be stopped. I'm going after her. Will you help me or not?"

Katla pushed her chair back, stood, and started walking away. She stopped and looked over her shoulder. "Are you coming?"

CHAPTER 30

Pain sizzled through Derek. Sweat covered him, and his vision went in and out of focus. He longed for unconsciousness, for any relief from the unrelenting throbbing of his wounds. Villette had healed his throat. He didn't know why. But she hadn't touched any of his other injuries.

He lay on a table in a gaping cavern. He wasn't bound but soon learned why when he attempted to rise. He could barely lift his head. The rest of his body wouldn't obey him. Worse, he still couldn't command his magic. He didn't know what was coming but knew it would be painful.

There was no sign of Kora. Had she found Villette? Had they fought? Derek refused to believe she was dead. He would feel it if she were.

"The poison worked to perfection," Villette said.

Her voice was close, but he couldn't make her out. Derek blinked several times to get his eyes to focus, but nothing helped.

He should've known Villette was responsible for the poison. He closed his hands into fists, imagining they were around her neck, squeezing.

Villette's fingers trailed down his arm. He tried to jerk away but only managed to cause himself more pain. Even breathing was pure agony. Regret threatened to choke him. If only he had helped Kora when she went after Villette. If only he had been honest with her from the beginning. If only...

"Bryok actually believed he would win against you," Villette continued. "He claimed he didn't need the poison to best you. I, of course, insisted. He never went against me. Not in all the eons we had together." She paused, her voice turning cold. "Unlike you. Why do you keep opposing me?"

"Because no matter what you do to me, I always see you for who you really are," Derek answered.

She snorted. "So did Bryok. Much sooner than you. That's what confuses me. He never cared about my true motives. All he wanted was to serve me."

"He couldn't think for himself."

"And you can?"

"Aye," Derek bit out.

Villette laughed softly as her fingers trailed down his bare leg to his ankle and then onto the next leg as she walked around the table. "You've not asked me why I keep you around. You've not asked why I sacrificed Bryok for you."

"I don't care." It wasn't true. He was desperate to know, but he wouldn't give her the satisfaction of asking.

"You're more powerful, but you've never known it. Not until today. I didn't give you the ability of ice. That came from within you. I had to enhance Bryok. But not you."

Derek stared upward at a ceiling he couldn't see because of his fuzzy eyesight. He had other senses, though. He strained to hear something that would tell him where he was but couldn't hear anything past Villette. It seemed his hearing was as affected as his eyesight. He tried to smell and failed in that, too. Fear coiled within him.

Villette reached his arm and stopped next to his shoulder. She leaned down so her lips were near his ear. "You are my weapon. In the past, I was careful when erasing your memories for fear of going too deep. I had hoped I wouldn't have to do this again, but the time has come for me to use you as I've always intended."

He went still as unease slithered through him. "Haven't I killed enough humans for you?"

"Oh, sweet Dederick," she said with a laugh as she straightened. "Your time harassing mortals is over. I'm going to send you across the border to the dragons. As you've always deduced, I've lied about them being held against their will. The Star People once enslaved the dragons and forced them to serve us. Until my meddling brother, Redis, decided they should be free."

All the breath left Derek. Merrill had spoken true. The dragons had been free all along. He'd known it, but he had been afraid to accept it. Because that would make him take a hard look at what he had done for Villette.

"Redis told no one what he planned. He created a new world just for the dragons. Somehow, he even managed to keep its location secret from the rest of us. So, we had no idea where to look when he facilitated their escape. Keeping Earth secret required all the magic Redis had. He readily gave his life to free the dragons and give them a home. They were slaves." She blew out a harsh breath. "In the end, I found Earth. It took me a very long time, but

I located it. And I intended to punish every dragon for leaving." She paused and barked a laugh. "I could have killed every one of them right there. With a snap of my fingers, I could've disintegrated the realm. But that would have been too easy. They needed to suffer."

A jolt of surprise went through Derek. There was another realm of dragons. Hunted by Villette, who he had killed for.

Her hands slammed down on the table near the top of Derek's head as she leaned over him. "It required patience. I planned down to the tiniest detail and wove such an intricate plot that no one could figure it out. Not even the great Constantine."

Derek flattened his lips at the name. It was no coincidence that Merrill had given him that name. If only he had reached out to Con as Merrill urged. Maybe he wouldn't be in this fiasco. His regrets kept coming.

Villette shrugged. "I could regale you with the details of my plot, but suffice it to say, I made sure the dragons and every King would be wiped from existence."

He waited for her to continue as she straightened and slowly walked around the table again. Then it came to him. "But your plan didn't work."

"I had contingencies if something went wrong."

"Which it did," Derek said with a smile. He couldn't wait to meet Con.

Villette pressed on his chest wounds. Derek bit his tongue, holding back the shout of pain. It felt as if his bones were disintegrating, and the very flesh was being eaten away.

"Don't be an ass," she told him. "I caused a great war on Earth. The Dragon Kings chose to send their own away rather than slaughter humans. All because they vowed not to harm them. The dragons came here, to Zora. Something led them here, but I have yet to figure out what that was. I followed and very quickly brought the first human to repeat what had happened on Earth. Except, this time, the Kings weren't here to lead the dragons." Her face was near his again. "Now, you're going to Con. Once he trusts you, you'll kill every dragon."

"Never," he stated.

She sighed wearily. "Do you have any idea how long it took to create you?"

Create? Had she just said *create*? Derek's mind went numb. He didn't have a family. He hadn't been born. He had been crafted by Villette's twisted mind and magic.

"Golds and Silvers are the largest of all dragons," she continued. "They are the only ones who can be the King of Dragon Kings. It's why I gave silver to you and gold to Bryok. Both of you needed that added potency to carry out the plan."

It took two tries before he found his voice. "And the eggs I've been guarding? You created those, too, didn't you?"

"That's right," she said, a smile in her voice. "There were six in all. It took so much power to get three of the eggs to hatch. One came out deformed. It had to be destroyed."

Derek's mind buzzed with denial and rage.

"The next steps in the plan were bypassed, thanks to Lotti."

He stored that name in his mind to find out who the woman was—if he remembered when Villette was finished with him this time. Would he remember his name? Who he was? What about Kora? Surely, he wouldn't forget her and his feelings for her. But what if he did? How long would it take for him to remember who he was?

Then another thought made him forget all the rest. What if Villette sent him to kill Kora?

"Lotti pushed up the timeline, so I didn't have a chance to get the other eggs hatched. But you'll be enough. And I have Merrill now." She laughed, then sighed longingly. "I never thought I would crave a Dragon King so. He wears the cuff now. That makes him mine. Now and forever."

Derek wanted to shift and roar, burn the entire city. Rip Villette limb from limb and crush what was left of her into dust.

"You want to kill me." She traced a finger across his cheek. "I can see it blazing in your eyes. I hope you enjoyed your freedom because it's all you will ever know. The dragons once belonged to the Star People, and the few I allow to live will serve us again."

"Kora will kill you."

"Oh, I've been waiting for you to mention her," Villette said excitedly. "Star People, dragons, and hellhounds. We three are bound for eternity. We all can kill our own, but only hellhounds can kill my kind, and Star People are the only ones who can slay Dragon Kings. And," she said with a smile in her voice, "dragons are the only ones who can exterminate hellhounds. Guess who I'm sending to take Kora's life."

He shook his head. It was just as he feared. "I won't do it."

"Oh, you'll do it, and you'll smile when you do. There will be nothing of Kora left in your head by the time I'm finished."

"Do you *ever* shut up?" Merrill asked irritably.

Derek rolled his head in the direction he thought Merrill was. He made out a silhouette against the wall.

"Bloody hell, woman, you do love the sound of your own fucking voice," Merrill said. "It's grating and annoying. You just drone on and on."

Derek smiled. Almost immediately, Villette's fingers were in his wounds again. This time, Derek couldn't hold back his bellow of agony. His body stiffened in pain. The edges of his vision began to blacken. He went limp when Villette removed her hand.

"You bitch," Merrill said. "If you're pissed at me, come take it out on me."

Her boot heels clicked as they moved toward Merrill. "Oh, I intend to, lover."

"You sure?" he taunted. "You're using a lot of magic to hide those burns I know still haven't healed."

Derek struggled to get his pain under control when Merrill groaned in anguish. A few moments later, Villette gasped and stumbled back a few steps.

"I'll get this fucking cuff off, and when I do, I'm going to make you pay for this," Merrill vowed, his breath coming in gasps

Villette's voice held a note of pain when she said, "It'll never come off. I'll make sure of it."

"We'll see about that."

Derek licked his dry lips. Villette was still weak—probably weaker than they realized. Derek might not be getting up from the table, but he could help Merrill—if there was time before Villette wiped his memories.

"Merrill?"

"Aye. I'm here."

"She's weak. We need to keep her that way so she can't take my memories."

Merrill's laughter filled his head. *"Got it."* Aloud, he said, "Where are your brothers and sisters? Why are none of them trying to enslave the dragons again?"

"Who says they aren't?" Villette replied.

"Well, Miena, for one."

Derek might not be able to see Villette, but he felt her fury.

"You dared to speak to her," she stated.

There was a grin in Merrill's voice when he said, "We had a nice, long conversation about you."

Villette's shout of anger bounced off the walls. Derek heard Merrill's grunts, and then Villette went silent.

"She's gone," Merrill said. "She can't control her anger. When she lashed out at me, it took the magic she was using to heal and hide the burns."

Derek heard the pain in his voice. "We need to keep using that."

"Aye."

"You okay?"

Merrill chuckled softly. "I'm a damn sight better than you. At least I'm healing."

"Can you get to me? I can remove the cuff."

"She has me chained to the wall."

Derek tried to roll over. The movement sent a surge of pain through him and had him gasping for breath. He heard Merrill call his name as he slipped into oblivion.

CHAPTER 31

Kora was three steps behind Katla as they neared the door. She had many questions for the woman, including what a Druid was, but Kora knew it didn't matter in the end. None of it did. The important thing was finding Villette and making sure her reign came to an end. It had been foolish for Kora to think she could take down Villette on her own.

Katla suddenly halted. Kora slowed on reflex and tried to see around the other woman. Katla rapidly pivoted to the right, moved to an empty table behind a boisterous group, and sat. Kora took the chair next to Katla and searched the tavern to find what had spooked the Druid.

"What's going on?" Kora asked.

Katla's lips were pinched as she swung her gaze to Kora. "This isn't a safe place."

"Then we should go."

Katla's hand covered Kora's arm as she started to rise. "Not yet."

"We're not safe anywhere in this city," Kora said.

Katla didn't answer. Instead, she ordered drinks.

Neither said anything until the beverages were delivered. Kora didn't want to sit there. She *wanted* to look for Villette. And Derek. Not knowing what had happened when she last saw him was driving her to distraction. She had to turn her mind off. Kora lifted the mug of ale to her lips and pretended to drink. "What are we waiting on?"

"I'm not sure," Katla said as she surreptitiously looked around the tavern as if searching for someone. "A feeling."

Kora accepted that answer. "How do you know our mutual enemy?"

"She wanted a war with the dragons. My people lived at the northern border with them. She sent raiders, and we ran to the only place we could."

"The border," Kora said softly. Toward dragons. She barely held back a shiver, imagining being surrounded by the beasts. Then she thought of Derek and Merrill. Maybe not all were beasts. The line that had so clearly been marked was blurred now, and she didn't know how she felt about that.

Katla nodded and turned her head to the side, listening to something from someone behind her. Then she sighed. "I believed I had watched my husband and daughter get devoured by dragon fire."

With those words, Kora was taken back to the day her brother, uncle, and cousin died. She could still hear their screams, still smell the burned flesh.

"Of my entire village, I was the only one left," Katla continued.

"I was consumed with levels of grief and rage you can't even begin to understand."

"I can."

Katla met her gaze. "I think maybe you can." She looked away. "Villette came to me and offered a solution. I didn't hesitate to accept it, not thinking beyond my pain and misery. That beautiful, fertile valley turned into a forest of vines so tall and dense they blocked the sun. Any dragon who ventured into it was trapped. The moment they were inside my domain, I handed them over to Villette."

"For what?"

"I believe she killed them. It's what I wanted. I intended to wipe out every one of the creatures."

Had Kora known, she would've been right there beside Katla. But then she wouldn't have met Derek or learned that not all dragons are the same. She wouldn't have known the taste of Derek's kisses or the safety of his arms.

"I paid no attention to the passage of time. I didn't realize thousands of years had come and gone until a woman rushed into the vines to save a young, pink dragon."

Katla's voice was so low that Kora barely heard the words. She leaned closer.

"That's how I learned that some dragons can change forms. The Dragon Queen fought against the vines' hold, and she wasn't alone. A man came after her. He's the one who figured out what had been done to me. He got the Queen out before Villette came for her."

"And?" Kora urged, needing to know the ending.

"I learned a lot that day. He called me a Druid."

Katla said the word slowly as if still testing it out.

"I confronted Villette, and she admitted everything. Even laughed about it. So, when the dragons and the others stood against her, I joined them."

Kora frowned and sat back. "After what they did to your family?"

Katla's gray gaze briefly slid away. "The one I believed had killed my husband and daughter actually saved them. She took them somewhere safe where they lived and thrived. While I was buried in revenge. We're the ones who crossed the border. Villette instigated that. She knew what the dragons would do. One did attack—the invaders, not my people. I trapped thousands of them to give to Villette, and somehow, they forgave me."

Forgiveness wasn't something Kora believed she could bestow upon those who had slain her family and people. Villette might have sent the dragons after hellhounds, but the dragons could have refused. She thought about Derek. Villette had filled his mind with lies. It made sense that she would do that to others, as well. Including dragons that killed hellhounds.

With that thought came another, one she wished hadn't formed. But once it was there, she couldn't stop thinking about it. Derek served Villette, and she had erased his memories. Could that mean he might have been one of the dragons who'd hunted her people?

She was too young to remember what the dragon that had attacked their village looked like, but she knew he wasn't the one who'd killed her brother, uncle, and cousin.

And if it had been him?

That wasn't an easy question to answer. She had uncovered some of Villette's treachery, and there was likely much more. Derek was part of that. Possibly unwilling. Did that make him less culpable if he killed hellhounds on Villette's orders? Before she knew him, she would have replied with a resounding, "*Aye*." Now, she didn't know.

It was difficult to reconcile the man she believed he was with the dragon she now knew him to be. He had stood against the amethyst for her. He had fought Bryok so she could get away. That wasn't even factoring in Merrill, who she didn't know at all. Yet he didn't hesitate to side with Derek. That had to mean something, didn't it?

And if she believed Derek had sided against Villette, then she had to believe he was a good man. Er...dragon. Since she had shared her body with him, and, if she were honest, her authentic self, then she had to admit that not every dragon was the fiend she had always believed them to be.

"We have to go. Now," Katla whispered urgently.

Kora rose to her feet. Katla quickly moved through the tavern. Someone pushed back a chair and cut Kora off. She had to go around another table and was nearly upon Katla when armored priests abruptly spilled through the entrance. Kora slid behind a pillar to hide. The conversation in the tavern went silent almost immediately.

"May I help you?" Katla's voice rang out, even and calm.

Kora winced. She peered around the post to find the Druid surrounded. A tall, stocky priest stepped forward and got right in her face. Katla didn't back down.

"We've come to detain you," the priest stated loudly.

"Have I broken some law by drinking ale?"

"You have magic."

Kora frowned. How could they know that? Daelya was still locked away with Miena. Unless Villette had someone else telling her about those with abilities. But then, wouldn't Villette have known about her when she arrived with Derek? She decided it had to be the priests looking for an excuse to take someone into custody. Yet it appeared as if they had singled Katla out.

"Do I?" Katla asked. "How interesting. And what did I do that was magical?"

"You know what you did," the priest replied.

"Since I've not done anything with magic, I believe I have a right to know."

"You have no rights in Stonemore. Take her!"

Kora could do nothing but watch in horror as the priests roughly grabbed Katla and dragged her out of the tavern. Just before Katla was through the door, she looked back and met Kora's gaze. Kora flattened her back against the support beam and tried to remain calm.

The conversation in the tavern returned as if nothing had happened. She soon realized they were celebrating Katla's capture. Kora had to get out without notice and preferably without any priests spotting her. She smiled and clapped with the others as she made her way to the door.

Once outside, Kora strolled leisurely through the streets. The moment she came to an alley, she ducked into it and touched the cuff to take her to the one place no one would think to look for her —the palace.

CHAPTER 32

Villette barely made it to her room before her legs gave out. She hit the floor so hard it jarred her body, creating more waves of pain. It snatched her breath and forced her limbs to go rigid. She couldn't stop herself as she fell to the side, slamming a blistered shoulder into the stone floor. She screamed—the only release she had.

Beings of such power didn't fall unconscious. There was no peaceful oblivion while the body healed. There was only constant torment. The persistent and unending pain as her body fought to heal the damage from the mixture of magic she had been doused with.

There had been little recovery in the days since she'd faced off with Katla, the dragons, and their mates. If she hadn't managed to get away, she would have died that day. But Villette had survived, and she had to heal. Too many things were at play for her to let them fall to the wayside simply because she wasn't at full strength.

She couldn't keep distributing her magic as she had been if she intended to heal. She needed all of it for herself. But if she stopped, it would leave Stonemore defenseless. And give her many enemies time to reach her.

But what choice did she have? She couldn't fight them off as she was. She couldn't even stand against Merrill and Derek at the moment. She had let her anger get the best of her and shown them weakness.

She could use that to her advantage, however. They wouldn't expect her to take the day or so she needed to fully regenerate. So, when she faced them again, they would still think her weakened.

Villette smiled through the pain. She couldn't wait to see the shock on their faces right before she scrubbed Derek's mind for the last time. Between him and Merrill, Con and the other Dragon Kings didn't stand a chance.

Everything she had set in motion millions of years ago was about to come to fruition. Her patience and planning had been worth every setback, every loss. Once the dragons were back under the Star People's control, her family could be whole again.

With a few minor adjustments. Miena and Lotti would have to die, but no one would miss them.

Villette looked at the bed. She tried to teleport herself from the floor to the mattress, but pain overwhelmed her power. She rolled to her hands and knees and crawled. Each movement was agonizing, but she didn't give up. No matter how many times her arms gave out, no matter how often she was overcome by anguish and screamed to release it, she kept getting up.

By the time she reached the bed, she was drenched in sweat and shaking from the exertion. She pulled herself to her feet, using the bed for assistance. Then, with slow, measured movements, she sat on the mattress and lay back.

Villette began to call her magic to her, piece by piece. She kept Merrill and Derek locked away and didn't touch the door leading to Miena, but everything else stopped.

As her power returned, she was able to breathe easier, and her body started to heal.

CHAPTER 33

Nothing felt right. Kora stood before the door where Miena and Daelya were but couldn't lift her hand to reach for it. At one time, she'd had Derek, Merrill, and Katla ready to help her. The Druid was now in the priests' hands, and Kora didn't know how Derek and Merrill fared or if they were even still alive. Surely, they would've returned to the city by now if they had been victorious.

Once more, everything rested solely on her shoulders. Perhaps it was the universe telling her this was how it was always meant to be. It made it easy for Kora not to have to think too hard about trusting Derek now that she knew he was a dragon. Her family would be outraged to know she'd had any kind of relationship with dragons.

But her family wasn't here. She was. She was the one making the decisions—the kind with no right choices. There only seemed to be bad and worse. Kora didn't know what that said about her, but there wasn't time to delve into that now. Maybe later. If she survived. Now, she had to focus on Villette.

Kora reached for the door handle and dropped her hand. She reached a second time but still couldn't close her fingers around the lever. She had already opened the door and spoken to both Miena and Daelya. What was the problem now?

She fisted her hand and lowered her arm to her side. It had to be Miena. As a Star Person, she posed the greatest threat. Although, she also claimed to want Villette. So, what was the problem? It wasn't as if Kora could release her.

Or could she?

What if she could free Miena? Sure, no Star Person could be trusted, but none of the others were siding with Villette. In fact, Miena wanted to stop her sister. Why not use that?

On the other hand, neither Merrill nor Derek had released Miena. That had to mean something. Or was it that they just didn't trust her? Kora didn't trust Miena at all, but sometimes, a person had to side with the lesser evil for a win.

All of it might be for naught. Kora didn't know if Miena could be released, and the only way to find out was to open the door. She flexed her hand before reaching out. Unease weighed on her, but she didn't stop. She wrapped her fingers around the handle, released a sigh, and pulled.

The door didn't budge. In fact, it felt as if something was sucking it shut. She frowned. Now that she had touched it, the apprehension that'd gripped her tapered off, but it wasn't gone completely.

She propped a foot on the wall and used both hands to pull. Her entire body strained against whatever held the door shut. She leaned as far back as she could, smoke wafting around her. The flames wanted to be released, but burning the door wasn't an option. It was there for a reason, and she wouldn't be the cause of it being destroyed.

Kora was about to give up when the door finally gave way. She quickly put her foot down, barely catching herself before falling. She shook out her arms and stared at the now-open door. Her grip was sure when she wrapped her fingers around the lever the next time. The door swung open more with barely a tug.

Kora spotted Daelya first. She stood against the wall, as limp as her strawberry-blond hair. Daelya's hazel gaze immediately slid to Miena. Kora moved to stand between the exit and the doorway to look at the Star Person.

"What could possibly bring you back to us?" Miena asked. "Is it perhaps because you lost Katla?"

Kora glanced at Daelya. She didn't blame her for telling Miena what was going on outside the palace walls. Kora would be hard-pressed to remain silent while alone with someone for weeks on end. "I didn't lose her."

"Right. The priests have her now. I wonder what they'll do to her."

The smile that filled Miena's face sent a chill through Kora. "She can take care of herself."

"More than you realize."

"What's that supposed to mean?"

Miena shrugged, making the chains rattle. "I doubt you came for a rousing conversation on the merits of uncovering things for yourself. Why are you here?"

"I want Villette's location."

Miena's bright green eyes flared with something before she looked away. "You still intend to go after her?"

"I'm a hellhound. She's weakened. It's the perfect time to strike."

"Not on your own. You need help."

Kora wiped the sweat from her forehead by swiping her face on her shoulder. "I came for her location."

"You need me."

Kora had known she would say it, but it didn't stop the chill from running through her a second time. "How do I know you won't betray me?"

"You don't."

"How do I know you won't take her place?"

Miena laughed. "Do you have any idea how many worlds there are? Can you even fathom the sheer size of the universe? Why would I stay when there are so many other places to visit and see? Are any of my siblings here? Don't you think they would do something if they were?"

To trust Miena was like embracing the sun and expecting it not to consume her. It wasn't a question of *if* Miena would betray her. It was a matter of *how* and *when*.

No one else was going after Villette. Vengeance had once pushed Kora toward Stonemore, but that emotion no longer ruled her. There were so many other reasons to bring an end to Villette's rule. And if Kora had to side with someone as wicked as Villette to do it, then so be it.

"And there it is," Miena said with a triumphant smile. "You recognize I can help. Now, do the right thing and release me."

Kora glanced at the lava. "How?"

"You're a hellhound. How do you think?"

"I can't walk through that. I might have fire within me, but that doesn't mean I can't be killed by it."

Miena rolled her eyes and sighed dramatically. "Must I explain everything? Dragon fire kills hellhounds. You can survive lava."

What if she couldn't? Then no one could take down Villette. Kora swallowed and considered Miena. She wanted out. Would she really put Kora's life in danger on the off chance she'd survive? That would never serve Miena's purposes. Which meant Kora really would survive.

She looked at Daelya. "I'm not stepping into the room unless you're here at the door, keeping it open."

"Forget the damn door," Miena snapped. "Once free, I can take us anywhere."

Kora felt the weight of the cuff against her wrist when she moved her arm. She had her own way out. She kept forgetting that.

"Are you insane?" Miena shouted. "Take the cuff off!"

"It's Derek's. It belongs to him," Kora argued.

Miena's nostrils flared with anger. "By all that is sacred. You humans are imbeciles. Who do you think made that piece of tasteless jewelry?"

Kora's eyes lowered to the silver cuff. "Villette."

"Aye. Which means she has sway over whoever wears it."

Kora immediately yanked it off. It tumbled through the air before hitting the ground and rolling to Daelya's feet.

"Kick it in the lava," Miena ordered.

Daelya looked at Kora. "She's right. It needs to be destroyed."

It was Kora's last link to Derek. She didn't know if she would ever see him again. She wanted to hold on to anything that belonged to him but couldn't put herself in a situation where Villette could control her. "Do it."

She watched the cuff sail through the air after Daelya reared back her foot and kicked it. It landed atop the moving magma and held for a heartbeat before the silver turned liquid and flowed into the red-orange river.

Chains rattled. "Time to free me, hellhound."

Kora lifted her head and took a deep breath. Every instinct told her not to leave the door unguarded, but she walked into the room. She jerked as the door banged shut loudly behind her. She didn't turn to look at it. She had made her decision, and the only way to see what happened next was to move forward. Her steps inched toward the lava, but she stopped at the edge.

"Call your fire," Miena urged.

Kora sought the fire inside her. Her skin cracked, revealing the flames beneath before engulfing her body.

Miena smiled and motioned her forward. "Now, walk."

Kora's clothes had disintegrated, along with her boots. She lifted her bare foot and set it in the magma. Nothing happened. She took another step, still expecting pain. Once again, there was nothing.

"I told you," Miena stated. "Trust what I say."

There wasn't a chance in all the universe that would happen, but Kora kept that to herself. Let Miena believe she had earned her trust. It might take Kora a few times to learn a lesson, but she *did* learn.

She waded through the magma as it deepened, rising to her ankles, then her calves and knees, finally halting at her thighs where it was the deepest. But why lava? There had to be a reason Villette had used it to hold her sister. Could it be to deter anyone who tried to get to Miena? That seemed too simple.

"The chains are locked below me," Miena instructed as Kora neared.

She looked at the flowing lava. "Below?"

"You'll have to go under."

"For?"

Miena shrugged. "I don't know what's there. I woke up to find myself here. First and last time my sister will get the better of me."

"Why lava, though?"

"Because my sister is a bitch."

Kora couldn't argue that point. But that hadn't really answered the question. "Villette doesn't do anything without a reason."

"You'll have to ask her if you want to know."

Kora was sure Miena was lying. Something about the lava bothered her, but since Miena stood in the middle of it, looking fresh and beautiful, it couldn't be pain. If not that, then what?

When Kora reached Miena, she walked around her for a better look. Then she traced the chains from Miena's wrists into the magma. Kora had to kneel, but even that wasn't enough for her to reach the end. She glanced at Miena before sucking in a breath and putting her head in the river of fire. Kora followed the chains down with her hand until she found where they disappeared beneath a small mound that Miena stood upon. Kora surfaced and gulped in air.

"It didn't work. I'm still chained," Miena snapped, angrily yanking again and again at the bindings.

Kora shot her a dark look and dove into the lava again. She swam down to the mound and felt around until she found a space big enough for her arm to fit through. She put her hand inside the opening and patted around until she found where the chains were gathered.

Something thin was coiled around the chains. Kora slowly began to loosen whatever it was. It was so long, and twisted so many times, that she had to come up for air twice before she pulled it free. She held it as the chains went lax.

Kora breached the surface to find Miena gone and the chains floating atop the magma. Daelya let out a sigh when she saw her. Kora got to her feet and looked down at her hand to see a small pink flower with eight slim petals. It hadn't withered in the lava. What was the flower, and what made it so special that it had been used to hold Miena's chains?

Kora walked to Daelya. "I guess I should've seen that coming."

No sooner were the words out than the door was yanked off its hinges and tossed away. Kora's clothes once more covered her body. Miena filled the doorway in a body-hugging green dress that matched her eyes, her long, black waves pulled elegantly away from her face.

"Come," she said to Kora. "I've waited a long time to bring my sister to her knees."

CHAPTER 34

The tormented screams pierced the silence in a never-ending cycle. Derek turned his head to the side and squeezed his eyes closed against reverberations of terror and agony so great they skimmed over his body like fingers seeking to grab hold.

"Derek!"

He tried to get back to the dream where he was with Kora and his pain was gone. She had vanished the moment the screams began. Where was she? He ached for her. It was a soul-deep yearning.

But he knew where Kora was. She hunted for Villette. And he wasn't there to help her.

"DEREK!!"

Merrill's voice perforated the shrieks. He focused on Merrill until the screaming dimmed and then fell away.

"That's it. Concentrate on me," Merrill said.

Derek tried, but the pain soon intruded. His attention kept shifting. Each time, the screams rose again.

"Open your eyes!" Merrill shouted. *"Derek, open your goddamn eyes!"*

It was as if Merrill's voice snapped him awake. His eyes flew open to stare up at the rock ceiling that towered above him. He could see it now.

"Look at me."

Derek rolled his head toward Merrill, who remained chained to the wall. He was breathing hard, and his hair was tangled and damp with sweat. *"What happened?"*

"You happened."

Derek frowned. *"Explain."*

"You tell me."

"I can't. I don't know what you're talking about."

Merrill blew out a harsh breath and dropped his head back against the stone wall. *"You passed out and almost immediately began screaming."*

Those bellows he'd heard had come from *him*? Derek shook his head. That couldn't be right. He swallowed and felt the rawness of his throat.

"You kept saying there were too many. That they were in pain. That they were begging you for help."

"Who?" Derek asked.

"I asked, but you didna hear me. Or couldna answer."

Derek met Merrill's gaze. *"But you figured it out."*

Merrill was silent for a moment before nodding. *"Look at the walls."*

It was the last thing Derek wanted to do, but he found his gaze lifting above Merrill. His eyesight wasn't what it usually was, but at least things weren't fuzzy now. He was able to make out the marks scored into the rock—the kind left by dragon talons.

"The scratches are everywhere," Merrill said.

"Where are the dragons?"

"No' here. No' anymore."

Derek tried to sit up, and pain slammed into him. *"I don't understand."*

"Long ago, an elder in my clan told me about one of the rarest dragon abilities. He said it was one no one ever wanted."

"Why?"

Merrill released a breath. When he spoke next, his words were barely discernable. *"Those unique few could see and hear the dead."*

"That isn't me. I've never seen or heard any dead."

"Have you been in this place before?"

Derek clenched his teeth. *"Not that I recall. My memories have been wiped, though."*

"They're trying to talk to you. Listen. They have something to say."

"I can't." Not if it caused him to scream. *"Why are you talking to me in my head. Villette is gone."*

"Aye, but we are no' alone." Merrill glanced past Derek.

He rolled his head to the other side and stared into the darkness. That's when he heard the unmistakable sound of breathing. Derek made out the shape of a dragon's head, but it wasn't just any dragon. It was the amethyst he and Merrill had both fought and killed.

"How is he still alive? I killed him. You killed him."

Merrill grunted. *"Without question. But he's here and alive."*

"Could there be more than one?"

"No' with that scar on its side. The one I fought had it."

Derek briefly closed his eyes but then turned his head and looked at Merrill. *"Villette must have done something to make sure he doesn't stay dead. What now? It isn't as if you can get free, and I'm not healing because of the damn poison."*

"Listen to the dead."

"I already told you I can't."

"You were," Merrill insisted. *"Whatever they said or showed you caused you great distress."*

"Which means I don't need to see or hear it again." Nor did he want to remember any of it. The very thought of such an ability seemed wrong. Why would anyone need to communicate with the dead? They were already gone and passed into another life.

Unless they were like the amethyst.

Derek lifted his head and looked down at his chest. Even that simple movement stole his breath. His body tried to heal, but whatever Villette had concocted ensured that it would deliver the most debilitating agony while also refusing to allow his body to heal. She wanted him weak and hurt. And that didn't bode well for anyone.

"You were given that gift for a reason," Merrill said.

"What about yours?" Derek interrupted. *"What is your ability? Why can't you use that?"*

"I'm no' sure a beam of searing light will help at this juncture."

"It might remove your chains."

Merrill shifted his weight from one foot to the other. *"Already tried. It did nothing but burn my skin."*

"Then we're fucked."

CHAPTER 35

Kora hurried out of the room after Miena. She took half a dozen steps before she realized Daelya hadn't followed. Kora stopped and looked back. "What are you doing? Let's go."

"I don't want to."

Kora motioned to what was left of the door with her hand. "There's nothing to close you in now. Anyone can find you. Why not stand against the one responsible for the loss of your family and your capture?"

"I'm not a fighter like you," Daelya argued.

"You don't have to be."

Daelya's lips compressed into a tight line. "I can sense other's magic. I can even see them using it. But I have nothing to defend myself with."

"You have your wits. I'd say that's plenty."

She shook her head. "I can't."

"I understand," Kora said. "Stay here. I'll be back when it's done."

She rushed from the room to catch up with Miena, but Kora couldn't find her. Shouting Miena's name didn't summon her either. Frustration bubbled within Kora, but she kept it together and headed down the stairs to where she had last encountered Villette.

When she reached the hallway, Kora slid to a stop. The door leading to Villette's room stood wide open. She slowly walked toward it and looked inside. She was sure her enemy was long gone. Kora was inwardly condemning herself for trusting Miena when her thoughts scattered at the sight of Villette on her knees with Miena standing behind her. Villette's eyes were wide with shock—the same emotion that had stopped Kora in her tracks.

Then Kora saw that Miena had her nails sunk into the back of Villette's neck. The burns had healed, but they were still visible. That meant they didn't have much time before Villette's power returned fully.

"What have you done?" Villette asked Kora.

The words were laced with panic. Kora's gaze jerked to Miena. She had made a choice. Had it been the wrong one?

"You never knew when to admit defeat, little sister," Miena said. "I told you I'd get free. I warned you what would happen when I did."

Villette's face was a mask of fury, but it was the hint of terror that stopped Kora in her tracks. She wouldn't feel sorry for Villette. Not after everything Villette had done to so very many. There were consequences for her actions, and it was time she paid.

"What are you waiting for?" Kora asked Miena.

Miena smoothed her free hand down her gown. As she did, the

color changed from green to pink. "I've been in that color for entirely too long. No one should have to wear the same thing every day."

"Kill her," Kora urged.

A horrified look filled Miena's face. "She's my sister."

"You said you were trying to stop her before. You promised to kill her for all she's done."

Villette snorted. "What *I've* done?"

Miena's nails sank deeper into Villette's neck, causing her to cry out in pain as blood dribbled over her neck and onto her clothes. But Miena's eyes were locked on Kora. "You are very demanding."

"We had a deal," Kora stated.

Villette peeled her lips back in a sneer. "Stupid hellhound."

"Where are they?" Miena demanded of her sister.

Villette stared into Kora's eyes as she answered, "I don't know."

"I'll rip your spine out right now if you don't te—"

Kora stepped back when Miena's voice halted mid-word, and a smile split her face.

"I should have known," Miena said with a laugh. "You are a creature of habit, after all." Miena's gaze then speared Kora. "You aren't going anywhere."

In the next instant, Kora found herself in a large cavern. Torches sat high on the walls as a red-gold light cascaded over the room. She saw Merrill first. He was chained to a wall. She started toward him when something caught her eye. Her heart lurched at the sight of Derek lying on the table, injured. Their eyes met, and she rushed to him. Suddenly, she was flying backward. She slammed into a wall and crashed to the floor.

Pain exploded in her head. Bones broke and punctured muscle

and cartilage. Somehow, she got an arm under her and lifted herself up. Raising her head was a challenge, but she had to see Derek.

"I'm going to fucking kill you!" he bellowed. His face was a mask of pain as he sat up.

Miena snapped her fingers, and he was lying flat again. Her laughter brought a chill into the already cool cavern. She withdrew her nails from Villette's neck and held out her arms as she turned in a circle. "I've waited for this for so long. My, but the taste of freedom certainly is sweet."

Nothing was going as Kora thought it would. She knew trusting Miena had been risky, but she had no other choice. Really, she had just been too scared to go after her enemy on her own. Making a deal with Miena had been a devil's bargain, and they would all pay the price for her mistake.

Miena walked to Merrill and stroked his face. "Tell me, hand-some, do the dragons remember when they served us?"

"We serve no one but ourselves," he replied frostily.

Miena laughed and glanced at Villette. "He doesn't know, does he?"

"Villette cheerfully shared the history lesson," Merrill retorted. "No' that it matters. We're free. Your brother saw to that."

Miena rolled her eyes. "Redis always did get in the way of my fun. Can you believe he felt sorry for you dragons? He had this notion that every being should be free. Such a radical thinker." Her voice deepened as anger sparked in her gaze. "He was smart, though. If I had caught on to what he planned, I would have squished him beneath my heel as he deserved."

"Is that what this is?" Kora asked as she sat up after her body had mended. "You plan to enslave the dragons again?"

Miena looked at her and smiled. "That was the original idea, but someone interfered," she said, shooting a withering glance at Villette, who hadn't moved from her knees. "I had a lot of time to think while locked away. I came up with a better plan."

Kora gingerly climbed to her feet. She looked at Derek, who was glaring at Miena. His gaze suddenly slid to her. She wanted to rush to him, wrap her arms around him, and feel his body against hers. The sight of his open wounds concerned her more than the fact that he couldn't get up.

"Anyone care to ask what it is?" Miena laughed as she slowly spun to look at each of them. "Come now. Surely one of you is curious."

Villette had a hand on the back of her neck where it still bled. "I'm not playing your games anymore."

"You most certainly will. All of you will," Miena ordered. She stared at Kora before a smug smile curved her lips. Then, she turned to Derek.

Kora dug her fingers into the rocks behind her to keep from shouting at Miena. If she discovered the depth of Kora's feelings for him, she would use it against her. Though Kora feared Miena already knew.

"Do you remember this place?" she asked Derek.

A muscle jumped in his jaw. "Should I?"

"Oh, absolutely. You spent a lot of time here."

A growl rumbled from Merrill as he yanked on his bindings.

Miena glanced at him over her shoulder and lifted a finger. "You've had your turn. It's Derek's now."

None of this should be happening. Kora couldn't figure out where everything had gone to shite. She had to salvage whatever she could while she had the opportunity because it might not come again. The gold cuff gleamed on Merrill's wrist. It didn't matter if Miena crafted it or Villette. It needed to come off. She inched toward him with painstaking slowness. If she got it off, maybe then he could break out of his chains.

Kora glared at Villette. Why wasn't she doing something? She might still be wounded and weak, but she could stand against Miena. But she wouldn't. Kora could see it in how Villette wouldn't look at her sister.

Miena slammed her hand on the table where Derek lay. Dust and small pebbles rained around them. "I grow weary of all of you."

"What's the plan?" Kora asked. If Miena wanted to play, then she would play. It might give them some time for...something.

Miena stood beside Derek and gazed down at his wounds. "Those look bad." She swiveled her head to Kora. "I knew you would be the one to break. I've seen the way you look at Derek. Do you have feelings for a *dragon*?" She grinned, laughing softly. "What would your parents say? Oh, that's right. They're dead. At Derek's hand." She gasped in mock horror. "Did I just let the big secret out?"

Kora had wondered if he was part of the hunt. But thinking it and hearing it were two different things. She'd thought she was past the pain of losing not just her parents but also her home. Her safety, her friends. Her happiness.

"Yikes, Derek," Miena said. "Whatever feelings Kora might have developed are vanishing rapidly."

Kora jerked at the half bellow, half growl that emanated from Derek. He thrashed on the table, causing his wounds to bleed again. She should hate him for what he did, but the only thing she felt was the need to get to his side and help him.

Miena lightly set her hand on his chest. He stilled immediately, his face contorted in pain.

"The plan, bitch," Merrill said through clenched teeth.

Miena shot him a side-eye and lifted her hand from Derek. "My conniving, backstabbing little sister took credit for all my hard work. Stepping in and twisting things to suit her. I admit, she made some decent progress, but she ultimately failed to get the job done. Just as she did on Earth."

Kora kept inching closer to Merrill. Miena drew in a deep breath and released it before moving to stand at the end of the table.

Miena rested her cheek against the side of Derek's head. "He is my creation. Villette and I each crafted three. Derek and Bryok came out perfect. Just as I formed them."

Tears gathered in Kora's eyes. Derek's hands were in fists, his body shaking from either pain or anger. Maybe both. She lifted her gaze to his face and met his olive eyes. The shame and pain she saw there nearly undid her.

"Villette's was a disaster," Miena said with a chuckle. "He had to be killed instantly. Of course, Villette destroyed my third egg out of spite. Leaving hers. Tell me, sister. Have either hatched?"

Hate burned in Villette's eyes. "You know they haven't."

"You were found lacking. Again." Miena moved her face to the other side of Derek's head, her lips twisting. "I wasn't exactly truthful earlier. Not just Villette has been tampering with your memories. I had fun messing around in that head of yours, too."

Kora had closed half the distance to Merrill. It wasn't nearly enough. She could continue to him or try to take out Miena. Villette would rise against her. Could she face two Star People at once? Not alone. She hated to admit that fact. She took a step and froze when Miena's gaze slid to her.

"Does she know, Derek?" Miena asked, loud enough for everyone to hear.

Kora found her gaze locked on him. A secret hung there, waiting to be revealed. Did she want to know? Whatever it was, it would only hurt her.

"Does Kora know you love her?" Miena asked, a smug smile curving her lips.

Kora looked from Miena to Derek. She saw the truth in his eyes. She was right. It was meant to hurt. Kora bit her tongue to keep her face from crumpling. She wouldn't give in to the tears distorting his handsome face.

"She didn't." Miena tsked. "You should've told her when you had the chance. Because you won't have another."

Villette rose to her knees when Miena walked to the amethyst dragon. "What are you doing?"

"You've had enough fun with your toys. They're mine now."

The words barely registered in Kora's head before Miena touched the dragon. The amethyst's citrine eyes opened. Miena stroked the dragon's scales and said something in a whisper. The dragon's gaze locked on Kora. Heart-stopping terror seized her. All thoughts of battling Villette and Miena fled. There was only one reason Miena had woken the dragon.

"Gordon is mine," Villette stated as she got to her feet, a feral look tightening her face.

Miena paid her sister no heed as she returned to Derek's side. She ran a hand over his chest. Kora watched his wounds heal. She was grateful that his pain was gone, but Miena did nothing without intention. Kora glanced at Merrill.

She was close enough to get to him and remove the cuff. Together, she, Derek, and Merrill could attack Miena. There was still a chance this all could end. She had to do something. It was her fault that Miena had been released. That meant it was up to her to fix things. Kora sidled closer. She just needed a little more time.

A deep, rumbling growl came from the dragon. Kora whipped her head to him and watched smoke billow from his nose. She froze, muscles stiffening in dread. Every fear that had haunted her returned tenfold.

Merrill fought wildly against his bindings. Kora was close enough that she could stretch out and touch him, but she didn't dare move. Even if she wanted to, her body wouldn't listen.

Miena snapped her fingers, and Merrill went silent. "I told you, all your toys are mine, sister," Miena said.

Out of the corner of her eye, Kora saw Miena smooth Derek's hair away from his face. "I'm going to wipe your memories one last time, Derek. I'm going to go in deep, scouring that brain to make sure there is nothing left for you to remember yourself or...anyone else."

Kora swallowed, knowing Miena was talking about her. She wanted to look at Derek, but she didn't dare take her eyes off Gordon.

"Then I'm going to send you to Earth," Miena continued. "Once you wipe out the Kings, you'll annihilate everyone else. I don't want anything left alive. My brother might not be alive to see it destroyed, but I can do the next best thing and make it uninhabitable. While Derek is having fun, I'll be making some adjustments here. Merrill will return to his friends. It won't take him long to bring Con to me. Once the mighty King of Dragon Kings is enslaved, the others will quickly fall."

Kora wanted to scream in outrage. At herself, at Miena, at Villette, at all of it. Villette had been a scourge upon Zora, but it was nothing compared to Miena. How could Kora have been so stupid as to believe Miena? She should've seen what Miena intended instead of worrying about facing Villette on her own.

"Do something," Kora urged Villette through clenched teeth.

Miena laughed. "She knows better."

Villette took a step forward. The exchange, when it came, happened swiftly. One moment, Villette was standing, readying her magic. The next, she was unconscious on the ground.

"She never learns," Miena said.

Gordon rose, towering over Kora. She shook uncontrollably. This was it. This was how she died. Her life flashed before her eyes. The screams of her brother, uncle, and cousin rose in her head. The ghosts of her ancestors cried out.

The dragon sucked in a breath. Kora watched in horror as his chest expanded. Her gut clenched at the sight of flames swirling between his scales. There was no escape. She was the only one in the cavern who could be killed by dragon fire. She didn't want the last thing she saw to be Gordon. She turned her head and locked eyes with Derek. He screamed her name and fought to get up, but Miena held him down with one hand, excitement on her face.

There was a beat of stillness, a silence like the universe holding its breath. And with that, her panic dissipated. A weird tranquility fell over her. Her mind cleared, and it allowed Kora to see a solution. She had come to Stonemore to kill Villette. Or at least that's what she'd thought. Maybe she had been brought here to help the dragons.

She might not be able to kill her targets, but she was a hell-hound, a fighter. And that's exactly what she would do. Kora dove to the side and ripped the bracelet off Merrill a heartbeat before fire erupted from Gordon. She smiled when Merrill wrenched from the chains and reached for her. She felt the heat of fire as it licked her skin. Merrill's arms roughly grabbed her, spinning her away.

The blast continued for what felt like an eternity. Kora's ears rang with the sound. The heat was sweltering. Merrill's arms finally dropped. Kora pitched forward and grabbed the wall for support. When she spun around, Miena and Gordon were gone.

And so was Derek.

THE END

Thank you for reading **THE BASTARD KING**.
I hope you enjoyed the book as much as I loved writing it.

* * *

To find out when new books release
SIGN UP FOR MY NEWSLETTER today at
https://www.tinyurl.com/DonnaGrantNews

* * *

Join my Facebook group, Donna Grant Groupies, for exclusive giveaways and sneak peeks of future books.
https://bit.ly/DGGroupies

* * *

Keep reading for a peek of THE UNCROWNED KING…

EXCERPT OF THE UNCROWNED KING

THE BASTARD DUOLOGY, BOOK 2

I would burn the world for him…

My people have been hunted to extinction by dragons. I am the last of my kind. Forever running. Forever alone.

Then I met him. Dangerous. Carnal. *Dragon.* And utterly magnetic. I had no defenses against the passion that claimed us. Each time his lips touched mine, each time his arms held me, I fell deeper.

And I fell hard.

My mortal enemy became my world. The very reason for my existence.

My one and only.

Until our forever was violently snatched away. Now, I'm hunted, once more.

But I'm not running this time. I'm fighting for love.

For him.

A hellhound facing her past. A dragon reclaiming his throne. Forbidden lovers will face the ultimate test. A Dragon King duology from *New York Times* and *USA Today* bestselling author Donna Grant.

Keep reading for an excerpt of THE UNCROWNED KING…

CHAPTER 1

Derek was gone. Vanished.

As if he never was.

Kora stared at the table where he had lain seconds before, screaming her name. Emotion swelled in her chest, pressing against it before rising to her throat, where it lodged awkwardly. The rest of her body was numb. Painfully so. She stepped forward, her hand reaching for him as if he were still there. As if she would be able to touch him.

Her knees buckled. Strong arms grabbed her before she hit the ground and propped her against the wall for support. Dimly, the sound of bickering voices reached her, but she was lost in thoughts of Derek. The alarming wounds on his chest, his fear for her in his pale olive eyes that soon turned to horror for himself.

Unbidden, Miena's voice broke into Kora's mind.

"Does she know, Derek?" Miena asked.

Kora found her gaze locked on him. A secret hung there, waiting to be revealed. Did she want to know? Whatever it was, it would only hurt her.

"Does Kora know you love her?" Miena asked, a smug smile curving her lips.

Kora looked from Miena to Derek. She saw the truth in his eyes. She was right. It was meant to hurt.

He loved her. And now, he was gone. Miena had taken him. She would wipe Derek's memory of Kora and everything else. For all Kora knew, Derek might have already forgotten her.

She swallowed in an attempt to wet her dry mouth. Sweat dripped from her brow near her temple. She wiped it away with her shoulder and caught sight of the black marks on the wall caused by dragon fire. It had been a blaze meant to kill her. If Merrill hadn't grabbed her when he did, she would be dead.

The haze of dismay began to clear. The voices she had ignored sharpened. And the stench of evil permeated the area, reminding her why she came to Stonemore. She turned to find Merrill and Villette quarreling. Villette had been Kora's intended target, the one responsible for the unyielding fist of evil that controlled Stonemore and the surrounding areas. The Star Person who traveled the universe, meddling and corrupting as she went.

The one only hellhounds could kill.

Flames erupted over Kora with a thought. They covered her body and flickered at the ends of her hair while consuming her clothes. She stalked forward, her gaze locked on the right side of Villette's face and neck, scarred from a previous encounter—likely with a hellhound. Miena might have gotten away, but Kora could still end Villette once and for all.

Villette's blue eyes grew round with fear at the sight of Kora. She raised a hand. "Let's talk about this," she begged frantically.

"I'm done talking." Kora had released Miena. She had believed Miena when she said she would kill Villette. How could Kora have been so naïve? So trusting? She knew what Miena was.

Villette backed up quickly, her long, blond hair whipping about as she glanced behind her. "You need me!"

Merrill stepped between them, his tall form blocking her. Dark blue eyes met Kora's. A lock of dirty blond hair fell across his forehead. He was the reason she was alive. Did dragon fire hurt dragons? She didn't see any marks on him. Maybe he healed quickly.

"I'd like nothing better than to see the end of Villette." The Dragon King sighed, his lips twisting ruefully. "But she's right. We need her."

"Nay." Kora had known when she came to Stonemore that she would have to face the powerful Villette on her own. Her family had been killed before they could slay the Star Person, and then Kora had run in an attempt to forget all she had lost. And in that time, thousands of innocents had died. No more. "She dies today."

Merrill didn't stop her when she started to walk around him. Instead, he said, "If you want Derek back, we need her alive."

Villette stood stiffly, her gaze moving from Merrill to Kora, injuries from a recent encounter with others still healing, her flesh pink and raised. "I know Miena better than anyone. I can find her," Villette pleaded.

"You had your chance to attack when she stood here with us and did nothing," Kora stated. The flames around her leaped higher with her anger, eager to devour the evil.

Villette's blue eyes narrowed. "My sister is more powerful than me. You have no idea what it took to capture her the first time."

"Exactly. You're useless."

Merrill turned and focused on Villette as he crossed his arms over his muscular chest, but his words were directed at Kora. "Perhaps she is when it comes to battle. But she has other uses."

"I don't like your tone," Villette replied acerbically.

Merrill ignored her and turned his head to Kora. "Trust me."

A week ago, Kora would've laughed at the very thought of putting her faith in a dragon. They were responsible for annihilating the hellhounds on Zora. Granted, it had been done on orders from Villette, but that didn't make the loss of Kora's family and friends any easier. And being the last of her kind had been unbearable.

Dragons were the enemy.

At least, they used to be.

When Kora met Derek, she'd had no idea what he was. It had never dawned on her that dragons could change forms to look human. If she had known, she never would've shared her body or her deepest confidences with him. She certainly wouldn't have fallen for him. But by the time she learned the secrets he so closely guarded, her heart had belonged to him.

Her throat constricted, and a deep, bottomless ache began in the center of her chest. She felt hollow, empty. Barren. As if a part of her had been stolen before she even knew it was there. The agony and excruciating anguish robbed her of breath. How would she go on? She couldn't stop thinking about Derek.

He could've taken her life the moment he discovered she was a hellhound. He could have informed Villette. But he had done neither. Instead, he had saved her from another dragon—and nearly got himself killed because of it.

Kora had barely accepted what Derek was when she learned that Merrill was also a dragon. Her world had spun out of control, and all she'd been able to do was try to stay upright and put one foot in front of the other. Suddenly, the lines dividing her from her enemies weren't as clear as they once were.

Merrill had asked for trust. She couldn't rely on her judgment since she had gotten it so wrong with Miena, but Derek had earned her trust time and again. And he believed Merrill. Which meant she should, as well.

"All right," she murmured to Merrill.

Villette snorted. "Do you honestly think any of your friends will come after you've ignored their calls for so long?"

Merrill slowly swiveled his head to Villette and gave her a hate-filled glare.

She threw up her hands. "Just wanted to put that out there."

The moment Villette turned as if to walk away, Kora threw out her hands. Balls of fire shot from them and landed on the floor, encircling Villette.

The Star Person drew up short, her head whipping around to pin Kora with a dark look.

"What is this for?"

Kora shrugged. "Insurance."

"I want to stop my sister," Villette said. "I could've left already, and you couldn't have done anything about it."

Merrill dropped his arms to his sides. "Perhaps. But you willna be going anywhere now."

"If we're going to work together, we need to trust each other," Villette argued.

Kora rolled her eyes. She had been betrayed by a Star Person for the last time. Villette couldn't do or say anything that would make her trust her. *Ever.*

She extinguished the flames on her body but then remembered her clothes were gone. She had gotten used to Derek using his magic to clothe her after she called her fire. Until she found new attire, she'd be walking around naked. Which meant she needed to find some immediately.

"I can give you clothes," Villette said. "With a wave of my hand. But you must lower the flames."

Merrill made a sound in the back of his throat. In the next instant, clothing covered Kora once more.

"So can I," Merrill stated.

Kora had expected Villette to be able to wield such power, but Merrill? She'd assumed Derek's magic came from the cuff Villette had given him. Had she been wrong? She knew next to nothing about dragons, other than that they'd killed her people. Maybe it was time she found out more.

If they were to be...friends.

Before she could come up with a question, Merrill said, "Rhi."

Kora frowned and looked from him to Villette. Neither gave anything away. "What is Rhi?"

"No' what. *Who*," Merrill replied. "She's a Fae."

"What's a Fae?"

Villette laughed and looked down at her nails.

"We're fucking magnificent," said a female voice behind Kora.

She turned at the odd accent to find a woman of incredible beauty sitting on the table, one long leg crossed over the other. Midnight locks fell past the newcomer's shoulders in soft waves. She wore all black from head to toe, and it didn't appear as if anyone would be able to stand on the high, slender heels of her boots. Silver eyes studied Kora before her gaze slid to Merrill.

"About bloody time," she said before flashing a bright smile.

If Kora had thought the woman was beautiful before, the smile lit up her face, transforming her into something ethereal. She couldn't stop staring.

"It's good to see you, Rhi," Merrill said, his lips softening.

Rhi lifted a slim shoulder. "It's always good to be seen." She looked at Villette before focusing on Kora. "Want to introduce me?"

"Rhi, this is Kora. Kora, Rhi." Merrill then motioned behind him with his thumb. "That's Villette."

The air crackled with tension as Rhi pushed off the table with her hands and landed nimbly on the impossibly high heels. Her gaze never left Villette. "And the fire?"

"That's all Kora. She's a hellhound," Merrill explained.

One of Rhi's brows rose as she looked at Kora with a grin. "Impressive."

"It seems hellhounds can kill Star People," Merrill added.

Rhi folded her arms across her chest as she and Villette stared at each other. "Then why is this one alive?"

"It's why I called for you."

There was an undercurrent of anger and resentment in the room that Kora didn't understand. She felt as if she were on the outside looking in, and it was an uncomfortable position to be in. However, she found it peculiar that Villette had decided to refrain from speaking. There was definitely something between them.

"Someone needs to get to Earth immediately and warn everyone at Dreagan that an attack is coming from another King. Tell them no' to kill him. Just incapacitate him," Merrill explained.

"Attack?" Rhi asked.

"Rhi," Merrill urged.

She was there one moment, and the next, she wasn't.

Kora stared at the empty space. With nothing but silence, Kora's thoughts returned to Derek. She hoped he wasn't in pain. She squeezed her eyes closed, trying not to think about what Miena might be doing to him. When Kora opened her eyes again, Rhi was there.

The Fae turned her back to Villette and let her unease show. She walked closer to Kora and motioned Merrill over. When she spoke, her voice was barely above a whisper. "Done. Now it's time to tell me what's going on."

Merrill exchanged a look with Kora. "A lot."

"Then you'd better start talking."

Kora glanced at the table, remembering how Derek had stared at her, his gaze pleading. "Derek is a dragon. They made him. And took him."

Silence met her statement. Rhi blew out a breath. "Shite." She briefly pressed her lips together. "We need to get to the others."

"We can no' leave Villette unattended," Merrill said. "She's our link to Miena."

Rhi shot him a flat look. "She's not coming with us. And you can't really think she'll help."

"We need her to find Derek."

Kora wished Merrill was wrong, but she knew he wasn't. "As much as it pains me to say it, we need her."

"All right," Rhi said. "Who's Miena?"

Merrill's lips twisted. "Villette's sister."

"I was afraid you were going to say something like that," Rhi muttered.

Kora longed for water to coat her throat and wet her mouth. "You two go. I'll watch Villette."

Merrill shook his head. "There are parts of the story only you can tell. And the others need to hear it."

"Others?" she asked, though she was afraid she already knew what he'd meant.

"Dragon Kings."

It was one thing to accept that not all dragons were evil, but to cross the border to their land and be surrounded by them? Kora wasn't sure she could do it. But then she thought about Derek and all he had done for her. She wanted him back. She wanted to rewind time and leave Miena locked away. She wanted to be in his arms once more.

She couldn't go into this fight alone. She needed Merrill and the dragons. She even needed Villette. Derek had risked his life for her. She owed him the same.

"I'll return after I take you two," Rhi said. "And I'll be sure to veil myself so no one can see me. If she tries anything, I'll stop her."

Kora shook her head, confused. "What is *veiling* yourself?"

"Veiling means that I'm invisible to others," Rhi explained. "I was veiled before I showed myself to you. It is something the Fae can do. Fae are magic, like you and the dragons. And we have some added benefits, like being able to teleport. If someone says my name, calling for me as Merrill did, I know where they are."

"Derek can teleport, but he uses a cuff."

"Ah. I see. It is rare to have such a piece. Let me take you to my mate, Con."

"So, he is real?" Kora wondered how different things would be now if Derek had gone to see Con.

Rhi nodded. "Aye, he is. And if any dragon is in trouble, nothing will stop him—or any of the Kings—from finding them."

"She's right. We willna," Merrill confirmed.

Rhi held out her hand. "Come. I'll take you both to Con."

BUY THE UNCROWNED KING NOW
at www.DonnaGrant.com

ABOUT THE AUTHOR

New York Times and *USA Today* bestselling author Donna Grant® has been praised for her "totally addictive" and "unique and sensual" stories.

She's written more than one hundred novels spanning multiple genres of romance including the bestselling Dragon Kings® series that features a thrilling combination of Druids, Fae, and immortal Highlanders who are dark, dangerous, and irresistible. She lives in Texas with her dog and a cat.

www.DonnaGrant.com
www.MotherofDragonsBooks.com

facebook.com/AuthorDonnaGrant

instagram.com/dgauthor

bookbub.com/authors/donna-grant

goodreads.com/donna_grant

pinterest.com/donnagrant1

TRAIL OF MADNESS

Jack McCall and the Killing of a Legend

Multiple Award-Winning Author
Michael Knost

www.LawlessTrailsPress.com

Trail of Madness

Jack McCall and the Killing of a Legend

Multiple Award-Winning Author

Michael Knost

*In memory of my father Earl Collins,
the man who introduced me to Westerns.
I miss you, Big E.*

Praise for Trail of Madness

"*Trail of Madness* takes the reader on a dark journey into the mind of the man who killed Wild Bill Hickok in a rip-roaring Western that smoothly blends fact and fiction into a gritty and compelling story." — **Michael Zimmer**, author of the Wrangler Award-winning novel, *The Poacher's Daughter*.

"Michael Knost explodes into the Western genre with a tour de force, a gripping yarn that takes a famous historical event and undoes everything we thought we knew about it. Highly recommended." — **Jeff Mariotte**, author of the Cody Cavanaugh Western trilogy and cofounder of Silverado Press.

"Michael Knost's *Trail of Madness* has more twists and turns than a sidewinder. A masterful mixture of traditional Western, mystery, suspense, and the true-life account of one of the most notorious assassins in Old West history. It is frontier storytelling at its finest!" — **Ronald Kelly**, author of *Timber Gray* and *The Saga of Dead-Eye* series.

"Saddle up and embark on this harrowing and gritty psychological Western tale as Jack McCall grapples with unsettling delusions from a traumatic brain injury. Or, is it that he's just experiencing sobering and equally bleak realities? Along a dusty and difficult trail of his own choosing, Broken Nose Jack eventually faces his darkest fears and uncovers shocking truths about himself and his father's death. Mark it down, *Trail of Madness* is certain to be the next Western classic!" — **F. Keith Davis**, author of *The Secret Life and Brutal Death of Mamie Thurman*.

Foreword

by Johnny D. Boggs

Unless you've never

    1.) read a historical Western novel

    2.) glanced at a history of the American West

    3.) visited Deadwood, South Dakota, or

    4.) have been living on Neptune all your life,
you know about Wild Bill Hickok and how he met his demise on August 2, 1876.

But let me insert a "spoiler alert" just in case.

Hickok was playing poker in Deadwood, an illegal gold-mining town in the Lakotas' Black Hills (and therefore off limits, supposedly, to white Americans) when Jack McCall, going by the alias Bill Sutherland, shot him in the back of the head. McCall was captured, released after being acquitted by a miners' court, then rearrested in Wyoming Territory and tried again in Yankton, the capital of

Dakota Territory. There was no "double jeopardy" since Deadwood was an illegal town and a miners' court had no legal standing. This time McCall was found guilty and hanged on March 1, 1877.

And that's about all we know about Jack McCall.

The late Joseph G. Rosa wrote several books about Hickok, including what most historians regard as the best biography, *They Called Him Wild Bill: The Life and Adventures of James Butler Hickok*, first published in 1964. Other Hickok biographers include A.M. Anderson, J.W. Buel, Tom Clavin, William Elsey Connelley, Wilbert E. Eisele, Edward Knight, James D. McLaird, Richard O'Connor, and Frank J. Wilstach. And that's just what I can see on the shelves in my office.

But Jack McCall has remained elusive. Rosa published a limited-edition book of 250 autographed copies, *Alias Jack McCall*, in 1967. (No. 30 is also on my bookshelves.) That book was based on a talk Rosa presented to the Kansas City Posse of the Westerners in 1966. But even Rosa pointed out that "surprisingly little is known of [McCall]" and that answers to the questions of why he murdered Hickok "are not yet complete, nor may they ever be."

Many novelists have tackled the story of that prince of pistoleers, Wild Bill (born James Butler Hickok in Illinois). There's Pete Dexter's *Deadwood*,

Randy Lee Eickhoff's *And Not to Yield*, Richard Matheson's *The Memoirs of Wild Bill Hickok*, and Max McCoy's *A Breed Apart*, just to name a few. Loren D. Estleman's *Aces & Eights* covers McCall's murder trial, and some Boggs character has put Hickok in a few of his novels, including *East of the Border*.

But McCall is a harder nut to crack.

So you have to respect Michael Knost for taking a swing at it. If you're expecting a biographical novella, however, you're in for a surprise. And a juicy treat. Because while Michael Knost might be a new name for many fans of Western fiction, he's well known in the horror—he's a Bram Stoker Award winner—science fiction, fantasy, and supernatural genres. And he twists the story of McCall into something completely different while keeping the history pretty much spot-on.

What's this? A horror writer taking on an iconic Western subject?

Well, the aforementioned Dexter is literary novelist and a National Book Award winner for *Paris Trout*. Estleman, though a multiple Spur Award winner and an Owen Wister Award recipient from Western Writers of America for his contributions to Western literature, is better known for his mysteries. The late, great Matheson wrote horror, fantasy and science fiction, including the classics *I Am Legend* and *The Shrinking Man.*

Most Western writers that I know don't just read Western fiction and nonfiction. Let's see . . . right now on my nightstand are Robert A. Caro's *The Power Broker*, Hal G. Evarts Jr.'s *The Talking Mountain*, Seamus Heaney's *100 Poems*, Wilson Tucker's *The Long Loud Silence*, and, yes, the most recent Wild Bill Hickok bio, Craig Crease's *The Wanderer: James Butler Hickok and the American West.* The audiobook in the Nissan Frontier, by the way, is Donald Hamilton's *The Shadowers.*

Not that *Trail of Madness* is a Weird Western, because Knost leaves the final verdict to the reader and the reader's imagination.

Either way, *Trail of Madness* is a treat. And I suspect this won't be Michael Knost's last foray into the Western genre.

I'm already looking forward to another good read.

Santa Fe, New Mexico, resident Johnny D. Boggs (JohnnyDBoggs.com) is a nine-time Spur Award winner from Western Writers of America, the 2020 recipient of the Owen Wister Award for lifetime contributions to Western literature, and a 2020

FOREWORD

inductee into the Western Writers Hall of Fame. A former newspaper journalist, he has also received the Western Heritage Award from the National Cowboy and Western Heritage Museum and the 2011 Distinguished Alumnus Award from the University of South Carolina's School of Journalism and Mass Communications. His most recent novels are *Longhorns East* and *Bloody Newton*.

Preface

Michael Knost

I'd first like to point out that this book is not meant to be taken as a literal account regarding the life of Jack McCall or the Death of Wild Bill Hickok. This is obviously a work of fiction, but I tried my best to remain as historically faithful as possible. And although this story includes people who truly existed in history, there is a very good chance that many of these individuals never actually crossed paths.

Myth and legend surround so much when it comes to the killing of Hickok. For instance, we get the term *Dead Man's Hand* being aces and eights as that is what is speculated Hickok held when he died. However, most historians will tell you that's nothing more than speculation. Oh, and that *Hickok Death Chair* hanging above the door of the Saloon #10 in deadwood today? It's hard to believe the original chair Hickok was killed in would have survived the fires of 1879, 1894, 1948, 1951, 1959, and 1987. And let's not forget the eyewitness account of bartender Sam Young mentioning that Wild Bill pulled "out the *stool* with his foot, from under the table, sitting down on it." Stool, not chair.

So there are a great number of myths, lies, and marketing deceptions surrounding this historic event. We know that history tells us Jack McCall, going by alias Bill Sutherland at the time, killed James Butler "Wild Bill" Hickok on August 2, 1876 at Nuttal and Mann's Saloon No. 10 in Deadwood, Dakota Territory. What we don't know is *why* he did it. Again, speculation points in a number of directions, some offering more plausibility than others, but in the end, they're all just mere speculation. Jack mentioned he did it to avenge his brother's death, saying Hickok had murdered his brother in cold blood. And yet records show us McCall had no brothers. Some say it was out of embarrassment from Wild Bill giving McCall money for breakfast the night before and telling him to take a break from the game until he could cover his bets. Plausible, yet still nothing more than speculation.

I wanted to approach the whole thing from a direction no one has looked before. A direction, again, nothing more than speculation, yet

PREFACE

finding a very interesting and entertaining story along the way.

From the book *The Plainsman* by Frank Jenner Wilstach: "Doc Peirce has given the writer a minute description of the assassin. He says that Jack McCall was known as Broken Nose Jack and that he was "'the most repulsive-looking man I have ever met. He was cross-eyed and his nose had been broken by being struck with a six-shooter.'"

My speculation is simply this: What if Jack McCall suffered brain damage from blunt-force trauma to the face that left him disfigured? And what if those issues had him seeing and experiencing hallucinations and paranoia as we know today as something that truly happens in some individuals with very similar injuries?

I'm not going to attempt to get into the medical or neurological aspects as those are well outside my fields, but I am so happy that Vic Kelly, MS is offering a professional opinion on the subject in his introduction so we get a better idea of what McCall may have been going through when it all happened.

Let me make this clear, I am not attempting to make an excuse for McCall's actions, nor am I saying I believe this is truly what happened. I am merely offering another speculation into the mix of speculations surrounding this historical event.

But I won't lie, it sure makes for an entertaining story whether it's fact or fiction.

And hopefully, by the time the reader has made it to the end, he or she is forced to make a decision whether McCall suffered brain trauma and hallucinations or the man actually encountered what he found down that Trail of Darkness.

That, my dear reader, is for you to decide.

Introduction

by Vic Kerry, MS

In my many years of working in the psychiatric field, I have encountered dozens, if not hundreds, and maybe even thousands of people suffering from some form of psychosis. That word has a wide range of meanings. Psychosis can be exhibited in delusions or false beliefs that cannot be substantiated by evidence. This would include paranoia. Psychosis can also mean disorganized and tangential thinking. This is when people talk about things that make no sense to the hearer but make sense to the speaker. It can include linking together things that are in no way similar.

An example might be that someone associates pigeons eating bread, meaning the Ford Motor Company gives him 1,000 stock options. The last symptoms that can be defined as psychosis are hallucinations. These are when a person hears, sees, feels, smells, or tastes things that are not there. Psychosis can also be a mix of all these things together. It is a difficult diagnosis to work with and unravel.

Modern psychology and psychiatry are not completely certain why people have psychosis. We know some diagnoses are more likely to have psychosis as a symptom. Schizophrenia cannot be diagnosed without some type of psychosis being present. When depression or bipolar disorder becomes severe enough, people with those diagnoses can have psychosis as well.

There is no definitive answer as to why people have psychosis. The current theory is that an imbalance of neurotransmitters causes psychosis. (If you're not sure what those are, they are the chemicals our brain cells use to communicate.) Most professionals agree that the neurotransmitter dopamine has a major influence on psychosis. Medications used to treat those symptoms, like Risperdal, Seroquel, or Zyprexa, are believed to balance out the amounts of dopamine in the brain. Professionals also think that serotonin and norepinephrine may also have an impact on psychosis. Antidepressants such as selective serotonin reuptake inhibitors (SSRIs) and selective serotonin-norepinephrine reuptake inhibitors (SSN-

RIs) help balance serotonin and norepinephrine, respectively. Mood stabilizers such as lithium and anti-convulsant medications like Depakote help balance the mania in bipolar disorder. The anti-depressant and mood stabilizers can also assist in ridding a person of psychosis.

How do those neurotransmitters get out of balance in the first place? Firstly, a person can be born with a predisposition to having an imbalance. This may come through inherited genetics. It might just be a fluke of in-utero development. Exposure to certain biological and chemical agents while in the womb may also cause imbalances. That's one of the reasons doctors are so specific about what pregnant women put in their bodies. We also know that trauma can cause psychosis.

The one diagnosis I have not mentioned is post-traumatic stress disorder (PTSD). Oftentimes, one of the major symptoms of PTSD is psychosis, especially delusions, and hallucinations in the form of reliving the traumatic event that caused the disorder. PTSD has to have a traumatic experience to be diagnosed. Some psychiatrists and psychologists believe that psychological trauma can cause neurotransmitter production and balances to go off kilter.

So why am I talking about all this psychological rot in an introduction to a Western? The answer is traditional Western characters lived hard-scrabble lives. Some went for long periods in solitude. Others lived in constant fear of being attacked either by bandits or angry Native Americans. And don't forget about the killings, as we know there were so many. Of course, there was the hard drinking as well.

In the Old West, people encountered things that count as trauma all the time. If a person starves for some time, they could develop PTSD. We know that sexual assault, witnessing violent crime, being a victim of violent crime, or perpetrating violent crime can cause it. That's one of the reasons I believe Clint Eastwood's *High Plains Drifter* is such a good example of a character with PTSD. If you watch this movie as a tale of revenge instead of a ghost story, you'll understand what I mean.

Another traumatic event has fairly recently been looked at in connection with psychosis. This is head trauma. Chronic Traumatic Encephalopathy (CET) has been in the news in recent years. It's the thing about chronic concussions that the NFL tried to hide. Numerous athletes across sports suffer from this. Many have died from it. One of the leading causes of their deaths is suicide, often because of psychosis that won't go away. If suicide isn't bad enough, sometimes they commit acts of violence due to the same cause. Chris Benoit, the

INTRODUCTION

pro-wrestler, is a prime example. The thing we now know is that one concussion can cause these issues. It doesn't even have to be a severe concussion. When the brain is damaged, it has a ripple effect. One of those ripples could and probably is damage to the production and regulation of neurotransmitters.

For me, with over 20 years of experience as a psychotherapist working with severe mental illness, it is not hard to imagine a person receiving head trauma and then hallucinating about voices telling them to do horrible things. I've seen it with my own eyes and heard it with my ears. The same is true for paranoia, which could lead someone to violent acts.

Psychosis is a serious mental illness. It can have multiple causes, from genetic heredity to substance use to psychological trauma to physical trauma. Something to remember is that it's been around as long as there have been humans. Many throughout history have suffered from psychosis for multiple causes. Just because it wasn't called psychosis in the old days doesn't mean it wasn't there.

I hope this hasn't been long-winded or condescending. I meant neither one. I simply wanted to explain something important to me, and the author of the following story, in a way that everyone could understand. Thanks for your patience.

Vic Kerry, MS

Vic Kerry is the author of five horror novels, two novellas, and a story collection. As V.M. Kerry, he published his first middle-grade horror novel (*The Thirteenth Halloween*) in September 2024. Kerry has an MS in clinical/applied psychology from the University of South Alabama. He is the director of the Crisis Residential Unit for Northwest Alabama Mental Health Center. Before this, he worked as senior psychotherapist for Walker Baptist Hospital's Behavioral Medicine Unit. All in all, Kerry has over 20 years of experience working with the severely mentally ill.

oving Craddock's horse out of one stall and into another, Jack gently stroked the Appaloosa's neck. "Don't get all jittery on me, girl. I'm just gonna shovel out your space so you'll have more room to do your business."

Manure and leather and straw lingered in the air, all the things he'd become accustomed to the past few months at the ranch.

"'Course if I ate as much as you, I'd be shittin' myself out of the barn as well."

The horse flicked its tail and quietly followed Jack's lead without resistance or hesitation.

"McCall."

It was downright spooky how Lucian Craddock could sidle up on a fella without a sound.

"Need you to go into town for supplies," he said, holding out a scrap of paper. "Here's the list."

"All right." Jack examined the handwriting that looked more like chicken scratches than letters or words.

"You *can* read, can't ya?"

"'Course I can read!" Jack hastily folded the paper as heat gathered in his chest and neck. "You and the ranch hands all think I'm some sorta idiot or something. Well I ain't, ya know!"

Craddock's wiry eyebrows converged at the bridge of his nose. "Boy, you *ever* take that tone with me again and I will cut that blamed tongue right outta your mouth." His eye twitched. "We clear on that?"

Jack nodded, the warmth spreading throughout his chest.

"Second of all, there ain't nobody here who thinks you're an idiot." Craddock's expression softened. "You're just a young'un is all—makin' the same mistakes every one of us made at your age."

The warmth advanced into Jack's cheeks and ears.

"Now get on into town and fetch them supplies like I asked." He gestured toward the horse. "You can finish things up here when you get back."

"Yessir."

"Better take the buckboard . . . some of them items will be a mite cumbersome."

Hitching the mule to the wagon, Jack kept his eye on Craddock as he left the barn just as quietly as he'd entered it. The grizzled rancher may have been a bit long in the tooth, but Jack remembered the old cuss beating the piss and vinegar out of a strapping young cowhand who'd somehow crossed the line.

"I'm gonna show 'em all one day, Jasper." The mule's ears perked up, twitched. "And they're gonna go on about how they knew me 'fore I made a name for myself. Just you wait and see."

The ride into town was a rough one in spite of the road's well-worn ruts. Jasper held a slow enough pace, all right, but the wagon somehow rattled and banged the entire way.

Craddock had gone on the past few days about getting a wheelwright to grease the axles and check the spokes, but decided against it when he learned the town's blacksmith could do the job cheaper. All Jack knew was the dang contraption jarred his guts almost as badly as that cantankerous bull the ranch hands coaxed him onto a few weeks back. The laughter still seared his conscience.

Stretching out like an ocean of crops and red Quinlan soil, the Kansas plains may as well been the surface of one of them planets Doc McDowell always went on about when compared to the Kentucky landscape Jack's family called home. The absence of mountains and hills was downright homesickening—it just wasn't natural to be able to see as far as one's eye could actually behold.

It seemed as though Doc McDowell knew a little something about everything. In fact, Jack's pa referred to the old man as the limey-know-it-all because he was always going on about planets or moons or the time he lived in a fancy railcar for several months . . . all in that fancy British way of speaking.

Maneuvering Jasper next to several horses in front of the saloon, Jack scanned the area for movement. The ruckus of laughter, music, and drunken revelry emanated from the establishment's batwing doors, where a tinny piano melody kept everything in some sort of chaotic rhythm.

Climbing off the wagon, Jack hitched Jasper to a post with several branded horses, something he'd only witnessed once in life.

"Well I'll be."

Tobacco smoke reached his nostrils, reminding him of his old man. Several months had come and gone since he'd gotten word that James McCall had been killed in Abilene.

Pushing through the doors, Jack found the saloon exactly as his ears pictured it. Tables spread out across the rough-wood floor with a few patrons playing poker and drinking. Others were in conversation and drinking. And some . . . well, some were just drinking.

A cold breeze washed over him as he located the gang at a table in the corner. Must have been seven of them, but he figured a few others were more than likely milling about with the regular crowd, keeping an eye out for anyone seeking to catch them by surprise. But those at the table were the big dogs. And right there in the middle of them all, just as big as life, was none other than Butch Carver.

Keeping his gaze fixed on those at the table, Jack made his way to the bar. No one gave him a second glance as he waded through the crowd, paying close attention as to not bump into anyone or jostle a table.

"What'cha want, boy?" The proprietor didn't bother looking up from the whiskey glasses he was stacking under the bar top.

"I have a right to be here as much as anyone!"

Glancing at Jack, the man shifted a cigar stump from one side of his mouth to the other. "To *drink*." He shook his head. "What'cha want to *drink*?"

Grunting, Jack scanned the bottles on the wall behind the portly man. "Just give me a whiskey. Somethin' cheap."

He slid a coin across the counter and knocked back the hooch in one gulp. The burn slithered into his throat and chest.

"Best take it easy on that rotgut, fella. It'll sneak up on you like a pissed off rattlesnake if you're not careful." Butch Carver moved next to Jack, holding up two fingers for the bartender.

"Ain't that the truth. But a rattlesnake will at least give you a warning 'fore it strikes."

"Sounds like you've been bitten a time or two." He handed Jack one of the freshly-loaded glasses. "Name's Butch Carver."

Taking the whiskey, Jack stood motionless. "You don't remember me."

"You know, every time somebody says that, I end up defending myself over something I did or said—or at least something they *think* I did or said." He dropped his hand close to his sidearm.

"Just a minute." Downing the liquor, Jack held up his empty hand. "I didn't mean it that way at all." A chill tingled up his legs. "My old man used to run with you fellers a ways back."

Butch cocked his head, squinted. "Good lord almighty, are you Jimmy's boy?"

The bright queasiness in Jack's chest softened. "I wasn't sure if any of you would recognize me."

"To be fair,"—Butch held up two fingers for the barkeep again—"you was just knee-high to a grasshopper the last time I saw you."

"You fellers gonna be in town a spell?"

Handing Jack another shot, Butch shrugged. "Hard to say." He knocked back his drink and grimaced. "Now *that's* snakebite good right there," he said, gesturing toward the empty glass.

Jack downed his own. "Much obliged for the drinks."

"Hey." Butch thudded Jack's chest with the back of his hand. "Come over and let me introduce you to the boys."

The crowd parted as Butch made his way toward the gang's table. Jack followed through the collapsing Red Sea of revelers.

"Guys." Butch put an arm around Jack's shoulders and offered a shifty grin. "Does this fella remind you of anyone?"

"My god, Butch, you let on like you've single-handedly sired every sombitch from here to Nacogdoches." The man tried to hide his gap-toothed grin before boisterous laughter overtook the others.

"Just doin' my part to replenish the earth, Henry," Butch said, joining in the laughter. "Just like the good book instructs."

"I think you overlooked the part where the Bible says you ain't s'posed to do that with your *neighbor's* wife!" Henry's face reddened from cackling.

Jack forced a smile, moving his gaze from Butch to the gang and back.

"Some of you were around when this fella was just a tyke. Anyways, this here's Jimmy's boy."

Henry rose to his feet. "I never would have guessed it in a thousand years." He took Jack's hand, shaking it. "Your old man was one of the best—as loyal as they come."

"Well I'll be roostered," the tall, black man said, getting to his feet. "I'm the one that made that slingshot for you when you was but a mere pup." He removed his hat as if standing graveside, paying respects. "Your pa was always goin' on about you and your sisters."

"Are you Elijah?"

"You gots a good memory!" His smile dampened. "We lost a good man when we lost your pa."

"What exactly happened to him?" Jack tried conjuring an inkling of spit in the desert that was now his mouth. "I know he got shot and all, but I never heard any details of who did it or why."

Butch retrieved his arm. "That burden is for those of us who was supposed to have been there for him."

Henry picked up a whiskey bottle. "He deserves to know the truth, Butch. After all, it's his pa we're talking about."

"It's too much for him to carry." Butch motioned toward Jack. "He ain't one of us, Henry. He ain't *like* us." He shrugged. "And what good is it gonna do him anyways?"

"It's his—"

"He'll end up getting his fool self killed!" Butch grasped Jack's shoulders. "Look, kid. When we find the bottom feeder who did it, you can rest assured *we'll* make him pay."

Jack dropped his gaze to his boot tips. "I may not *be* one of you fellers, but you ain't got no idea as to whether or not I'm *like* y'all."

Butch grinned. "Sounds like something Jimmy would have said."

"So if none of you was there when it happened, then how do y'all know who did it?"

"We got the culprit's description from somebody who *was* there," Henry said, prompting a glare from Butch.

"So you're saying you don't really know *who* did it, you just know what the guy looks like."

"Well, to be honest"—while still speaking to Jack, Henry eased his gaze to Butch—"there are a bunch of men who fit the description."

"So you're saying—"

"Listen, Jack." Butch removed his hat, wiped his forehead. "The details we gathered could describe at least a half-dozen men in this saloon at this very moment: tall, long hair, mustache." He shrugged. "There's more, but I don't want to take a chance on you going over the deep end every time you see someone with that depiction."

"You know, Butch, we've been in need of another gun since Jimmy's death." Elijah gestured toward Jack. "Maybe he could take his pa's place."

"That's not a bad idea." Butch leaned forward as though searching for some kind of fire in Jack's eyes. "How would you like to be part of the gang when we catch up with your father's killer?"

"You serious?"

Butch smiled. "You got a horse?"

Jack jutted a thumb over his shoulder. "Back at the ranch."

"Better go fetch it. We need to brand that beast if you're gonna ride with us."

"We'll camp here." Butch climbed off his horse and pointed toward the landscape. "These rock formations will make good cover."

Stirring dust finally caught up with them, silently passing among their ranks like spirits of the past, oblivious to the here and now.

"Let's gather some firewood," Henry said, tugging Jack's arm.

Darkness moved in, stretching shadows across the scorched earth. Most of the trees and vegetation looked to have been dead for years without a single drop of rain.

"Where we headed?" Jack picked up a few broken branchlets. "Nobody's said nothin' about anything."

"We got a job in Wyoming."

"Doin' what?"

Henry broke a limb across his knee and cradled the pieces in one arm. "Hunting buffalo for the railroad."

"Buffalo?"

"Yep. Quick and easy money." He paused a moment. "You seem surprised."

"I just expected a little more . . . lawlessness, I guess."

"Being on your own out here is dangerous." Henry snapped a twig for demonstration. "Truth is, we band together for protection." Bundling several twigs in his grip, he feigned a failed attempt of breaking them. "It's not about being outlaws, it's about improving our chances of survival."

"Funny how that worked out for my old man."

Dropping the branches, Henry grabbed Jack by the lapels. "Don't you be spoutin' off with a bunch of malarkey you know nothin' about!" The words came through a smattering of gnashed teeth. "Your pa was more family to many of us than our own flesh and blood."

"I didn't—"

"Yeah, yeah." Henry shoved Jack away and started retrieving the scattered wood. "You'd best keep that foolish talk to yourself. And just so you know"—he aimed an unwieldy bough at Jack's chest—"*Shedding* blood with someone is just as much kinship as *sharing* blood with them."

"Honest, I meant no offense."

Henry stared at the ground a moment before finally moving back toward camp. "This should be enough to get the fire started."

"Henry?"

"Yeah?"

"Did Pa kill anybody?"

Henry looked as though he'd just took a swig of clabbered milk. "Now why would you go and ask something like that?"

"Just curious is all." He rubbed the back of his neck. "Pa never talked about his work . . . or you fellers, for that matter."

"Well if Jimmy'd wanted you to know any of that stuff, *he* woulda told ya himself." Shifting the tree limbs in his arms, Henry started toward camp. "Let's get some vittles rustled up."

The campfire crackled and popped as heat and flickering light ebbed and flowed in the darkness.

The grub was warm, but that's about the only positive thing Jack could say about it. The beans were bland, the coffee was stale, and the hardtack was nothing short of barely-edible rocks.

But the men didn't seem to be too put off with any of it.

"You gots a gun, Jack?" Elijah had that bewildered look on his face again—the same look he always had while seemingly in deep thought.

"I lost the only one I had a few weeks back in a poker game."

"Lord have mercy." Elijah rummaged a grimy saddlebag. "Here," he said, handing over a Colt Single Action Army. "I'm returning the favor in your pa's honor."

"I can't accept this."

Taking Jack's wrist, Elijah forced the weapon into his hand. "It be the least I can do." He sat back, nodded. "After all, Jimmy gave me my first one. And besides, you'll be needin' it."

Jack opened the revolver's loading gate and gently rotated the cylinder. "I had no idea you were in the army."

"Not me." Elijah chuckled. "No sir, I acquired that piece from a genuine enlisted fella."

"So . . . you stole it?"

His eyes grinned as broadly as his mouth. "Now you knows it ain't polite to kiss and tell!"

The weight and feel of the revolver was comfortable in Jack's hand—almost too comfortable. "Thank you."

"Best keep it in an oiled rag or somethin' to

make sure it's good and protected. Last thing you want is it jammin' up on you when you needs it most."

Flipping the revolver over, Jack scrutinized the grip. "How long did you know Pa?"

"I'm guessin' right close to fifteen years or so." His bewildered expression developed into a sneaky grin. "That old buzzard saved my hide the very night I met him in Kansas."

"Really? What happened?"

"I was waitin' on a freight boss to finish up some paperwork in town." He raised an eyebrow. "Couple a drunken mudsills accused me of lookin' at 'em crossways or somethin'. 'Fore I know'd it, I was starin' straight down the barrel of a six-shooter."

A faint breeze washed over them, carrying light embers and smoke.

"Then this big fella walks up and puts a gun to the ear of the man pointin' his'n at me." Shaking his head, Elijah grinned. "Jimmy cocked back the hammer and told that fella, 'Go right on ahead if you feel froggy, son . . . but just you remember, frogs with glass asses only jump but once.'"

"Pa said that?"

"He sure did." Elijah slapped his leg and laughed. "Hard to say who was ready to mess their britches more, them mudsills or *me*!"

"What'd they do?"

"Them boys tore off down the way like scalded dogs." He shrugged. "I bought your pa a few rounds of whiskey and he invited me to ride with him and Henry."

"So that's . . ."

"That's how we got started."

Jack stared across the campfire, watching the flickering shadows contort and warp Butch Carver's face. "You reckon he'd teach me how to quick draw?"

Elijah followed Jack's gaze. "You mean Butch? To be right honest with you, I don't think he knows *how* to draw fast, I think he just can."

"Ever seen him draw on somebody?"

"More than *one* somebody." He turned back to Jack. "Different folk have a God-given talent for stuff. They don't learn it, they just does it." He shrugged. "I know'd a shopkeeper in Kansas who could remember *everything* he read . . . word for word. That fella remembered every bill of sale, every inventory list, and every single number on a tally sheet." Shaking his head, Elijah grinned. "It was like he was readin' those pages and numbers right from his naked brain."

"I ain't never heard tell of anything like that."

Elijah motioned toward Butch. "*His* talent is killing men 'fore they can kill him. He can draw and shoot straighter and faster than most can blink. To be real honest about it, I don't think that's something anybody can teach."

"Maybe." Jack pushed a smoldering log deeper into the flames. "But he just might be able to offer some advice on getting started."

"Come take my rifle, Jack." Butch's whispers were nearly lost in the wind as a dozen or more ambling buffalo grazed just down the hillside. "I want you to focus on that one right there." He gestured toward a specific cow to the left. "That's the leader."

"How can you tell?"

"Just do as I say. We'll stay downwind of the herd, getting as close as we can without spooking them." He put a hand on Jack's forearm. "Tell me what's next."

"I'm gonna drop the leader first, and then I'm gonna take my time picking off those around it—one shot, one kill each."

Butch nodded. "Don't forget, you're going to *squeeze* the trigger, not pull it or yank it like you did earlier."

Crouching as they moved, the two men inched quietly ahead while Elijah stayed behind on the hillside. The bison's pungent muskiness overwhelmed them the closer they approached.

"I don't think—"

Putting an index finger to his lips, Butch surveyed for movement, and then motioned toward the lead cow. "Do it," he mouthed.

Perspiration trickled around Jack's eyes, threatening to blur and sting. *You can do this.*

"Remember, ease your breath out while *squeezing* the trigger."

Jack put a bead on the behemoth and made an effort to clear his thoughts from the thundering heartbeat in his ears.

You can do this.

The blast caught him by surprise as the recoiling buttstock rammed into him, sending pain to his shoulder and the Winchester to the ground.

Reaching to retrieve the rifle, Jack fell forward and recognized the panicked movement from the bison.

"Move!"

Just as he caught sight of the lead cow barreling down on him, Jack grabbed for his hat while Butch drug him away from the imminent impact by his collar.

Another gunshot roared with the creature collapsing just feet from Jack's legs. The stampeding herd was like rolling thunder echoing throughout the valley.

Butch holstered his pistol and hefted Jack to his feet. "Are you all right?"

"I think so," he said, rubbing his shaky legs. "I'm not sure what happened."

Blood flowed from the buffalo's mangled eye as its front legs jerked and quivered.

Retrieving the rifle, Butch cranked its lever and fired into the creature's head. "Now do you see why the details are important?"

"I don't know what happened. I tried doing everything you said, but the rifle went off before I was ready."

"That's why you always leave your finger *outside* the trigger guard until you're ready for the shot." Butch cranked the lever again and collected the spent casings. "Keep your finger stretched out, pointing forward, until you're ready to squeeze. How many times have we gone over this?"

"I'm sorry, Butch."

"You two scared the wits outta me." Elijah came up behind them, placing a hand on Jack's shoulder. "You hurt?"

"I don't think so." He rubbed his shoulder. "Gonna be a tad sore for a few days, though."

"Here." Butch handed the rifle to Jack. "You and I are following the herd so we can finish this." Turning to Elijah, he gestured back toward the hillside. "Get someone to help you with cleaning this one, then follow after us for the others."

Jack held out the Winchester. "You better take this, I've caused enough problems."

"No sir." Butch pocketed the casings. "You're going to finish what you started."

Jack pushed the beans around his tin, waiting for the campfire ribbing to commence. Neither Butch nor Elijah, or any of the others for that matter, had so much as snickered or poked fun at him over the day's blunders.

"This may be the best buffalo I've ever gnawed on," Elijah said, cutting into another piece. "What you got on this, Henry?"

"Just salt."

"I don't normally take to buffalo"—Elijah gestured toward his plate—"but this here's mighty tasty."

"May be the best I've had as well," Butch said. "And we can all give thanks to Jack for felling this beast, feeding us all tonight."

The agreeing grunts and cheers didn't last long as the men refocused on their food.

Scanning faces for any smirks or giggles or sneaky grins, Jack shoveled another spoonful of beans into his mouth.

Henry cleared his throat in that way when you want everyone's attention. "I heard tell that Jim Leavy is about these parts."

Butch pushed his hat back on his head. "Jim Leavy? *Here*?"

"Is what I heard."

"What's that no-good sidewinder doing here?"

"Other than looking for a fight?" Henry shrugged. "I wouldn't have the foggiest."

"He'll find *exactly* what he's looking for if I run into him." Butch lit a cheroot and traipsed into the darkness. "I can promise you that much."

Jack waited a moment before leaning into Elijah. "Who's Jim Leavy?"

"Mostly a gambler and gunfighter. Gots a mean reputation as fast and efficient." He glanced into the darkness. "Gunned down Butch's cohort, Mike Casey, back in Nevada."

"You think he's here for Butch?"

"Hard to say." He sopped a biscuit in his beans. "But if Butch catches him out somewheres, it ain't gonna be pretty."

"I wouldn't know the man if I laid eyes on him."

"Oh you'd know Leavy if you happened upon *him*." Elijah's bewildered look soured. "One of Casey's friends shot the Irish bastard in the jaw, leaving him disfigured and downright grotesque."

"Think Butch could beat him to the draw?"

"I imagine it'd be close, for sure. But Leavy's got more of a reputation for calm accuracy than just fast-draw theatrics."

Soft harmonica notes emanated from somewhere about the campfire, intermingling a familiar, yet unidentifiable melody with the popping and cracking.

"How did Butch end up joining the gang?"

"He come to us, asked if we had room for another gun. Didn't take long at all to realize just how good he was."

"Was Pa the leader back then?"

"Sure enough." His smile widened. "But Jimmy was groomin' Butch almost from the very beginning."

"To take over as leader?"

Elijah went back to sopping. "To grow up and take responsibility for more than just his own self."

Jack rode next to Butch on horseback as they led the wagon into a mud-filled valley entrance. Shifting in his saddle, he spat an amber stream of tobacco. "This has to be the smallest town I've ever witnessed."

"Ain't a town," Butch said, surveying the surroundings. "It's a trading post."

"Well it's the smallest *trading post* I've ever seen."

The building was but a house made from crude logs and daubing. A covered porch gave shelter to the front door as well as a window to its right.

"Stay close when we get inside." Jabbing a thumb over his shoulder, Butch slowed the pace. "The others will unload everything while we negotiate."

A single horse stood hitched at the bottom of the sloped knoll where the building rested at the top. Rocks jutted from the muddy footpath leading to the entrance, encouraging hope of sure footing and dry clothing.

"Let me handle the conversations," Butch said, dismounting. "Your job is to watch my back. That is all."

"Got it."

Dank hides and burnt coffee lingered in the air just inside the main room, where an elderly woman smiled from a cluttered counter. "You boys like something to drink?" Her voice was shaky, thin.

"No thank you, ma'am." Butch made his way toward her. "But we sure do appreciate the hospitality."

"Looking for anything in particular?"

"Got a wagon full of buffalo hides." Butch motioned to the door. "Like to see about selling them."

Squinting, the woman leaned forward. "You boys don't look much like skinners."

"We thought we'd try our hands at hunting for the railroad." He rubbed the back of his neck. "While we're moving through the territory."

"Let me guess." A perceptive smile wrinkled her face. "You boys have *extra* pelts you're now aimin' to sell on the side."

Butch grinned. "Yes, ma'am. That about sums it up."

Jack studied the room, taking note of an open doorway leading to another room to the right.

"These hides. They ain't gonna put me in a stinky predicament, are they?"

"No ma'am, these were not acquired while hunting on railroad time."

A single chuckle shook her chest and head. "That don't mean nothin' to the railroad folk."

"I can promise you, the men in our camp who felled these beasts are not even signed up by the railroad."

"I gotta hand it to you." Her smile widened. "You're pretty sharp for a dull fella."

A crashing came from the next room, sounding as though something had been knocked over or dropped.

Butch met Jack's gaze and nodded in the direction where the ruckus came from.

Removing the Colt from his belt, Jack crept through the doorway, scouring the room for movement.

Among the stacks of hides and blankets and cookware, the shelving was filled with every imaginable item a man would need on or off the trail.

"Sorry about the racket."

Jack jerked his aim toward the voice as a rush of adrenaline stabbed his nerves.

"W-whoa, whoa!" A tall figure emerged from the darkness of the far corner, hands raised. "Didn't mean to startle you."

Jack held his stance and aim. "What are you doing in here?"

"I was—"

"Everything all right?" Butch stood in the doorway with a hand on his sidearm.

"I was just trying to tell your friend here that I accidentally knocked over these shovels while reaching for that frying pan."

Butch moved his gaze from the man to the shovels and then to the shelf. "Put away your piece, Jack." He stepped closer to the man. "I apologize, we've been on the trail a bit too long."

"No need to apologize." The man took the skillet from the shelf and made his way to the main room. "The trail can make a fella right jumpy, it can."

After the stranger was gone, Butch placed a hand on Jack's shoulder. "I'm gonna go fetch one of the hides for the old woman to look over." He picked up a plug of tobacco and tossed it to Jack. "Gather all the items we discussed."

"Will do."

Jack carried several things to the counter where the woman was preoccupied with folding blankets.

"Where do you keep the cookin' flour?"

The woman finally looked up. "Your name Butch Carver?"

Jack squinted. "Why do you wanna know?"

Handing him a slip of paper, she shrugged. "Fella who just left told me to give that to you."

Jack glanced at the door, then back to the woman, who had already gone back to her folding. Opening the note, Jack made his way to the seclusion of the next room before Butch returned.

"I'm going to give you a fighting chance," the words read. "I will be waiting at the Palace Hotel. If, however, you choose to take the yellow trail, you will find my generosity sorely lacking."

Jack's stomach roiled at the sight of the signature. "Jim Leavy."

He's here for Butch. Jack read the note again, searching for anything he could find between the words. *He's come for Butch.*

"Everything all right?"

"Yeah." Jack tucked the note into a pocket as he turned to Butch. "Just makin' sure I got everything."

The late-morning heat squeezed Jack's lungs, oppressing his *innards* as much as his *out-tards,* as his Aunt Bessie used to say. And just like the sweltering Kentucky summers, the manure-laced breezes here did very little in the way of cooling anything in the torrid Wyoming pot.

"Gimme a hand, Jack." Henry tossed a rope across the wagon's buffalo hides. "Tighten that down and tie it off."

Feeding the braided hemp through a slat, Jack pulled it taut before working a simple knot. "Come see if this is up to snuff."

Henry tugged at the rope, nodded. "Hey, why don't you ride into town with me and help get these hides to the railroaders?"

The arid soil carried the scent of rain—yet not a hint of cloud could be found.

"Sure. Just let me visit the necessary first."

Finding a spot behind a decent bull pine, he gazed into the big blue sky where a Red-Tailed Hawk circled in silence and majesty. Jack shivered—either from the sight of the bird or from the relieving sensation of making water.

On his way back to the wagon, he clutched the slip of paper inside his pocket while fixing his gaze to Butch, who appeared to be cleaning his rifle on the far side of camp.

"Where you off to in such a trot?" Elijah seemed to step out from nowhere. "You let on like they handin' out sorghum cake in town or somethin'."

"Sweet Jesus, you scared the ever-lovin' bird turds outta me."

"I guess so, you was comin' through here like you was paintin' the camp with peyote."

Jack ran his thumb across the note still in his pocket. "I'm on my way to help Henry take the new hides into town."

"Then you best get to it." He slapped Jack on the back. "You sure don't want to keep that cantankerous buzzard waitin'."

Jack's gaze moved to the figure cleaning the rifle in the distance. "What do you think *he's* up to?" he said, jutting his chin toward Butch.

"If I was a bettin' man, I'd say he makin' preparations for Jim Leavy." Elijah smiled. "But I ain't no bettin' man . . . and I *still* say he makin' preparations for Leavy."

"Butch ain't gonna have to worry none about that feller."

Elijah turned back to him. "Now what on earth is *that* supposed to mean?"

Jack shrugged. "I just figure that Leavy feller don't really want no part of Butch Carver is all."

Another bluff of heat washed over them and was gone as quickly as it showed up.

"You best not be workin' up any preparations on your own, you hear?"

Jack let go of the note in his pocket and adjusted his hat. "I better get going. Like you said, I don't want Henry fussin' and sworpin' any more than usual."

Even though there wasn't much to speak of, the town bustled with activity. Wagons coming and going, men loading and unloading items of all sorts and sizes, and folks standing around waiting for something or someone or seemingly nothing in particular.

"Everyone keeps calling this place *town*," Jack said as they neared a mass of buildings. "Just plain ol' *town*. I don't reckon I've heard anybody use its name."

"Evanston. Named after some railroad official."

Jack leaned forward, pointing toward an enormous structure in the distance. "What in tarnation is *that*?"

"Roundhouse. It's where they work on engines and such."

"Is that where we're going?"

"No." He motioned toward a two-story building that seemed to be the center of business in town. "*That's* the Union Pacific office."

A distant clanging came from the direction of that immense edifice down the tracks—a metal to metal rhythmic dinging you'd normally hear from a blacksmith's shop.

"Seeing how the saloon is just next door, reckon we could have a few 'fore we head back to camp?" He grinned. "I mean, when we're done with business, of course."

"We'll see." Henry climbed down from the bench, stretched. "You stay with the hides while I go settle up with these high-benders."

The clanging continued in the distance, intermingled with an occasional steam whooshing.

Jack's stomach gurgled when he spotted the Palace Hotel just on the other side of the saloon. Long pull-down flags and pleated fan bunting gave the front of the establishment a very patriotic and official appearance.

"Newspaper?"

The boy standing beside the wagon couldn't have been more than ten or eleven, but something about the darkness around his eyes revealed life had aged him more than his years.

"What?"

"Newspaper." The boy held one up for Jack to see. "*Uinta County Herald*. Wanna buy one?"

"I ain't got no use for a blamed newspaper."

"Can't read?"

A familiar figure stepped out from the saloon's door. He wasn't carrying the pan he'd bought, but he was definitely the fellow from the trading post.

"I can read, you little bastard! Now go on and git!"

The man in front of the saloon turned his gaze toward Jack and instantly darted between the buildings.

"Hey!" Jack yelled as he leaped from the wagon. "Come back here!"

The man slipped into a doorway on the saloon side and disappeared into the darkness.

"I've got questions for you!" Jack put a hand on his Colt. "Stop acting like a coward and come face me!"

Stepping through the doorway, Jack scanned the space, which was obviously the saloon's storage area. Wooden crates lined the back wall, barely visible in the darkness. The ruckus from the main hall was muted, yet synonymous with nearly every saloon he'd ever frequented.

The stranger stood in the shadows at the far corner of the room. "Leave me be," he said without moving.

Jack raised his piece as he eased forward. "You're gonna tell me about that note you left at the tradin' post."

"I ain't got nothin' to say."

"You better have *plenty* to say." Jack inched closer, maintaining his aim on the silhouette. "You're ridin' with that Jim Leavy feller, ain't ya?"

The silhouette shifted without a reply.

"Answer me!"

Movement from the darkness at Jack's right caught his attention, just as pain exploded in his hand when something knocked the Colt from his grip.

A weathered boot quickly pinned the weapon to the floor as Jack scrambled to recover it.

"You're not Butch Carver." The voice made an odd slushing sound with each syllable. When the light from the door revealed the man's scars and misaligned jawline, Jack stepped back with a coldness in his gut.

"Jim Leavy." The name came out of Jack before he could stop it.

"Thatsh right."

Jack barely had time to blink when he caught glimpse of the pistol butt barreling toward his face.

The darkness shifted with garbled and glugging sounds that reminded Jack of swimming the depths of Green River as a kid.

He forced his matted eyelids open and winced at the sunlight coming through what appeared to be ornate parlor windows of some luxury locomotive car.

Mahogany wainscoting, velveteen curtains, and opulent gas lamps stood out among the cabin's countless decorative features.

Attempting to sit up, Jack caught his balance when he realized he'd actually been standing the entire time.

What in blazes?

He quickly ran his hand over his nose and face but found no pain, no blood, not one thing out of the ordinary.

"There you are."

Turning, Jack found a refined gentleman seated on a leather burgundy sofa, combing his hair to the side.

His single-breasted morning jacket was brown ribbed worsted coating with the edges and cuffs bound with fine braid, a collarless waistcoat of white fancy quilting, and bright brown stripe trousers.

"Please . . ." He motioned toward a matching wingback chair. "Make yourself comfortable."

Jack held his gaze to the stranger's cold blue eyes while trying to put a finger on why his voice sounded familiar. "Where am I?"

"I have to admit." The man pocketed the comb and lit a rotund cigar. "I have searched the world high and low to locate you."

"What are you talking about?"

"I'd like to offer you a job, Mr. McCall—one that will make yours a household name for generations to come."

"How do you know my name?" Jack sat forward, scanning the quarters. "Are you with that Jim Leavy feller?"

Rising, the stranger made his way to a mirrored shelf and poured a glass of whiskey from a lavish decanter. "I'll get right to the point. There's a certain individual whom I wish to become . . . let's say . . . bereft of life."

There was something about the way the man spoke that was very much reminiscent of Doc Mc-Dowell—especially his accent and use of highfalutin words and phrases.

Jack got to his feet. "So you *are* with that lowdown murderer! Well you can get it outta your head right now, Mister . . ."

"I fear you misunderstand my intentions." Extending a hand, the man stepped closer. "For the sake of anonymity, why don't you just call me John Varnes."

Jack refused the handshake. "I'd just as soon die as to help you kill Butch Carver!"

"I assure you, Butch Carver is *not* my concern." He shrugged. "And neither is Jim Leavy, for that matter."

"I don't think I—"

"In exchange for your services, Mr. McCall, I'm willing to make you . . . bulletproof."

Jack cocked his head. "You some kind of politician or somethin'? Promisin' to keep the law outta my hair if I do as you ask?"

"I'm afraid not." Varnes poured another whiskey and handed it to Jack. "I mean precisely what I say—you will *physically* become bulletproof."

Pain exploded throughout Jack's face as he awak-
ened on a saloon table, stretched out on his back,
with a cluster of men standing over him.

"He's coming to!" The booming voice startled
Jack into sitting up.

"Easy there," an older man soothed while
gentle hands moved his shoulders back to the table.
"You've been out for a while. You had us worried."

Squinting from the painful light, Jack reached
for his face, searching for the source of agony.

A hand caught his wrist and moved his arm
back to his side. "Take it easy, son, your nose is
busted up pretty bad and both your eyes are turning purple."

"Where'd he go?"

"Who?" The man pulled one of Jack's bottom
eyelids down and leaned closer. "Barkeep found
you in the back looking like you'd been kicked in
the face by a bank mule. Found your Colt a few
feet away."

"The fella from the train." Jack's own voice
brought misery to his head. "Where'd he go?"

"Just settle down." The man checked Jack's
other eye. "I'm Doc Zornes. I'm gonna give you
some laudanum for the pain."

"I don't need no laudanum." Jack moved to
sit up again, and again allowed the hands to ease
him back to the table.

"Son, you're gonna need all you can get your hands on when I start working on resetting that snout of yours."

Scrunching his nose, Jack immediately winced as another stab of pain came as quickly as the welling tears. "Shit!"

Zornes chuckled. "Do you see what I mean? That's why I'm giving you the—"

"Listen to me!" Jack groped at the man's lapels. "There was a fella here just a few minutes ago...well, not *here*...he was inside some fancy railcar."

"You took a terrible blow to the head, son. You're probably seeing things that aren't really there. It's a common thing with head trauma like yours."

"I know what I saw!"

Pulling away, the doctor motioned toward the doors. "You mean that fella with the wagon of buffalo hides Leavy took after?"

"What?" Jack pushed hands away as he sat up. "I need a horse!"

"Son, you're in no shape to—"

"Listen to me!" Jack moved to his feet, stuffing the Colt into the waistband of his trousers. "I need a horse *now*!"

Whistling wind carried dirt and debris through camp as Jack tied the mare he'd appropriated from the front of the saloon in town.

Scanning the area for activity, he noticed a few men standing over something. "Hey, did Henry come back this way?"

The individuals turned to Jack and steadily parted when he made his way toward them, revealing a figure on the ground at their feet.

"Henry?" Jack pushed past the men, dropped to his knees, and pulled the bloodied figure toward him. "Henry!"

Someone tugged at his arm. "It's too late. He's dead, Jack."

"No . . ."

The men pulled him to his feet. "Come on, Jack. We've got to get outta here before that maniac returns."

Jack straightened. "Leavy?" He studied each man's face. "Did Leavy do this?"

One of the fellas shrugged. "It was some guy with a mangled-up face."

"Where's Butch?"

"Him and Elijah took after the fella."

"Which way did they go?"

"Don't know what's going on, Jack, but that man was here intentionally for Butch."

Jack focused on the man's face for the first time. "What are you talking about, Burgess?"

"It was like that fella knew Henry'd lead him straight to Butch." He shrugged. "It's bound to be the reason he chased him."

"Why would you say that?"

"After he killed Henry, he rode through camp yelling Butch's name." Burgess dropped his gaze to the ground. "He tore outta here when Elijah and the rest of us started sending lead in his direction."

"He was ridin' through so fast, I don't reckon nary a bullet found a lick of flesh," one of the other men added.

Burgess cocked his head. "Next thing I know'd, Butch and Elijah tore outta here on horseback, yelling for us to stay with Henry."

Jack waited a moment, moving his gaze from one man to the next. "Well?"

Burgess stood motionless, maintaining a baffled expression.

Lifting his arms with an exaggerated shrug, Jack shook his head. "Which way did they go?"

Jack followed the trail of stirring dust as he scoured the valley for anything that could point him in the right direction.

Leavy must have knew Henry and Butch rode together.

The cumbrous sun weighed around his shoulders and neck—an albatross soaking his grubby collar with perspiration.

Reaching for the anguish in his face again, Jack winced as the searing stabs thrummed with every heartbeat, the wind against his face forcing tears toward his earlobes.

Why else would he go after Henry?

Gunshots rang out from a short distance ahead, instantly halting the gelding, the poor critter bobbing its head in protest.

"Let's go!" Jack yelled, striking the reins.

The agony in his head grew with every movement of the ride, seemingly as though something was expanding inside his skull.

The trail eventually opened into a fog of thick dust settling in every direction.

Slowing to listen closer, Jack turned in the saddle when a breeze rustled through twisted, shabby trees, carrying a hint of cigar smoke.

"We have some unfinished business, don't you think?"

Jack fumbled for his piece as an icy stab ran the length of his spine. The coldness swelled when he found John Varnes sitting cross legged on a wingback chair in the middle of the wilderness, a smoldering cigar just inches from his face.

"Shit!" Jack took aim. "How did you—"

"We don't have a lot of time . . . especially with what you're about to encounter."

Jack searched the surroundings for a horse or wagon or anything that could make sense of any of this. "You some kinda haint?"

Smiling, Varnes drew on the cigar. "I'm afraid you are about to embark on a situation where my offer would be quite advantageous," he said, exhaling smoke.

Jack tried to steady his aim. "What do you mean?"

"Very shortly, in just mere minutes, you are going to find yourself in a situation where the benefits of our agreement could mean life or death for you." He rose to his feet. "And you are of no use to me dead."

"Where is Butch and Elijah? Did they come through this way?"

Retrieving an envelope from his jacket's inside pocket, Varnes stepped forward. "All you have to do is take care of my problem, and your issue will no longer be an issue."

"Look, I ain't no murderer. I don't know what gave you that idea. I don't even know who you are . . . or *what* you are for that matter."

Varnes removed the folded paper from the envelope and held it out. "You don't have to pretend with me."

Jack took the document, looked over the fancy handwriting. "There's not even a name listed for the feller you want—"

"You'll know him when you meet him." Varnes smiled. "You won't have to worry about that."

Jack studied the man's eyes. "What if I say no?"

"I'll just find someone else." Shrugging, Varnes held out a writing instrument. "Possibly sooner than it will take for anyone to find your rotting corpse out here."

"You threatenin' me?"

"Not at all." Varnes sank back into the chair. "In fact, I'm trying to save you."

The quietude on the trail brought a sourness to Jack's stomach as he rode further into the openness.

He poked at his chest with an index finger, examining the pressure and tenderness of fingernail against flesh.

What am I doing? He wiped his finger down his jacket and refocused on the surroundings. *Varnes is a lunatic.*

A darkened spot in the distance stood out from the landscape's dust, rocks, and vegetation.

Holding his gaze on the motionless shape, Jack urged the horse along with caution.

He massaged his forehead, hoping to relieve the misery. "Shoulda asked to be *painproof* instead of bulletproof."

Jack drew his piece, directing it toward a silhouette when he caught a glimpse of movement.

"You best turn back if ya know what's good for you," a strained voice said from the bleeding man on the ground.

"Elijah?" Jack dismounted and dropped next to him. "Are you ok?"

Elijah stared off to the right. "Is that you, Jack?" He put a trembling hand on his chest and coughed. "You needs to git on outta here."

Jack leaned closer. "Where's Butch?"

"Don't you worry none about Butch. Butch can care for his own self." He coughed again, sending specks of crimson onto his cheeks and chin. "Git on that horse and head back the way you came."

"You know I can't—"

"You should lishen to your friend."

Coldness bloomed in Jack's legs and torso as he turned toward Jim Leavy. The man's stance was a confident lean with a palm resting on his sidearm.

Jack couldn't tell if Leavy was offering a smirk of a grin, or if the scars just twisted up his mouth that way. "Go to hell."

"Thatsh just downright rude, boy." There was no doubt it was a smile now twisting into place. "I'd exshpect a bit more gratitude from someone I left with little more than a busted nose."

"Where's Butch?"

Leavy squinched his eyes. "Amid the flames o' hell by now, I'd wager."

"You . . ." Jack turned his piece toward the Irishman and began firing.

Report from Leavy's gun intermingled with Jack's as the two men moved for cover.

Jack's legs weakened and his chest tightened as he searched for a safe spot to retreat.

The horse Jack brought fidgeted at the ruckus before buckling swiftly to the ground.

Gun smoke lingered in the air with the faintest of a breeze.

Trying to keep his gaze to Leavy, Jack tripped over a rock and came down hard on his side. The pain in his ribs seemed connected directly to his throbbing face.

He examined his side with a trembling hand but found no blood, no bullet wounds.

Upon realizing the shooting had ended, Jack noticed Leavy was no longer in the place he'd been firing from.

"You all right, Elijah?"

The sounds of a galloping horse echoed as Leavy came into view as he rode back toward town.

Turning to Elijah, Jack noticed the fresh bullet hole in his friend's forehead. "Elijah?"

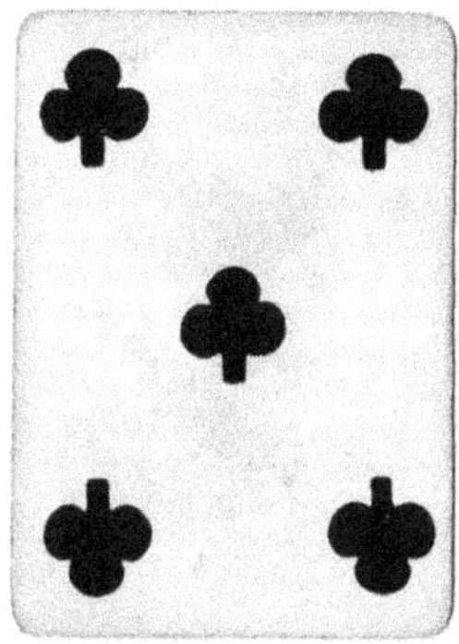

The campfire crackled and popped as the night air washed over the handful of men gathered at what was left of their camp.

"What are we to do now, Jack?" The dirt stains on Burgess's undershirt was a mournful reminder of the three men they'd buried just hours earlier.

"I ain't got no clue." Jack stared blankly ahead. "Why are you askin' me?"

"I reckon it's the thing to talk over." Burgess spit tobacco toward the fire. "Should we head out in the morning or stay put for a day or so?"

One of the other men leaned forward. "Word in town is Leavy has already packed and gone."

Jack lifted his chin. "What direction they sayin' he took?"

"Nobody's made that clear."

"Just so you know, I'm leavin' first thing in the mornin'." Jack focused on the fire. "I'm headin' out on my own."

"You oughta stay with us for a few days longer," Burgess said. "We can all use some time to think before we start making decisions."

"I ain't stayin' here any longer than I have to."

"I understand." There was resignation in Burgess's voice. "You've been through quite a bit today. And Lady Luck seemed to have been by your side the whole time."

Jack gently touched his aching nose. "If Lady Luck was with me, I'd sure hate to think of what my day woulda been without her."

"Elijah got a bullet smack-dab twixt his eyes." Burgess shook his head. "That horse you road out there on took a bullet to the side of the head and was probably dead 'fore it hit the ground." He shrugged. "You survived without a slug one, and *you* were the one Leavy was shooting at."

"Yeah, well maybe he's just not as good as they let on."

"You know better than that. That fella shot Henry from a distance while riding through camp." Burgess forced air from his lips. "We all know how good Butch was, right? And you saw what the man did to Butch . . . no sir, Lady Luck was practically holding your hand."

Jack stared deeper into the fire. "Y'all ever heard of John Varnes?"

One of the men took a swig from a bottle and handed it to Jack. "Who?"

Jack wiped the top with a shirtsleeve before taking a drink. "John Varnes." He handed the whiskey to Burgess. "I met him in one of them fancy rail cars."

"I don't recall anyone named Varnes," Burgess said with a shrug. "Is he from around these parts?"

Jack reached for the whiskey again. "I'm fairly certain Varnes ain't from around here."

The front of the trading post appeared abandoned when Jack pulled the wagon to the hitching rail with his horse ponied.

He shifted his Colt in his waistband as he headed toward the open door where the old woman stood staring out at him.

"Can't be good news when you come traipsin' in here all by your lonesome."

Jack removed his hat, wiped a gritty sleeve across his forehead. "You'd be correct in that assumption, ma'am."

Stepping out on the porch, the woman shielded her eyes from the sunlight. "You wouldn't be bringin' trouble with you, now would you?"

"At this point, I don't rightly know what to expect."

"You look like you could use a bit of bourbon." She turned to go inside. "I can already tell I'm gonna need some myself."

There was a sweet smell just inside, but not in a pleasant manner.

"You looking to sell those hides?"

Placing his hat back on his head, Jack nodded. "Looking to sell the whole rig . . . except for my horse."

She put a half-empty bottle on the counter and stared into Jack. "I got myself a bad feeling about this."

Jack uncorked the bourbon, took a drink, and slid the bottle back across the counter. "Tell you what, you let me collect a few supplies and I'll just leave the rig and hides."

She took a drink. "I fear the trouble it's bound to bring me."

"What's a proprietor to do when someone just abandons things right outside their door?"

A grin eventually stretched across her face. "You got ten minutes . . . and I better never see you around here again."

On his way back toward the wagon, Jack noticed a tethered horse that hadn't been there when he'd gone inside. He scanned the landscape without moving his head, just as Butch had taught him.

Keeping his Colt at the ready, Jack secured the supplies to his horse, mounted up, and eased back to the trail.

The mysterious critter wasn't Leavy's, nor was it the horse of the fella running with the Irishman as best Jack could recollect. *I woulda surely heard if someone had entered the building while I was gathering items.*

He kept glancing over his shoulder as his horse trotted along without any sign of alarm or caution.

Where the hell am I goin'? He yanked at the collar that kept riding up his neck. *And which direction would Leavy be heading?*

It only took a few hours in the saddle before Jack was rubbing at his backside. After a bit of numbness and soreness, he found a clearing and secured the horse.

Stretching, he gazed over the area before finding a spot to relieve himself. Darkness would be upon him soon so he decided to set up camp for the night.

Once he had a fire started, he took a few pieces of jerked beef from his pack and nibbled. He'd been riding west, but not intentionally or with a specific destination in mind.

The fire's warmth permeated his clothing, rebuking the night air, soothing his nose and face.

A warbling groan came from the horse as it shifted.

Turning to check on the beast, Jack recoiled at the sudden cold metal against his temple.

"Keep your hands right where they are." It was a soft, growl-of-a-voice from behind. "Hand me that piece you've got tucked at your side. I don't wanna kill you, but I will if you force me to."

The man's voice wasn't familiar, but Jack strained to attach it to someone he may have encountered in the past. "Who are you with?"

"Just keep your mouth shut and do as I say."

The stench from the stranger reminded Jack of his days working with the hogs back at his grandfather's farm.

"Give me the money and I'll leave you with your horse and supplies."

Jack dug into a pocket and retrieved a small leather pouch. Holding it out, he noticed the wrinkling in the stranger's hands and face. "You gonna leave my piece as well?"

"Shut up." The man opened the pouch's mouth and emptied the contents into a filthy palm. "What's this?"

Jack moved his gaze from the coins to the man's face. "What do you mean?"

"What do I mean?" His frown turned to clenched teeth. "Where's the money?"

"I don't think I follow what you mean." He nodded toward the coins. "You've got the money right there."

The man balled his fist around the silver pieces. "Drop the simpleton routine, boy!" He stepped closer, keeping the muzzle against Jack's head. "I followed you from the trading post after you sold them hides and wagon. So where's the money?"

Heat spread into the back of Jack's neck. "I didn't sell anything. And if that old hag said I did, then she lied to you."

"I'm going to give you one last chance." The words came through still-clenched teeth. "If you don't tell me where the money is, I'll spread your brains across this fire and search for it myself."

"Look, I'll empty my pockets, strip down naked if you want . . . and even unpack everything from the horse." Jack shrugged. "But what little bit you got in your hand is all the money there is."

The man's eyebrows came down together. "Just shut your yappin'." He stuffed the bits into a pocket and shook his head. "I can't believe I followed you all this way for little more than a handful of nickels."

A branch shifted in the fire, sending a light burst of embers into the air.

"And I can't just let you go now, can I?"

The warmth drained from Jack's neck and chest. "Listen— "

"I said shut up!" He added pressure to the muzzle against Jack's temple. "I need to think."

Jack closed his eyes and tried to slow his breathing.

"I'm sorry, fella." The man ratcheted the hammer back. "But I can't take any chances."

Jack braced himself, squeezing his eyes shut. But the firearm offered nothing more than an empty click.

Without hesitation, Jack knocked the gun from his head and wrestled the thief to the ground.

The man wasn't as large as he'd appeared to be when he was standing over Jack. And now on the ground, he seemed nothing more than a scrawny old timer.

Clenching the fella's throat with one hand, Jack struggled to regain control of his own pistol. "You ain't so tough now, are ya?"

The old man abruptly clutched at Jack's grip with both hands, giving up the Colt in the struggle. His gasping turned to coughing, his coughing to dry heaves.

Putting the muzzle of his piece to the man's forehead, Jack grimaced. "Are you alone?"

The man's face reddened from his struggles. "Please don't kill me."

"Answer the question."

"I swear I'll ride in any direction you tell me to go. Just don't kill me." He held his hands up in surrender. "I have young'uns to feed."

"I'm afraid your young'uns are fixin' to starve."

Blood spattered Jack's arms and face when the gun went off.

He sat quietly until the ringing in his ears subsided before retrieving his money. "Those kid's oughta be old enough to fend for themselves by now anyway."

The saloon table looked as though it may have been used for shelter during some horrific battle. Deep scarring marred the wood, along with cigar-shaped burns at its edges.

Shoveling another spoonful of stew into his mouth, Jack kept tabs on the activity taking place between his seat in the far corner and the door.

The beef was tough and damn near tasteless, but as long as customers kept buying whisky, the grub was complimentary.

Four men occupied a nearby gambling table, each focusing so intently on the hands they'd been dealt, anyone who wasn't familiar with the game would probably think they were ignoring one another.

"If you'd spend a little more time shuffling the deck instead of running your mouth, we wouldn't keep playin' the same hands over and over," one of the men finally said, tossing his cards to the center of the table.

Grumbles and murmuring followed as the others surrendered their hands to the pot.

The ride had been a long and arduous one, especially with the efforts of being more vigilant along the way.

Leavy could be anywhere by now.

Cold air washed over the room when a husky fella came through the door sporting a clean shirt and britches that didn't quite match his stature.

A Colt hung high on his hip, cavalry-draw style, with the flap clearly cut from the holster.

Smiling at the bartender, the man ambled toward the bar, revealing another figure who'd followed in behind him.

The fancy attire of the second individual stood out among the common folk, yet no one seemed to pay him any mind as he made his way toward Jack's table.

"I'm glad to see you are traveling in the correct direction," John Varnes said, taking a seat.

"I ain't got no clue as to what you're up to." Jack tapped an index finger to his temple. "But there ain't a doubt in my mind, you're tetched in the head."

"In spite of last night's altercation, you still don't believe yourself to be bulletproof?"

"For one thing, the thief's pistol jammed when . . ." He paused a moment. "How did you know about last night?"

"Do you play?" The man lit a cigar.

Jack noticed the bartender studying him as he turned back to Varnes. "What the hell is that supposed to mean?"

"Poker." He gestured toward the men still playing. "Do you know how to play?"

"Of course. I'm more familiar with Faro, but I've taken part in about every gambling game you can imagine."

"Good. It will come in handy when you get to Deadwood."

"Deadwood? Dakota Territory?"

"That's right." Varnes fiddled with one of his cufflinks. "The gentleman I have contracted you to . . . deal with . . . will be there." He drew on his cigar. "I use the term *gentleman* very loosely here, mind you."

"Who are you really?"

Varnes leaned back in his chair. "Why, Mr. McCall, I've already explained that you may call me John Varnes."

"I got that. But you know damn well that ain't what I'm gettin' at."

It took a moment before Varnes smiled. "I know you are interested in more details, Mr. McCall." Leaning forward, he fixed his gaze to Jack's. "But for anonymity purposes, *John Varnes* will have to suffice."

"The only thing I'm interested in right now is finding Jim Leavy."

"I'm afraid vengeance will not satiate the hunger you now carry, my boy."

Jack raised his eyebrows. "Says the man that's hired me to kill some feller in order to satisfy his own vengeance."

"Ah, but *that* is where you are incorrect. I am but a mere debt collector. Vengeance is not mine, emotions do not rule my motives." He flicked ashes to the floor. "And you, my good man, are simply collecting a debt on my behalf."

"Call it what you will, but it's all the same if you ask me."

"Tell me something." Varnes put his elbows on the table and leaned in. "Why are you so hell bent on Jim Leavy?"

Jack searched the man's eyes. "You're joking, right?" He stole a glance at the door before turning back. "He killed Butch, killed Elijah, and killed Henry!"

"Let's be rational. How do you know he was the one who committed all those atrocities?"

"Waddaya mean *how do I know*? I was there."

Varnes drew on his cigar, leaned back in the chair. "Well, to be fair, you only *heard* that Leavy killed Henry." He stared at the butt of his cigar. "Sure, Elijah died during a gun battle between you and Leavy, but you can't be certain it wasn't a ricocheting bullet of his or yours that did him in. And there are absolutely no witnesses to the death of Butch Carver."

"Leavy was the only other person out there!"

Varnes tilted his head. "Can you be certain of that?"

"Leavy even said—"

"Jim Leavy speculated that Butch was *amid the flames of hell* when you asked where he was." He brought the cigar closer to his lips. "A far cry from admission to murder, I would think."

Jack started to stand but leaned closer. "What are you gettin' at?"

Varnes shrugged. "What if it was someone else?"

"Do you know something you ain't tellin'?"

"I don't know, do I . . . Jack?"

"What the hell is *that* supposed to mean?"

Varnes drew again from the cigar. "You've talked quite a bit about Jim Leavy, but you haven't said one word about what you found when you discovered Butch."

Jack picked up his whiskey and immediately put it back on the table. "I don't want to talk about it."

"Oh, I think you *want* to talk about it." His gentle tone did little to soften the lingering chill in his eyes. "And I understand your worries of being overcome with emotion."

Jack tried to swallow the tightness that crept into his throat.

"After all, this is one of your closest friends we're talking about." Varnes barely nodded. "More than likely, you regarded Butch Carver far more closely than you did your very own family. Why, I would even go so far as to say you probably thought of him as a brother."

The saloon's quietude produced a ringing in Jack's head, very similar to what is experienced after one fires a scattergun.

Cigar smoke stung Jack's eyes as the tightening in his throat became a lump of dryness. "He looked to be sleepin' on a small plateau of rocks." Trying to swallow again, Jack closed his eyes. "Just as peaceful as could be."

"Tell me what you saw."

Rubbing a knuckle over an eyebrow, Jack shook his head. "I just remember there was so much blood." The ringing seemingly grew. "Front of his shirt was soaked with it."

"Was there anything that seemed . . . *odd* to you?"

"There was no blood on his face. I remember that vividly for some reason."

"What about his hands?" Varnes blew smoke toward the ceiling. "Did you notice anything strange about his hands?"

Jack flinched at the returning images. "No blood either."

"Did you notice what he was *holding*?"

Jack shrugged. "He wasn't holding anything."

Dipping his chin toward his chest, Varnes lifted his brows for effect. "Nothing at all?"

"Nothing. He just looked as though . . ." Jack rubbed his aching forehead. "His pistols were still in their holsters."

"It sounds as though someone else could have took him by surprise."

Jack caught another glimpse of the gawking bartender. "Is there anything I can help you with?" he called across the room.

The proprietor turned away as though embarrassed, straightening bottles on the backbar as he moved.

"I've gotta watch my back now closer than ever before."

"After everything thus far," Varnes said, shaking his head. "You still do not believe yourself to be bulletproof?"

"I'll be honest with you, at this point, I don't believe much."

Varnes got to his feet. "Well then," he said, picking up his chair. "Let's make you a believer, shall we?"

In one fluid motion, he raised the chair over and behind his head and hurled it toward the bar where it crashed against the big man standing there.

Jack rose, watching as the crimson-faced fella turned toward him and Varnes.

Except Varnes was no longer there.

"If you're looking for trouble, boy, you've sure found it." The man shoved an empty table out of the way as he approached.

"Now hold on." Jack held up his hands. "There's been a misunderstanding."

"You better believe there's been a misunderstanding," he said, yanking Jack by the lapels. "A very *big* misunderstanding."

Scrambling for his piece, Jack barely had time to wince before the ham-of-a-fist slammed into his face, intensifying the pain that was already there.

Had the man not been holding him with that other ham, Jack would have been sprawled out on the floor, counting ceiling beams.

"So help me, if you manage to get that pistol outta your belt, you're gonna have an even bigger misunderstanding on your hands." The man's

Colt was now directed at Jack's head as he finally released him.

"I didn't—"

"Shut your mouth!" he said, motioning his revolver toward Jack's. "Just hand over the Peacemaker before you start taking heed to any other unhealthy ideas."

"If you'll just listen, I can—"

The man pulled back the hammer. "This is your last chance, boy."

Sourness crept from Jack's stomach into his chest and throat. "All right. All right." He carefully pulled the Colt from his belt, holding it close.

"Hand it over."

The sourness festered in Jack's throat. "I tell you what," he said, bringing the piece up, aiming it at the man's head. "Why don't you come and get it."

That intensive stare never wavered, it was as though the big fella hadn't heard Jack's words, hadn't noticed the Colt's bead on him. But then his left eye twitched.

At first, Jack believed his was the only report when he fired, but the sting in his shoulder, and smoke wafting from the man's piece, told a different story.

With blank eyes fixed on something unseen, the big fella groped at the widening bloodstain on his chest before dropping to the floor like a felled oak.

A warm breeze circulated the room as a few patrons scrambled out the door.

"Hells bells," the bartender said, moving closer. "You killed Virgil."

"He tried to kill *me*! You saw the whole thing." Jack returned the Colt to his belt. "He even got me in my shoulder." He reached for the wound and brought back a dry hand.

"You don't look hit." The bartender stepped closer to inspect. "What's your name?"

"Jack McCall." Jack closed his eyes almost immediately, shaking his head. "I mean—"

"You got a few holes in your shirt, but nary a bloodstain." The man turned to the remaining patrons. "Somebody go and fetch the sheriff."

Sure enough there were two holes, but no pain, no blood, and no explanation. The fact that the two holes were so closely situated they could easily be mistaken for one long one did little to ease Jack's mind. "You seen where I tried to keep from fightin' that feller."

"Everybody knows Virgil's got a temper, and when you hit him with that chair . . . why you're lucky to be alive. He just don't miss like he did with you."

"I didn't throw that chair. It was that fancy feller that came back to the table. John Varnes. That's his name, John Varnes."

The barkeep's eyebrows came together. "Look, kid, I'm not trying to put the blame on you. I'm just saying you're one lucky man to be alive right now."

The gamblers were back to their card game as though nothing had happened.

"I best go fetch the sheriff myself." The bartender tossed a rag behind the counter and made his way toward the door. "Hopefully he's not too drunk to come by."

Jack touched his shoulder again before downing what whiskey remained in his glass. *Shit.*

The gamblers didn't bother looking up from their cards as he quickly made his way to the door and his horse.

When first coming up to the tail end of a wagon train, Jack slowed his pace while focusing on getting a head count.

Looked to be just a few wagons with several flanking riders, but Jack made the effort to ride in the open, at a respectable distance. The last thing he wanted was to startle them with an unexpected approach.

It didn't take long before two riders split from the caravan and headed toward him in a reserved gallop.

The one leading the way had a dark brown beard with graying tufts at the chin, while the other looked to be too young to even shave.

"Didn't mean to startle you fellers," Jack called out before the two made it all the way to his position. "I wasn't expectin' to encounter anyone else out here."

"I reckon you're heading to Deadwood as well?" the older man asked, pushing his hat back on his head.

"That's the plan."

The man looked over Jack and his horse. "Ain't safe to be ridin' alone out here." He leaned over to his right and spat. "You runnin' from somebody or somethin'?"

A bead of sweat trickled Jack's backside. "Just got some business to tend, is all."

"I'm Luther Jackson." The man nodded toward his companion. "This here's my son, Clarence."

With the briefest of a nod, the younger fella moved his gaze anywhere he could to seemingly avoid Jack's.

"Nice to meet you fellers."

"I'm sure you understand our cautious nature. We can ill afford nary a chance on the trail."

Jack nodded. "I understand more than you know. But if you let me pass 'round you folks, you won't have to burden yourselves with maintaining an eye on a tailing stranger."

Luther daubed at his neck with a dingy bandana. "When's the last time you had a proper meal?"

"Other than jerked beef and hardtack? It's been a while."

The man nodded as though he knew the answer before Jack replied. "We're gonna set up camp here shortly. Why don't you let us get something in your belly before you move on?"

"I ain't lookin' to impose myself on y'all. But I sure do appreciate the gesture."

"You're *invited* . . . ain't the same as imposin'." He smiled. "Besides, I'd feel a whole heap better knowing we sent you ahead fully sustained."

"Suit yourself. I ain't about to turn down a hot meal."

"I think I should warn you, though." Luther pulled the reins to turn toward the wagons. "We have an old woman who'll want to speak with you at some point before you head out."

"Why is that a warning?"

Pulling the hat back where it belonged, Luther lifted his brows. "Let's just say Gran Mary's a different breed of cat altogether. That's all."

The woman plopped another slab of thick-cut bacon onto Jack's tin. "I'm going to bundle up some of these vittles for you to take with you on the trail."

"Thank you, ma'am." He tore off a hunk of bread. "If you don't mind me sayin' so, you sure don't look old enough to be called Gran Mary."

Putting a hand on her hip, the woman stared into him. "That's because I'm *not* Gran Mary."

"Oh . . . my apologies."

"None necessary." She pointed toward a sun-leathered woman sitting just behind the back end of one of the prairie schooners. "*That's* Gran Mary."

"It's my fault." Luther wiped his mouth with a shirtsleeve. "I shoulda introduced you to everyone already. This here's my wife, Betsy."

"Nice to meet you, ma'am."

Luther turned to Jack with a narrowing gaze. "Come to think of it, I don't recollect you ever giving your name."

"I didn't?" Jack rubbed his neck. "I'm Bill Sutherland."

"Well . . . you've already met—"

"Bring the stranger to me." The raspy voice came from the direction of Gran Mary.

The couple glanced at each other before Luther turned to Jack. "Don't say I didn't warn you."

"Warn me about what?"

"Stop it, Luther." Betsy gently slapped his arm before turning to Jack. "Gran Mary is just a bit odd is all. Luther and the boys let on like she's some kind of witch or something."

"She's really harmless," Luther said with a nod. "But you'll see what I'm talking about."

Gran Mary was threading a sewing needle when Luther led Jack to the wooden crate where the old woman sat. Her dress came all the way down to her feet and seemed to be made from old feed sacks.

"Here he is," Luther said with elevated volume. "His name is Bill Sutherland."

Gran Mary didn't look up as she matched the ends of her thread before tying a knot. "He'll be just dandy without you, Luther. Go on about your business."

Luther glanced at Jack. "Yes, ma'am."

An open jar sat on the back of the wagon near the old woman, its varied contents glinting in the setting sun. Next to the jar was a tin of colored threads and cloth patches.

"You from Wyoming?" She maintained her focus on her busy hands.

Jack eased onto a nearby crate. "Kentucky."

"Hmm." She pushed the needle into a thick fabric and pulled the thread through. "What did Luther say your name was?"

"Sutherland. Bill Sutherland."

She met Jack's gaze but kept working the needle. "Hmm."

Warmth gathered in Jack's cheeks, spreading to his ears and neck. The old woman's stare was like an imminent branding iron.

Clearing his throat, Jack gestured toward the back of the wagon. "What's in the canning glass?"

Gran Mary followed his gaze. "Oh . . . that's my crow jar."

Jack waited a moment for an explanation, then cleared his throat again when none came. "I don't reckon I've ever heard of a crow jar."

"A while back I started feeding the starving things when they came near." She tied a knot in the thread and trimmed it with a knife. "And before long a few of the crows brought back gifts to say thank you."

Jack leaned forward. "Gifts?"

"Uh huh." She retrieved the jar and poured a few of its contents into a wrinkled palm. "Shiny trinkets of metal, small slivers of painted wood, bone pieces, and beads."

"And they bring these things to you because you feed them?"

Her smile carried a glint of pride. "The kindness we show others will *always* develop into friendships and treasure."

Cocking his head, Jack squinted. "Are you sayin' they actually *put* the items in the jar?"

"Oh, no," she said with a laugh. "No, they leave the things in the same area I feed them so I can gather them up myself."

"I ain't never heard tell of anything like that." He shook his head. "I reckon this all took place before you folks started on the trail."

"That's where it *started*," she said, dumping the items back into the jar. "See that one getting closer? That's Maxwell. He was just a little thing when I first started feeding them."

"What? So the crows you're feeding on this here trail are the same crows you fed at home?"

"Oh yes." Her smile widened. "We reap that which we sow, you know. Sowing kindness will ensure kindness in return. And it will follow you for the rest of your days." Her smile faded. "But if we sow pain or hate or evil . . ." Her branding-iron gaze returned. "Then we can expect our remaining days to be a harvest of the same."

The warmth spread to Jack's chest and stomach. "Sounds like Sunday preachin' if you ask me."

"What happened to make your nose all crooked like that?"

Jack reached for his face but stopped short. "Feller hit me with a pistol."

"Hmm." She swirled the jar's items with a few fingers. "Just be mindful, evil almost always enters through our pain."

"Well." Jack slapped his knees and rose to his feet. "I best be headin' on out." He tipped his hat. "But I sure do appreciate the hospitality."

"Before you traipse off, I want to give you something." Retrieving several beads from the jar, she began stringing them onto a long piece of thread. "These are ghost beads."

"I feel like you're puttin' me on."

She added a few more without looking up. "They're made from dried juniper berries. The Navajo say these bring about peace, harmony, and safety."

Jack forced a smile. "What makes you think I need them?"

She tied the ends of the thread and cut the excess. "Because they're said to ward off evil spirits, ghosts, and nightmares."

"How do you . . .?"

Handing the beads to him, she offered a resolute expression. "You don't have to wear them, but be sure and keep them with you at all times."

A flurry of wind washed over them with stinging grains of sand and debris.

"Have you ever heard of . . ." Jack shook his head.

The old woman studied his face a moment. "Have I ever heard of *what*?"

Jack tried to keep his focus away from the jar. "Oh, nothin'. I don't mean to keep you from your stitchin'."

She placed a smooth, cold hand on Jack's forearm. "You don't have to follow the shadow." She squeezed his arm gently. "Let the shadow follow behind *you* . . . Where it belongs."

The breeze picked up again as Jack searched her eyes. "What's that supposed to mean?"

Gran Mary went back to her sewing. "Look at the sun. Tell me what it's doing."

"Uh . . ." Jack searched the sky. "Setting?"

"Correct. And the exact same sun that is *setting* for you right now is, without a doubt, *rising* for someone else at this very moment." She smiled. "What's the difference?"

Jack shrugged.

She squeezed his arm. "It's where you stand, and when."

Jack considered her a moment before stashing the beads into a pocket. "Once again, thank you for the hospitality, ma'am."

eadwood's mud-encrusted streets bustled with activity amid the mining supplies and saloons on seemingly every corner.

Jack breathed in the late July heat and winced at the heaviness in his lungs.

"Let's get you some water," he said, patting the horse's neck. "To be honest, I could use a drink or two myself."

A couple of young men lounged atop a small pile of lumber just next to a shabby tent with several shovels and tools set out for display.

"I can help you find the cheapest livery in town, mister." The young man scooted toward the edge of the lumber. "And they take real good care of the critters."

"Cheapest, huh?" Jack rubbed the stubble on his chin. "How much of a cut are they givin' you?"

"My uncle owns the place. I get a bed and regular meals." He shrugged. "That's about it."

The boy's oversized boots possessed far more years of wear than the young fella could possibly account for.

"Lead the way," Jack said.

Moving through the streets like a raccoon searching for food, the young man paused every few moments to make sure Jack was still following.

The thing that stood out more than anything was Deadwood's pace. It seemed as though everyone was in a rush. At least when compared to other towns and hollows.

No leisure strolls. No gallivanting about. No time to take in the stench from the strewn oddments and food scraps.

The livery was a bit larger than expected with rough-wood stalls lining the interior along with rough-cut saddle stands and piles of hay.

"Told you it was the best in town." The boy took Jack's horse by the reigns and waited for him to climb down. "My uncle can also re-shoe if'n the need arises."

"What's the cost per week?"

Gesturing toward a handwritten list on the wall, the boy revealed a rotten front tooth when he smiled. "Five dollars . . . seven with feed."

Glancing at the door, Jack patted the horse's chest. "Somebody here at all times?"

"Yessir."

Jack looked over the space. "Who's here while you're out rustlin' business?"

"That was Uncle Zeke sittin' near the door when we came inside." The boy flashed that rotten tooth again. "Me and my cousin, Ora, take turns keepin' watch overnight."

"The price seems a little—"

"Our prices ensure the best care," the boy said, trying to stand taller. "Come over here and let me show you something."

Jack tied the reins to a rail and followed the boy through the stables.

"We just got this one a few days ago." The boy stopped at a particular stall where a beautiful black horse stood. "What do you think?"

Jack moved his gaze to the boy. "About what?"

"This horse. What do you think?"

"Look, I ain't got no use for another critter." Jack jutted a thumb toward the door. "Got my hands full with the one I got."

"Oh no." The boy's face soured immediately. "This horse ain't for sale. This here horse belongs to Wild Bill Hickok."

"No kiddin'. So this is the horse that climbed up on the billiard table in Missouri, is it?"

"No sir, Black Nell died a few years back. This one goes by the name Buckshot."

"Wild Bill Hickok . . . here in Deadwood. What do you reckon he's doing here?"

"I ain't got no idea. But it just goes to show how our livery is the most trusted in town."

"Well, if it's good enough for Bill Hickok, then it's good enough for me."

"I'll go fetch my uncle." He started toward the door but turned back. "Oh, what'd you say your name was?"

Jack held his gaze to the horse. "Bill Sutherland."

Jack studied his cards as well as the faces of the other players. Perspiration heavied his limbs, causing his shirt to cling to his back and chest. "I'm out," he said, tossing the cards to the table.

The town's streets bustled just outside with a culmination of wagons and horses and what must have been the indistinct murmurings of men, women, and children.

"I heard Bill Hickok is in town." Charles Rich flipped his cards to the table as well. "Reckon he's aiming to get into the gold business?"

"From what I understand, he's here to do some gambling," said a man with a name that escaped Jack. "Heard he has a real knack for poker."

Jack knocked back what whiskey was left in his glass. "I laid eyes on his horse at the livery when I first came into town."

"I wouldn't mind playing a few hands with the man." Charles offered a sneaky smile. "I'd love to someday be able to tell my grandchildren I beat Duck Bill Hickok."

Laughter filled the room.

"I'd be a little more cautious about saying things like that too loudly if I were you." The man Jack couldn't remember a name for shook his head. "It's been said he's got a cantankerous disposition."

Jack rubbed his temples, hoping to quell the burgeoning pressure. "Whereabouts is he set up?"

"From what I was told, he's taken to Nuttall and Mann's Saloon." Charles released his smile. "Heard they're giving him a cut in hopes his fame will draw more lappers."

"You gonna deal, or are we just gonna yammer on about some dime-novel hustler?" The player to Jack's right scrunched up his sweaty face.

"There's no reason to get all worked up, Albert." Charles slid the cards in front of the man. "Here, cut the deck before you keel over with a coronary."

"I just don't understand why we're wasting so much—"

"Then stop wasting time, Albert." Charles gestured toward the cards. "Christ almighty, we're sitting here waiting on *you*!"

After making the cut, the man slid the deck in front of the dealer. "You're makin' me ill as a hornet, Charlie. If you ever get the chance to gamble with Hickok, you should do yourself a favor and keep your dad-blasted mouth shut."

Laughter erupted again.

"Point taken, Albert. Point taken."

The dealer made quick work of distributing the cards.

"Hold on a second." Jack filled his glass again before placing the contents from his pockets onto the table. "It appears I'm running low."

"You talking about your whiskey bottle or money?" Charles squinted toward the pile of items in front of Jack. "How in the world did you get your hands on ghost beads?"

Jack raked them into a closed fist. "Some old woman gave 'em to me while I was ridin' out this way."

"Navajo?"

"She didn't look it to me. But if there was such a thing as a *Loco* tribe, she sure as hell woulda been the queen chief."

Charles held out a hand. "Mind if I take a look?"

"We're wasting time with all the—"

"Good lord, Albert!" Charles turned on his stool. "Does your wife have you on a curfew or something?"

The man's face reddened. "Of course not!"

"Then what in God's name has put you in such a rushed tizzy?"

Albert briefly set his tongue to the corner of his mouth. "Don't mind me. I was just under the impression we were playing poker here."

Charles rolled one of the beads between a forefinger and thumb. "My wife's been searching for a strand of these for well over a year now, but none of the Indians will sell them to us for some reason."

"You should tell her the beads are meant to protect from ghosts and evil," Albert said with a grin. "Not ugly husbands."

Laughter erupted again.

"You willing to part with these?" Charles lifted an eyebrow. "I'll give you five dollars for them right here, right now."

"Five dollars? Are you serious? I had no idea they were worth anything."

"Do we have a deal?"

Jack nodded. "I reckon we do."

"Well I'm sure relieved we got that settled." Albert held up is arms. "Hopefully we can get on with the game now."

The young man who first led Jack to the livery sat at the establishment's front doors with a lantern that held back the darkness.

The night air seemed to cut into the soul's quick in spite of an absence of breeze or storm.

Jack finished what was left of his whiskey and tossed the bottle to the side of the walkway.

"You're out and about mighty late, Mister Sutherland." The boy climbed to his feet. "If you're worried about your horse, I can assure you I fed all the animals a few hours ago."

"Just out for a walk and thought I'd stop by and check on things. Gotta make sure the old gal knows I haven't abandoned her or anything."

"Ain't nothin' wrong with that, but . . ." The young man lit another lantern and held it out. "Trust me, you're gonna need this when you go in yonder."

Leather and hay and manure stirred the air, along with shuffling hoof movement and neighs.

The mare stuck her head over the gate and nickered.

"There you are," Jack said. "I wanted to be sure they were carin' for you properly."

The beast nudged into him as he patted its broad neck.

"Sure is a different place 'round these parts, ain't it?" Jack retrieved a carrot from his pocket. "Especially when you ain't got no law houndin' over you."

The horse snorted, stretching toward Jack's hand.

"Oh, you see what I brought you, don't you?" He snapped the carrot into several pieces and held them out in a cold palm. "I know how you love these."

Nibbling gently, the horse inched closer.

"I'm sorry for pushing you all this way." He held his other palm to his forehead, hoping the coolness would ease the ache. "But it looks to me like you're getting rested good and fed well."

Once the carrot was gone, Jack rubbed the sides of the horse's face. "You're all I've got now. From here on out it's just me and you."

A light emerged at the front doorway, bobbing and swaying with each footstep.

"You've done a mighty fine job takin' care of my critter," Jack said, turning toward the approaching figure. "Much obliged."

"I'd love to say it was all my doing," a deep voice said as the man drew closer. "But I'm only here checking on mine as well."

Jack was surprised the rafters didn't graze the man's hat as he walked.

"My apologies. I thought you was the stable boy comin' in."

"Ain't hardly nothing."

Jack immediately recognized the man's features from the drawings of Wild Bill Hickok he'd seen over the last few years. "I'd better let you be about your business."

Nodding, Hickok edged past Jack, moving toward the stall where Buckshot was stabled.

Ain't hardly nothing. The words seemingly implied he didn't take Jack's comments as an insult ... *or was he really sayin' I wasn't much*?

Just outside the door, the boy peered past Jack, eyes wide. "Did you see him? That was *him*! That was *Bill Hickok* in the flesh."

Handing the lantern to the boy, Jack started back toward the saloon. "Ain't hardly nothin'."

Pushing his hands deep into his pockets, Jack staggered through town kicking dried mud clods as he went along. It was a queer experience as to how quickly the sweltering days could turn so frigid at night.

But it barely fazed the townspeople as the streets bustled with as much activity in the evenings as they did during the heat of the day.

"Could I interest you in some of the finest mining implements available?" John Varnes held out a long-handled shovel while standing next to a tent with items stacked around it. "Why the gold wouldn't stand a chance with you being so well equipped."

"You nearly got me killed with that chair-throwin' stunt you pulled a few days back."

"You sure have a thick skull, don't you?" Varnes set the shovel against the tent wall. "What is it going to take to get you to finally understand you're bulletproof?"

"I'm just lucky that man missed his shot."

Brushing dust from his lapels, Varnes rolled his eyes. "Give me your pistol."

Instinctively putting a hand to his piece, Jack drew his lower lip between his teeth. "Why?"

Varnes held out a hand. "I'd like to settle this once and for all. Now hand it over."

"You plannin' to shoot me?"

"You leave me no choice." He lifted his chin while keeping his gaze fixed. "I want you to know, beyond a shadow of a doubt, that you have nothing to fear."

Jack stepped to the side. "That's all right. I'll take your word for it."

Keeping his hand outstretched, Varnes smirked. "Just give me the Colt and let's get this over with. The sooner it's done, the sooner we can move on without worries."

The searing pangs in Jack's forehead and face dug into his ears. "I ain't giving you my piece. You can forget about that."

"I am sorry, Jack, but I simply cannot allow you to relent to fears of the flesh."

Coldness washed over Jack at the sight of his very own Colt now in Varnes'shand and no longer tucked in his belt. "How'd you—"

"I can ill afford you reneging on our agreement."

Jack held up his hands. "I believe you. I believe."

"If that was the absolute truth, Jack McCall, you would not have a problem with this at all, now would you?"

"Like hell! I don't reckon I'd be comfortable with someone holdin' a pistol on me even if my skin was made of locomotive steel."

Varnes lifted his aim to Jack's head. "Keep your eyes open and on me. I want you to see the whole thing."

The pressure in Jack's bladder was like a knife twisting inside him. "Jesus Christ. Just give me the Colt back."

Varnes smiled. "You'll get it back."

Darkness came almost as quickly as the gun's report.

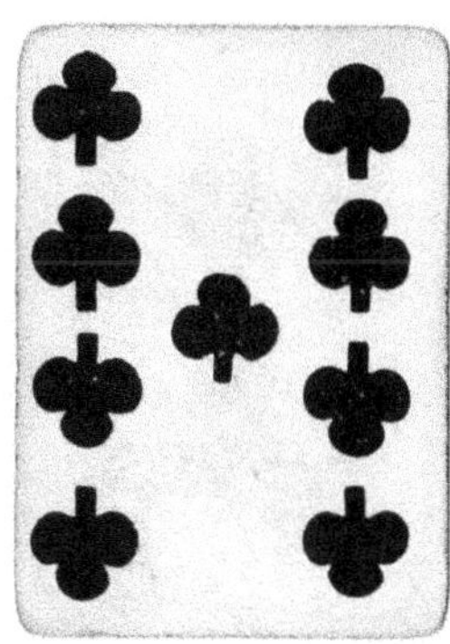

“**W**ake up!”

Jack's head burned like a festering boil.

"Don't act like you can't hear me, boy." Someone was kicking at Jack's foot. "I said get up!"

Sunlight only intensified the pain as Jack tried to open his eyes. "All right. All right."

Searching for the lingering sourness, Jack reached for his side where the shirt clung to his skin with wetness.

"Go on! Get to moving." The man's face was beet red and twisted with rage. "I can't sell a tarnal thing with a vomit-covered drunk passed out in the middle of my goods!"

Climbing to his feet, Jack steadied himself with the shovel handle leaning against the tent.

"Sorry." He searched the immediate area. "Let me find my pistol and I'll be on my way."

"Are you still drunk, boy?" The man pointed at Jack's waistline. "It's right there in your belt."

Jack's stomach raged as he put his hand on the revolver's butt and started off down the street. "Sorry for the trouble."

He brought back a dry hand every time he inspected his head and face, which worked miracles in settling his stomach and nerves. The only wetness he could find was the disgorge on his shirt.

Am I losing my wits?

Pulling the Colt from his belt, Jack took a seat at the back of an empty walkway. He opened the revolver's loading gate and turned the cylinder.

Sure enough, one of the cartridges was spent. *I'll be jiggered.*

His stomach roiled again as he went back to probing for wounds.

The pain seemed a little worse than usual, but that was more than likely due to the added pressures of an obvious hangover.

"You're looking mighty rough." Charles Rich reached out a hand to help him to his feet. "Are you okay?"

"I'm fine." Jack returned the Colt to his belt and took the outstretched hand. "Just feelin' the effects of last night's bender."

"You certainly appear as though you accomplished quite a bit of bending." Charles gestured toward Jack's shirt. "As well as airin' the paunch."

Pinching at the wet spot, Jack lifted the cold material from his flesh. "I reckon it's been one of them nights."

"I reckon so," Charles said with a laugh. "I wanted to let you know I'm going to Nuttall and Mann's Saloon later to try to get on the same table as Hickok."

"Is that right? I may join you after I get cleaned up."

"Just don't bring Albert." His smile spread into a chuckle. "God knows he'd have Hickok shootin' up the place within a few minutes."

"How'd your wife like the beads?"

Charles pulled the strand from a pocket. "She's helping her sister with a newborn and won't be home for a few more days."

"You really think you can get on a table with Hickok?"

Charles shrugged. "I'm sure gonna give it a shot."

Nuttall and Mann's Saloon was far too quiet despite the multitude of people drinking and milling about. Most patrons were no doubt there just to catch a glimpse of Deadwood's most famous visitor, but at least they were doing so with a drink in hand.

And Wild Bill Hickok certainly did not disappoint—his demeanor was nearly as stoic and intimidating as his immense stature.

Brownish blonde locks hung to his shoulders in twists and waves—a defiant provocation for bloodthirsty savages wanting to carve them from his scalp.

Sitting with his back to the furthest wall, Hickok volleyed his gaze between his cards and movement throughout the saloon.

Jack nestled up close to the bartender and waited for him to finish with another customer.

"What'll it be?" the man finally said, moving some peanuts in front of Jack.

"Give me a bottle of the cheapest whiskey you got."

The bartender smiled. "That bad of a day, huh?"

"You could say that."

The man placed a bottle in front of Jack before wiping out a glass and setting it closer to Jack's hand. "Two bits."

Sliding the coins across the bar top, Jack nodded. "Much obliged."

"I'm pretty good with accents, let me guess." The bartender cocked his head. "You're from . . . Tennessee?"

Jack filled his glass. "Kentucky."

"Ah, I always get the two mixed up." He held out a hand. "Harry Young."

Jack downed his glass before shaking the man's hand. "Good to meet you, Harry. I'm Bill Sutherland." He filled his glass again. "You from these parts?"

"Truth be told, nobody is *from* Deadwood." He wiped the bar top and leaned against it. "I ran away from my home in New York when I was fourteen so I could see the West for myself."

"I reckon that's been a while back." Jack took a drink. "Or so it would seem."

"Eleven years now."

"I bet this place is a whole lot different than New York." Jack chuckled. "I bet you carry a whole lot bigger pistol now than you did back then."

"I don't even own a piece." He shrugged. "Never had a need for one while working here."

"I see." Jack downed what remained in his glass. "They keep one under the bar top so you don't have to buy one for yourself."

"No, that's not the case at all. But I've thought about buying one from time to time. Never know when one could come in handy out here."

Jack filled his glass again. "Probably a good idea."

"Sutherland!" A voice came over the roar of the crowd. "Bill Sutherland!"

Jack couldn't believe he'd overlooked Charles Rich sitting at Hickok's table.

"That's Bill Sutherland," Charles said to the other players. "He could take Morgan's place."

Tobacco smoke settled throughout the room—a tapestry of stagnant gray haze.

"Come join us, Bill!" Charles was grinning like a possum eating sand briars. "Morgan here is leaving the game."

Jack collected the bottle and glass. "Mighty good meetin' you, Harry."

"Same."

At the table, Hickok shuffled the deck while boring his gaze into Jack. "We've met."

Jack glimpsed at Charles before turning back to Hickok. "That's right. At the livery."

"Have a seat." Hickok nodded toward the empty stool. "Anybody that will go the extra mile for their horse is always welcome at my table."

"I ain't too fond of sittin' away from the door," Jack said, easing into the seat. "But I reckon havin' a man of your reputation watchin' my back is good enough."

Sliding the cards to the dealer, Hickok fixed his attention on Jack. "What unit did you serve with?"

"I ain't been in no uniform."

"He looks a bit young to have served." Charles's salesman smile stretched across his face.

"I ain't never served."

"Then where'd you acquire that Army-issued Colt you got in your belt?" Hickok asked.

A bead of sweat trickled Jack's spine. "Friend of my old man gave it to me back in Wyoming."

"Where'd *he* get it?"

Jack cleared his throat and leaned forward. "He told me it was rude to kiss and tell when I asked him that very question."

Laughter erupted with Hickok offering a crooked grin. "Let's get back to the game."

Always welcome at my *table.* The words kept sloshing through Jack's brain, competing with the abundance of alcohol. *He acts like he owns this table or something.*

The first hour came and went as fast as the whiskey, but Jack's pressured bladder made the second hour seem like it drug on forever.

The dealer's eyebrows lifted with a persistent stare. "Bill?"

An elbow from Charles jolted Jack back to the game.

"What is it?"

The dealer shook his head. "Are you in?"

Downing what was left of his glass, Jack fidgeted with his pouch while still clinging to the empty bottle. "Anyone care to spot me on this hand? I'll repay double tomorrow."

"It *is* tomorrow," Charles said, sparking laughter. "It's pert near two in the morning."

"All right then, I'll repay double later *today*."

Laughter again.

"Here," Hickok said, holding out a small stack of change.

Jack stared at the coinage, warmth filling his cheeks and ears. "Thank you."

"This ain't a loan," Hickok said, pulling back his hand when Jack reached for it. "*This* is for you to get yourself something to eat." He dipped his head slightly. "I'm advising you not to play again until you can cover your losses."

The warmth returned, spread.

Hickok's expression did not falter. "Do you find this agreeable?"

Jack unclenched his teeth. *Thinks he can get rid of me as easy as that.* His stomach grumbled again.

"Well?"

The bottle slipped from Jack's hand and rolled across the tabletop where Charles barely saved it from crashing to the floor.

"All right." Jack jarred the table as he clamored to stand. "I'll get something to eat."

The pancakes were not as thick as the ones Jack's mamma made when he was growing up in Kentucky, but they were nearly twice as big in diameter.

A cast-iron smokiness filled the room from the abundance of frying bacon—along with a sweetness from maple syrup and sorghum.

Low down bottom-feeder.

Taking another bite, Jack gripped the fork so tightly his palm ached.

Thinks he can just brush me off that easily— goin' out of his way to humiliate me in front of all them people.

Sunlight spilled across the table, adding warmth where shadows stretched toward every nook and cranny.

"I hope you are finding everything to your satisfaction, sir."

Jack recognized the voice before John Varnes stepped into view. The curious man wore an apron over his gaudy suit while brandishing a dish towel draped over his forearm.

"Why can't you just leave me alone?"

Varnes allowed his smile to soften. "Why, Mr. McCall, are you dissatisfied with our agreement?"

"Keep your voice down," Jack said, scanning the room. "You know I'm going by Bill Sutherland."

Varnes pulled a chair from the table and shrugged. "Please, pardon my error, *Mr. Sutherland.*" He lowered himself into the seat. "But it's time for you to live up to your end of the bargain."

"About that—"

"I think you should be aware of the fact that should you renege on our agreement, the bullets you defied while under the contract will instantly succeed as they would have, had you not been bulletproof."

"What the hell does that even mean?"

With eyebrows lifting, Varnes raised his chin. "It means you will meet your demise the moment you break our compact."

The headache was now in Jack's teeth. "Well I guess I have no choice in the matter, now do I?"

"On the contrary, you made your choice when you signed your mark on the contract."

Jack pushed the remaining portions of pancake around his plate. "Well I still don't know who I'm supposed to be—"

"Shouldn't you follow your own counsel and keep your voice down?"

Jack glared at a few patrons staring from a table on the other side of the room. "I'm tired of you stringin' me along," he continued in a hushed tone. "I just want to be done with it all."

"That's certainly understandable." Varnes pulled the apron over his head. "But you already know the person in question."

"See? That's just the problem. I really *don't* know who the person is."

"I'm not saying you know the person's identity, I'm merely stating that you've met the individual here in Deadwood."

Jack dropped his fork into his plate. "That don't tell me anything, I've met quite a few people while here."

"That's right." Varnes nodded. "But you and this man have even shared a gambling table."

"Well that still doesn't narrow things down for me. I've played poker with a dozen or so folks since coming here."

"That is true." Varnes leaned forward. "But only one of those individuals insulted you in front of the whole saloon. Only *one* of those men treated you like a Judas—offering thirty pieces of silver and advising you to stay away from the table until you can cover your bets."

Jack wanted to stand but remained where he was, his legs now sluggish, heavy. "Hickok."

"That is correct."

"Jesus, Mary, and Joseph." Jack's stomach churned. "You can't be serious."

"Oh I am quite serious."

Jack cleared his throat. "Why are you so hell-bent on Hickok?"

"Let's just say there was an incident in Denver." His face twisted with what must have been resentment. "The fool ended up breaking a deal we had agreed upon."

"Hold on a second. Are you telling me Hickok is bulletproof as well?"

"I can assure you of this one thing." His widening smile seemed intended more for himself than for Jack's benefit. "James Butler Hickok is far from bulletproof."

"So what did his contract—"

"I suggest you focus on your own agreement." He sat back, lifted his eyebrows. "But after what Hickok has stolen from you and your family, I'm surprised you're not more eager to see the job through."

"What are you talking about? Are you sayin' Wild Bill killed my father?"

"Your father and Hickok have never been in the same territory at the same time." He moved to his feet, leaving the apron on the table. "On the other hand, it was Hickok who, in cold blood, gunned down your brother in Abilene."

Jack shook his head. "I ain't got no brother."

"Your father never told you about him, but you had a brother."

A queasiness tickled Jack's throat. "That ain't so. I had three sisters when I was growin' up, and that's it. Besides, the old man would have told me otherwise."

"He didn't tell you because he didn't want your mother to find out about your illegitimate sibling."

Jack laughed. "That's crazy. He would have told me about him no matter what."

The smirk on Varnes's face turned into a crooked grin. "You mean like how he told you everything about the men from the gang and what they did together? Or how he confided in you about the dozens of people he'd killed?"

"Dozens?"

Varnes retrieved a cigar from his inside coat pocket. "It's just a shame that Hickok robbed you of any hope you may have ever had in meeting your only brother."

"That doesn't sound right to me." Jack quickly got to his feet. "But what about my old man, do you know who killed my father?"

Lighting the cigar, Varnes eased back into his chair. "I tell you what, *Mister Sutherland*, let's get this ordeal behind us and I promise to tell you everything you want to know as to the death of your father. Is this agreeable?"

The livery was a different place during the day. Sunlight stretched through the gaps of the walls, bringing heat and a heightened sense of barnyard odors.

Jack rubbed his horse's nose while the mare craned her neck toward his hand.

"I ain't got nothin' for you to nibble on this time."

The horse shook its head.

"I know. I know. I'm real sorry. I shoulda brought you an apple or something."

He couldn't get the image of Hickok's smug face out of his head. There was something about the stoic blankness he'd held while he was offering the money.

"We ain't gonna stay here much longer," Jack said, grooming the critter's neck with a brush he'd found nearby. "I promise. But I've got something really important I need to do before we can move on."

The livery boy walked by carrying a flake of hay before entering another stall several feet past, and then, almost immediately, came back out empty handed. The young man didn't so much as look in Jack's direction as he headed toward the front door.

"Get yourself rested up, girl. We're gonna have some miles ahead of us real soon." He rubbed the horse's nose again. "And then things are gonna be different. You'll see."

Was Varnes really telling the truth about a brother Jack had never heard of before? And that Hickok killed him in cold blood?

Should've asked what the brother's name was.

A small breeze whistled through the cracks in the planked walls, carrying grit and grime, as well as stirring hay and odors.

"She's well mannered," the boy said, pushing past Jack with a couple more hay flakes. "Most of the time the horses are ornery or demanding."

Jack stepped aside from being startled. "I'd like to take credit for that, but to be right honest about it, she's never been a lick of trouble."

The boy scattered the hay on the dirt floor and checked the water. "Uncle Zeke says feeding from the floor makes 'em healthier. Says it helps drain their noses so they can breathe better."

"Is that right?"

"Yessir. I reckon he knows just about everything there is to know about horses and mules and such." A prideful smile stretched across his face. "Why I bet Uncle Zeke knows more about 'em than anybody."

The horse munched on the hay without movement or noise.

"Sounds like your uncle has taught you quite a bit." Jack placed the brush back on the ledge. "Has he taught you any shoein' skills?"

"Not yet, but he says we'll get around to it someday. I've watched him so many times I could probably do it with my eyes closed, though."

Jack cut off a piece of plug tobacco and crammed it into his mouth. "My grandfather tried to teach me how to shoe when I was a boy back on the farm in Kentucky."

"What do you mean he *tried* to teach you?"

Jack worked the tobacco a bit before situating it into his cheek. "Well I reckon he stopped tryin' because it didn't take."

"What happened?"

"Apparently I wasn't too good at it and the old man feared I would end up injuring one of the poor critters and he'd have to put it down."

"Makes sense."

"He did teach me something I was good at, though." Jack moved the tobacco to his other cheek. "I was real good at killing the hogs for slaughter."

"Yeah?"

"I remember grandpa bragging to anybody who'd listen about how there wasn't a soul alive who could put one down any better than me."

"Saw my daddy kill one before. That thing screamed and squealed like nothing I've ever seen or heard."

Jack nodded. "You gotta know where and how to shoot it. This ain't like waitin' out buffalo, you see. Pigs only sit still without movin' when they're either sleepin' or eatin' or drinkin'. So I always started preparing for the kill the day before."

The boy perched himself on a nearby railing. "What do you mean?"

"You don't want to give 'em any water the day before. That's the key, you get 'em good and parched. Then the next day, while they're drinkin' their fill, you walk right up on 'em and lay a bead an inch or so up from between their eyes." Jack shook his head. "Nary a squeal or a scream—they never know what hit 'em."

"So while they're focused on quenching their thirst, you shoot 'em when they're not paying attention to anything else."

Jack spat. "You could even put the rifle's muzzle right against the poor thing's thick skull if you wanted and it wouldn't pay you no more mind than a worn-out fence post."

"That's pretty smart."

"It ain't shoein', but it's somethin', that's for sure." Jack rubbed the mare's neck. "I reckon I better let you get back to work 'fore your uncle catches you sittin' around in here and gives you what for."

It seemed to be a bustling late afternoon at Nuttall and Mann's Number Ten Saloon, where the rumbling of many voices spilled out onto the street where Jack paced.

The front window revealed that although a number of the usuals were already set up at the back table, Hickok was nowhere to be found.

Of all times for him not to show up.

Wiping sweat from his forehead, Jack moved across the street to keep out of sight while taking note of who went in or came out.

It was funny how a place named Deadwood was actually the liveliest place in the territories, with dozens of miners and fortune seekers arriving in town every day.

It didn't take long before Hickok came down the planked walkway, weaving through the populace, heading for Nuttall and Mann's. He paused a second or two at the door and adjusted his hat before entering.

Jack scrambled across the street to peek through the window. Inside, Hickok had a short conversation with someone at the bar before heading to the back table where a game was already in progress.

As the legendary gunman approached the game, the player sitting with his back to the door rose and gestured that Hickok could take his place as he was leaving.

Hickok then appealed to Charles Rich to trade seats so he could sit facing the door, but Charlie refused. He apparently asked again—and again, Charlie refused. Jack couldn't hear the conversation from the window, but it was obvious that's what was being discussed.

Removing his jacket, Hickok finally pulled the stool out from the table with his foot and sat as the game seemingly picked up right where it left off.

This is as good as it's going to get.

Scanning the patrons and activity of the entire saloon, Jack focused on the hands dealt at the table, and waited for Hickok's shoulders to slouch with complacency.

Someone brushed against Jack's arm while opening the door to go inside. Jack quickly followed, slowly making his way toward the bar.

The rambunctious crowd noise did little in the way of drowning out the pulsing heart in his nose and face, or quelling the misery that accompanied it.

Nodding to Harry Young as he approached the bar, Jack couldn't figure out what to do with his hands. The very thought of acting normal only made things worse.

Just get on with it.

Averting his gaze, Jack slowly moved down the length of the bar and paused where the gold-weighing scales rested at the end.

Coldness expanded in Jack's chest when Hickok turned toward the bar and said, "Bring me fifty dollars worth of checks, Harry."

Jack didn't move, the coldness quickly spreading to his legs and feet.

Harry placed the stack on the table in front of Hickok and waited just off to his side.

Hickok gazed up at him, gesturing toward a player Jack didn't recognize. "The old duffer broke me on that hand."

Jack's first step was wobbly as he made a beeline for the table. Each succeeding footstep felt like the quick, jarring paces made when drunk.

The coldness turned to fire as perspiration beaded his forehead, threatening to move into his eyes.

Stepping just behind Hickok, Jack brought the piece from his belt and aimed it mere inches from Wild Bill's head.

The recoil and report startled Jack as much as it apparently did everyone else.

"Damn you, take that!"

Gasps and grumbles erupted, along with a piercing ring, as Jack stepped back and surveyed the room.

The crowd went silent at the sight of Hickok's slumping body, as well as Jack's smoking pistol. They were all on their feet now, focusing solely on Jack, faces rife with confusion and fear and anger.

Waving his Colt around as a warning, Jack eased his way to the back door before taking off down the alley where he found, to his surprise, a tethered horse a few feet away.

He released the reins, put a foot in the stirrup, and tried pulling himself up by the saddle horn, but the whole rig slid from the horse as he fell to the ground.

Clambering to get back to his feet, Jack recovered his Colt and scrambled down the alley away from all the shouting and commotion.

In addition to his ringing ears, aching face, and the unbearable heat, Jack's gut churned and rumbled with threats of regurgitation.

The clamoring and shouting drew closer, louder. It was evident that many of those from the saloon were following in an attempt to apprehend Wild Bill Hickok's killer.

Slipping through an open back door, Jack found himself in the darkened storage area of a butcher's shop, and locked the door behind him. The coppery scent reminded him of his early years helping his grandfather butcher the hogs he'd killed.

"You always want to take your time when stickin' and guttin'," his grandfather would say while working on the carcass. "One poor move of the blade and you can ruin the meat."

There must have been a search party just outside with yelling and running and shuffling about.

"You clearly have not lost your touch," John Varnes said, stepping out from the shadows wearing a bloodstained butcher's apron. "Congratulations on fulfilling the deal."

Jack moved closer. "Our business is all done with and I'm gettin' the hell outta here."

"And you certainly deserve it." Varnes wiped his blood-mucked hands on the apron. "How does it feel to have finally avenged your brother's death?"

"I told you, I ain't got no brother!"

"My boy, if you know what's good for you, you'll embrace the loss of your brother."

"I've had enough of this." Jack pointed a finger at Varnes. "I did exactly what you asked, now get me outta here."

"Excuse me?"

"Get me outta here!"

Shaking his head, Varnes offered a weird smile. "You know quite well that that is not part of the contract."

The growing chaos outside seemed to close in on Jack as coldness returned to his chest and stomach. "No," he said, raising the Colt to Varnes's head. "I don't care what it takes, just get me the hell outta here!"

"I honestly do not understand why someone who is bulletproof can be so concerned about a horde of men chasing with bullets and anger."

Jack cocked the hammer. "I ain't gonna tell you again."

"Pull the trigger." Varnes's face was icy. "Or better yet, since you don't think you're going to get out of here alive, why don't you put the muzzle to your own head and end it now."

"Listen—"

"Why give those bloody mongrels the satisfaction? If you *truly* do not believe to be bulletproof, or that you will not make it out of this building alive, then do the deed yourself and be done with it."

The crowd noise was growing outside.

"But if you turn that revolver on yourself and you come out unscathed, well then what do you have to worry about?"

Jack lowered his piece. "I'm not afraid to die."

Someone attempted to open the door from outside. "This one's locked as well!"

Gesturing toward Jack's Colt, Varnes nodded. "Prove to yourself once and for all. Or take from them the very thing they seek."

A commotion came from the front side of the butcher's shop this time.

Jack lifted the muzzle to his temple and cocked the hammer. "I'm not afraid to die."

"Then stop being afraid to live!"

Jack closed his eyes and pulled the trigger to an empty click. He peeked a bit while thumbing back the hammer and pulling the trigger again . . . to yet another empty click. He began laughing as he went through the motions three more times . . . all to empty clicks. "I really *am* bulletproof," he said. But Varnes was no longer with him.

Another ruckus came from the front again as several men burst into the storage area. "There he is!"

Jack was still laughing when the men wrestled him to the ground.

"I said to wake up!" Someone jostled Jack's shoulder. "We ain't got all day, now move it."

Trying to sit upright from his side, Jack struggled with getting his arms to cooperate. "What's goin' on?"

"Here." A hand pulled Jack's arm to move him into a sitting position. "We've gotta get you to your trial."

The binding on Jack's wrists left reddened skin and an irritating fire. "Trial?"

"That's right. You killed Wild Bill Hickok yesterday, remember?" The man's face was red and sweaty. "Or were you too drunk to even remember?"

"Who are you?"

"Joseph Brown." The man used both hands under Jack's arm to pull him to his feet. "I'm the new sheriff."

"What town are you taking me to?"

Brown turned Jack toward the door. "Your trial is going to take place at the theater."

"Now hold on a second, I thought there weren't no law in Deadwood."

Brown shook his head. "There wasn't any until you done what you did. A bunch of us got pulled into duties we never asked for. I was appointed sheriff for this ordeal, thank you very much."

There were a few armed men waiting outside who took up walking with the sheriff and Jack. "Just so you know, this here trial and everything was thrown together so the townspeople wouldn't string you up on the spot."

Men and women watched as Jack and the new lawmen made their way through the middle of the street.

"Just keep your head down so we can get you there with no bullet holes or neck burns."

Jack laughed.

"I'm glad *you* think it's funny." He squeezed Jack's bicep while continuing to pull him ahead. "Because me and these men are risking our necks to ensure you make it safely to trial, you jackass!"

The faces of the gawking people gave the impression they were saddened or tired. Not one of them tried to intervene or intercept, but just in front of the theater, a smile stood out like a fiddle in a box of mouth harps.

"There's Varnes," Jack said, stretching his neck to get a better view.

"Shut up." Brown jerked Jack's arm forward. "We're almost there."

Varnes offered an open-palm wave before disappearing into the crowd.

Jack couldn't get over how quiet the crowd was—no screaming or yelling or throwing things like he'd seen with captured fellas in the past.

"When we get inside, I want you to keep your mouth shut until it's your turn to speak." Brown kept his gaze in front of him. "Understood?"

"Who's the judge?"

"I just told you to keep your mouth shut until it's your turn to speak!"

Jack tried to stop walking but found himself pulled forward again. "You said *when we get in there*! If my eyes aren't deceiving me, we ain't in there yet!"

"The judge's name is William Kuykendall."

"Well with a name like that, I can sure understand why you was avoiding the question."

"And does the defense have any other witnesses to call?"

The lawyer next to Jack rose. "Yes, Your Honor. If it pleases the court, we would like to call the defendant to the stand."

The spectators broke into excessive murmuring and chattering.

Taking the chair just to the right of the judge, Jack crossed his arms and squinted past the numerous stage lamps reflected on him. It was as though he was standing in mid-July heat right next to a brush fire.

"It's been pointed out by the prosecution that your name really isn't Bill Sutherland." The lawyer meandered about with as much showmanship as any actor the very stage had previously graced. "But that your given name is John McCall."

"Jack."

"That's right, your preference is *Jack* McCall." The lawyer pulled back the side-front of his jacket to place a dramatic hand on his hip. "And there's a very good reason you went by an alias, correct?"

"That's right."

"Would you kindly explain as to why you took use of this other name?"

"Survival."

"Please explain to the court what you mean by that, and testify as to what happened."

Uncrossing his arms, Jack leaned forward. "Well, men, I have but few words to say. Wild Bill killed my brother, and I killed him." He straightened a bit. "Wild Bill threatened to kill me if I crossed his path, and I'm not sorry for what I did. As a matter of fact, I'd do the same thing over again!"

The murmuring and chattering swelled again, this time louder than before.

"All right, that's enough," the judge called out as he rose from his seat. "Keep it down! We're still in session."

A quietness came over the auditorium with the exception of faint shuffling in the crowd.

Turning to the lawyer on the other side of the stage, the judge lifted his hands. "The witness is yours."

The man rose just briefly enough to state, "The prosecution rests, your honor."

"How long has it been?" Jack shifted his rear on the floor.

"Hard to tell." Sheriff Brown stared back from a chair next to the door. "Been hours, I'm sure of that much."

"What do you reckon they're gonna do?"

Shrugging, Brown pushed his hat back on his head. "I ain't got no idea. A lot of folk wants you dead for what you did, but I think a bunch of others are a little more understanding after hearing about your brother."

Jack fiddled with the rope around his wrists. "I reckon we'll know one way or another 'fore too long."

"You don't seem too flustered for a man standing trial for murder."

"Ain't much to fret about. Won't do any good anyways."

"That's a bold way of looking at it." He offered a nod. "Especially for someone who could be facing the noose."

"Ain't worried about that at all."

"You don't think they'll hang you if they find you guilty?"

"I ain't worried if they do." He gave a slight grin. "I can't die."

"What in God's name do you mean by that?"

Chuckling, Jack leaned back against the wall. "I reckon you'll see."

"I'm not playing any games with you, McCall. I'm not about to put my neck on the line, or the necks of any of the other men for that matter, to keep you safe just so you can do something stupid and get us all killed."

"You ain't got nothin' to worry about with me, constable. No sir, I ain't about to make trouble for anybody."

"That's what I want to hear." He adjusted his holster and crossed his legs. "Now what are you talking about when you say you can't die?"

"I mean exactly that, I can't die." He took in a deep breath and released it. "It's a long story, and you won't believe it no ways."

"Now you need to—"

The knock at the door caused Brown to wince.

"They're ready," a voice sounded from the other side.

"All right, McCall, let's get moving." He helped pull Jack to his feet. "You better not be scheming up anything. You hear me?"

"You ain't gonna have to worry about me."

"Has the jury reached a verdict?"

A man among the secluded jurors rose to his feet. "We have, Your Honor."

"What say you?"

The man straightened himself. "After nearly twelve hours of—"

"We're not looking for any formalities or lengthy expository, all I want to hear is *guilty* or *not guilty*. You understand?"

Nodding, the man stared forward. "Not guilty."

The crowd erupted with yelling and gasps and grumblings, shifting and moving about as they shoved one another within the confines of the hall.

"Order!" The judge banged a block of wood against the table in front of him. "I will have order in this court!"

As the crowd started settling, the judge turned to the sheriff. "Get him to the back somewhere. Cut him loose, but keep him there until I get a chance to come back and speak with him."

The back stage area was dark and empty and smelled of paint, tobacco smoke, and lamp oil.

"Does that mean I'm free?"

Brown led Jack into a cramped room in the far corner. "That's right, but you heard the judge say he wants to speak to you before we let you go."

"But I'm free?"

Nodding, Brown began cutting the rope from Jack's wrist. "Jury found you not guilty, so yes, you're free."

Jack rubbed the rope burns once the ties were cut away. "Are you stayin' on as sheriff now that this trial is over?"

"Hell no." He peeked out the door for a moment. "Going back to digging gold as soon as I can."

The crowd noise was faint from the distance, but still very much active.

"Well I wish you all the luck in the world. I really do. You've been nothing but fair and decent to me during this whole ordeal."

"Tell me something." Brown scratched at his beard. "What did you mean when you said you couldn't die?"

Jack smiled. "Let's just say I made a deal and now I can't die."

"What exactly do you mean you made a deal?"

"I know it sounds—"

"There you are." The door opened as the judge stepped inside. "I believe we have everyone calmed down and out the door." The man's ruddy face glistened with perspiration. "Thank you for everything, Joseph. You served honorably as sheriff during this fiasco."

"I'd like to say the pleasure was all mine, but I think you know I would not be telling the truth."

"And for you, Mr. McCall." He turned toward Jack with a stern face. "If you know what's best for you, you'd head out of Deadwood as quickly as possible."

"I plan to do just that."

"Good. We'll have your horse saddled and brought over once it gets a little darker." He touched Jack's chest with an index finger. "Once you're on that horse, you're on your own, boy."

After nearly a month on the run, Jack made his way to Wyoming—first to Cheyenne before moving on to Laramie.

The first saloon he came to in town was a bit larger than those in Deadwood, but nowhere near as busy or raucous.

"Give me a whisky," he said, placing a few coins on the bar top.

"You got it." The bartender took down a bottle from the back shelf and poured. "You look familiar."

"Been through here a time or two."

"That seems to be the case with everyone." The man corked the bottle and moved it to the side. "Seems like everybody just stops by Laramie on their way to wherever they are going."

"Oh? And why is that?"

"I reckon the rocky dirt makes it damn near impossible to properly set roots." He smiled. "It's easier to travel across, than to dig into, I suppose."

"So why are you here?"

"I'm saving up enough money to head out to Deadwood and see if I can't find me some of that gold everybody's talking about."

Jack knocked back the whiskey and slid the glass forward. "Give me another."

The bartender refilled. "Where you headed?"

"Anywhere but Deadwood."

"I heard somebody killed Wild Bill Hickok out there."

"You heard correctly." Jack downed the whiskey, jutted a thumb to his chest. "And you're lookin' at the feller who shot him."

The man stared blankly. "No fooling?"

"That's right. Son of a bitch killed my brother and said he'd kill me if he ever got the chance. But I was acquitted of all charges by a court of law."

"I reckon a fella has to be pretty dang quick to kill Wild Bill Hickok."

Nodding toward the empty glass, Jack slid a few more coins across the bar. "You don't have to be quick when you're quiet."

He stopped pouring the whiskey and scrunched up his face. "You mean . . ."

"Keep pourin'." Jack gestured toward the glass. "Listen, when a practiced killer says he's gonna gun you down, you better believe every word he says." He gulped the whiskey and ran a sleeve across his mouth. "And if you wanna live, then you better beat him to the draw . . . no matter how you do it."

"So what'd you and your brother do to put Wild Bill Hickok on your scent?"

Placing the glass on the bar, Jack studied the man's face. "What?"

"Why was Wild Bill after the two of you in the first place?"

"Well . . ." His gaze roamed the saloon. "I reckon he just wanted to kill somebody."

The man placed the bottle back on the shelf. "Uh huh."

"Whereabouts is the nearest livery?"

"If I was you, I'd keep moving. And if not, I wouldn't go around bragging about what you did in Deadwood." He wiped out Jack's glass and placed it under the bar top. "I don't think folks around here will take too kindly to your story."

Taking a step back, Jack lowered his hand near the Colt. "I can take care of myself."

Jack spread his cards on the table and smiled. "I hope you fellers don't mind, but I brought some ladies to the dance." He scooped the money from the center of the table. "Three queens have never looked so lovely."

Groans and grumbles came as cards landed at the table's center.

"Jack McCall?" the voice said from behind him.

As he turned to look up, Jack felt someone jerking the Colt from his waistband. "Hey!"

Two men dragged him from the chair by his arms. "Put the shackles on him."

"What's this all about?" Jack tried pulling away. "I ain't done nothin' but played cards."

"You're under arrest, McCall." A big fella stepped in front of him.

"Arrest? For what?"

"For the murder of James Butler Hickok."

"I was acquitted! Ain't you heard?" He tried pulling away again. "The jury declared I was not guilty."

"Make sure he doesn't have any other guns or anything." The man turned to Jack. "I'm Deputy Marshal Balcomlie. And the jury you mentioned was just as illegal as the court itself."

"What the hell are you talkin' about?"

"There's no law in Deadwood, son. And that's because the town is illegally set up inside Indian territory that was established by the federal government."

"That can't be right. There was a judge and lawyers and—"

"All illegal." The marshal pulled at the shackles on Jack's wrists. "But you're fixin' to stand trial in a real courtroom."

"At least let me take my winnings." Jack nodded toward the table. "I just won a bunch of money. Hell, I'd be willin' to share if you'd let me go."

The marshal pulled him toward the door. "Son, you ain't gonna need any money with where you're going."

"Where are you taking me?"

"We'll be leaving for Yankton as soon as your preliminary hearing is over here in town."

Jack took in the darkness when they finally made it outside. "Wild Bill killed my brother, you know. Said he was gonna kill me too, but I beat him to the punch."

"You know damn well, you don't have a brother, McCall." Balcomlie jerked at the shackles. "You've been too stupid to realize all your bragging about it would catch up with you."

"I'm telling you a man named John Varnes hired me to kill Hickok over some dispute the two of them had in Denver."

The jail cell was small, dark, and carried what must have been the smells of past sins.

"And I told you we sent someone to Deadwood about that." The attorney pushed his shoulders up to his cheeks. "And there's nobody there by that name."

"There's gotta be something we can do."

Placing a hand on Jack's shoulder, the lawyer shook his head. "I'm afraid unless we get some kind of a miracle, or a stay of execution from the governor, the jury has found you guilty and the judge has set your date."

Jack gazed at the ceiling. "Well I sure didn't think about all of this when I agreed to the deal."

"I'm sorry? What deal are you referring to?"

"It don't matter now, I reckon." He gently rubbed his forehead. "Say, how long do they leave a feller hangin' 'fore they cut him down?"

"Your sentence states the guilty party is hanged by the neck until dead. So it depends on how long that takes, I imagine."

Jack sat forward. "What happens if the feller gettin' hanged doesn't die?"

"I'm not sure I understand your question."

"Oh just forget about it. We'll get there when we get there."

The lawyer rose to his feet. "Unfortunately, I have a great deal of paperwork to finish. But if I'm not mistaken, they have a priest who wants to speak with you if you'd like."

"I don't want no damn priest in here."

Shrugging, the lawyer moved toward the hall. "Suit yourself."

The bars clanged shut, leaving a ringing in Jack's ears. Dripping echoed from somewhere without a sign of water or dampness.

He rubbed again at his throbbing forehead, working to ease the pressure. Closing his eyes, Jack found the flashing colors and lights he'd been used to for a while.

"Bless you, my son," John Varnes said, stepping in front of the bars. He was adorned with a priest's robe and a crucifix around his neck. "I have come to hear your confession."

Rising from the threadbare cot, Jack stepped forward. "Damn you, Varnes. Get me outta here!"

"My boy, how many times must I tell you that that was never in our agreement?"

Jack grasped the bars as he moved his face closer. "Don't you see what they're planning to do? They're gonna hang me!"

"There is no question about that, I'm afraid."

"And you're okay with that? You don't care a bit in the world that they are going to string me up just like that?"

"I have no say in the matter, I'm afraid."

"*You're* the reason I'm in this mess!"

"That's not true." Varnes put his hands behind his back. "You are in this mess because *you* failed to take precautions in not getting caught."

"Don't you see what's going to happen? They are going to string me up and leave me hanging there for . . . who knows how long before they realize I can't die!"

Varnes scrunched his eyebrows together. "What did you say?"

"You heard me!"

"I fear you have misunderstood our agreement. The contract you signed only stated that you would be *bulletproof*." He shook his head. "It most certainly did *not* state that you would be deathless."

Acknowledgments

This book would not have been possible without the collective efforts of a number of people. So I would like to say thank you to Tony Acree and the entire team at Lawless Trails Press, Johnny D. Boggs for the foreword, Vic Kerry, MS for the Introduction, Andy Thomas for the gorgeous cover art, and Alex Mcvey for the amazing interior art pieces. I also would like to thank Joe R. Lansdale, Michael Zimmer, Jeff Mariotte, F. Keith Davis, Ronald Kelly, James Aquilone, Joe Mynhardt, Keith Lansdale, Jennifer Collins, Bella Collins, Crystal Adkins Wagner, Brian J. Hatcher, Lee E.E. Stone, Darrell Taylor, Tim Ooten, Dianna Toler, Mary Trent, Teri Wells, Hattie Newsome, Brian Carter, Brittany Dove, Kennedy Dove, Elijah Hooker, Michele Moore, Cassandra Vance, Kelly Jacobs, Shelly Parker, Shelly Stewart, Angela Dotson, Aaron Blankenship, Meghan Shell, Roger Williamson, Lillie Teeters, Cheryl Thacker, Paula Maynard, Roberta Carter, Susan Meade, Patricia Brooks, Shannon Williams, and Elizabeth Evans.

Michael Knost is a two-time Bram Stoker Award®-winner of science fiction, fantasy, horror, Western, and supernatural thrillers. He has written in various genres and helmed dozens of anthologies. His *Writers Workshop of Horror* won the 2009 Bram Stoker Award® in England for superior achievement in non-fiction. His *Writers Workshop of Horror 2* recently won the 2021 Bram Stoker Award® in Denver for the same category. His critically acclaimed *Writers Workshop of Science Fiction & Fantasy* is an Amazon #1 bestseller. Michael received the Horror Writers Association's Silver Hammer Award in 2015 for his work as the organization's mentorship chair and was recognized as the 2021 Mentor of the Year from the organization. He also received the prestigious J.U.G. (Just Uncommonly Good) Award from West Virginia Writer's Inc. His novel *Return of the Mothman* has been filmed as a movie adaption. Michael currently resides in Chapmanville, West Virginia with his wife, daughter, and a zombie goldfish.